CW00676014

THE
FENCE
AND THE
Musician

CANDICE CLARK

Content Warning

THIS BOOK CONTAINS DARK SUBJECT MATTER THAT MAY BE TRIGGERING TO SOME. IT IS INTENDED FOR MATURE READERS ONLY. PLEASE REVIEW THE LIST BELOW AND CONSIDER THESE CAREFULLY BEFORE CONTINUING. YOUR MENTAL HEALTH MATTERS.

MURDER (ON PAGE)

KIDNAPPING

SEXUAL ASSAULT (ON PAGE)

DOMESTIC ABUSE (ON PAGE)

DRUG ABUSE (MENTIONED)

DRUG OVERDOSE (ON PAGE)

DEATH OF A LOVED ONE (ON PAGE)

DEPRESSION/THOUGHTS OF SUICIDE

DISSOCIATION

ANXIETY

BODY DYSMORPHIA

Spotify Playlist

KD. LANG - SKYLARK
JAMIE FINE - YOU'RE LIKE
CELESTE BUCKINGHAM - RUN RUN RUN
HOZIER - NO PLAN
YEARS & YEARS - EYES SHUT
TINASHE - COLD SWEAT
JENNIFER PAIGE - CRUSH
WIZTHEMC - DEATH OF ME
STILETO, KENDYLE PAIGE - CRAVIN'
FARR - REBEL SOUL
WESLEE - GASSED
SLEEP TOKEN - LIKE THAT
LOSTBOYCROW - DEVIL'S IN THE BACKSEAT
BLACK ATLASS, JESSIE REYES - SACRIFICE
STUDIO KOLOMNA - VENUS
A!KA - I WON'T SAY (I'M IN LOVE)
DISCLOSURE, SAM SMITH - LATCH
JAMES ARTHUR - NEW TATTOO
SAM HUNT - TAKE YOUR TIME
BLACK ATLASS, SONIA - BY MY SIDE
DRAMATIC VIOLIN - SWEATER WEATHER
RUEL - DAZED & CONFUSED
MIGUEL - SURE THING
LAINEY WILSON - HEART LIKE A TRUCK
JAYMES YOUNG - FEEL SOMETHING
JACK U, SKRILLEX, DIPLO, KAI - MIND
OH WONDER - LIVEWIRE
VOILA - FIGURE YOU OUT
BANKS - BEGGIN FOR THREAD
JAMES ARTHUR - I AM
NEW RADICALS - MOTHER, WE JUST CAN'T GET ENOUGH

https://open.spotify.com/playlist/2MlZt70uWpRvCtQoDclQIW

"Healing cannot be counted or weighed or measured.

It's redefined every day, simply by opening your eyes."

I SEEM TO HAVE GOTTEN THE ORDER OF THIS BACKWARDS. I DEDICATED MY FIRST BOOK TO THE WOMEN IN MY LIFE THAT GAVE ME THE CONFIDENCE TO BELIEVE THAT I COULD WRITE A WHOLE ASS NOVEL. NOW, AT THE BEGINNING OF THIS VERY FEMALE-DRIVEN SECOND BOOK, I'M GOING TO BE THANKING MY HUSBAND, WHO'S A MAN, AND MY DAUGHTER.

FOR RICHARD, EVEN THOUGH YOU'VE NEVER READ A SINGLE WORD I'VE WRITTEN, YOU ALSO NEVER ONCE DISCOURAGED ME FROM DOING IT. THANK YOU FOR LISTENING TO ME COMPLAIN EVERY DAY FOR TWO YEARS ABOUT HOW BADLY MY HEAD HURT (CHRONIC PAIN IS A BITCH) AND STILL NEVER TELLING ME NOT TO GO FOR WHAT I WANTED. YOUR SUPPORT MAY BE QUIET, BUT IT'S BEEN FELT IN EVERY LITTLE THING YOU DO.

FOR CHARLOTTE, I HAVE NO DOUBT THAT ONE DAY YOU'LL DECIDE TO PICK UP AND READ ONE OF MY BOOKS AND FOR THAT, I SAY, I AM SO SORRY. NOT SORRY BECAUSE I REGRET WRITING THEM, BUT BECAUSE YOU'LL NOW NEVER BE ABLE TO MAKE EYE CONTACT WITH YOUR MOTHER EVER AGAIN. ALSO, THANK YOU FOR BEING AN EVEN MORE CONSTANT ANCHOR FOR ME THAN YOUR FATHER. YOU PROBABLY WON'T REMEMBER THE NUMBER OF DAYS THAT I PUSHED MYSELF SO HARD AND FELT SO BAD, ONLY TO HAVE YOU COME UP AND HUG ME AND TELL ME EVERYTHING WOULD BE OKAY AND TO JUST GO TAKE SOME TYLENOL. YOU WON'T REMEMBER THOSE DAYS, BUT I WILL. THOSE ARE THE DAYS THAT GOT ME THROUGH TO THE NEXT ONE. FOR THAT, YOU CREATED THIS BOOK AS MUCH AS I DID ... I JUST WROTE ALL THE SEX SCENES. LOL!

LOVE,
CANDICE (MOM)

"A SKY FULL OF STARS, AND
HE WAS STARING AT HER."

—Atticus

"I AM THE SEA AND
NOBODY OWNS ME."

—Pippi Longstocking

PROLOGUE

Siren

    Somewhere in my foggy brain, I register the sound of music. That, in itself, isn't unusual. I hear music in my head all the time. Music has been an integral part of my life for as long as I can remember. Being the daughter of two affluent—albeit neglectful—parents meant being exposed to many of the finer things in life. But in terms of music, I think I felt the beauty of it long before I came to recognize the part it played in cultural status. It didn't matter if it was classics played to a packed house by an orchestra or a street performer playing blues music for three or four people on the corner. If it was done well, music of any kind could be transcendent. It was that connection to instruments, lyrics, and composition which led me to my chosen profession as a violinist with the Charleston Symphony. So, it would be safe to say that music has always been a part of who I am. I, like most people, had my favorite pieces. Each one evoked different emotions within me, which was why I loved music so much.

As I try to open my bleary eyes and bring my consciousness back online from whatever is causing the brain fog currently clouding my mind, the first emotion that hits me is fear. As my mind clears and the music begins to register, I recognize the reasoning behind that fear. I know this piece. It's Bach's Chaconne. A hauntingly beautiful work of art that I used to adore listening to and playing. Now, the sound of it causes a rush of terror to coarse through my veins, replacing my blood with battery acid. I haven't heard this piece in years. I haven't wanted to. This particular song is associated with both the best and worst years of my life. They're years that I wished I could wipe from my memory but, unfortunately, you couldn't do that when the scars of the past weren't only figurative but literal.

My brain feels fuzzy with confusion. I never would've put this song on myself, and I'm having such a hard time focusing on anything other than the panic associated with the music. This has happened a handful of times in the past. In the early days, I'd unerringly hear the song and immediately dissolve into a full-blown panic attack. It's taken me a long time to come to terms with the knowledge that this song is now a trigger for me, serving to remind me of the horrors of my past. The only thing that helped me recover was the constant reminder that I'd survived. Well, that and the sheer pigheadedness of my innate personality.

Fighting to shake myself awake, I wonder if I'm stuck in another nightmare. They've plagued me off and on for years, ever since I escaped from that Hell on Earth that had once been a fantasy come to life. As I force my eyes open, I blink hard to adjust my vision until I realize my eyes aren't the problem. I'm surrounded by darkness. The music is loud now. Maybe it's been loud this entire time, and I was just too out of it to notice. The piece seems to swell in time with my anxiety as my vision fully clears, and I'm able to take in more details of the room around me. Even with the blurry film gone from my eyes, it's difficult to see because the light is so dim. Some things register immediately, however.

I'm in a bed that's not my own. In a room that's not my own. In a house that's not my own. I don't recognize anything in this room, but whoever owns it clearly has money. Every piece of furniture is ornate and ostentatious. It reminds me of the furniture that surrounded me in my parent's home when I was growing up. Lifting my arm, I bring my hand up to rub my eyes, but it's as though my entire body is working on a delay, and my limbs weigh a hundred pounds. Fighting to sit up, I feel like I'm under water, struggling to kick my way to the surface. The pressure on my chest is immense, but that's probably the oncoming panic attack. I think my heart is beating a mile a minute. Racking my brain, I try to recall what I was doing before this. The last thing I remember was texting Amelia before going to sleep, but that was definitely in my own bed. I have no idea how I got to wherever I am now, and the unknowns are causing all sorts of crazy scenarios to run rampant in my mind. Squinting, I wish I could locate a lamp or light switch somewhere so I can take in more of the room surrounding me. Maybe I could get a better idea of where I am and how I got here.

"Hello, *mia* Sirena."

The blood in my veins turns to ice, and it isn't long before every other part of my body immediately follows suit. That voice. It's the voice from my nightmares. A voice that I never thought I'd have to hear again. At least not outside of my own head. No, no, no, no. It's not possible. He's dead. I killed him. I watched the blood drain from his body. Gaze-tracking the voice, I see the dark silhouette of a prominent figure sitting in an armchair in the corner of the room. It's only now that my senses register something else. Something they hadn't before. The smell of cigar smoke. A very distinct cigar. As I watch, the figure brings the cigar to his mouth, the bright orange glow on the end momentarily illuminating a face that still haunts me to this day but one that I thought was dead and buried. Feeling my insides begin to tremble, those tremors soon turn into full-body shakes. This can't be happening.

"You don't look happy to see me, *bella*," the voice croons. "Did you think I'd let you go that easily? You should know me better than that."

Pulling my knees to my chest, I blink past the tears streaming down my face. If I'm here and that voice is real, no one will know where to find me. By the time they even realize I'm gone, there'll be no saving me. I won't be lucky enough to make it out alive twice. Once was a fluke; twice would be defying fate. That voice once told me that he was my destiny. Has anyone ever spit in the face of destiny and lived to tell the tale? I did, or so I thought. I guess I was wrong. It looks like destiny has finally caught up with me. Every instinct in me already wants so badly to dissociate. To revert to the coping mechanism that used to get me through moments, hours, and days of misery with this man. But my fight-or-flight responses are on full alert. Without moving a muscle, my eyes track the distance of the door relative to where I am and where he still sits. If I'm fast enough, I might make it. I wasn't always fast enough before. On those nights, in particular, I prayed for death. If I don't make it to the door before he catches me, I know how quickly I can end up back there. After nearly three years of waiting, I can only imagine the pain he has in store for me. I have to run, to get as far away from here as I can, and hide, until I can figure out how any of this is possible and how I can fix it. I can't afford to fall apart right now, and I can't mentally check out either, as much as I'd like to.

The voice from the corner comes again. "I disapprove of the pictures you've put all over your body, Sirena. It's almost as if you were trying to cover my artwork. My signature, painstakingly written over and over in your flesh. How are people going to know who you belong to now?" Making a tsking sound, he says, "I can't have other men out there thinking they can touch what's mine. I suppose I'll just have to redo all my hard work. It will hurt me ... and you ... but you brought this on yourself."

Releasing a sob, I bury my face in my hands. I shouldn't cry. I know he likes it. But despite my tough exterior, I can't seem to stop myself. The iron grip that this man has had over my life reaches far beyond the six years I spent with him in Hell. The only thing that kept me alive was when my pain turned to rage. The fear was always there, but at that point, I had nothing to live for and, therefore, nothing to lose. I would either get away or die in the process. I'd resigned myself to either fate, though I'd gotten away in the end. I remind myself again ... I'd gotten away. I could do it again. My body makes the decision even before my brain has a chance to catch up. I spring from the bed, thanking God that the man was arrogant enough not to believe that I should be tied down. Sprinting in the direction of the door, I hear movement behind me and know he's giving chase. I try not to choke on the heart that's suddenly jumped up into my throat. I race the handful of feet to the door, blessedly reaching it before him. Blindly gripping the knob, I turn it quickly and wrench it open, managing only a few inches before an impossibly large palm slaps against the door directly next to my face, effectively slamming it closed again. At the same time, another hand roughly grips my hair in a tight fist, pushing the side of my face hard against the wood as a massive body presses into me from behind.

His mouth hovers close to my ear, and I feel his breath a second before the tip of his tongue darts out, running along the length of the shell. Hissing through gritted teeth, he grinds himself into me from behind, and I can feel the erection that he's not even attempting to disguise. I meant it when I said he liked to hear me cry. He liked to hear me scream, too. Even knowing that, terror has my mouth opening on a high-pitched wail that's abruptly cut off when my head is jerked back sharply and then slammed into the hardwood of the door. As spots begin to swim at the edge of my vision and I feel my body slowly sliding down the length of the door, I hear a deep chuckle, followed by a whisper.

"Haven't you learned by now, *bella*? You'll never escape me. Even when you thought you were free, you were just on a longer leash. You seem to have forgotten your place. We'll just have to start back at the beginning of your training."

As another sinister laugh escapes him, he eases back enough to allow me to fall to the floor in a heap. That laugh is the last thing I hear before blackness swallows me whole. Not for the first time in my short life, I pray that I never wake up.

CHAPTER 1

Deacon

I hate shit like this. As I pull at the knot of my tie, I try for the hundredth time to loosen its chokehold around my neck in an effort to not feel like I'm strangling to death. It doesn't work. This is one of the many reasons why I can't stand attending formal functions. Ties. They're literally torture devices. This scene was Merrick's forte, not mine. Unlike me, my best friend had the ability to blend seamlessly with both the upper crust of society and the seedy underbelly. Truthfully, I'd always been most comfortable as a faceless individual behind a computer screen or facilitating shady deals in back alleys. Though these days, I've upgraded to conducting those shady business deals in lavishly furnished offices and palatial estates.

As a man who proffered the sale of stolen art, gems, and antiquities, I'd come a long way from my humble and turbulent youth, as I like to put it. I tried to blend into the wealthy lifestyle more befitting my regular clientele but in reality, "humble" meant broke and "turbulent" meant shitshow. The first part of my childhood had been more than a little rough. Hell, my entire childhood had been rough. But at least for the first 14 years of my life, I'd had my mother. Granted, she hadn't been without her ... problems. But she loved me, that I knew. She made sure that, no matter what her mental state was, she showed me every day that I was her reason for being. She'd bought me my first computer, and even as a young child, it was clear I had a penchant for technology. She'd encouraged me to play to my strengths and nurtured my newfound obsession as best she could, given the fact that she was addicted to opioid medication for the majority of my life. Then, not long after I turned 14, she died of a drug overdose. Even though I knew in my heart that it was an accident, because she never would've voluntarily left me, the nightmare that had plagued me for years had finally come true. Suddenly yanked from the only home I'd ever known, I'd found myself a ward of the state. We didn't have any family to speak of, and even though it wasn't long after that I found out who my father was, mama never listed him on the birth certificate, so little was done to locate him. During the years that were supposed to be my most impressionable, I found myself caught up in the circus that was the foster care system. Don't get me wrong, I'd had a few caseworkers that actually seemed to give a shit about my wellbeing, but for the most part, they'd all been overworked and overwhelmed. The system was a joke. I'd watched countless kids, both older and younger than me, fall victim to sexual predators. Countless more used simply for a government check, but ultimately being neglected or physically abused. Even more turned to drugs or alcohol themselves to escape a vicious cycle so full of flaws that no one ever really *saw* them.

Driven by determination and probably sheer luck, I narrowly avoided those harrowing paths. Being the son of a junkie, albeit a functioning one, cemented the conviction that I didn't wanna be anywhere near the stuff. So instead of an addict, I'd become a criminal. Sure, I could've taken what happened to me and turned myself into some type of advocate or social justice warrior, but I didn't have much tolerance for bullshit and a life like that would've been rife with bullshit. Pandering, hand-shaking, and debating. No, thank you. So, by my 15th birthday, I'd run from what would become my last neglectful foster family and started carving my own path. It wasn't easy, I can't lie. Living on the streets as a teen wasn't a dream come true. It was dangerous, and if you wanted to survive, you had to learn who and what to watch out for. It hadn't taken me much time to decide that I didn't wanna be just another petty criminal. Call me delusional but my ultimate plans had been much more grandiose. I lived for two things: money and revenge. The first, I'd begun amassing in small amounts when my mother was still alive but no longer able to care for us. Even at that early age, I knew I was a natural-born salesman. But you wouldn't find me on some car lot hawking lemons to suckers. Instead, I'd used my knack for technology to create a mystique for myself. A reputation as a pirate of the criminal underworld. An online savant that could access any information that existed on the internet ... for a price. My other persona was as a trustworthy go-between for thieves and those who had no problem receiving stolen goods as long as said goods were of the highest quality. Both dual sides of my personality helped fund the comfortable yet modest bachelor lifestyle I now led. The extra, I hoarded like a dragon. If I did take from my sizable nest egg, it usually went toward my ultimate goal of doling out retribution to a particular United States Senator. The man at the root of everything that had ever gone wrong in my life.

This explained why I was currently sipping a glass of single malt whiskey in the back of a crowded room full of ageing debutantes and wrinkly old bastards with more belly than balls. And, of course, money. Always money. It was changing hands via unmarked white envelopes or auction bids at a table full of items nobody really wanted. It was all one big circle jerk to see who would rise in the ranks of power and who would become a used-up husk thrown to the side and ultimately forgotten.

The pretense of tonight's fundraiser was to shine a light on … actually, I didn't really know what the hell the purpose of this gathering was. All I knew was that Senator Hawkins was on the guest list, which meant so was I. Well, not technically, but I was a halfway decent forger, too. Party invitations, even ones like this, were child's play to me. As I skulk around the edges of the room, looking for my target, I keep as much to the periphery as possible. It only made sense considering both of my alter egos are perfectly at home in the shadows. I also don't wanna be recognized. Not that I think anyone who sees me will make a connection to the beloved senator, but you could never be too careful. I take after my father, after all.

Senator Martin Hawkins was happily married with two fully grown kids, both of which seemed to be using their connections and wealth to follow in their noble father's footsteps of philanthropy and do-gooding. At least, that was the public image. In private, the good senator fucked anything that moved, his wife couldn't function without a glass of red wine in her hand, and the kids were spoiled little shits who wouldn't know a hard day's work if it bit them in the ass. As for me, the only thing I'd inherited from the man was my strong jawline and eyes, which were as blue as the sky on a clear day. My sandy blonde hair was a trait passed down to me by my mother, even if it was too long to be considered stylish by this crowd. As it was now, it was pulled back in a small knot at the base of my skull, and to anyone looking at me head-on, I'd blend in well with the rest of the slicked-back rats in this room. Once again, I make a futile move to pull at my tie. I swear, each time only seemed to make it tighter and tighter. I would feel a hell of a lot better if Merrick were here tonight. While I don't think he enjoys these types of parties any more than I do, he definitely schmoozes better. The man was a fucking chameleon, having the uncanny ability to camouflage himself into the pattern of any setting. It was probably one of the traits that led to his chosen profession as a world-class thief. But as much as Merrick's presence would ease some of my anxiety, I wasn't ready to share with him just how close to this situation I'd put myself. Don't get me wrong, Merrick knew all about my father and nearly all of my reasons for despising the man. But I hadn't yet let him in on my plans to systematically break down and destroy every aspect of his life. To say I was bitter would be an understatement. Martin Hawkins had ruined my mother, refused to acknowledge my existence, and thrown us both away like trash. For that, he would pay with nothing less than everything. I'd make sure of it.

A sudden commotion near the entrance of the large banquet hall has my head swinging towards the doorway where I can just make out the dark hair lined with silver that was Senator Hawkin's signature look. My gaze turns to stone, and I track the man's movements as he shakes hand after hand, flashing a set of pearly whites that I'm sure cost a pretty penny. I'd bet my life they weren't his pennies, though. The man was as crooked as they came. If you looked up the word "corruption" in the dictionary, you'd see a picture of his face. My face. I hated that. Hated the fact that I looked anything like the man that had sired me. The man who had cheated on his wife by seducing a 17-year-old girl, promising her the world, and instead, got her pregnant. Who'd discarded her like garbage when she refused to have an abortion. The man who now stood as a pillar of the community and the epitome of Southern class.

As he works his way through the room, I watch from the sidelines as his wife, drink in hand, follows three feet behind him like some peasant made to walk in deference behind the king. Thankfully, the asshole's other children weren't in attendance tonight, which would make my mission that much easier to accomplish. I'd picked up a tip that, like many other parties of this nature, one of the many meetings taking place here tonight was to discuss the upcoming auction at the estate of Mr. Eugene Kingsley. The annual auction was one I've attended before. It was invitation-only and ridiculously exclusive, mostly because of all the illegal shit that happened there. Mr. Kingsley's yearly party was a who's who of black market buyers and sellers. The construction magnate had his hand in a lot of sketchy pies. Art, jewels, antiques, exotic animals, you name it. On paper, his forte was land development, and the city contracts he received through bribes and blackmail made him a very rich man very quickly. There was never an official list of items for sale before the party, but it was rumored that there was going to be a valuable gem among the many things up for auction. A gem I'd been obsessing over since I was a child. It had changed hands illegally several times since its last legitimate sale through an auction house to a private bidder. The current owner of the stone was somewhat of a mystery, though, making it hard to pin down. Couldn't get your best friend to steal something for you that neither of you could find. The name Dante Gaspari had been thrown around a few times, but I took that bit of information with a grain of salt. I'd heard of Gaspari before—an eccentric Italian with too much money and a sick streak a mile long. The stories told about him were the things nightmares were made of. Especially his treatment of women, though I'd heard his reputation for savagery didn't extend only to the fairer sex. I didn't buy into the possibility of him being the owner of my sought-after jewel because, quite frankly, the man was currently feeding worms in a cemetery somewhere. I, like the rest of the criminal underworld, knew that Dante Gaspari had died under mysterious circumstances nearly three years ago. His killer was never caught. The irony wasn't lost on me, considering the man had had a reputation for making others disappear, among other things.

Obviously, whoever this new seller was, he was a mystery to me. And I didn't like mysteries. In the same way, I didn't like mint-flavored gum or anyone over 80 with a driver's license. So, whenever possible, I needed to get to the bottom of these mysteries. It was almost like a compulsion. I was currently the number one fence on the East Coast. The one with a reputation for getting the ungettable, and right now, I wanted to get my hands on that jewel. Especially if the correspondence I'd intercepted was true and my father planned on attending that auction. I didn't believe he was going for the same reason I was, though. That ship had sailed a long time ago. Twenty-eight years ago, to be exact. But I also didn't believe in coincidences, so my reason for attending the auction would be twofold. I needed that jewel, and I needed to find out exactly what my father would be doing there. If I could, I might finally have enough leverage to topple the delicate house of cards he's built up around himself.

Just then, I see my target lean down to whisper something into his wife's ear. As I watch, she obediently moves away to chat with some of the other trophy wives in attendance. Clocking the senator's movements, I see him shake hands with an unknown male before they both stealthily exit the room through a door at the back. As they disappear through the doorway, a guard I hadn't noticed before steps in front of the now closed door, effectively blocking the entrance to wherever that door leads. Narrowing my eyes, my gut tells me this is the moment I've been waiting for. I sit my unfinished glass of whiskey on a side table and shove my hands into the pockets of my slacks, making my way over to the entryway that leads to the foyer at the front of the house, moving casually, as though I'm on my way out. I know what I need to do. Exiting through the front door, I stroll around to the side of the house, taking out my phone and putting it to my ear. I'm not actually calling anyone, but if someone were to look out of a window and see a random man wandering the grounds, at least it would appear as though I have a plausible reason. Clearly, I needed to step away from the noise of the party to take a very important phone call. A call that I needed privacy for, hence the wandering. In reality, as I walk the perimeter of the house, my eyes catalog the windows along the side that match up to the direction of that door. My father and this unknown man are in one of those rooms. Looking in both directions to make sure no guards are patrolling the grounds, I quietly slip along the line of shrubs bordering the house. Luckily, several trees provide me with a good amount of cover as I make my way to each window, peering inside. When I get to window number three, I peek through the open curtains before ducking my head back quickly. Bingo. Backtracking to the window of the last room I passed, I make Merrick proud with how quickly I jimmy the lock, and lifting the window, I climb inside. This room is dark and thankfully empty, but I can hear faint voices nearby. The deep baritone that I recognize as my father's and that of the man he left the ballroom with. Locating an air vent near the top of the wall that separates the two rooms, I grab a chair, quietly place it beneath, and climb up. The voices are louder now and I can hear exactly what's being said next door.

"I need you to speak with him, Greg. He's the only one that can take care of it. I'm already having issues with the IRS and missing campaign funds. My accountant must've fucked up somewhere. Either that or the bastard is embezzling my money. If I don't get re-elected, I'll lose everything! I can't afford for my seat to go to that smug little shit, Sykes."

That's definitely my father. I can't stop the smirk of satisfaction that crosses my face at his words, knowing that I'm the reason he's missing money. The other man, whose name and information I'll have by the end of the night, replies soon after.

"It's a difficult situation, Martin. He's not a man you can just throw money at, even if you have it. He's got money. Hell, he's got everything. If you want him to help you, you'll have to come up with something more than just cash, and that's if you can even get a meeting. It's not like he's got an open door policy at this point."

My brows draw down in confusion. Who the hell are they talking about?

"I heard he's going to be at that auction, and I'm just desperate enough to go and try to find him myself if I have to, but I'd rather not have to. That's where you come in. You can get me a meeting. Tell him I'll give him whatever he wants. There's gotta be something he doesn't have. Whatever it is, I'll get it. I need this problem taken care of."

The other man sighs heavily. "I'll see what I can do. If I can get him to see you, it'll definitely be in LA. He won't trust that any other meeting place will be neutral enough to talk."

"Fine. I'll be there. And I'll get him whatever he wants."

As I listen to the sound of footsteps, followed by a door opening and closing, I quietly lower myself down from the chair, backing against the wall behind the door, just in case someone enters. After a few minutes, when the door remains closed, I know my father and the other man must be gone. Exiting the room the same way I entered, I keep to the cover of the shadows near the house as I make my way back around the front. As I wait for the valet to pull my car around, I turn back to take one last look at the house—no yelling, no guards running out, and nothing out of the ordinary. When my car pulls up in front of me, I take the keys from the valet and leave the ridiculously large house in my rearview mirror. I don't need to be here anymore. I got what I came for. As I make my way back to the highway that will take me home, I take stock of what I know. My father is clearly desperately trying to win his re-election bid. His opponent, Cole Sykes, is currently leading in the polls. Whoever this man is that they were discussing is someone with enough money, power, or both to take Sykes out of the running. Whether by physical harm or ruination remains to be seen. I'm going to have to do a lot of digging when I get home, but there's one thing I know for sure. Whatever's going to happen next, it's gonna happen at Eugene Kingsley's auction. Looks like I'm definitely going to LA.

CHAPTER 2

Siren

I've destroyed this entire fucking room. As I sit on the bed, surrounded by shredded sheets and marveling at my handiwork, I wonder why Dante hasn't come in to punish me yet. It's been two days since I realized that I was trapped in an empty house with the devil. I haven't slept more than a few minutes at a time since I got here, worried that I'll wake up to find myself trapped under the weight of Satan himself, the cold steel of his favored blade pressed to my skin. The blade that still gives me nightmares. But so far ... there's been nothing. There is no sign of him, and as much as I dread coming face to face with him again, the not knowing is slowly killing me. In the past, he was always quick to dole out pain, but then again, he always liked his mind games, too. I can only guess that that's what this is. There's no other reason I can think of that would answer the question of why he's let me destroy everything in sight and hasn't come in once to try and stop me. I would take solace in silence, but he never was a kind man. Despite the anxiety it causes—or more likely because of it—the music has continued. Bach's Chaconne plays on a loop from somewhere not too far away. It's another mind game. One that's working because I'm starting to feel like I'm on a carousel that never actually stops.

I know I'm being watched. I can't see the camera, but I know it's here. It was always there in the past. Even knowing he's looking, I've turned this room upside down searching for something I can use as a weapon for whenever he inevitably returns. Because I know it's only a matter of time. So far, I've gotten nothing. All the furniture here is old, ornate, and, unfortunately, made with better craftsmanship than anything you'll find at IKEA. Even trying to remove the leg of the chair that Dante occupied when I first woke up here was fruitless. It reminded me of that old saying about things not being made the way they used to be, only in reverse. The chair was too well made. When I realized I couldn't do more than knock things over and shred the bedding, I'd done just that. The old me would've cowered in a corner, doing nothing and waiting for my inevitable punishment. That was the version of me that Dante had systematically broken down over the course of six years. The woman I'd become since I'd escaped him was different. Stronger. If he thought for one second that I wouldn't fight him every step of the way, he was dead wrong. And if given even the smallest chance, I'd make that *dead* part stick this time.

There was only one window in the room. Before I even checked, I knew it would be locked and probably have bars on it. I'd still checked. Frustration bubbles inside me like a witch's cauldron, and I swear, if I make it out of this alive, I'm gonna familiarize myself with an arsenal's worth of hexes. As Bach continues to play in the distance, I grip my hair in my hands, pulling hard on the strands. Anything to keep myself grounded. It would be so easy to dissociate. To float away and never come back. Old Siren would've already checked out. But if I allow myself to do that, I'll never be able to catch Dante unaware. And I need to get the hell out of here. Since that fateful night nearly three years ago, I've built a new life for myself. One that I'm proud of. One that I miss. So, for now, I sit in the middle of the ruined bed and wait for the devil to reappear.

I don't have to wait much longer. Soon, the click of a key in a lock has my eyes shooting to the door. It takes Dante a moment to realize that he can't get it open more than a few inches, with the upturned dresser in the way. Guess his stupid fucking camera missed that. The sound of a low chuckle has me grinding my teeth seconds before a series of loud bangs erupt. Kicking the door several times, he finally manages to get it open enough to enter. I don't move from my place in the center of the bed. Legs crossed, I straighten my spine and watch him warily. He takes his time surveying the damage even though I know he will have seen the worst of it from his vantage point at the other end of a recording. As I watch, he looks down and brushes a piece of invisible lint from the tie of his immaculate three-piece suit, the picture of sophistication.

Wanting to catch him off guard, I speak first, setting the tone of the conversation. This, too, is something new. "You should've stayed dead."

Arching an eyebrow, he cocks his head and stares at me. One minute turns into two, and still he says nothing. But I refuse to squirm. It's what he wants, after all. Soon, his husky voice comes. "Something's changed. You're ... different. I think I might like it," he says, humor lacing his tone. His Italian accent is just as pronounced today as it was eight years ago when we first met. Only now, instead of sounding romantic, it makes me wanna barf.

Narrowing my eyes, I say, "I don't know what you have planned, but I won't make it easy for you. I'll fight you every step of the way. I'm not the same scared little girl you used to know." Make no mistake—a healthy dose of fear still ran through my veins like ice, but the heat of self-preservation was fast on its heels.

"I hope you do. It will be like our first time, all over again. Do you remember Sirena? The night I took your virginity? The first cut I ever made on your beautiful skin?"

Subconsciously, I run my fingers over the small raised scar on my left collarbone, barely visible beneath the Treble Clef tattoo there. His eyes track the movement, and a small smile plays at the corners of his lips. Dropping my hand back to my lap, I say, "A girl always remembers her first. Though, the many men that came after you have made that memory a bit hazy."

I know I'm courting disaster. In addition to his penchant for pain, he was always jealous and possessive. Even at the beginning of our relationship, before I knew what kind of monster I'd gotten into bed with, he would become enraged if he ever caught another man's eyes on me. Confirming that I've slept with other men since I got away from him will only make him angry. I know this, yet I can't stop myself from needling him. If I learned nothing else from our relationship, it's that people tended to make mistakes when their emotions came into play. Anger was an emotion Dante was on a first name basis with. As I watch, his eyes darken, and his jaw tightens. Hands balling into fists, he does exactly as predicted, charging towards me. Pretending to cower away, I skitter to the opposite side of the bed. As he makes a move to grab me, I fist the strip of torn bed sheet I've been holding in both hands, circling it around his neck. Heavy hands grip my biceps in a punishing hold even as I pull both ends of the sheet, tightening it as hard as I can. We grapple for several long seconds before he manages to drag me down to the floor. I land with a thud, my head knocking against the hardwood. Spots swim in my vision, and for a brief moment, I lose sight of his face. My grip on the sheet falters, and then his hands are around my throat.

"You've got more fire in you now, Sirena, but I'll still break you, just like before," he says, though I can hear the exertion in his voice and know the fight has winded him.

As his grip tightens, the spots in front of my eyes begin to bleed together, forming a haze that I know will soon lead to unconsciousness, and yet, I still have enough breath to get out two final words.

"Fuck you."

CHAPTER 3

Deacon

I'm driving through downtown Savannah when the phone call comes. Glancing down at the screen of my cell, I see Merrick's name.

Lifting the phone to my ear, I say, "Whatever it is you're selling, I'm not buying." It's a funny joke, at least in my eyes, considering Merrick is a thief, and I frequently buy and sell things for him.

"Deacon..." he says, tone grave. Merrick's tone is always serious. He's the yin to my yang. The stoic to my sarcastic humor. And he frequently uses my name in a tone that says *if you don't cut the shit, I'm gonna lose it on you*. But this ... this is something different. All my senses go on high alert. I feel the smile slip from my face. The worry in his voice is crystal clear, and that doesn't happen often.

Immediately pulling my car onto a side street, I park along a random curb before saying, "What's wrong?"

"I need you to come to Charleston. Something's happened to Siren."

Immediately feeling my heart jump to somewhere in the vicinity of my throat, I say, "Tell me everything." As I listen to him talk, I absently rub at a spot in the center of my chest. There's a twinge that only worsens as Merrick details the situation.

"Amelia hasn't been able to get a hold of her for three days. Finally, we went over there together because no way in hell was I letting my pregnant wife go alone. It was clear someone had broken into her place. A window connected to the fire escape was smashed in. They must've reached through and unlocked it because it was still wide open. Thankfully, Amelia had a key, so I didn't have to climb through that same window. After we finished fighting about who was going in—a battle I won by the way—I found her place in perfect order, except the bedroom."

I can hear my heartbeat in my ears as I ask, "Is she hurt? Where is she?"

"That's the thing ... we don't know. She wasn't there. Her bed was unmade, and all her clothes had been pulled out. Amelia says her suitcase and a bunch of her toiletries from the bathroom are missing. Her phone was still on the nightstand, but her violin was gone." There's a heavy pause before he continues. "I think someone took her while she was asleep, then packed her shit to make it look like she just left."

The thudding in my ears is so loud now that I barely hear the end of his sentence but the phrase *someone took her* plays on a loop in my head over and over. Calm tone belying my emotions, I simply say, "I'll be there within the hour." I don't wait for a reply before disconnecting the call. When my eyes finally focus again, it's to find my hands white-knuckled on the steering wheel. The urge to beat them against the front dash is nearly overwhelming. I wanna say my visceral reaction is a surprise but if I'm honest with myself, Siren's been like an itch between my shoulder blades for months, one that I just can't seem to reach. We slept together once and only once, but not because of anything I did. In fact, even now, I can still feel the strands of her long black hair in my hands. I can still see her brown eyes turn to melted chocolate seconds before she came beneath me. Unfortunately, I only got the privilege of one night with her. You see, Siren has a chip on her shoulder the size of the iceberg that sank the Titanic. I would've gladly gone more than one round, but she wouldn't give me the time of day after, and as much as that stung, when I sat back and thought about all the shit going on in my life, I knew I wasn't boyfriend material. It just isn't in my genetic makeup. But the fact that we aren't in a relationship doesn't mean I want anything bad to happen to her. And from the sound of it, something bad has definitely happened. Putting the car back into drive, I punch the accelerator and make my way to the interstate that bridges the gap between Savannah and Charleston. Doing nearly 100 mph, I pray that there aren't any state troopers lying in wait to catch me in a speed trap. To be honest, I don't really give a shit. I've done high-speed chase before; I'll gladly do it again. I just know that I've gotta get there so I can assess how bad the situation really is, and as soon as I've done that, I'll be online, following every single digital footprint made by Siren or anyone who's had any contact with her. It baffles me how this could've happened without me being alerted. Unbeknownst to her, I've been keeping tabs on Siren since before Merrick and Amelia even got married. Over the months, we've formed something of a ragtag group of friends. Even the Fed has managed to wedge his way into our lives and pop up whenever it suits him. So for something like this to happen and neither myself nor Alexi get

31

any type of notification is ... not right. I can't help but think that someone out there is making moves against us, and not even I saw them coming. I don't like the idea one bit.

The drive to Charleston is tense but it's late and the streets are blessedly quiet at this time on a weeknight. Thankfully, I'm meeting Merrick at Siren's place instead of having to go all the way out to the house Merrick and Amelia now share. That would've tacked on another half hour to my drive. As I make my way through Downtown Charleston, I seem to get stuck at every fucking red light in the city, and I can feel my frustration mounting with each press of my foot on the brake pedal. At this rate, by the time I get to her place, my blood pressure will be so high I will have given myself a stroke. Finally, I make it into the French Quarter. Parking my car along the side of the street, I get out and hurriedly lock up. I don't even give a second thought to the idea of someone sideswiping me, nor do I care if I get a ticket for not feeding the meter. At this point, my car doesn't matter. Funny, I would never have thought anything could make me think those words. My feet eat up the sidewalk pavement as I make long strides toward the front door of Siren's apartment building. Even from the outside, anyone walking by would be able to tell they cost a pretty penny. From the bit of digging I've done into her background, I know that Siren grew up with money. Her parents, Blake and Vanessa Sinclair, are members of Charleston's elite circle. But like most parents of that social class, having kids is more about carrying on the family name and less about actually wanting to know them. They spent most of their time abroad or on the family yacht, while Siren spent her early childhood being raised by nannies and then shipped off to boarding school. That's where she and Amelia met, and that's about as far as I've allowed myself to dig. Invading someone's privacy for their own protection was one thing. Wanting to find out whether they ate white or brown gravy on their fried steak was another. The need was there, but I fought it.

As I punch in the code that will allow me to enter the building, I don't even pause to take in the scenery. I've been here before, and I know where I'm going. From the outside, you'd never guess that the interior of the building has been hollowed out in the center, allowing the sun to shine down onto what I can only imagine is a replica of the Garden of Eden during the day. Around the garden are numerous staircases, each leading up to an individual loft, allowing the tenants to come and go without being bothered while also providing a measure of security. Or so we thought. That security is obviously lacking if someone could break into an apartment and get a woman and a shit ton of her belongings out without anyone noticing. Taking the staircase to my right, I'm banging on Siren's door three seconds later. Three seconds after that, the door opens, and I come face-to-face with Merrick.

He immediately steps back to let me in, closing the door behind me. Amelia is sitting cross-legged on the couch across the room, worry written all over her face. I have no idea how she's able to sit in that position being six months pregnant. The female body was a wonder.

Not wasting any time, I ask, "Have you called the police yet?"

Amelia shakes her head, twisting the large emerald ring on her finger nervously. I'm just turning back to Merrick when he says, "No, I didn't think it was a good idea. We don't know who took her or for what purpose, and if it turns out to somehow be connected to either of us, the cops will only fuck things up."

He's right. Merrick and I have made a lot of enemies over the years. Most of the criminal underworld has no idea who the real faces are behind our metaphorical disguises, but I have no doubt that there are a few who could find out if they really wanted to. While I've taken care to wipe every string tying that of our alter egos to our true identities from the web, I don't discount any possibility. It wouldn't be that much of a leap for one of them to take something we care about and use it as leverage against us. The idea that this could in some way be my fault causes a tightening in my chest.

"What about the Fed?" I ask. It was only fair that we could call on him for favors when he'd made it clear that he wanted something from us, even if we didn't really know what that something was yet. What I do know is that he has a lot of connections we could utilize.

Just as Merrick opens his mouth to answer, a knock sounds at the door. I'm now closest, with Merrick having moved to stand near his wife right after I came in. I go over and look through the peephole. Fucking Hell. Swinging the door wide, I roll my eyes. *Ask, and you shall receive.* I guess that answered my question. Looking grim instead of smug for once, Agent Alexi Kapranov enters the apartment. I wanna be annoyed that he's here, but if dealing with him means locating Siren, I'll just have to grit my teeth and bare it.

Alexi gives Merrick and I each a nod before granting Amelia a small smile. An incredibly hard feat for him, I'm sure. Without even a hello, I say, "What do you know?"

He doesn't make a comment about the bluntness of my tone. I think he recognizes how dire the situation is and that now isn't the time for levity. Instead, he just replies, "Not much, I'm sorry

34

to say. There's no visual of her leaving on any of the surrounding cameras in the area. One camera, located across the street outside of a restaurant, did catch a large SUV pulling up to the curb, but it only captured the front of the car. It sat there for less than 10 minutes before backing out of camera view. I can only assume to keep their plates from showing. Whoever it was, they knew where the cameras were and how to avoid them. They had to have done extensive recon on the area. If she was taken, it wasn't by some low-level criminal. This was a professional job. Someone with experience or a lot of money to pay the right people."

I'm surprised my teeth haven't cracked from how hard my jaw is clenching. I should've known nothing good would come out of befriending the Fed. He knows next to nothing. Even though I know I could've gotten that information with my eyes closed and one hand tied behind my back, if I think about it objectively, it's possible that I'm just being salty because I feel ... helpless. Granted, I haven't gotten behind my monitors yet, so I can't say if what he came across is all there is to find, but at least now I have a starting point.

"I need my computer," I say to the room in general. I was in such a hurry to get inside that I didn't even think to bring up the laptop I usually carry with me. Without another word, I walk to the door. Merrick makes a move as if to stop me or say something, but the look I give him has him immediately turning stony-faced, and with a nod, he goes back to stand near his wife. The normally funny Deacon is gone. What's taken his place is a facet of myself that I rarely allow people to see. Mainly because it's dangerous and full of rage. But right now, that might be exactly the motivation I need. Siren may very well turn out to be *the one who got away*, but she's not getting away like this.

CHAPTER 4

Siren

Three days. That's how long it's been since I woke up from my last fight with Dante. Three days with no food and no water. Three days of endless music and solitude. I hate it. I guess he didn't like the differences in me as much as he thought he did, because he hasn't come back. I wanna rage. I suppose I should be grateful that he's left me alone. If he's not here, at least he can't cause me physical pain. But I'm not grateful. A part of me, a very big part of me, wants him to come back in here so that I can at least attempt to get the hell out. I know he's physically stronger than me, and I know that there's a good chance I'll lose in another one-on-one altercation, but at least then I wouldn't feel like I'm just sitting here doing nothing. Not even trying to save my own life. I can't do anything if he never opens the goddamn door. At least he's allowing me to make use of the toilet, for the time being, anyway. The water to the sink and shower has been shut off, though, so I probably have nowhere to drink from. In the past, he would systematically take things away whenever I misbehaved. It started small, and looking back, I've realized that

39

it was such a gradual process that I've stopped beating myself up for not noticing it right away or for all the times that my brainwashed mind made up excuses for his behavior—because that's exactly what he did to me. Brainwashed me. It's hard to see the world for what it is when you're young, starved for affection, and wearing a pair of rose-colored glasses. But what started as tiny restrictions evolved into things much worse, and the time came when I could no longer pretend that what I felt coming from him was his own uniquely warped version of love. His love included pain, and while I knew that sometimes love hurt, I finally came to terms with the fact that it wasn't supposed to hurt like this. Unfortunately, by the time I had that epiphany, I was already broken down and desolate. A shell of what I once was. There was no joy anymore. No laughter, no more shades of pink and red. Only gray. Only shadows and what had once been a head and heart filled with beautiful music had been reduced to one song. When that song wasn't playing, there was only silence. Right now, I'd welcome the silence with open arms. The fact that this man had single-handedly ruined Bach for me was like a simmering fire in my gut.

As I stand in front of the bathroom mirror, I'm at least thankful for the use of the toilet. You never quite appreciated indoor plumbing until you had to pee in a bucket in the corner of a room that was locked from the outside. Thankfully, things haven't reached that point yet. I keep telling myself that I know how to play the game better now. What Dante doesn't know is that everything he put me through before did nothing but condition me to be stronger. To fight harder. I think my newfound rebellion has thrown him for a bit of a loop. I'd bet he's taking time to reassess and decide how best to handle me. The joke's on him; I won't be handled this time. I'll fight tooth and nail for as long as I've got breath in me. This man, if you can even call him that, has already taken enough from me. For six years, I lived in misery. A gilded cage. One in which I was beaten, tortured, humiliated, and ruined. After my escape, I somehow managed to take what small pieces were left and stitch together something resembling a human being. Someone with goals and dreams and friends. Eventually, even the music came back. Not this particular song, but the melodies that had always been a constant companion inside my head, filling the silence left on the outside by parents who were never there. After all the hard work of finding myself again, I refuse to go back to being Dante's broken little doll. I'd die first.

The sound of raised voices in the hall has my ears perking up. I noticed the volume of the music was lowered about half an hour ago. I have no idea why. At the time, all I could think was *thank God*. Maybe the voices outside my room have something to do with it. Tiptoeing from the adjoining bathroom, which is probably ridiculous considering there are eyes on me at all times, I press my ear to the wood of the door. I hear several men talking heatedly. I recognize one of the voices as Dante's but I don't know the others and they sound too far away for me to make out what they're saying. Shit. I *need* to hear what's going on out there. If he's planning something and is foolish enough to discuss it near my room, it may give me the advantage I need to get the drop on him. Unfortunately, no matter how hard I press my ear to the wood, it's just too thick. The voices are still too muffled to make out what they're saying. Feeling discouraged but not giving up by a long shot, I begin to turn back towards the chair in the corner to strategize. I refuse to sit on that bed again. If he wants to get me on it, he'll have to drag me there. Just as I'm taking my first step away from the door, I feel a small waft of air and glance down. My eyes bounce back and forth from my bare feet to the bottom of the door. The one that's got about an inch worth of gap between it and the floor. Yes! Lowering myself down to my stomach, I peer through the crack. I can make out the legs and feet of three men at the end of the hallway, right in front of the door that may serve as Dante's office. One set of those feet definitely belongs to him. I'd recognize those shoes anywhere. The pretentious fuck. He was always very particular about brands and price tags. Dante grew up dirt poor, the son of a barber with a drinking problem. His father spent more money on booze than he ever did on food for his family. How he still managed to idealize the man, I had no idea. But it's no wonder that when Dante inevitably turned to a life of crime and actually got some money of his own, he developed severe delusions of grandeur. Rolling my eyes at his feet, I press my face as close as possible to the gap beneath the door, trying to see if I can figure out who the other men are. There's no way to tell by the legs, but based on the shoes on their feet, they're definitely not guards. Whoever they are, they must've just come out of Dante's office. Taking my eyes from the crack is a gamble, but one I'm gonna have to take. Tilting my head, I press my ear to the opening, finally able to make out some of their conversation.

"Are you sure you want to do this?" one of the unknown men asks. His Italian accent is thick but I don't recognize the voice. "You know it's only a matter of time before he comes after you."

The other unknown man tacks on, "Exactly my thoughts. Right now, he doesn't know you're the one with the diamond, but if you try to sell it, the trail will eventually lead him right to your doorstep."

The reply comes from Dante's voice. "Once it's out of my hands, it's not my problem anymore. He can chase down the poor bastard that buys it. But even so, I'm not worried about Ilya. He's getting old; from what I hear, no one respects his successor. His true heir is nowhere to be found, and really, at this point, all he has is his reputation. That type of fear only invokes loyalty for so long. There are many in the Bratva that think he's gone soft and is ready to be replaced," he says. I can see his feet pacing back and forth in the hall as he continues. "You both know my situation. I don't want to sell the stone, but I don't have a choice." Dante's voice lowers before he says, "It's all I have left. If I'd gotten rid of it three years ago, the way I planned, I'd be sitting on an island somewhere, with Ilya Kapranov none the wiser. Instead, I spent years recovering and reclaiming what was mine. I came from nothing, and I'll be damned if I go back to being nothing, all because of a fucking woman."

Three years ago? A woman? He's gotta be talking about me. I wonder if the circumstances of my escape wrecked some deal he had in the works. Maybe I cost him a lot of money? And what diamond are they talking about? I thought that by eavesdropping, I'd get some answers to the questions that have been rattling around my brain for days, but instead, all I have now are more questions. Most of what they said meant nothing to me, but one thing certainly stood out amongst the rest. The name, Ilya Kapranov. Russia is a big place, but surely it can't just be a coincidence that the sexy Russian FBI agent who's been popping in and out of our lives for the last few months has the same last name as this Ilya person. Could they be related? Ugh, the unknowns are going to drive me insane. The low hum of the music isn't enough to disguise how deafening the silence in the hall is. Worried that he will come in soon, I begin to push up from the floor when I hear one of the other men pipe up.

"Speaking of the woman, do you think it was wise to take her with everything else going on? She was the cause of your ruination before, after all. What if she manages to do so again? If it's a matter of revenge, just kill her and be done with it."

So it *is* me they're talking about. When I left Dante the first time, he obviously survived, but what I did to him clearly cost him greatly. Good. I hope I do get the chance to do it again. Pressing my ear harder to the gap, I wait for Dante's reply with bated breath.

"I know what I'm doing. She won't escape me again. She's developed something resembling confidence since the last time, but I'll break her, just like before. It's only a matter of time. I have plans for her, and those plans require her to be with me at all times so I can control her movements, her mind, and, eventually, her spirit. A spirit that I *will* break. But no matter what happens, I won't be parted from her again. *She's mine.*" The other two men remain silent, which is probably wise. Maybe even they recognize that he sounds more than a little unhinged, and it would be in their best interest not to oppose him.

As the voices from the hall grow fainter, I put my eye under the door again and see that they're heading down the stairs. Thank fuck. I need time to sit and think about everything I've just heard. The irony of the fact that I was spoiling for a fight with Dante only moments ago, and now I'm thanking my lucky stars that he's not coming in here isn't lost on me. God, I wish I could call Amelia. She'd tell Merrick, who'd tell Deacon, who'd tell Alexi, and between all of them, they'd figure out what's going on. But I can't. I'm stuck here in a kind of endless purgatory. That, in itself, is its own type of torture, and maybe that's exactly what Dante intended, leaving me alone for the last three days. I can't stand seclusion. I hate being alone with my own thoughts almost as much as I hate him. Being in this house with this man and listening to that music is essentially killing me slowly. Finally standing, I begin to pace back and forth from one side of the room to the other. With my arms crossed over my chest, I try my best to dislodge the whispers floating around my head. They're always in his voice, things he used to croon to me, and the tone always belied by the weight of his words whenever he was hurting me the most.

"*You deserve this.*"

"*You and I are destined to be together.*"

"*No one else ever wanted you, not even your parents. No one else ever will.*"

"*I'm the only one that loves you.*"

Gripping the sides of my head in both hands, I shake it violently back and forth. No, no, no. Lies. They were all lies. Lies he told, to keep me docile. To keep me dependent on him. To keep me under control. Suddenly overwhelmed with the urge to scream, I give in and let loose a shriek of rage that would make a banshee proud. I scream out all my built-up frustration at being stuck here, all the fear about what comes next, and all the hate I still harbor inside me for this bastard. I scream until I run out of breath and my throat burns. Running my fingers through my still-damp hair, I swivel around to pace back in the other direction and come face-to-face with Dante. As we stare at each other, I try to analyze the look in his eyes. It's menacing, sure, but what I really see in the dark depths is ... pleasure. He likes seeing me lose my cool. It's an indication that he's getting to me, and in his mind, he'll assume that means I'm reaching my breaking point. But he doesn't know me. He used to, but that's not who I am anymore. This version of me is vengeance personified. I will *not* go down without a fight. So I don't step back when I realize he's there. I stand my ground but still watch him carefully. He cocks his head to one side, studying me. Like a child or a dog would when they're trying to figure something out.

Finally, he says, "I'm glad I still have the ability to make you scream, Sirena. Though, I wish you would've waited for me. I had to handle some business, but we can finally begin now."

Begin what?? When he talks about me screaming, I know he's referring to torture, but whether it's of the physical or sexual kind, I'm not sure. Either way, I'm not interested.

Without warning, I rear back, attempting to headbutt him in the nose. At the last second, he turns his head, sidestepping me and causing me to graze his cheek instead. Not very ladylike of me, but you know what? Fuck ladylike. If he doesn't like the person I've become, he can take me back home and drop me off right where he found me. He turns back to face me slowly, deadly intent written all over his features. I watch warily as he takes off his suit jacket and lays over the back of the nearby chair. I brace for whatever's coming next because I know whatever it is, it's gonna hurt. I expect a slap or maybe even a punch. But when he reaches his hand into the pocket of his slacks and removes something rectangular that glints silver when it catches the light above, my blood runs cold.

"That wasn't very nice, Sirena. Do you remember what I said to you the first night I brought you here?" he asks.

As he lifts the old-fashioned barber's razor that I know belonged to his father, I finally allow a healthy measure of fear to take over and take a slow step backward. It's not a retreat, just self-preservation. At least, that's the excuse I tell myself.

"I told you, I spent so much time and energy turning your body from a worthless lump of clay into a beautiful work of art, and you go and ruin it with these unsightly blemishes. Tell me, when you look in the mirror, do you still see my name on your skin?"

I shake my head no, even though I know it's a lie. I hate looking at myself in the mirror. I always have, even before him. As a child and throughout my teen years, I went through the motions, not realizing there was a term for what I was experiencing—Body Dysmorphia. Those issues were only ever reinforced by my parents, other students at school, and young people of my own social class. Adults could be cruel, but kids were even more so, and Dante knows this. He knows how I felt about my body when we first met and, how self-conscious I was about my weight, how I hated nearly everything about myself. But that's not the focus of the conversation now. No, now he's referring to all the cuts that he painstakingly made in my flesh during the time we were together. The ones that I've spent the last two years covering with tattoos. Most are on my back and upper shoulders, but some are in places like my thighs and ribcage. Any place he put his blade, I wanted a needle full of ink there afterward.

He laughs low under his breath, moving towards me. "Don't lie to me, Sirena. I know you better than that." Flicking the blade open, he continues, "Unfortunately, I will have to punish you for what you've done. But after that, we'll start fresh. There's still more than enough left of you to mold, after all."

CHAPTER 5

Deacon

It doesn't take long to get from Siren's apartment to my house when you're speeding at about the same rate on the trip coming back as you were going. Not that I have it in me to care. Just like before, the thought of being pulled over by a cop is the furthest thing from my mind right now. As I guide my car down the long, familiar dirt road that stands as my driveway, my mind may very well be racing faster than my car. On its surface, the possibilities of who could've taken Siren are endless. There are dozens, if not hundreds, of people out there who would love to get to Merrick or me. But if this had anything to do with Merrick, they would've gone after Amelia, not Siren. No, this is either about me and something I've done, or it's not about any of us. I have a hard time believing this is just a random act by some stranger, though. The fact that so much care went into packing her clothes and even her violin tells me that this is personal, most likely to her. Someone spent time watching that apartment and learning her routine. Time planning this abduction. This isn't the act of some rando.

As the driveway ends and the space opens up, my home finally comes into view. If I'd been anyone else, silent alarms would've been tripped the second I turned onto the dirt road. As it is, the recognition software I developed is programmed to scan both my car and my face, then disengages all of the security measures surrounding the most inconspicuous house you've ever seen in your life. Which is a good thing because right now, I don't have the patience to deal with phone alerts and passcodes. Bringing my car to a stop, I jump out and seconds later, I'm bounding up the stairs. Opening the front door that's already been unlocked by the system, I walk inside, going straight through the living room, dining room, and kitchen. On the other side of the kitchen is the laundry room, which no one would ever pay any attention to. That was the whole point. Hidden behind a sliding wall that would make Tim Curry's character from Clue proud, is a door. Unlike the rest of the house's décor, this door is made of solid steel and about four inches thick. Similar to the type you'd find on a bank vault, what lies behind it is just as valuable. Information. Opening a panel activates a three step biometric system that requires voice, fingerprint, and iris scans. If someone were to actually reach the door and open the panel, the system was created to automatically lock down if the required verifications aren't entered within 15 seconds. This is plenty of time for me, considering I have all the required documentation, as it were. As the door releases with a sound very similar to an airlock container being opened, I enter my favorite room of the house. The one that nobody besides Merrick knows exists. Three short steps down, and I'm standing in the center of my own version of paradise. The wall directly in front of me is devoted to nothing but monitors. Large screens that automatically go dark when no one is in the room but that now light up with wave after wave of information. The system here is synced to my laptop, so to save time, I booted it up in the car on the drive home. I put my laptop down and sit in a chair positioned behind the main desk, directly in front of the wall of screens. I stare up at a large picture of Siren on one of the monitors. Next to it lists all her personal details. Not just the ones that are a matter of public record but everything from her social security number to the time and date of her next doctor's appointment. Do I feel bad about prying into her background? Before today, maybe I would've said yes. Now, not in the least. Because if there's the possibility that I'm able to uncover something that can point me in the direction of the person who took her, I'll gladly let her scream at me for invading her privacy when I've got her standing in front of me again. As I stare at the screens, my fingers fly furiously over the keyboard. As new documents and details flash in front of my eyes, one after the other, I just become increasingly frustrated. Every bit of new information I learn about Siren piques my interest and only makes me want to know more about her. But that's not the point of this fact-finding mission. Nothing I uncover gives any indication that it could be related to where she is or who may have abducted her.

Scrubbing my hand over my face, I glance at my watch and have to blink hard at the time before I accept the fact that I've been sitting here for four hours. As much as I'd like to keep going and pray that something jumps out, I know that if I don't get some sleep, I'm not only gonna be useless when it comes to gathering information, but I'm also gonna be crabby as fuck tomorrow. Well ... today, technically. Also, tired people make mistakes, and I'm not a person who makes mistakes when it comes to digging up info. Pushing back from the desk, I rest my forearms on my knees and hang my head in defeat for a moment. There's something I'm missing. There's gotta be. Something I've either overlooked or just too exhausted to recognize as significant. I finally force myself to stand up and wearily make my way over to the same door I entered through. Closing up everything behind me, I drag myself back through the house and down the hallway that leads to my bedroom. There, I fall into bed, still fully clothed. Booted feet hanging off the side, I barely manage to toe them off and lay my head back on the pillow before it's lights out for me. Tomorrow's a new day and a new opportunity to look at the situation through fresh eyes. I can only pray that whoever has Siren isn't hurting her in the meantime. This isn't the first time that the little curvy firecracker is the last thing on my mind before I fall asleep, and I'm sure it won't be the last. I just wish that this time it were under better circumstances.

A buzzing in my skull wakes me, and it takes me a solid minute to realize it isn't coming from inside my head but from underneath my pillow. Realizing that it's gotta be my phone because I haven't actually turned on my ringer since about 2010, I barely look at the caller ID before I hit the green button and bring the phone to my ear.

Merrick's voice cuts through the fog, clouding both my mind and vision like a knife through room-temperature butter. With little effort and with extreme purpose. Fuck, now I want a toasted muffin.

"... hello? Deacon, are you listening to me?"

Shaking off the remnants of a very lucid and possibly sexy dream featuring a currently missing woman, I berate my twisted brain while quickly glancing at the time before I reply, "I fell asleep three hours ago. Sorry, I'm not more attentive, darling. Maybe if you'd shown up with a cup of coffee and a muffin, I'd be more inclined to play the doting housewife and hang on your every word."

See? Crabby. Sighing, I say, "Shit. Sorry, I'm just tired. Though, I really do want a coffee and a muffin. Blueberry preferably."

I'm greeted by silence for several seconds before I hear, "Did you find anything?" See, that's one thing I love about Merrick. He's the only person alive who can navigate my ever-changing moods and let the ups and downs of my personality roll right off his back. Or, to put it in layman's terms, he tolerates my bullshit really well.

Sighing heavily, I say, "Not much. Or should I say, not much that I didn't already know. Not that I've been stalking the woman before this." I may have been stalking the woman before this.

"I talked with Amelia after you left last night. She thinks you should look into Siren's whereabouts from when she was 16 until just after she turned 22. According to Amelia, Siren left town mysteriously at 16 with some guy, and something bad must've happened because all she'd tell me was that when she went to pick her up six years later, she was in a bad state. She isn't sure, because Siren never wanted to go into detail about what happened during those six years, but she knows that during that time, someone hurt her. Where that person is now, she doesn't know."

Sitting up, I throw my legs over the side of the bed, looking down to see that I'm still wearing yesterday's clothes. Putting Merrick on speakerphone, I stand and tug my shirt over my head. The light pouring in through the window catches and highlights the many tattoos littering my chest as well as the ones that comprise both full sleeves. Heading for the bathroom, I turn on the shower before coming back into my bedroom to drop my pants and pull my socks off, nearly falling over in the process.

"What's that noise?" Merrick asks.

"Oh, nothing. Just me nearly killing myself. Please continue."

He is not the least bit dissuaded by my sarcasm because, let's be honest, he's used to it by now. He does indeed continue.

"Amelia said that one night, right after her 22nd birthday, she got a phone call around 2 a.m. from an unknown number. When she answered, it was Siren. She said she was in trouble and asked Amelia if she could come pick her up. Amelia said she gave her directions to some seedy motel not far from Palm Beach, Florida. She drove through the night and got there around 10 a.m. the next morning."

I realize I'm standing stark naked in the middle of my bedroom when Amelia speaks up for the first time. Obviously, I'm not the only one that uses the speakerphone function. Even though neither of them can see me, the fact that I'm talking to Merrick's very pregnant wife while standing in my birthday suit skeeves even me out a little. I feel guilty for being naked, which is absolutely ridiculous since I'm in my own damn bedroom.

"Deacon, when I opened the door to the motel room, it was pitch black inside. She was huddled down on the floor between two double beds. She'd lost about 50 pounds since I'd last seen her. Her hair and face were a mess, and she just had a cheap motel towel pressed to her front." She pauses, and the ominous feeling that things are about to get much worse is confirmed when she continues. "I think she had on a shirt at one point but had to take it off because her back was covered in cuts. Slashes made by some kind of knife or blade. There was blood everywhere. It was dried up in her hair and all over her hands. I assumed it was her own because a lot of the cuts on her back were still bleeding. But she also had what looked like cigar burns on other parts of her body. Some healed and scarred over, some fresh. The minute I crouched down in front of her, she burst into tears. I tried to hug her but I couldn't even put my arms around her. When I finally got her calmed down enough to speak, she would only say that she'd done what she had to do and that she wanted to go home. So I helped her gather the few things she had with her, and we drove straight back to Charleston. She stayed with me for nearly a month before she'd even face her parents, not that they gave a shit. But during that month, she'd wake up every other night screaming. Something happened to her during those few years, and I think it's got something to do with whoever has her now."

Sitting back down on the edge of the bed, I stare at the phone, trying to process everything she's just said and reconcile the image of the barely there girl from that motel with the busty dynamo that I've come to know. I can't picture it, and I realize that the harder I try, the tighter my grip on the phone becomes until I can no longer feel my hand. Deliberately loosening my hold, I say as calmly as possible, "I'm gonna have a quick shower, then I'll get back to the computer."

"Thank you, Deacon. Thank you so much." Amelia says. The dueling worry and relief in her voice are palpable but she shouldn't thank me just yet. I may be good with technology but I don't tell her that, in my experience, those with enough money and a high desire not to be found usually aren't. And from what it sounds like, during that time, whoever had Siren wouldn't just be doing that type of shit to her out in the open. Which means tracking them won't be a cakewalk. Sucks for them that I happen to be a muffin kinda guy anyway.

Saying my goodbyes with as much reassurance as I'm capable of giving at this point, I hang up, stand, and make my way back into the bathroom in a kind of daze. Sitting my phone on the counter, I step under the hot spray, letting the water wash away the remnants of sleep and try to shake the sick feeling that things are gonna get a lot worse before they get better.

CHAPTER 6

Siren

Something is tickling my nose. The feeling of fabric against the side of my face has confusion rushing through me. I try to bring my hand to my face to scratch at the itch, but when I tug at my arm, I'm met with resistance. Turning my head, I push my face into the fabric, which must be a pillow, and rub it back and forth to satisfy the need to scratch. Wait. Pillow? The last thing I remember was finding a bottle of water underneath the bed. Assuming it'd been forgotten there and desperate with dehydration, I'd guzzled it down. Everything after that is a blank. I don't remember falling asleep; even if I had, it would never have been in this bed. Nevertheless, as I try to open my eyes, my lids feel like they weigh a thousand pounds. That mother fucker put something in the water. He must have. It's the only thing that makes sense. He planted that bottle there and fucking drugged me. Fury rising by the second, I finally manage to crack my eyes open, but it takes several seconds for my vision to adjust to the bright light in the room. Tugging at my hands again, I look up to find them tied tight to the bedposts with thick silk ribbon. Panic liquifies my insides into soup, and as I crane my head around to see that my ankles are also tied to the opposite corners of the bed, the urge to vomit has my mouth watering. Lifting up slightly, it dawns on me with horror that I'm naked. Spread-eagle upside down on the same bed that I've refused to sleep in since I got here. Hysteria threatens to take over when my brain finally registers the music. That fucking song! Pulling fruitlessly on the ties, I desperately yank and yank until blood begins to trickle down my wrists. The thought crosses my mind that even something as soft as silk can be weaponized if done by the right person. Or, in this case, the wrong person.

Even as the silk rubs my wrists raw, I pull, trying to free myself. When I've exhausted myself and still made no progress, I open my mouth and let out a scream full of frustration, pain, and anguish. It's happening again. and I'm helpless to stop it. The sudden sound of a deep laugh cuts through the music playing from an old fashioned record player in the corner of the room. Trying to turn my upper body around enough to see him, I can barely make out the figure sitting in the chair near the bed. The red tip of his favored cigar glows as he puffs, and clouds of smoke waft over towards me, making the sick feeling in my stomach infinitely worse. Bile rises up my throat but I manage to swallow it back down, along with the lump that's suddenly formed there. The urge to cry is nearly overwhelming, but I refuse to give him the satisfaction. No matter what happens next, I'll hold out for as long as possible. I won't break as easily as I did the first time. I like the new me and refuse to give her up without a fight.

Between panting breaths, I say, "I'm gonna fucking kill you, you bastard! Not just try but actually succeed this time!"

Standing from the chair, Dante slowly walks over to the side of the bed. I try to recoil away from him, but it's impossible, and based on the smile that spreads across his face, he knows that. Reaching down with the hand still holding the cigar, he trails a finger down the length of my spine. The touch causes every hair on my body to rise in alarm. I jerk as hard as I can in the opposite direction, but before I can dislodge his hand, he's flipped the cigar over and pressed the lit end against the skin at the base of my spine. I grit my teeth to keep from crying out.

"I told you, Sirena. It was a mistake to cover my marks with all this ink. Do you think I want to have to hurt you again?"

I puff out great gusts of air around the pain he's causing and say, "Yes. I think you're a sick fuck that gets off on causing other people pain." As I say it, I can feel the burning sting from the cigar radiating outward. A fresh wave of anger pulses through me, nearly as hot as the fresh wound. Even knowing I'll pay for it, I turn my head to face him, craning my neck as far as my bonds will allow, and spit in the general direction of his face.

Ever so slowly, he reaches up and wipes the side of his bearded cheek. Staring at the tip of his finger for a moment, he meets my eyes before bringing the finger to his mouth and sucking it clean. Just when I have the thought that the sick bastard actually liked that, a powerful hand grips the back of my neck, pushing my face hard into the pillow. I can't breathe. My moment of defiance quickly morphs into one of terror, and that moment seems to last hours as I struggle desperately to twist my head around enough to get to the air hovering just out of reach. Bright colors burst behind my closed eyelids, and there's a ringing in my head that starts off so loud, but as the rest of my body flails, trying to buck his hand off, that ringing begins to drift away, fading into a blissful silence. Just when I'm sure that I'm about to suffocate to death, the pressure on my neck lessens, and I jerk my head to the side, taking great pulls of air into my lungs, all the while coughing and trying to see past the spots swimming in my vision. He doesn't remove his hand from the back of my neck, but instead of pressing downward again, he squeezes it tightly, bringing his mouth close to my ear as he speaks his next words. I can tell that he's breathing nearly as hard as I am, but I know that it's not from the effort of holding me down. It's from excitement.

"I want to be angry that you seem to have forgotten all the lessons I taught you, but I'm not. Before, you were like unmolded clay. Mine to shape and so easily manipulated. You're like a wild horse now, and I will take even greater pleasure in taming you." Hot breath fans my ear, and I grit my teeth to keep the retort that's on the tip of my tongue inside. I know I have to pick and choose my battles.

Voice dropping an octave, he hisses, "You will submit to me, Sirena. Neither of us has a choice in this. You were mine from the moment I laid eyes on you, and you will be mine until you draw your last breath. Whenever that may be..." He trails off, but the threat is clearly implied. Before I realize what he's doing, he's sat the cigar in the ashtray on the bedside table and is straddling me. I know what's coming before I even hear the quiet swish of the barber's blade being flipped open.

"AHHH!! Don't you fucking dare!!" I scream, but my words fall on deaf ears. Within seconds, I feel the sharp stab of pain as he drags the blade over the skin of my right shoulder blade. As crazy as it sounds, I can feel every movement of the razor. It's a heart. He's cutting a heart into my skin. Soon, the pain becomes unbearable, and I can't stop the scream that tears from my lips, echoing around the room, effortlessly blending in with the rising swells of the music. The sliding of the blade in and out of my skin seems to last for hours. With every cry of pain and every tear that manages to slip through my closed eyelids, I can feel the length of him hardening against my lower back. He's loving this. Even knowing that I can't help the sob that's muffled by the pillow as I bury my face deep into the soft cotton. Sliding down my body like the snake he is, I hear the sound of a zipper being pulled down seconds before I feel the thick weight of his erection sliding up and down my backside as he grinds himself against me.

All of my resolve to be strong and not allow him to take what small parts of me I still have left fly out the window. I'm prepared to beg, even knowing the effort is futile, so I say, "Dante, please! Please don't do this. I'll behave, I promise." It's a lie, but one that falls easily from my lips because, at this moment, I'll tell him anything he wants to hear to keep him from what he's about to do.

"I know you will, Sirena. You'll be my good girl now, and eventually, when I feel you've earned it, you'll be my wife. I'll give you the world. All you have to give me in return is this: your body, your pain, and your music. Your cries are better than any symphony could ever be. You'll sing for me now, then later I'll get your violin, and you can play for me too."

Without warning, he pulls back his hips, positions himself, and thrusts to the hilt inside me. Crying out at the searing pain, I can do no more than break down as he leans in and runs his tongue over one of the cuts on my back. As the revolting sound of a groan releases from his throat, he pulls back and shoves into me again and again, all the while cleaning up the bloody mess left by his blade. Soon, agony turns to numbness, and my voice goes horse from all my screams. As the tears pour from my eyes, soaking into the pillow beneath me, I turn my head towards the wall adjacent to the bed and stare at nothing. Because that's what I'll be when he's finished. Nothing. And right now, I'm okay with that. I want nothing. I pray for nothing. No more Siren, no more music, just ... *nothing*.

CHAPTER 7

Deacon

12 YEARS OLD

Mama was high again. Most kids my age wouldn't even know what that meant, much less be able to recognize it. But this has been my reality for as long as I can remember. It took me a long time to understand that there were different types of addicts in this world. The high-functioning types that were able to get through everyday life while simultaneously touching the clouds, and the types that hit the ground hard and stayed there. Mama had started out the first type. She took her "medicine" every day. Little white pills that, over time, had become yellow and were now red. When I was younger, I thought she got them from her doctor, and maybe she did in the beginning. But now, I know she buys them illegally. Doctors don't meet you in empty parking lots and accept only cash. These days, Mama wasn't so high-functioning. She slept a lot, and the small house that had always felt like a home was falling apart around us. I loved my mother but didn't know how to help her anymore. There used to be a time when I was younger, she'd look at my face and just start crying. I'd think I'd done something wrong, but then she'd pull me in for a hug and tell me how much she loved me. I believed her. When she says it now, I still do. Though, sometimes I can't help but wonder which she loves more, me or the pills?

It didn't used to be like this. Sure, we've always been poor, always had to scrape by on the rent, electricity, and other bills. But Mama always made sure I had food and clothes. When summer breaks ended and school time came back around, she'd find money to get me pencils and paper and new shoes. Granted, they weren't brand-name shoes but they were still new. Over the years, though, our life seems to have begun to crumble, and now I don't even think she knows what day it is most of the time. It scares me. I know I shouldn't be scared because I'm 12 and about to be a teenager, but I am. I've tried to talk to her about her medicine, but whenever I do, she just brushes me off or says everything's fine. But it's not fine, and I don't think it ever will be. That thought scares me, too.

Because Mama isn't capable of providing for us the way she used to, I've begun to do things. Things I know aren't strictly legal. I was good with computers. Better than good, actually. I knew how to do things that most grown adults working for the government couldn't do. When I'd figured that out, I'd started taking money from places I shouldn't. Skimming small amounts from bank accounts that belonged to God only knows who. Just enough to pay the bills and get food. I knew I wouldn't get caught. I was good at covering my tracks. But no amount of money would fix what was wrong with Mama. Sure, there were places she could go to get off the pills, but I knew she'd just end up going back to them. Mama's problems were in her head. Unless she could get rid of those, she'd never stay clean. And I had a feeling that, just like the pills, I was both the cause and cure for that problem. I knew just by the way she looked at me when she was sober ... and the way she looked at me when she was high. I wondered more and more if it had anything to do with my father. The one she refused to talk about when sober, but I think she saw him in her head when she was high. Maybe that was why she took so much. Maybe she preferred his company to mine.

A loud clattering sound from the kitchen jerks me out of my head and back to reality. Surveying the damage from my vantage point on the threadbare couch of the living room, I see that the commotion was a mountain of old tupperware falling from the highest cabinet to the floor.

"Shit!" I hear Mama murmur under her breath. Leaning down to pick up one of the plastic containers, I watch as she loses her balance and nearly falls over. Jumping up from the couch, I rush to the kitchen to steady her.

"I'll get it, Mama. Don't worry about it." I say.

Attempting to brush my hands away, she says, "No, no. I can do it, baby. It's my mess. It's not your job to clean up behind me."

I sigh internally. Because it *had* become my job, it had become more frequent as the years went on. It was just a fact of life now. Taking my mother's hand, I pull her toward the living room sofa and ease her down. I can feel the blue stone she wears on her left hand pressing against the inside of my palm where it's been twisted around. It's a testament to how far away she is mentally that she allows me to drag her to the couch without protest. As she sits, she places her hands demurely in her lap, and after a few seconds, just like many times before, her gaze lands on the ring.

She turns it around so it's facing the right way and rubs her opposite thumb over the gem, staring at it with a fixated look that makes it clear she isn't here anymore. At least, that's what I think until she opens her mouth and says, "Your Daddy was gonna get me a real one, you know. He promised ... someday, he'd get me a real one, and we'd get married."

I look down at the fake stone. Even though it's clearly costume jewelry, the blue still catches the light and shines brightly back at me. Set in a simple silver band, the ring stands out like a rock on Mama's frail hand.

"No matter how hard I wished, he never kept his promise," she whispers, still absently rubbing at the jewelry. Then, as if waking up from some hypnotic state, her eyes shift to focus on mine. They're cloudy, but she still manages to keep them trained on my face. As our gazes hold, she reaches up and cups the side of my face, stroking her thumb over my cheek. In a small voice, she mutters, "Just like stars ..." I know she's talking about my eyes. *His* eyes. She's said similar things before. "He promised me the stars too. I guess I got em' ... just not the way I thought." Her voice is melancholy, as though she's going to burst into tears at any moment. Sometimes, she does, so I brace for it. But she just drops her hands back to her lap, eyes returning to the ring.

I gently place my hand over hers to still the rhythmic motion of her thumb on the stone, and, while I have her attention, say, "I'll get you a real one someday, Mama." Smiling sadly at me, she takes a long blink, and a tear rolls down her gaunt cheek.

Leaning her head back, I watch as she closes her eyes. For a split second, panic surges up inside me, and I stare hard at her chest, waiting for the lack of movement that would signal that she's stopped breathing. But her chest rises and falls slowly and after a minute or two, my panic subsides somewhat.

Eyes still closed, she says, "I'm just gonna take a little nap, baby. I'm tired, that's all. When I wake up, we'll go out for dinner. How does that sound?" She asks the question, but I can tell that she's not gonna hear my answer. I say it anyway.

"Sure, Mama. That sounds good," I reply, but I know that dinner time will come and go before she wakes again. Either way, I'll cook something so she can eat when she wakes up. She would usually forget to eat unless I reminded her. Leaving her there on the couch, I go to my room and get one of the thin blankets off my bed, bringing it back to cover her. She's asleep now, and as I look at her face, she suddenly appears so much older than her 30 short years. Sighing heavily, I get up and go to the little kitchen to pick up the spilled tupperware and restack it in the cabinet. I take down a pot, fill it with water, and begin making some boxed mac and cheese for dinner, all the while stealing glances at Mama's chest ... just in case.

CHAPTER 8

Siren

During the brief periods of time that I allow my consciousness to surface, everything hurts. The pain is so overwhelming that it takes very little effort to let myself sink back under again. I'd rather be drowning than breathe in air that smells like copper and sweat. The copper is mine, the sweat is his. It was a pairing of scents I'd hoped to never smell again. Despite my resolve to fight him, each time it takes less and less effort on his part to overpower me. My refusal to eat or drink anything else hasn't helped and even though I know I need to conserve energy to keep my stamina up, I can't stomach the thought of being drugged again. What he does to me when I'm awake is bad enough. What he does when I'm unconscious isn't something I can think about or I risk breaking permanently. He's always here now. Every day, several times a day. For the first few days, he kept me tied to the bed, only allowing me free long enough to use the bathroom. I lost the skin around my wrists and ankles pretty quickly, soon turning to open wounds. Since my release from the ties, they've just barely begun to heal. Add it to the list. When he's here, he cleans and dresses the cuts he's made on the rest of my body, only so he can ensure the scarring will turn out exactly as he wants, then he makes new ones. He hasn't let me shower. I know it's because he wants me to smell like him. I know that because he's a creature of habit, and we've been through this song and dance before. I may not be tied up anymore, but I'm still a puppet with strings pulled by a master who takes no care with his toys. During the more brutal of our "lessons," he whispers to me. He tells me how much he missed me, how he forgives me for what happened before, how much he loves me. *Love.* Despite his vehement claims, he doesn't know the meaning of the word. But I don't think I do either when I sit back and think about it. My parents never loved me. Call it the curse of our social class. My only friend growing up was Amelia, and while I knew she'd always be there for me and I'd do anything in the world for her, I wasn't sure if what I felt for her was love. How could you know you were feeling something that you've never been the recipient of before? It took me a long time to realize that it was difficult to recognize how truly being loved made you feel, but it was very easy to recognize the feeling of being without it. I think that's why, when Dante first entered my life, I was so infatuated by him. Because he made me feel something I'd never felt before. I'd handed him my heart, body, and soul on a silver platter, and in return, he'd given me my first true taste of what love really felt like. It felt like a thousand cuts, a hundred bruises, dozens of humiliations, and one rule. Obey.

After a while, I became adept at following that rule. Whether by accident or design, when pushed past a certain point, my mind and body went into a kind of autopilot. Operating with the sole purpose of living another day, even when there were plenty of days I wished would be my last. I guess somewhere in the back of my subconscious, I knew that at some point, he'd have to slip up. Allow me the tiniest window through which I could escape. And eventually, he did. It only took six years. For two years after that, I worked to rebuild my life. I was never the same as before, but I liked to think I became a better version of myself. A smarter version. I'd never again let a man have power over me. Never again allow a man to dictate to me what I could do, where I could go, what I could wear. When I could bathe or when I could use the bathroom. No, at least on the outside, I projected a confident and independent woman. On the inside, I was still very much the scared little girl who smelled copper and sweat everywhere she went.

Blinking hard to dislodge the memories, I realize that it's night-time now, and I'm finally alone. He hasn't cut me over the last three days, and though I'm unsure why, I almost wish he had. The things he chose to do to me instead are somehow worse. After our most recent "lesson", Dante left me here on the blood and tear-stained mattress, allowing me a few precious hours of sleep. As much as I wanted to, sleep eluded me. Curled into a ball on my side, I stared at that familiar wall next to the bed because I'd never even think about laying on my back. We were friends now, the wall and I. It kept my secrets and, just like the trappings of a prison cell, helped me keep track of my days. Not long after I'd gotten here, I'd used one of my nails to make small indentations in the wall, counting the days as they went by so I'd know exactly how long I'd been gone. I had a feeling, however, that I may have been here for a bit longer than I thought, having missed a day here and there when my mind just couldn't handle reality anymore. It still made me feel slightly better, though, because, with each passing day, I knew that my friends would search for me that much harder. Digging that much deeper.

As I stare at that wall, my gaze starts to blur at the edges, and I know that I'm about to enter that headspace where nothing and no one can hurt me. Suddenly, something in the room catches the moonlight coming in through the barred window, and two bright blue spots appear on the expanse of white across from me. Immediately, I think of Deacon. Of how his blue eyes glitter when he's laughing or making some kind of sarcastic joke ... which is always. How they darkened whenever they looked at me. I wonder what he's doing right now. If he's helping Amelia and Merrick search for me. If he even knows or cares that I'm missing. I'd like to think so, but just like the dozens before him, Deacon was a blip on my radar. Blips didn't care about me any more than I cared about them. Blips couldn't hurt you. Even so, as the two spots of blue shimmer in the moonlight, I finally drift off, not into my safe space but to sleep, those bright blue eyes across from me promising rescue and retribution. In my imagination, at least.

The sound of a door slamming open has me jerking awake, the movement causing white-hot flames to erupt all over my body, but especially my back. I can't stop the involuntary yelp of pain. Quickly clamping my mouth shut, I gingerly turn my head towards the door to see Dante striding into the room, holding a white box. Immediately, my brain conjures up images of all the new torture scenarios that he has planned with whatever's in there. Everything inside me starts to tremble, and I know I'm shaking outwardly. I can't help it. Most likely from a mixture of terror and weakness, the combination manifests symptoms that I can no longer control. I stare at him wide-eyed, waiting for news of my next "lesson." However, when he speaks, saying I'm shocked would be an understatement.

"Get up. We have somewhere to be," he says, his accent seemingly more pronounced than usual. As I continue to stare at him as though he's grown a second head, I take in more details that seem ... off. His suit is wrinkled, and his hair is slightly disheveled, as though he's run his hands through it several times. Which he definitely doesn't do. His words are clipped, and he looks frazzled, also, very unlike him. Dante is never frazzled. Frenzied, often. Frazzled, never. When I don't immediately make a move to sit up, he drops the box down on the end of the bed, coming around and gripping my arm in a punishing hold. Pulling me up to my knees, the flames licking at my back combust into an inferno, and he brings his face so close to mine that I can feel the small particles of spit fly from his mouth when he says, "I said move, Sirena! And don't tell me that you're still hurting from the other night. I've let you rest, no? This is why. We have to go out. I'm going to take your bandages off; then you're going to shower and put on what's inside that box. Do something with your hair and face, too. I need a trophy tonight, not a zombie."

The fact that he considers sexually assaulting me instead of slicing open my skin as "letting me rest" would be laughable if anything about this situation was funny. Looking into his eyes, I remember all those years ago when I would've been happy to fall into those dark depths. And so I did, not knowing that there was no bottom. Just an endless cycle of falling, never knowing what chaos I'd go through on the way down. An image of Alice in Wonderland flashes into my mind, and chalking it up to hysteria, I can't stop the laugh that bubbles up my throat and out of my mouth, right into Dante's angry face.

The open-palmed slap is a shock to the system, but the stinging pain in my cheek barely registers. He's done far worse, and I'm sure he'll do worse yet. So when I don't immediately cry out or beg for forgiveness, rough hands release my arm to fist in my hair, dragging me from the bed and towards the now locked bathroom. At this point, I do cry out, but this time in rage.

"Let me go, you son of a bitch!" Kicking and screaming, I try to wrestle his hands from my hair, feeling the strands being ripped from my scalp the entire time. I know I'm probably doing more harm than good but I've cut off my nose to spite my face so many times since I got here that I've lost count and, honestly, I don't give a shit anymore. If he wants to kill me, he can just kill me and get it over with. Within seconds, he stops us in front of the bathroom door, releases one hand from my hair to reach into his pocket, and pulls out a key. Quickly unlocking the door, he pulls me inside, throwing me down hard onto the cream-colored marble. Unlike the bedroom, this room is sparkling. Probably because the bastard has barely let me use it since I got here. I watch from my place on the floor as he steps over to the shower stall, pulling back the frosted glass of the sliding door and turning the water on. My eyes quickly dart between him and the open bathroom door. I could try to run. I might make it past him. If I do, I might be able to get out of the bedroom before he can catch me, and ... then what? I don't know how many men he has in this house or the surrounding grounds. I don't know what weapons they possess or what orders they've been given in regards to me. If I manage to escape, are they supposed to capture me alive or shoot on sight? Surely, he'd want me back alive. Right? Unless he'd rather see me dead than run the risk of losing me twice. As the internal struggle wages, the opportunity passes right before my eyes. Hope dwindles as he turns back to me and points to the shower.

"Get in and wash yourself, Sirena, or I'll do it for you. If you make me do it, I promise to take the same care with your body during the process as I've done thus far."

Meaning he'll make it hurt. Of course he would. He'd like nothing more than an excuse to inflict more pain. I know that fighting him further would be futile, and probably only serve to weaken me more, possibly ruining any future escape attempts. Even knowing that, I glare daggers at him before giving one small nod of my head. He lets out a small chuckle that almost has me changing my mind and making a run for it, but I don't. I keep my jaw clamped tightly shut while he exits the bathroom and leaves me to bathe and get ready, for what I don't know. When I hear the bedroom door slam shut, I let out a harsh breath. As I stare down at the cream tiles that were so spotless before, I notice a smear of fresh blood across the one closest to me. I'm bleeding from somewhere. Either a barely healed wound has reopened, or a new one was created when Dante threw me to the hard floor. It's a testament to how desensitized I've become that I can't even pinpoint where the blood is coming from. At this point, the pain receptors in my body are all firing at once. I put my palms on the floor and attempt to push myself up to a standing position. As the tender skin of my back stretches with the effort, I let out a low moan before my arms give out, and I collapse back to the hard tiles. On my hands and knees now, I pant for breath, letting out a small sob that's full of frustration and exhaustion. How did I get back here again? To a place that I told myself I'd never have to return to. For two years, I repeated those words to myself over and over. Every time I woke up screaming or thought I caught a glimpse of his face in a crowded room. Every time I let a man touch me, he was always there in the back of my mind. Tainting everything I did. The only thing that survived was the music. But as I stare at that streak of blood across the floor through watery eyes, I realize there's only silence now. As I blink, a tear falls to mix with the bright red painting the cream tile. Despite my resolve, the negatively intrusive thoughts bombard me. I'm never gonna get out of here. If my friends were going to find me, they would've done it already. No one is looking for me. No one cares. I'm alone ... again.

Eventually, I manage to pull myself up from the floor and step into the shower. I welcome the sting as the water hits my skin, running over every cut and bruise. I take advantage of the gift Dante has unwittingly given me by cupping my hands together and drinking gulp after gulp of the tepid water. As I hang my head, I watch the water turn from clear to red, then red to pink, before eventually running mostly clear again. The same process happens when I work up the energy to shampoo my hair. My arms shake with the effort and I realize that I'm weaker than I thought. I feel like I'm stuck in an impossible position. I know if I don't start eating and drinking, I won't be able to escape, even if the opportunity arises. But the idea of what Dante would do to my body, should I be drugged again has me terrified. I either starve myself to death or allow him unfettered access to every part of me without my consent. Without even being able to attempt to defend myself. Either way, I'm fucked. Despondent, I turn off the shower, drying myself and wrapping my hair in a thick white towel. *White.* I release a humorless laugh. Not for long. As I step out of the bathroom in an almost trance-like state, I stare at the large box on the end of the bed. My stomach churns as I remove the lid to find a pile of black lace, silk, and some makeup and hair products. The thought briefly crosses my mind to question why Dante would want me to go anywhere dressed in this. It's nothing more than black lingerie and a thin silk robe. But as quickly as the thought comes, it drifts away. The whys don't matter anymore. I've finally been pushed past the point of caring. As my body goes through the motions, I dress and do my hair. When I look into the mirror to begin putting on my makeup, I see ... nothing. Blank eyes stare back at me from a face sporting sunken cheeks and dark circles. I try to focus, and as I do, the picture becomes clearer. Releasing another bitter laugh ending in a coughing fit, I realize I recognize this person. I've met her before, and she is nothing. Like a light switch being flipped, Siren takes a backseat to Sirena. Dante's whore. A worthless nobody. Any tears I might've shed over the death of my old self are blotted away as I apply a liberal coat of foundation, knowing Dante won't want any of the bruises to show. When I've finished putting on my makeup, I return to the bedroom. Slipping my feet into a pair of black heels left by the door, I sit obediently on the bed and wait for the next phase of my condemnation to begin. I'll go through the motions until I can't anymore. Until my warped mind makes the decision to remove me from this Earth. Not that it'll matter. In all the ways that count, I'm already dead.

CHAPTER 9

Deacon

As my car approaches Eugene Kingsley's estate, I do a mental checklist of everything I brought with me that I may need tonight. Both physically and figuratively. I'm having a hard time concentrating, which is never a good thing. I need to stay focused on the task at hand, but the situation with Siren is plaguing me. Despite the hours, days, and weeks I've spent combing through every piece of data I can get my hands on, there's still no sign of her. There is nothing on traffic cameras. No credible tips. Nothing on the dark web. It's as if she disappeared into thin air.

I don't believe in magic, only science. Technology. What you could see with your eyes and hear with your ears. Unfortunately, all of those avenues have so far come up empty. I don't like it, not only the fact that I, the man frequently relied upon to find information that even the most intelligent people tired to keep hidden, couldn't find anything. But also my mind is constantly running rampant with thoughts of what could be happening to her; I feel like I'm slowly descending into madness. With every passing day, my nerves become more and more frayed. Three weeks. She's been missing for three weeks and could be God knows where with God knows who. I think that's the part that bothers me most. Not the jab that my ego is taking at not being able to find her, but the very real possibility that someone is hurting her, even now.

After speaking with Merrick and Amelia, I know more about Siren's history. With renewed purpose, I'd dug deep into the missing years after she left home. Again, there wasn't much to find, which made me even more uneasy. Whoever she'd been with when she was a teenager was someone with money, power, and connections. There was no way to go through life without leaving at least a digital footprint unless you were someone who knew how to cover your tracks. Whoever this is, either has their own arsenal of technological skills or they have some seriously influential people in their back pocket. I knew the man was someone important but, to date, I haven't been able to discover his identity. Based on the information I do have, I would guess that he's significantly older than Siren. Probably cultured and so-phisticated. Contrary to what people believed, there were many different classes of criminals and you couldn't run in ours unless you met specific criteria. So, tonight's auction would serve dual purposes. Considering that I'd be rubbing elbows with some of the underworld's elite, I was hoping to not only intercept and spy on the meeting with my father and try to get a lead on Siren's location. All I needed was a whisper, a nugget of information, something. Even if I only had one thread to pull, I could use it to lead me somewhere else. Maybe that thread would lead to another, and eventually, things would unravel, and I'd find her at the other end.

If I was honest with myself, it wasn't only her connection to Amelia that drove me to find her and bring her home. We'd had ... something. I wasn't sure what it was, but she'd disappeared before I had a chance to figure it out. And that just pissed me off. Shortly before Amelia had been shot by her psychotic mother, Siren and I had spent one night together. One ridiculously hot night, in which I'd had her on her knees, putting that smart-ass mouth to good use. Something I'd bet she didn't allow often. *Fuck.* I couldn't think about that night without getting hard. Which was inconvenient and a little disturbing, given the circumstances of her now being missing. The bottom line was I wanted her back. I wanted to explore this thing between us. I wanted her beneath me, covered in sweat and my scent, while I feasted on her body until she was cursing my name. She'd done that before, but it wasn't in the context I wanted. Most importantly, I wanted to save her from whatever trap she'd fallen, or in this case, been locked into.

Shaking my head in an attempt to clear it, I have just enough time to get my mind back on track before reaching the end of the long gravel driveway. Finally, seeing the main house come into view, I let out an audible snort at the over-the-top décor. The mansion definitely befits a construction tycoon with questionable morals and more money than he knows what to do with. It's big and, honestly, ugly as fuck. Made up of large white stone sides with virtually no windows, it looked more like a fortress than a house. I had no doubt that Kingsley had chosen this location to build his monstrosity of a home because of its remote surroundings that were far enough away from prying eyes that the owner could get up to all kinds of misdeeds while still remaining within driving distance of the city. Sitting on a flat piece of land that's been cleared of all trees, the open space surrounding the house was a security guard's wet dream. Unfortunately for them, Mr. Kingsley's annual auction occurred at night, making visibility a bit more difficult. For whatever reason, bad people seemed to believe that the appearance of their sins was somehow diminished in low lighting. The bad people that would be in attendance tonight were no different. Hence, the house sat dead center in the dark expanse of space, sans a handful of tiki-style torches that had been lit and surrounded the house. Shorter versions in a similar style lined the circular gravel drive that already sported a row of cars more expensive than most people would make working a 9-5 job for the rest of their lives. In comparison to this view, my house in Savannah wouldn't be good enough for Mr. Kingsley to take a shit in. I knew people like him. People who were born with a silver spoon in their mouths but spent their entire lives preaching about how hard they'd worked to get where they were. All while stepping on people they considered their inferiors and hoarding every penny from those who so desperately needed it. I had once been one of those people in need, so I recognized Eugene Kingsley as someone who would've spit on me as he passed by while I begged for change on the corner just to get something to eat. I hated men like him. They did nothing but perpetuate the cycle of the wealthy taking everything while giving nothing.

Tonight, I would enact step one of my plan to take a little something back from his type of criminal. Over time, I'd take everything else until these men knew what it was to feel like less than nothing. Gathering up the dirt on my father was my first priority. My need to dish out retribution for everything that man had cost me, was a burning pit deep in my stomach. It ate away at

86

all the good parts of me. The parts my mother had tried so hard to nurture while battling her own demons. I wasn't sure how much of those parts were left, but whatever there was, I needed to preserve them, and the only way to do that was to ruin my father: his good name, his happiness, his life. I would take it all and then some. It was only fair. Men like him didn't deserve to prosper. They deserved to rot. And I had more than one promise to keep.

Pulling my Maybach Exelero to a stop in front of the house, I step out and narrow my gaze at the valet that hustles around the vehicle. Unlike the modest home I live in, this car has an insane price tag. It was one of the few things I'd treated myself to when I got older and began committing serious cyber crimes that stole from the rich to give to the poor. Except this version of Robin Hood had a horse worth around nine million dollars.

As I glare at the snot-nosed little shit that's come to stand in front of me with his hand out, waiting for me to pass my keys over, I channel my inner villain and say, "If anything happens to my car, there won't be enough left of you for your mom to bury."

The kid's eyes widen before he nods frantically. "Yes ... yes s-s-sir," he stutters nervously. Reluctantly handing over my keys, I straighten the jacket of my tux, ensuring the loose-fitting pants and long-sleeve t-shirt underneath are well hidden. I always wore a comfortable change of clothes beneath the monkey suit required for functions like this, just in case I found myself in a tough spot. I'd feel a hell of a lot better if I had a weapon of some kind on me, but this isn't my first rodeo. I know Kingsley will have security at the doors, sweeping guests with discreet metal-detecting wands, in addition to giving them an ocular pat down. That man was rightfully paranoid and had a strict no-weapons policy at these events. His way of keeping people honest was to make sure no one got the drop on him or one of his shady business partners. I couldn't blame him. If I had this many sharks shoved into one tank, I'd be worried about their teeth, too.

Stepping inside, I go through the motions of allowing the guard to sweep me for weapons. He gives me the all-clear, and a blonde in a skin-tight red dress steps up to me and asks for my invitation. Though I'm sure it could've been done, the heavily embossed cardstock I pull from the inside of my jacket pocket isn't a forgery. In the handful of years I've been working with high society's criminal underbelly, I've garnered a reputation that lent me a certain level of respect. And that was only based on what they knew of me as a fence. None of these idiots had any idea about my online persona. The one that could do the most damage. I did everything in my power to keep it that way. When the time came that I chose to make my presence known, it would already be too late for them.

Handing over my invitation, I give her a moment to check its authenticity while I take a seemingly casual glance around the room. I recognized many faces, though not all of them would recognize me in return. I'd never met most of the posh men and women littering the foyer but I knew *of* them. I'd taken care to research many of the key players in the buy/sell/trade game. When it came to art, gems, antiques, guns, drugs, women ... I knew who to keep my eye on. And who not to give my back to. Just glancing around the room, I see Katrina Herrera, Michael Beck, Holly Tucker, and Ray Cooley. Katrina was in the business of drugs, specifically heroin, while Michael's drug of choice had a pulse. The scumbag was one of the biggest sex traffickers on the East Coast. Holly Tucker was a gem dealer and seemed to at least have *something* of a conscience, based on the little face to face interactions I'd had with her in the past. Ray, on the other hand, was another literal piece of human garbage. He sold guns, and didn't give a shit whose hands they fell into after that deposit hit his offshore bank account. Three out of the four were on the list of people who would be wiped clean at the end of my long game.

As the blonde in the red dress nods and welcomes me inside, I head straight to the bar that's been set up along the left side of the foyer. Bypassing all the bottom feeders in designer suits, I order an expensive label whiskey that I won't be drinking and meander to the back of the room. Scoping out the best vantage point, I make my way there so that I can take in the entirety of the room and what lies beyond. Just off the foyer, a large ballroom has been transformed into a showroom of sorts. An empty space devoid of chairs surrounds a large stage that's been erected along the back of one wall. An empty podium stands next to the beginning of a short catwalk, illuminated by bright theater spotlights. As I look on, I can see people doing last-minute audio equipment and lighting checks. As it has for the last few years, the big-ticket items that happen to come in small packages will be put to bid there. Another wall of the room sports a long table full of iPads, presumably showcasing more of the items up for auction, letting people place early bids for some of the lesser valued items that won't be deserving of the stage spotlight. I'm not even gonna bother looking at those. I know what I'm after, and it definitely won't be found on that table. Bringing my glass to my lips, I discreetly appear to take a sip while not actually drinking anything. I wasn't opposed to alcohol, but at a function like this with people like these, I didn't need anything impairing my judgment.

Just then, a man in a uniform so starched I'm surprised he can walk straight steps into the room and says, "The auction will begin in five minutes time. Please make your way into the ballroom if you wish to bid."

Showtime. As I take another sweep of the room, I look around for any hint of my father. Considering that he wouldn't actually be here to bid on anything, I'm not all that surprised when I don't see his face in the migrating crowd. He must not be here yet. That's fine. It'll give me time to verify if the rumors about the jewel I'd come here to get my hands on were true. As I start to make my way into the ballroom, following the rest of the crowd, the blonde from earlier catches my eye. Leaning against a far wall, we make eye contact, and her gaze bores into mine. As I watch, she not-so-subtly glides her hands down the sides of her breasts before sliding them down her stomach and pausing a little too long on the area hidden beneath her extremely short skirt. Cocking an eyebrow at her blatant flirting, I almost bite back a laugh as she licks her lips hungrily. In another lifetime, I'd already be across the room and dragging her into the nearest closet. But as sexy as she is in that tiny red dress, tonight I've got my heart set on something a little more ... blue.

The Oppenheimer Blue, to be exact. The largest vivid blue diamond in the world. I have no doubt that the uptick of guests in attendance tonight has something to do with the rumor that an unknown seller will offer the elusive stone to the highest bidder. I intend on being the highest bidder. Whatever the gem ended up selling for, it wouldn't even be close to the price it fetched at its last *legitimate* sale, which was close to 60 million dollars. It might sell for half that tonight, considering it was now listed as stolen and would be nearly impossible to flip. Well, impossible for most people. I wasn't most people. Not that it mattered. I have no intention of selling it. Giving the blonde a wink and a small shake of my head, which I hope comes across as a little regretful, I enter the ballroom and take a position near the back wall. From this vantage point, I'd be able to see the majority of the people bidding while keeping the stage in clear view. First, I'd get my diamond, then deal with my father. So far, I haven't seen hide nor hair of him. I happened to know that Kingsley only allowed one entrance and exit during this party, which was the one I came in through, so his meeting with this mystery man must be later tonight.

As a man in a sharp black suit steps out from behind a curtain at the back of the stage, a buzz of excitement runs through the waiting crowd. Straightening from my slouched position against the wall, I look on with hooded eyes as the man steps up to the microphone that's been set up at the podium. Soon, the auction begins. As the bidding of each item commences, I notice one significant difference between this year's sale and the ones that have taken place previously. As each piece is brought out to display to the waiting crowd, it's being carried by a woman. A different woman each time, and each one dressed in what I can only imagine is very expensive lingerie to match or accent each item up for bid. Interesting. I have the fleeting thought about whether the women are here voluntarily or if they've been loaned out by one of the many flesh peddlers in attendance. As much as the southern gentleman in me clamors to defend a lady's honor, I know that I can't. I've got more pressing matters to deal with tonight, but I make a mental note to follow up on this later.

That is, until a woman steps out from behind the curtain holding ... nothing. As opposed to the previous girls, who carried paintings or other high priced antiquities, this girl's hands are empty. As she comes to stand next to the podium, a hush falls over the crowd. Unconsciously, my hands ball into fists at my sides as the woman begins to slowly make her way down the catwalk towards the end. Dressed in black lace and some sheer fabric that seems to float around her toned legs like smoke, my eyes track her every move as she nears the end of the runway. My gaze sweeps up her body from the black stilettos that sport straps that twist all the way up her calves; I take in her short but generously curved figure. As my eyes slide over her soft belly and full breasts, they pause only briefly on the large blue diamond that's been set into an intricate silver necklace before finally landing on the girl's face. Aggression gnaws at my insides like a beast attempting to break free of its cage, but it has nothing to do with the stone. It's the girl. As she comes to stand at the end of the catwalk, the men closest to the stage press forward. Trying to get a better look at the stone or to leer at the woman, I don't know. Feeling my blood burn through my veins, I have the sudden uncontrollable urge to barrel my way through the crowd and start throwing punches, not because of the diamond but because I know that face. I know those curves. I recognize them because I've had them beneath my hands, in my mouth, and against my flesh. As I grit my teeth, my eyes return to the woman's face. Hazel eyes clash with mine, and for a brief moment, time seems to stop, along with my breathing. As we stare at each other, I see the second my features register to her, and I transform from being just another faceless man in the crowd. The recognition is almost instantaneous. It only takes a moment, but that's all I need. Despite the thick layer of makeup painting her features and the 14-carat blue diamond hanging heavily around her neck, I'd recognize that beautiful face and long dark hair anywhere. All thoughts of my father and whoever he's meeting flee my brain as a loud buzzing begins to sound in my ears. She may have lost a good amount of weight, but I could never forget that body or those features.

It's Siren.

CHAPTER 10

Siren

Like a deer caught in a pair of headlights, I gaze unfocused at the crowd beneath me. From my slightly elevated position on stage, I can see the outlines of dozens and dozens of sharply dressed men and women filling the room. The spotlight pointed directly at me would blind an average person, but I've spent most of my life on a stage. Granted, I'm usually wearing a lot more clothing. Even so, after my glassy eyes give a cursory sweep of the faces closest to the platform, my gaze is inexplicably drawn to the back of the room. In an area made dim by shadows, my eyes clash suddenly with a pair of bright blues that seem to see more than the rest. A piercing blue that sees past the stone hanging around my neck like an anchor to the woman beneath. I feel those eyes like a zap of electricity, reanimating a spark of hope I thought was lost for good. I know those eyes. Unlike all the other men I've been with in the past when those eyes had stared into mine during sex, I'd felt something other than the pleasant buzz of an impending orgasm. Those eyes had seemed to peer beneath my fake bravado and sarcastic mouth. The feeling had scared me, so I'd pushed him from my mind just like the others. I was terrified of letting another man get close to me. I was still living in the nightmare created by the last one.

As I stand on stage, staring into Deacon's eyes, I know what he sees looking back at him. Nothing. I'm so numb inside now. Over the past three weeks, I've screamed or cried out any lingering emotion I may have had. I don't have anything left in me to give. Not to Deacon, not to Dante, not to anyone. Don't get me wrong, I still feel the pain Dante inflicts on me, but during those moments, I go somewhere else. Somewhere far from here, where there are no cuts or burns or bruises. A place free of vile Italian words spoken through lips made only to wound. To bite and tear at the parts of flesh no one else is allowed to see. Parts that have been claimed by a demon. Claimed and reclaimed, over and over. Ever conscious of the shadow at my back, I know he's watching from behind the stage. If I give any one man in the crowd more attention than the rest, he'll notice. He sees everything. So, as much as every fiber of my being is screaming to call out for Deacon's help, I have no choice but to break eye contact and move on. Turning left and right, I go through the motions of being nothing more than a prop for the sale of Dante's latest acquisition—The Oppenheimer Blue diamond. I overheard Dante and the auctioneer talking about the necklace. I don't know exactly how he came by the gem, but when it was placed on my neck, I was reminded of the conversation between Dante and the two other Italians in the hallway outside my room shortly after I was taken. I can't help but wonder if this is the diamond they were referring to. If so, it belonged to Ilya Kapranov, and he wants it back. Did Dante steal it? The thought of that meeting reminds me of another that took place only moments ago: two more men, one a stranger but the other very well known. I'd recognized him, even from the small glimpse I'd gotten before Dante had locked me in the room next door. It was Senator Martin Hawkins. Try as I might, I wasn't able to hear much through the closed door between the office and the room I'd been shut up in. I was pretty sure I'd heard the name Sykes, and I know they were talking about money, but that wasn't much to go on.

For as long as I've known Dante, he's had money. A seemingly endless amount of money. Since I've been taken, things feel ... different. It's almost as though I can see the cracks beginning to show in the sophisticated and debonair picture he's painted himself into. All I need is for one of those cracks to get large enough for my voice to be heard through it. Then maybe I'll have the opening I need to get as far away from here as possible. Glancing back over towards the shadowed corner where Deacon was just standing, my stomach bottoms out when I see he's no longer there. Trying to keep my facial expression as blank as possible, my eyes dart from one end of the room to the other, frantically searching for him. Would he just leave me here? I have to believe that, even if he didn't feel anything more for me than lust, he wouldn't want me in this situation. I have to believe that he'd try to do ... *something*.

A sudden movement at the base of the stage directly in front of me catches my attention. Looking down, I see that Deacon is indeed still here and has shoved his way to the front of the leering men. In fact, he looks like he's planning to jump on stage at any second. Terrified of what Dante will do, I meet Deacon's ice-blue gaze again and give an almost imperceptible shake of my head. I want help, but I don't know how many of these people are allied with Dante, and I don't want Deacon getting hurt or, worse, killed trying to save me. As I stare into Deacon's eyes, his stare conveys hours of words that can't be spoken here. He's not gonna leave me to fend for myself. If his posture and the righteous fury on his face are any indication, he'll do whatever he has to do to take me out of here. Or at least I pray that's what the unspoken exchange is trying to tell me. Looking away, I stare straight ahead, seemingly uninterested in the man who's literally pulsing with aggression below, but I give a slight nod of my head, letting him know that I understand. Since my first escape from Dante, I've done my best to be my own savior. To never count on anyone to rescue me. This time, though, I know I need help, and that help may very well come in the form of a smartass that sells stolen goods and sports a man bun.

As I listen to the auctioneer list the details of the diamond, I stare blankly at the wall on the opposite side of the room. As the bidding begins, I hear millions of dollars worth of bids thrown out like candy to children on Halloween. Thirty million, forty million, forty-five million. That amount of money clearly means nothing to these people. It's just chocolate bars and lollipops. A deep baritone suddenly seems to rise above the others, ringing clear as a bell, even in the loud and crowded room.

"Eighty million dollars."

It's only by sheer force of will that I keep my eyes from flying to the source of that voice. Even so, I can't stop my eyes from widening at the ridiculous amount. It's well above the market value of the diamond. Nearly double, in fact. I don't know what Deacon is thinking. Does he even have that kind of money? As I listen to the rest of the room fall silent, I can physically feel eyes burning into my flesh—two sets in particular. One loathed, the other longed for. As I wait to hear someone speak up with a higher bid, all the air going in and out of my body seems lodged in my throat. I'm not sure if I'm hoping for it or dreading it. I pray this is part of Deacon's plan, whatever that may be, to get me the hell out of here.

The auctioneer calls, "We have a new high bidder! Eighty million dollars! Do I hear ninety?" Holding his gavel out to the crowd, as though he works for Christy's, he pretends he doesn't know that every person in here is a criminal with either a notorious or vile nature. I wait to hear the next words, knowing they'll be sealing my fate, one way or another. My eyes finally flick back down to Deacon. Blue and brown gazes collide, and for whatever reason; I can't look away. A long, heavy look passes between us, desperation pulsing from both sides, though for different reasons.

"Eighty million, going once … going twice … sold!" the man calls out loudly. The bang of the gavel has me jumping involuntarily. Eyes still locked with Deacons, I watch as his jaw tightens to what I imagine is a painful degree. He looks furious. I'm not sure if it's with me or the situation. But I'll take Deacon's fury over Dante's torment any day. Finally tearing my gaze from his, I turn on unsteady legs and make my way back down the catwalk towards the curtain at the back of the stage, willing Deacon not to fulfill the promise in his eyes and jump on stage to follow me. Just as I reach the curtain, I glance to my left to find Dante standing off to the side, partially hidden behind the curtain and the auctioneer's podium. With his gaze intent on my face, I do my best to school my features and present an outwardly neutral expression. Even so, I don't miss the displeasure and suspicion I see staring back at me. Pretending as though I don't see it, I step behind the main curtain to the backstage area that's been set up. There I stop, waiting for the devil to come retrieve me. It doesn't take long.

"Well, I see I chose a good display for my necklace. That amount was definitely unexpected," he says in his smooth Italian accent. I'm not at all surprised to hear him refer to me as inanimate property. It isn't the first time. I spent years being treated like a possession, used and abused. I'm used to it. He makes a twirling motion with his index finger, and he indicates that I should spin around. Though the last thing I want to do is give him my back, I do as I'm told, knowing there will be dire repercussions if I disobey. Coming up behind me, close enough for me to feel his body heat against my back, he lets his fingers trail over the skin of my neck. It's only years of practice that keeps me from recoiling. Unclipping the chain at the base of my neck, he removes the heavy stone. As I turn back around, I see another man standing nearby, holding a velvet box. He steps forward, opening the box to allow Dante to place the necklace inside. He must work for Mr. Kingsley or the auctioneer. Taking my wrist in a tight hold, Dante pulls me along behind him as he and the other man walk down a hallway and open a door that leads into what appears to be an office. Entering behind the two men, their backs obscure the complete view of the room until we're well inside, and the door is shut firmly behind us. Only once Dante and the other man move do I see two men waiting in the room already. Mr. Kingsley sits behind a massive oak desk. Sitting in a chair opposite him is Deacon. At our entrance, the two men look over. Blue eyes meet mine again before looking down to where Dante grips my wrist. I watch Deacon's gaze narrow to slits before he stands, and I have a moment of panic, wondering if all hell is about to break loose. Just as I brace myself to duck for cover, Mr. Kingsley stands as well, seemingly unaware of the mounting tension in every muscle of Deacon's body. The man who entered with us moves over to hand the necklace off to his boss. Opening the velvet case, Mr. Kingsley lets out a low whistle of appreciation. Passing the open case over to Deacon, he hands him a jeweler's loop, standing watch while Deacon inspects the gem. Closing the case with a snap, he hands it back to Mr. Kingsley with a nod.

Smiling hugely, he hands Deacon a small slip of paper and says, "Mr. Taylor, if you'll initiate the transfer of the funds to the account number listed there, minus my 10%, of course, the transaction will be complete."

Instead of pulling out his phone, Deacon pauses momentarily before meeting Dante's eyes for the first time since we entered the room. Watching the silent exchange between the two men is terrifying. The animosity coming from Deacon is so thick you could cut it with a knife. Alternately, Dante's usual air of sophisticated danger has me on edge. Between the two of them, the air in the room feels like molasses in my lungs. Eyes darting back and forth between them, I stand awkwardly in the ridiculously revealing lingerie. I'm not shy by any means but I've never been entirely comfortable with my body. Having it on nearly full display is just one more blow to my already battered psyche. I can only pray that Deacon wasn't able to see the fresh cuts on my back beneath the bright lights of the stage. I don't think he did because, if he had, I have a sneaking suspicion that Dante would be dead already. I'm honestly not used to this intense side of Deacon. The only time he's come remotely close to being this serious was when he was inside me. I give myself an inward shake because, after everything I've been through these last few weeks,

I can't think about anything even remotely sexual right now. I also can't afford to lower my guard for even a second.

As Deacon maintains eye contact with Dante, I wonder if he can see the evil lurking within. Maybe it's because of that evil that he now won't look anywhere else. Not at Mr. Kingsley, not at the unnamed lackey, not even at me. Just when I'm sure I'm going to suffocate under the weight of the tense silence, he finally speaks.

"How much for the girl?" he asks. He still won't look at me, but I don't need him to, to know that the girl in question is me. He's taking the direct approach. I didn't expect this. I would've tried to warn him that it wouldn't work if I had. There's no way Dante will let me go. Not for any price.

Lips turning up in a sinister grin, Dante says, "I'm sorry to disappoint you, Mr. Taylor, but *mia* Sirena is not for sale." Funny, he doesn't sound sorry.

Not the least bit deterred, Deacon says, "Name your price."

Dante gives an unexpected tug on the wrist, still held in his grasp. I'm not prepared for the move, and I stumble towards him on the heels he forced me to wear tonight. Drawing me back against him, he brings his other hand up, wrapping it around my throat. The hold isn't tight, but it's threatening all the same, and his message is crystal clear. Staring at Deacon, I see the hands at his sides ball into fists, but he and Dante are too busy mean-mugging each other for Dante to notice. Or at least, that's my sincere hope.

Chuckling under his breath, Dante says, "Ah, but you see, she's my most prized possession. Just look at her. I cannot blame you, Mr. Taylor, but the only way I will part with her is in death."

My bottom lip begins to tremble, and I blink back the tears threatening to spill over. I watch as a blank mask comes down over Deacon's features and I suddenly realize I don't know this person. In fact, he scares me nearly as much as Dante. He's ... cold. All hints of the playfully sarcastic man I met at the bar all those weeks ago, is gone. He's gonna leave me here, I know it.

Nodding slowly, he takes his phone from the inside pocket of his tux, punching in the numbers for what I can only assume is one of Dante's offshore bank accounts. Hearing a ping sound from behind me, Dante finally releases my neck in favor of pulling out his own phone.

"Pleasure doing business with you, Mr. Taylor," he says. Mr. Kingsley comes around his desk, shaking hands with both men. I stand between them, little more than a piece of furniture now. It's as if I don't exist. Trying my best not to hyperventilate, I remind myself that I'm no worse off than I was before the auction. I'm still in the same position. The internal pep talk doesn't work, though. How is it possible to feel so bereft after only such a tiny sliver of hope to begin with? Standing there, everything within me begins the process of shutting down again, trying to distance myself from the situation, from all the men in the room, from the world.

"Come, Sirena," Dante says. Not a request but a command, like a dog. Dutifully, I turn and follow behind him without a backward glance. I can't look back. If I do, I'll fall apart. My future lies bleak and painful in front of me. Internally, I'm screaming. But on the outside, I'm numb again.

CHAPTER 11

Deacon

That mother fucker's gonna die. It takes every ounce of willpower I possess to watch Siren walk out of Kingsley's office with that sick bastard. I nearly snapped when she turned to leave, and I saw the red marks on her back—fresh wounds made by some kind of blade. I might have missed them if I hadn't been staring so intently at her leaving form. As I watch the door close behind them, I have a sudden gnawing sensation in my gut, like some monster that I thought I'd buried deep long ago has finally woken up and is trying to claw its way out. I feel sick to my stomach. Releasing the beast from its cage for a split second, I allow my rage to get the better of me. With a roar of fury, I pick up the nearest chair with one hand, hurling it into the wall. "Fuck!" Kingsley lets out a yell and ducks behind his desk, probably going for a weapon, but I don't give a shit. I should've known this simpering fuck in front of me would change up the rooms for his shady deals this year, especially after Merrick broke in and stole a painting from his study upstairs after the last auction. Maybe if I'd thought that far ahead, I could've had an escape route mapped out and Siren never would've been allowed to walk out that door. But I fucked up, and now I've got to fix it.

Turning to the now cowering man, I brace my palms on the desk. Leaning down so that we're nearly nose to nose, I say, "I want every piece of information you have on that man."

Kingsley blusters, but I don't allow him even to get a word out before I'm cutting him off. "You'll give it to me, or I'll have the FBI on the phone in the next 10 seconds. I have more than enough dirt on you to put you *underneath* the prison. Give. Me. His. Name," I say through gritted teeth. I know if I dug in myself, I'd be able to find out who he is, but I don't have time for that. I've gotta get Siren out now.

He stares into my eyes for only a millisecond more before nodding reluctantly. As he shakily pulls himself up into his chair, he opens the laptop sitting on the side of his desk. After several clicks on the keys, he turns it around so I can see the screen.

Dante Gaspari.

Son of a bitch. Taking out my phone, I open a cloning app that I developed myself. Sitting it down next to the laptop, I initiate the transfer of information. Within minutes, everything Kingsley knows, I'll know. Staring at me with wide eyes, he says nothing. He could be actively planning to have me killed the moment I walk out of this room, and it wouldn't even phase me. I've dealt with far scarier things than Eugene Kingsley.

After successfully cloning his device, I pick up the velvet box holding the Oppenheimer Blue and walk towards the door. Placing my hand on the knob, I turn to see him still staring at my back. Pausing, I say, "If you try to warn him, you'll be dead before morning." Not waiting for a response, I open the door and walk out of the office and this monstrosity of a house. I'll have Siren away from that bastard before the night is out. If I'm lucky, I'll get to kill him in the process, making sure he actually stays dead this time.

Once I had that thread, finding Gaspari wasn't difficult for someone like me. The information from Kingsley's laptop wasn't much, but it gave me a starting point. The address listed for Dante Gaspari in the records Kingsley kept for the auction was little more than a warehouse. This would be a dead end for a normal person, one where they'd admit defeat and give up. Unfortunately for him, that phrase isn't in my vocabulary. Sitting in my car, I pull out my laptop and look into the ownership of the warehouse. It was owned by a shell corporation. It takes me less than 10 minutes to find out that the owner of that shell corporation is a well-known associate of Gaspari's. I don't believe in coincidences, so I pull up every other property registered to the man. Most are businesses and other warehouses, but he did own several residential properties throughout the city and surrounding areas. To narrow that down, I hack into the local power company's server to see which properties are actively using considerable amounts of electricity. There are only three. One is the man's primary home, and the other is in a high-rise, smack dab, in the middle of the city. I have a feeling Gaspari won't want the prying eyes of neighbors keeping tabs on his comings and goings, so that leaves only one location. A large estate about an hour from LA. Pulling up Google Maps, I put in the address and look at the street view images as well as the 360 view of the property. I can barely make out the roof of the large house because it's surrounded by dense forest. It's a risk, but my gut tells me that's the place.

Speeding through the city, I make it there in 40 minutes. I pull my car off to the side of the road, easing my baby into the cover of thick shadows provided by the surrounding trees. As I turn off the car, I open a hidden compartment that I had custom-built beneath the passenger's seat and take out the loaded handgun that I keep there for emergencies. I wasn't a huge fan of guns, but in my line of work, it was just good business sense to keep a weapon handy, in case someone decided they wanted the merchandise without paying for it. Double-checking the clip to make sure it's loaded, I step out of the car and sit the gun on the trunk while quickly shrugging out of my suit jacket before tucking the gun into the waistband at the back of my slacks. I don't have time to remove them or my dress shirt. I'm hyper-conscious of the fact that every minute Siren remains with Gaspari is another minute he could be using to hurt her. Tossing my discarded clothes into the passenger's seat, I take out the small flashlight I keep in the middle console, along with a handful of zip-ties. I close the door quietly, leaving my precious car behind. Doing my best to jog through the thick brush without tripping and breaking my neck, I finally reach the tree line where I can see the house just past a large expanse of neatly manicured lawn. It's another monstrosity of a home. Clearly bought for property value and tax deductions, but I imagine that pretentious fuck Gaspari feels right at home inside.

During the few precious minutes I'd spent researching earlier, I'd done a quick check into Dante Gaspari. He'd been born into nothing, just like me, though he hadn't stayed that way long. I hated rich people, with the exception of a very select few. However, Gaspari would fall into the category of those deserving of my hate. Instead of using his newfound wealth to add something of value to the world, he'd chosen to use it to form alliances with every crooked politician, mob boss, and criminal from Sicily to California. Once he'd realized he had a talent for ruining people's lives, he'd decided to contract that talent out ... for a price. Based on everything I'd read, the man had delusions of grandeur and presented the image of a well-educated and classy gentleman to the world—a patron of the arts and a lover of all the finer things in life. In reality, he was a thug, albeit a thug in an expensive suit.

I watch the house, clocking two guards that are alternating between covering the front entrance and patrolling the grounds. Keeping to the inside of the tree line, I make my way around back. As suspected, there's another guard stationed at the back door. This guard, however, doesn't seem to be taking his job quite as seriously as the others. As I watch, he steps away from the door, lighting a cigarette before pulling out his phone to scroll through something as he wanders further away and into the grass between us. I count the seconds as I will him to walk closer to the spot where I'm currently hiding behind a large pine tree: thankfully, he does, and I realize it's now or never. This is my chance and I may not get another one. Quietly stepping out from behind the tree, I bum-rush the guard, taking him down to the ground. He flails but doesn't cry out for help, probably because he's still got the lit cigarette clamped between his lips. Straddling the man, I pull my fist back and cold clock him right in the face, knocking him unconscious. Dragging him into the cover of the trees, I quickly bind his hands and feet with the zip-ties I brought with me in my back pocket. I remove a handkerchief from my other pocket, and use it as a gag. Conducting a quick search, I find only his wallet, which, surprise surprise, has no ID, and a slip of folded paper. Opening the paper up, I see a six-digit number. I'm not sure what it goes to, but I think I'll hold onto it, just in case. I sprint to the back door, looking left and right for anyone else. Quickly inspecting the area, I see a panel to the left. It's a keypad, not for an alarm system but for keyless entry into the house. Pausing, I actually laugh a little under my breath. No fucking way. Taking the piece of paper out of my pocket, I punch in the six numbers written on it. A click sounds, and I turn the knob on the door and push it open an inch or two. This fucking idiot actually wrote down the code to the back door on a piece of paper in his pocket. Jesus. I guess it was hard to find good help these days. Taking a few deep breaths, I ease the door open and glance inside. I don't see anyone, but I'm still careful as I slip into the house, closing the door quietly behind me. Standing in what appears to be a mudroom, I give myself a second for my eyes to adjust to the new level of light before moving further inside. Slowly checking each room on the main floor, I find them all empty. Fuck. As I reach the front of the house, however, I can hear music coming from upstairs. It's a violin. Bingo. Knowing I've got the right place, I breathe a sigh of relief. That is, until a scream rises above the crescendo of the music, traveling down the stairs and hitting me like a punch to the chest.

CHAPTER 12

Siren

I knew he was angry. Just like I knew he was going to hurt me. However, when I come to think of it, he's never really needed to be angry in order to hurt me. But tonight, he seems ... enraged. At what, I don't know. All I know is that whatever he has planned for me, it's probably gonna be much worse than anything before. From the moment we walked out of Mr. Kingsley's office, leaving Deacon behind, I've felt like a robot. Whatever hope that had started to build in me when I looked out into that crowd of jeering men and saw those blue eyes staring back at me in utter shock is gone. Like the last dying note to a beautiful song that turns tragic at the end before silence reigns. I'm not sure what I expected. I should've known better. Dante is a force to be reckoned with; he always has been. The fact that he's let his iron control slip several times since I've been here is telling, but that doesn't make him any less dangerous. In fact, he seems more unstable now than ever. As we near the house, the silence in the car is deafening. My muscles are tight and bunched up as I sit next to him on the leather seat in the back of the Rolls Royce.

When we'd first gotten in the car, the driver had asked Dante if he wanted the partition put up. Despite the pleading in my eyes that I knew the man could see from his vantage point in the rear view mirror, he'd still complied when Dante said yes. As that tinted glass rose, I could feel myself bracing for the blows I knew would come. I was still braced for them, even now. Yet, Dante hadn't moved since we left the estate. He'd poured himself a drink from the small bar built into the car's side panel and then spent the rest of the time staring out the window while stroking his goatee with an index finger. This move, too, was telling. Dante only did that when he was in deep thought about something. In the past, that something was usually some creative way to punish me for some transgression, I didn't even know I'd committed, which was why I was currently taking the most defensive position in the backseat that I could without making it too obvious. I honestly wish he'd just go ahead and hit me. A punch I could take. Waiting for it was torture. The longer we sat in silence, the more time I knew he had to think of some new and demented way of making me pay for whatever he perceived from the interaction with Deacon because I have no doubt that that's the cause of this deep contemplation. Knowing Dante, he probably felt disrespected. He was big on respect. He demanded it, along with total obedience. Any deviation would set him off.

As the house comes into view, I should be breathing a sigh of relief. Instead, the panic and terror inside me only mounts. Once we're inside and alone, I'm his to do with as he sees fit. I know there are guards outside the house, but there's no one inside. Dante doesn't like an audience when he inflicts my punishments. He still believes that I'm one of his many possessions as he told Deacon, perhaps his most prized possession. Pressing a hand to my stomach, I try to quell the churning that's threatening to have me throwing up my guts right here in the backseat of this car; not that much of anything else would come up. But that would only make him angrier. So, instead, I close my eyes for a brief moment and take deep breaths through my nose, trying to regulate my breathing and thundering heart. As the car pulls up in front of the house and the driver gets out, Dante exits first, then helps me out of the car. Ever the gentleman. Or so it would appear. Guiding me up the stone walkway, we pass the guard posted outside the front door. The man nods to Dante but doesn't acknowledge me whatsoever. I'm used to this, too. The men work for him, and even if they felt some measure of sympathy for me, they'd never put their lives on the line to help me.

Following Dante inside, I walk past him as he closes the heavy oak door with a resounding thud. Like the first shovel full of dirt thrown atop a freshly lowered coffin. As I stand in the foyer of the large house, I keep my back to him. I don't bother turning around now. I don't need to see the face of my judge, jury, and executioner. It's been burned into my brain for years. Instead, I stand still, waiting, but I don't have to wait long. Soon, I feel one of Dante's strong hands wrap around the front of my throat, giving it a light squeeze. Not enough to cut off my air but enough to send a lightning bolt of fear through my body.

Circling around until he's standing in front of me, he brings our faces close as he asks, "Did you know that man, Sirena?" I'm shaking my head before he's even finished his question, but I can tell by the look in his eyes that he knows I'm lying.

The hand around my throat tightens. "Who is he to you, Bella? An acquaintance? A friend?" I don't realize a tear spills down my cheek until he flicks out his tongue. As he licks up the side of my face, he whispers, "A lover?" It sounds like blasphemy when he says it, and the cooling trail of saliva left in the wake of his tongue is enough to make my stomach pitch.

"He's n-no one. I've never even met him before tonight." I stutter out. I don't know why I bother lying. I know he's going to punish me regardless. Using his other hand to grip my hair roughly, he jerks my head back so hard my eyes water, only adding to the wetness already coating my face. Slanting his mouth over mine, I feel his tongue push roughly inside. I don't fight him but I also don't kiss him back. Even though I know it'll anger him further, I just can't bring myself to participate in my own rape. Releasing the hand around my throat, he moves it to my right wrist, twisting my arm painfully behind my back, causing me to cry out. With a shove, he releases me entirely, and I fall to the floor in a heap. Even as I attempt to scramble away from him, some part of my addled brain tells me that there's no getting out of this house alive. If Dante doesn't get to me first, the guards outside will surely stop me before I get too far. Even so, my heels screech across the marble tiles as I try to gain purchase enough to pull myself up. The weakness from what little food and water I've allowed myself that plagued me earlier returns in full force, and it takes me longer than it should to kick the shoes off and leave them behind. I finally make it onto my feet but only get as far as the kitchen doorway when a foot planted firmly into my back sends me flying forward. As I hit the floor again, I try to catch myself, but the wrist Dante twisted before does little to break my fall, and I feel my face hit the linoleum floor hard, top teeth breaking through the skin of my bottom lip. As blood pours down my chin, I once again make to get up, but before I can even get up to my knees, a rough hand grips my hair again, and soon, I'm being dragged through the house kicking and screaming. Pulling me up straight, Dante turns me to face him just as we make it to the landing leading to the second floor of the house. A backhand to the face has spots swimming in my vision. As my equilibrium turns my world upside down and my legs into jello, I feel myself being lifted off the floor. Vaguely, I'm aware that I'm being carried up the stairs but I can't seem to get the world to right itself so that I can prepare for what's coming next.

As I'm dropped roughly onto a bed, I'm finally able to blink the room around me into focus. Just as I orient myself to my surroundings, the music begins to play—Bach's *Chaconne*. With renewed purpose, I make a move to crawl off the bed. Immediately, Dante is on top of me. Teeth gritted with barely controlled rage, he says, "Did you let him fuck you, Sirena?? Did you let him put his mouth on *my* skin?? Did you let him taste the pussy that belongs to *me*???" Ripping open the lapels of the robe I'd been allowed to put back on in the car, he bares my lace-covered breasts. Not to be impeded by anything, he grabs the cups, jerking them down roughly, exposing flesh that he's spent the last few weeks marring. Hissing between his teeth, his eyes full of hunger and madness, he traces his fingertips lovingly over the bite marks, bruises, and small cuts made by his favored weapon of choice. Knowing the razor belonged to his father makes me wonder if he was anywhere near the monster that his son grew into.

As he paws my breasts roughly, I come to the realization that my hands are finally free. I swing for his face but narrowly miss when he jerks back. The move costs me dearly. Within seconds, he manages to wrangle both my wrists in one of his powerful hands, holding them high above my head. With the other hand, he grips my right nipple hard, twisting brutally. Against my will, I let loose a scream that practically shakes the very walls of the house. Probably less than a minute later, I'm dimly aware of a series of loud bangs in the hallway outside.

BANG! BANG! BANG!

It isn't until the door to the bedroom swings nearly off its hinges, hitting the wall behind it, that I realize the banging sounds must've been the doors to the other rooms on this floor of the house being kicked in. As Dante jerks his head around at the sound, I use the opportunity to reach for the inside pocket of his suit jacket, where I know he keeps his precious blade hidden. I have no idea who just burst in, but I know I have to take advantage of the distraction. I may not get another chance. Hand closing around the heavy weight of the weapon, I jerk it from his pocket, using the momentum to release the blade from the shield. Quick as a flash, I swing my hand in the direction of Dante's throat. With his head turned towards the door, he never sees the blade coming. Suddenly, blood is pouring down on my face, making it difficult to see. Shaky hand still gripping the now slippery razor, I scramble out from under Dante as he falls onto his side, gripping his throat. There's so much blood that it's hard to see exactly where I cut him, but the look of shock on his face would be comical under any other circumstances. Breaths heaving, I stand there next to the bed. I want to watch the life drain from his body. I want to see the light fade from his eyes. I want to make sure he stays dead this time.

A gentle hand on my shoulder has me swinging around, blade at the ready. But my eyes soon clash with a set of sky blues. Instantly, all thoughts of Dante are forgotten. Any need for eternal retribution is diminished in the wake of that soft gaze as it roves over me. I know I must look like something from a horror movie, but I don't care. Dropping the razor to the floor, I finally let down my guard and reach for Deacon just as his strong arms wrap around me, lifting me off the floor. Holding me close to his chest, he cradles me with one arm, using the hand of the other to pull my robe closed, concealing my torso before slipping that arm under my knees. With one last glance at Dante's prone form on the blood-soaked bed, Deacon takes me from the room, barely pausing to grab my violin case from the nearby table before we're heading down the stairs and out of the house. No guards appear to try to stop us, but I know that unless Deacon actually killed them on his way in, they'll be on our heels any minute. His sure stride and the gentle way he's holding me against him culminate to create a perfect storm of emotion. Burying my face in his neck, I finally allow myself the freedom to release a loud sob out into the night. One tear turns to two, and soon, I'm crying rivers. I'm crying for all the pain, anguish, and torture I've endured over the last few weeks. And crying because I know I'll never be the person I was before. A person already damaged, now possibly broken beyond repair. And I cry because I've been saved not only by my own hand but by the man now holding me as though I'm the most fragile piece of glass. As my tears run down the skin of his neck, I allow myself to shatter in his arms.

CHAPTER 13

Deacon

Siren won't stop shaking. As I gently lower her into my car's passenger seat, I get a slightly closer look at her appearance. Blood-soaked skin and ripped clothes. Bruises and cuts and what look like teeth marks where that sadistic fuck must've bitten her. With the amount of blood pouring from his neck a few minutes ago, he should be good and dead by now. If he wasn't, I'd go back in there and inflict the worst types of torture on him in return. Right now, though, my main focus is getting Siren to safety and assessing her injuries. More so than the obvious ones, I'm worried about the pain I can't see—the emotional toll this has and will continue to take on her. I'm afraid. Not for myself but for her. Afraid that this ordeal will permanently alter the vivacious yet snarky bombshell I met all those weeks ago. I'm afraid that that sick piece of shit may have pushed her mind past the point of no return and that she won't be able to claw her way back from this.

As I ease the seat belt over her partially covered chest and then carefully close the passenger's side door, my mind whirls with thoughts of what to do next. I need to get her some place where I can have a doctor look her over, but I know if I try to take her to a hospital, she'll freak out. I also worry that if, by some miracle of Satan, that bastard in there manages to survive that slice to the neck, he'll try to come for her again. I need to get her somewhere safe. I could call the Fed and ask for a favor, but we aren't that close, and without Merrick as a buffer, I don't know how that would work out. And there's no fucking way I'm calling Merrick right now. Merrick and Amelia are attached at the hip, and while I know both of them have been worried about Siren's whereabouts, I also know that if Amelia sees her in her current condition, she'll lose it. Somehow, I don't think Merrick will thank me if I cause his wife to have a meltdown. His overprotectiveness knows no bounds, and that stood steadfast even before they found out she was pregnant. I could always just find a safe house somewhere off the grid. Drop her off, send someone to clean her up, and nurse her back to health. But for some reason, that felt wrong. It felt cold, detached, and the polar opposite of everything I'm feeling right now. My gut instinct screams at me to keep this woman by my side indefinitely. Which is weird because it's usually telling me to grab my underwear from the floor and run as quickly as possible. After ensuring she's secured in the passenger's seat, I get in the car, start it, and pull onto the road. Heading towards the airport, I pick up my phone and make a quick call to have Merrick's plane, which I'd used to get to the auction, ready for takeoff within the next half hour. I had more money than I knew what to do with, but I still didn't own my own fucking plane. I wasn't that full of myself. Instead, I chose to invest my money in gadgets that someone like Merrick wouldn't even know how to turn on. To each his own.

The ride to the airport is silent, except for the light sniffles I hear coming from the passenger's seat, each evoking a reactionary flinch in me. I've glanced over a few times, but each time, Siren's face has been turned toward the window, so I haven't been able to quite make out what kind of headspace she's in. For some reason, the urge to pull the car over and drag her into my lap is nearly overwhelming. I don't know where these instincts to console and protect are coming from but I do my best to push them from my mind so that I can make rational decisions and focus on getting us where we need to go. Thirty minutes later, we're pulling onto the tarmac, and I'm carrying Siren up the stairs into the spacious private jet cabin. I spoke briefly with one of the guys working to ready the plane, who assured me he'd make arrangements to get my car back home. I think he could tell by the look in my eye that if my car made it back down south with so much as a scratch on the door, he'd be walking with a limp for a week. The threat was half-hearted at best, considering my attention had been monopolized by the woman in my arms.

I'm just about to sit Siren on one of the leather seats when I look down to find her asleep against my chest. She'd seemed a little out of it when I'd taken her from the car, but I'd just chalked it up to her being fucking traumatized beyond what most people would be able to comprehend. Looking down at her now, it's clear that she's exhausted. Hell, this may be the first time she's been able to relax in weeks. Moving away from the chair, I gently lay her down on one of the plush couches instead. She makes a slight whimpering sound that causes my chest to tighten painfully but she doesn't fight me as I settle her into the soft material of the sofa. I pull a blanket from the back of the couch to cover her sleeping and half-naked form and stare down at her for another long moment. Before I even realize that I've made up my mind, I'm already heading to the cockpit to inform the pilot that we'll be flying not to Charleston but to Savannah.

Cementing my resolve, I dispel all the reasons why this is a bad idea. I don't give a shit. Until I know that Gaspari is indeed dead, she's staying with me. I have this visceral need to make sure she's alright. Not just physically but emotionally and mentally as well. I won't change my mind on this. I'm taking Siren home to *my home*. For the first time in the history of ever, there'd be a woman in my house. My sanctuary. God help us both.

The town car that picked us up at the airport slows down to make the turn off the main road and onto the long dirt driveway leading to my house. When I loaded Siren into the back seat, the driver didn't ask any questions. He was paid well enough not to. The ride from the airport to my home was a quiet one. Siren's awake now but still hasn't spoken. I can feel my anxiety rising with each passing minute. Not just at the possibility that that mother fucker Gaspari has permanently broken her but also at the idea of her being in my home. I've never taken a woman here. Usually, when I spend the night with someone, it's at their place or a hotel, and I'm usually sneaking out before they can wake up and ask what I want for breakfast. I liked to eat my eggs alone, thank you very much. Even so, as my house comes into view, I make a quick glance at Siren to gauge her reaction.

My home isn't anything elaborate. Hell, I'm only one person. What the fuck do I need with a big ass house? The small cab-in-style home is made from thick logs meant to blend in with the surrounding woods. As a man that had the ability to invade other people's privacy at will, it made me value mine all the more. As I briefly glance back and forth between Siren's face and the house, I wonder what she sees. Is she disgusted by my meager dwelling? The wooden home sports a wraparound porch barely visible past the many shrubs that encircle the house. The bushes are large and could probably use a trim, come to think of it. There's one giant window that looks out onto the porch but even at night, no one would be able to see inside. The glass of all the windows of the house is coated in a product that essentially makes them like that of the kind of two-way mirror found in interrogation rooms. Besides the main porch window, you can't see much else of the house from this vantage. Unfortunately, Siren's face gives nothing away. Staring at the house stoically, she barely waits for the car to come to a stop before she pushes the door open and attempts to haul herself out. I know she must be in pain, and I'll bet she's weak from all the weight she's lost, but she doesn't even wait for me to get out and come around to help her. It's clear that the old Siren, the one that snuck out even before I could, the morning after our one night together, is making a resurgence. At least mentally. Physically, she's not quite there, and as I reach the other side of the car, I catch her just as her legs go out from under her. The driver, who's also gotten out and rushed around the front of the car, looks to me for direction. Giving a nod that conveys both thanks and dismissal, I lift Siren into my arms and watch the man get back in the car and leave. Taking a steadying breath that has nothing to do with the weight of Siren in my arms and everything to do with the heavy sensation that I'm standing at some type of life-altering turning point, I force my feet to move and take the handful of steps up to the porch.

"I can walk, you know. You don't have to carry me everywhere."

It's the first time the woman's spoken since I got her out of that hell hole, and, of course, the first words out of her mouth would be something sassy. Fuck. How is it possible that even traumatized and covered in dried blood, she still manages to cause my own to burn through my veins like fire? The instinct to protect and coddle her wars with the memories of our single night together and the many other ways I'd like to put that sassy mouth to use.

"I'm just trying to help you. Don't bite my damn head off," I reply.

She lets out a huff but doesn't say anything more. Keeping an arm under her knees, I use the hand of the one at her back to open the security panel hidden behind the old-fashioned letter box mounted next to the front door. Not having my car, the alarms and locks haven't auto disengaged, which is inconvenient, but at least going through the motions of entering reminds me of how secure my home really is. After entering a 10-digit code, a series of quick beeps prompt me to press my thumb to the screen. The system reads my thumbprint, and the sound of several clicks comes from just inside the door, indicating that the deadbolt and door have been unlocked. Using the same hand, I turn the handle and push the door open enough to allow us through. Kicking it shut behind us, I don't give Siren much time to look around before I stride over to the couch along the left wall of the living room and gently place her down. Pulling out my phone, I wander a few steps away as I call a very discreet physician I've worked with in the past when a few jobs have gone south on me. The man was known to most only as "The Doctor". I knew Theo Aristille to be a first-generation American of French Creole lineage with strong ties to his home state of Louisiana. Raised by his grandmother after his mother died giving birth to his younger sibling, he traveled frequently between Louisiana and Savannah. The 35-year-old doctor catered to a very specific type of clientele. Rich, secretive, and criminal. From everything I knew about him, including everything he didn't know I knew, he seemed like a genuine, if eccentric, man. Right now, I didn't give two shits about his upbringing or who else he made house calls to. All I cared about was that he was near enough to come out and look Siren over. After a brief conversation, I'm thankful he's in Savannah "on business" and said he could be here within the hour.

As I turn back to Siren, it's to catch her inspecting the living room around us. Unlike the outside, when I wasn't sure what she was thinking about the appearance of my home, this time, I know what she sees—a warm and inviting space with a large couch and several cushy armchairs. A coffee table, handmade from driftwood, sits between the seating area and the large fireplace on the opposite wall. An equally sizeable flat-screen TV hangs just above the mantle. A mantle decorated with framed photos of me with the few people I consider family. Me and Mama on the beach. Me and Merrick on the day that he and Amelia got married. Me, photobombing the two of them during one of our many outings together. There's also one of Siren and I dancing in a bar. That was the night Merrick went all caveman and threw Amelia over his shoulder and hauled her outside for having the audacity to let another man touch her. Neither of them knew that Siren and I had shared a dance after they left. I'd gotten the picture from hacking into the bar's security cameras and pulling the feed from that night. Quickly stepping in front of the mantle, I grab the frame and pull it down, hiding it behind my back before she has a chance to see it. As I watch, her eyes narrow on me and I'm sure if she had the strength, she'd already be across the room and attempting to snatch it out of my hand. As much as I hate the idea of her in pain, I thank my lucky stars that she's not able to wrestle me for the picture. She's already given me shit about being obsessed with her. If she realized I had a photo of her in my house, I'd never hear the end of it.

"I've called a doctor. He should be here within the hour to check you out. Do you need anything? A drink? Something to eat? Some ... Band-Aids?" I ask, wincing after the last part. I don't know how to make small talk with women. Don't get me wrong; I could turn on the charm with no problem when I was trying to get into their pants. Whenever I had to have a real conversation that didn't revolve around sex, I was actually awkward as fuck. It was the curse of being part computer nerd, I guess. Thank God I had my looks to fall back on, or I'd still be a virgin, getting my jollies from lurking around OnlyFans.

"You're more attractive when you're nervous," she replies with a snort, but her tone holds only a fraction of its usual bite. For some reason that I can't quite put my finger on, I don't like that fact.

"You're more snarky when you're injured," I say in return, waiting to see if she'll take the bait and come back at me the way she's done in the past.

We stare at each other for a long moment before she breaks eye contact to gingerly bring her legs up onto the couch, laying her head down on one of the several throw pillows that litter each end. She lets out a heavy sigh and closes her eyes, effectively dismissing me. I can't explain why I'm disappointed, but I am. Within minutes, I hear her breathing even out and know she's fallen asleep again. Quietly, I move to the couch, repeating the motion of taking the fleece blanket off the back and putting it over her, just like I did on the plane. Easing myself down into one of the nearby chairs, I stare at her blood-stained hand that's gone slack from where she was clutching the two halves of her top together and can't stop myself from remembering another time that I sat next to a couch, staring at a woman.

CHAPTER 14

Deacon

14 YEARS OLD

"Oh, come on, Deacon, it's just a little fun," Troy says. "You never come out with us. Always running back home to Mommy. What are you, some kinda Mama's boy?"

"Yeah, it's not like she'll miss you anyway," Matt adds with a roll of his eyes.

I can feel my ears starting to burn. I wasn't very popular at school, what with being late all the time and missing so many days. People thought I was weird just because I didn't go out and create havoc like a lot of the other kids my age. I was a freshly minted teenager, and with my hormones raging and my body changing more and more every day, I knew I was in that awkward stage between being a boy and becoming a man. Considering all this and my general demeanor of gruffness, I'd managed to make exactly two friends. And they were both fucking idiots.

Against my better judgment, I'd snuck out tonight to meet up with them. Rumor had it that Vickie Kincaid was having a sleepover at her house, which was only two streets over from mine, with a bunch of other girls from our year, and the guys wanted to go over and play peeping Tom. I knew this was what kids our age did, but I still thought it was pretty stupid. Although Vickie *had* come back to school after Summer break with boobs that definitely weren't there last year. So I'd had the thought earlier that maybe the guys weren't quite as stupid as they appeared and so here I am. Looking at them now, I'm reminded of why I formed my original opinion in the first place.

"Shut the fuck up, you guys. Y'all don't know shit," I retort.

Problem was, they did know shit, and that's what was so embarrassing. Everyone in school knew about my mama's ... issues. That was the problem with small southern towns. People loved getting into other people's business. For the millionth time, I wish I could just be nobody. No name, no face, no story. Maybe someday. Mama had been doing really good the last few months. Maybe if I could come up with a plausible lie to explain where I'd gotten the little nest egg of money I kept in an account no one knew about, we could move and start over. Looking at my only friends, I don't feel the expected tug of sadness at the idea of leaving them behind. They were morons. I knew it; our classmates knew it, and hell, they even knew it. But even knowing this, their needling about my mother has the desired effect of prompting me to do stuff I normally wouldn't.

"You guys are dumb," I finally say with a shake of my head. "Fine, let's go."

Two yells of excitement echo in the still night air. Shushing them, I lead the way as we cut between houses, skirting flower beds and cyclone fences. As Vickie's house comes into view, I quickly look around to make sure no one is watching. Pulling Troy, who's now in a whispering match with Matt about whether the girls sleep in their underwear, we finally make it to the bushes that border one side of the house. I don't know the layout, but Matt claimed Vickie's bedroom is somewhere towards the back. Keeping as low to the ground as possible, we scurry around the back side of the house and, sure enough, there are three windows, all of which have lights shining from inside. Crouching down beneath the first one, I peer over and look inside. It's the kitchen. I watch as Vickie's mom empties a bag of microwave popcorn into a large bowl and then carries it out through a doorway that leads to the hall. As she goes right, so do we. The next window is much smaller and, at first glance, appears to be an empty bathroom. As I'm about to move on to the third and final window at the back of the house, movement within the small bathroom catches my eye. Before my brain even has a chance to register what I'm seeing, the guys are rushing past me to the last window. Peeking their heads up, they quickly duck back down in a fit of giggles. What a bunch of little girls.

"Deacon, come on! They're in here! Holy shit, Chelsea's lying on the bed and the back of her nightgown is hiked up. I can see her ass! You gotta see this!" Matt whispers over to me.

His excitement is palpable, but still, I don't leave just yet. Ignoring my friend, I stare hard through the window, trying to locate the source of the movement I just saw. It's difficult to see anything through the tiny sliver left open between the closed curtains and most of the window is all fogged up. Just as I'm about to chock the movement up to a trick of the light, I see it again. My eyes squint hard before turning into saucers. Vickie Kincaid just stepped out of the fucking shower. Even though my mind knows that spying on her like this is wrong, something inside me ignites, and flames eat at my skin. I'm starting to sweat, and I lick away a line of beads that've formed above my top lip. I'd like to blame southern humidity for my sudden attack of perspiration, but I know the heat has nothing to do with the climate outside and everything to do with the sight of Vickie's newly developed breasts. As does the sudden hard-on that's pushing against the zipper of my worn-down jeans. What must only be seconds seem like hours before I'm able to tear my gaze away from Vickie and look towards my friends. They're still alternately peeking into the bedroom window and ducking down to laugh and talk shit amongst themselves. They're so caught up in what they're doing that I might as well not even be here. I open my mouth to call out to them, to tell them what I've found, and to come quick, but at the last second, I stop. I close my mouth again without saying anything. Why should I share this with them? After the way they razzed me earlier, they don't deserve to see Vickie naked. So I say nothing, instead turning back to the crack in the curtains. As Vickie stands in front of the mirror, towel-drying her hair, I stare at her body. It's not the body of women I've watched in my abundance of online porn surfing, but it's real and right here in front of my face. I remain there, crouched down outside the small bathroom window, until Vickie finally pulls on a pair of panties and an oversized t-shirt. Brushing her hair in front of the mirror, she opens the door and leaves, having no clue that someone was watching her the entire time. The act and the idea that I've done something forbidden sends a bolt of lightning up my spine. My breathing is fast, and I know that if I don't get out of here right now, my cock is gonna explode in my pants.

"Guys, I gotta go. I've got shit to do," I whisper over to Troy and Matt. They both groan, calling me a pussy and taunting me about how I'll miss out on the pillow fight the girls are probably gonna have. Who gives a shit about a pillow fight? That's nothing compared to what I just saw, but they don't need to know that. Flipping them both the bird, I slink back around the side of the house and cut back through the way we came. It takes me about five minutes to walk to my house from where I met the guys, and every step is agony on my poor dick. Finally making it home, I stick my fingers under the crack I deliberately left beneath my window and lift it up, quietly climbing back through and into my room. Closing the window behind me, I pull the curtains tight. The last thing I need is for the guys to come back around and see me jacking off in my bedroom. The house is quiet, and as I reach for the button on my jeans, it dawns on me that it's too quiet. Looking at the clock, I see that it's only 11 p.m. Mama may think I've gone to bed, but she wouldn't be asleep already. She said earlier that she was gonna stay up a while and catch up on her soaps, but I don't hear the TV. In fact, I don't hear anything.

A sudden, overwhelming sense of unease settles over me, and I'm plagued by a feeling of dread that I just can't shake. All thoughts of Vickie are gone now, replaced by a pitching in my stomach, like wave after wave of unending nausea. I stare at my closed bedroom door. I'm actually afraid to open it. I can't explain why I'm afraid, but I am. Closing my eyes, I take deep breaths. In through the nose, out through the mouth. The way Mama taught me when I was younger and had the flu. I know I have to open the door. I have to make sure nothing bad has happened. But I can't make my feet move. It feels like I'm trapped in quicksand, slowly sinking into a bog of panic and nightmares. Nightmares that haven't come true yet but that have always been there in the back of my mind. With great effort, I finally force myself to take the few short steps toward the door. My hand shakes as it reaches for the knob. It takes me three tries to get the lock turned and open the door. The living room of our small house is dark but not so dark that I can't see the figure sitting prone on the couch, head laid against the back, as though simply taking a nap. But somewhere, deep down, I know that's not the case. The sludge weighing me down only seconds ago disappears as my body jerks into hyperspeed. Rushing over to the sofa, I reach out my hand to gently shake my mother's shoulder, but that hand pauses in midair when my eyes finally adjust to the darkness, and I'm able to get a good look at her face. Her eyes are open, staring at the cobweb-covered ceiling. Sightless. She doesn't move at the sound of my presence. She doesn't tilt her head and smile at me as she looks into my eyes.

"... *just like stars.*"

Everything inside me begins to tremble. I feel like I'm coming unglued from the inside out. Forcing my hand to breach those final few inches is probably the hardest thing I've ever had to do. I place my palm over her eyes and slide them close. Her skin is cold. All of the warmth from only hours ago is gone. Feeling my own blood turn to ice in my veins, I close my eyes, too, letting the tears fall as silent sobs wrack my thin body. Sliding down to the floor beside the couch, I sit next to my dead mother and cry until I can't anymore. Until there's nothing left inside of me but a hole that I know will never be filled again. I've got no one now. She was the only person that ever loved me. Even with all her problems, she made sure that I knew I was the center of her world. That everything began and ended with me. I felt it in everything she did. Even when she was high and her eyes were glazed over, they looked at me like I was the best part of her. Laying my head against my mother's knee, I bring my own to my chest and stare at the empty bottle and the few remaining pills that must've scattered across the ratty rug when it fell from her hand. As I stare at those pills, it isn't resentment that I feel. It never even enters my mind that, in the end, my mother chose the high over me. Instead, there's something else taking over, and suddenly, that hole isn't so empty anymore. It takes me a moment to recognize the emotion slowly filling up all that negative space.

Rage. This never would've happened if it hadn't been for *him*. Our lives would've been so different if he'd kept his promises. As I sit there on the floor, I make a promise of my own to my mother and myself. There were three deaths here today. Hers, mine, and his. He just doesn't know it yet. But he will.

CHAPTER 15

Siren

A series of loud pings followed by what sounds like a dog's growl drags me from the deep sleep that I must've slipped into after we got to Deacon's house. It didn't take me long to figure out that it was his, not some random hole in the wall. The framed photos of Merrick, Amelia, and even me gave it away. Plus, the house just felt like a home. Well-worn furniture and little nick-nacks everywhere. I have to admit, it's not exactly the type of home I would've imagined Deacon having. I know he has money. After everything that happened between Amelia and Merrick, the secret of their chosen professions have been aired for quite some time. But whereas Merrick gave the aura of tasteful money, Deacon's choice of living conditions is quite the puzzle. One I'd have to think on. In the meantime, I need to open my eyes and figure out what that sound is and where it's coming from. That task is easier said than done, unfortunately. After so many weeks of fitful, terrified bursts of sleep, the ease with which I drifted off and the depth at which I slept amazes me. Maybe it's this house. Or perhaps it's the man. The one that I can now hear cursing from another room.

I manage to pry my eyes open just in time to see Deacon actually tiptoeing across the living room. The scene is almost comical. This big, tattooed, surfer-looking guy is trying to tread lightly across creaky old wooden floorboards. For some reason, the action makes me smile, and I realize it's the first time I've done so in weeks. Honestly, I wasn't sure if I'd even remember how. As I watch, Deacon reaches the front door, jerking it open to reveal a tall, deeply tanned man I'd peg to be in his early to mid thirties. The man is leaning casually on the doorframe and holds a leather duffle bag in one hand. Surely, this can't be the doctor. Never in my life have I seen a doctor that looks like this one. Along with his bag comes a well-worn leather jacket and dark jeans. His boots are the type a biker would wear. With a head full of windblown dark curls and actual dust on his pants, I wonder if he rode some type of bike here. It would make sense and coincide with the growling sound I heard before. Definitely a motorcycle.

I watch as Deacon holds his finger up to his lips in the universal sign to be quiet. That's when the man's gaze turns towards me. Even through dark sunglasses, I can tell when his eyes land on my curled-up form. His posture stiffens, and I watch his fist tighten around the handle of the bag. Immediately, I'm put on guard. Sitting up as gingerly as possible, I pull my knees to my chest and wait. I don't think Deacon would've let him get close to the house if he didn't trust him somewhat. Even so, I eye the man warily at the same time that he eyes me. As Deacons steps back, the other man enters slowly, boots thudding lightly on the hardwood. He takes slow, deliberate steps, the way one would when trying to approach a wounded animal.

"I don't think there's much need for quiet, *mon gars*. Your guest looks to be awake. Aren't you, cricket?" the man says. His voice is deep and gravelly, adding to his overall roughened appearance. He's also got a slight accent. Not much, but it's definitely there. Based on whatever he called Deacon, I'd say French. As my brain tries to process the overall picture, it takes me a minute to comprehend what he said. Did he just call me a cricket? Like the bug??

Deacon turns his head towards me at the man's words. Letting out a heavy sigh of resignation at my awakened state, he moves closer, whether by design or subconsciously, putting himself in between me and the other man. Letting out a low chuckle, the man stays where he is but leans his head to the side to glance at me again before straightening and addressing Deacon again.

"You called me, remember?" he says before following up in a more hushed tone, "Don't worry, *mon gars*, I won't hurt her."

Reluctantly, Deacon moves to the side and takes a seat in the armchair next to the couch. Gesturing towards the other man, he says, "Siren, this is Dr. Aristille. He's here to look you over." At my sharp glance, he continues, "He looks scarier than he actually is." Eyes boring into mine, he says, "Trust me." And for some reason that I can't quite explain, I do. Even so, as the man walks forward and crouches down in front of me, I can't help the involuntary jerk backward. Aside from a slight dimming of his grin, he gives no other indication that he's noticed.

In a soothing tone, he says, "Easy, cricket. I'm here to help you. Let me see how badly you're injured. I promise not to do anything you don't want me to."

The sudden softness of his tone belies the tough-as-nails exterior and somehow works to put me at ease. Lowering my legs slowly until my feet are touching the floor between his spread knees, I give a slight nod. Taking my consent for what it is, he opens the leather bag at his feet and takes out a small flashlight, going through the motions of shining it in my eyes to test my pupillary responses. Next, he listens to my heart and lungs, takes my blood pressure, and then my oxygen saturation with a small device on my finger. It takes everything in me not to freak out when he asks me to lie down on the couch so he can check for any broken ribs. I take deep breaths, and my head turns towards Deacon's chair as he pushes on different parts of my stomach before allowing me to sit back up slowly.

Gesturing towards my neck, he says, "May I?"

Nodding again, I allow him to run his fingers over the hand-print-shaped bruises I know are there. From my peripheral vision, I see Deacon stiffen in his chair. His reaction is surprising, considering the doctor isn't hurting me. His touch on my neck is feather-light, and even though it's not menacing in any way, I can't help the jitters that come with having another man's hands on me. Quickly enough, he pulls them away, after turning my face this way and that, and I see some of the tension leave Deacon's body. For some reason, the sight dispels some of my unease.

"Well, cricket … my professional opinion is that you've got a mild concussion, a few burst blood vessels in your left eye, a busted lip, and lots of cuts and bruises. The older cuts are already healing. The fresher ones, along with the bruises, will heal in time. You're also severely dehydrated and probably malnourished. Aside from that, I think you're okay." After a short pause, he adds, "Is there anywhere else you'd like me to check before I go?"

I know what he's asking. Do I want him to do a rape kit or some type of vaginal exam. And the answer to that is *hell no*. I was violated, yes. But I've been violated before. I'll live. Shaking my head, I say, "No, thank you. I'm fine."

He stares at me intently for a long moment before finally saying, "You will be, cricket, you will be. And you can call me Theo, by the way."

After another moment, he stands up, brushing a cloud of dust off his pants, and motions to Deacon to follow him to the room next door. If I had to guess, probably the kitchen. While they talk, I lay my head back against the couch and try to breathe past the lump that's formed in my throat. I'm not a crier; never have been. Unless you counted the tears I shed over music. As a rule, though, I never made a habit of crying. Not before I met Dante, at least. I cried when Amelia got shot, and we didn't know whether she was gonna make it, but aside from that incident, I haven't cried since I escaped the first time. I thought the period of my life that involved Dante was over, and I swore I'd never shed another tear because of that bastard until I was taken again. Even though I know I've gotten away a second time, the urge to let loose more useless tears is nearly overwhelming. I don't know why. It's not like it'll change anything. Closing my eyes, I try my best to push away the memory of the night that kicked off my years of torment and the first time I ever cried over a man. Refusing to be squashed, however, the flashbacks wash over me like the ebb and flow of the ocean right before the inevitable happens and it takes you under.

CHAPTER 16

Siren

16 YEARS OLD

As I walk out onto the empty stage, the bright lights warm my skin, and even if every seat in this entire theater was empty, they'd be all the accolades I need to know that this is what I'm meant to do with my life. But the seats aren't empty. The house is packed, and everyone who bought a ticket tonight came to see ... me. It still blows my mind that anyone would want to pay actual money to listen to me play. My best friend, Amelia, would tell me to shut up and accept the fact that I was a musical genius. I know because I've said the same thing to her about her paintings. She's so talented, and rarely gives herself the credit she deserves. As I glance to my left, I see her standing in the backstage area that can't be seen from the center of the theater, and I give her a small smile. She winks back at me and gives me two thumbs up of encouragement. I appreciate the sentiment, but I don't really need it. I was practically born with a violin in my hand, and I've never felt more at home than when I was holding it. It wouldn't matter if I were playing only for my own shadow or to this packed auditorium at Charleston Music Hall.

I was only 16 and in one of the best all-girl's private schools in the country. I'd been raised with money. I'd had private lessons and tutors and was given the best of everything. To say I was privileged would be an understatement. The one thing I was never given, though, was the one thing money can't buy. Love. My parents' neglect wasn't what most people would think of when they thought of neglect, but it was neglect all the same. I wasn't being beaten, malnourished, or left home alone while they went off on benders for days on end. Well ... that last one wasn't entirely true. They did, but my parents preferred to experience their benders on yachts instead of in back alleys or bars. I'd been raised by nannies, fed by chefs, and dressed by maids. It was just the way of our social class. A fact I'd come to accept a long time ago. That didn't make the hurt any less or excuse it, but it did explain it. Like many others in Charleston's elite circle, my parents were absent, save for a few annual functions they hosted in the city. By now, I'd learned the only person I could really rely on was myself. It was a hard lesson to learn before you actually reached adulthood, but I liked to think that, in many ways, I was ahead of the curve. Especially when it came to music. My listening tastes ranged from 80s British punk to today's hits and everything in between. But the area of music I felt most comfortable in, the place where I felt what I imagined the warmth of love must feel like, was classical. There was something to be said for the simple yet complex feelings that a single violin and a bow string could evoke. Sometimes, the sounds could bring you to tears. Other times, more than I'd care to admit, it quite literally picked you up off the floor. All you had to do was listen. Not just to the notes themselves but to the space in between, where silence reigned. That was where you found yourself. Where you figured out who you really are. And I'm a badass who doesn't need anyone to make me feel whole. All I needed were the strings.

So, as I stand in front of the only other thing on stage, a microphone stand, I bring the violin to my chin, lift the bow, close my eyes, and let the audience see the real me. The strong and the vulnerable. Because when you were good at something, truly good at it, you had to give it everything in you. It was a hunger that would never be satisfied with just the crumbs. You had to feed it your heart and soul. That was true love. Or what I imagined it must feel like, at least. So, I begin with one of my favorite classical pieces, Bach's Chaconne. I don't need sheet music. I don't need a conductor—only the heart and soul. As the melancholy song reaches its first peak, I can feel a tear slide down my left cheek. It's not the first time I've cried while playing, and I know it won't be the last. I love this piece because there's nothing here but honesty. There is no room for pretense when playing Bach—no place to hide. So I play every note with precision, integrity, and, as I would imagine the composer himself would want, wholeheartedly. There's a brief second of silence as the song comes to a close, during which I lower my instrument and open my eyes. A millisecond later, I'm met with thunderous applause. As the crowd comes to their feet in a standing ovation, it's not arrogance I feel. It's not even pride. It's humility and I close my eyes again, a small smile forming on my lips as a few more tears escape. To be able to share this part of me with people is the greatest gift I've ever been given. And, as my tutors can attest to, it cost absolutely nothing. I was born with this inside me. It may have taken a little coaxing to get it out, but once it was free, it took on a life of its own and became my parent, friend, lover, and most trusted confidant. So, no, I don't feel pride. I only feel grateful because not many people out there get to take this feeling with them everywhere they go.

Opening my eyes again, I take a bow, only because it's expected of me, then wait for the curtain to come down for intermission before hastily swiping away any running mascara and turning to stage left. Amelia is still there; I can tell she's also been crying. She claps along with the applause that try to break their way through the heavy red curtain.

Smiling as I walk up to her, I say, "While Bach is deserving of much praise, please, save your tears for my own work."

Laughing, we get in a quick hug before I'm whisked off to the backstage area where my dressing table is. I know my makeup is in desperate need of repair, but I'm honestly not sure there's any point. It'll be destroyed again in 15 minutes. Still, I let the assistant use a makeup remover wipe under my eyes before reapplying foundation and powder. Nerves churn in my stomach like a thousand tiny butterflies, and I know it's stupid to feel that way because the minute I walk out there again and begin to play, they'll evaporate, but it's the getting to that point that always has me wanting to throw up. I'd much rather play for myself and only myself, but I've been told that a gift like mine should be shared with the world. So, at least for the next two years, while I figure out my next steps, I'll stay the course that my parents put me on before they even knew that I was the one secretly holding the map.

As the makeup artist finishes her work, I thank her and stand up, lifting the skirt of my red velvet dress to keep from tripping over it as I make my way back to the side of the stage. I know my parents would prefer that I wear something black because black is slimming and as they like to remind me at every available opportunity, I need as much help in that department as I can get. But fuck what they want because they couldn't even be bothered to show up tonight. I loved red. Not a bright red like the color you see around Christmas, but a deeper, blood red. It made me feel powerful and just a little less inferior to other girls my age.

Stepping up next to where Amelia still stands offstage, I feel her hand reach out for mine and give it a light squeeze. Immediately, half the butterflies disappear, and I'm left feeling only slightly nauseous. She may be my best friend, but even those have their limits. Still, I appreciate her presence here. She's never missed a recital, even though I know her mother hates me. I'm too loud, too ballsy, and too unladylike. AKA, I'm the opposite of the deadhead wallflower she and the rest of society would like me to be, so obviously, I'm a terrible influence on her daughter. The knowledge brings a mischievous grin to my face. It was true that of the two of us, I was the more brash, but Amelia was her own person with her own spirit and there would come a time when her mother would no longer be able to keep her on society's proverbial leash. Lord help humanity when she was let loose. I, personally, can't wait.

As the curtain rises again, I reluctantly release Amelia's hand and return to the microphone. This time, when I bring the violin and bow up, a large smile blossoms across my face because the next song I'll be playing is mine. I composed it, developed it, and perfected it. It's poignant and beautiful. I'd titled it "Siren's Call." It was a little on the nose, but I guess I was a romantic at heart. Keeping my eyes open this time, I begin to play. As the song progresses, I allow the tears to run freely, but the smile never falters. The song is as full of me as I am of it. Full of longing, despair, secrets, insecurities, optimism, and so many other emotions that would take a lifetime to put into words. In music, it takes about 13 minutes. When I finish, I bow for myself this time because the original piece would never have made it out into the world if I hadn't set it free. Now, I feel the pride. Now, I look at the faces in the audience, and I absorb their applause like a sponge, soaking up every bit of admiration and adoration as my due. Despite all my other issues, I have unwavering confidence in one thing. This. So, this time, I don't bother wiping away the tears. I leave them there for the world to see, taking another bow as the curtain lowers again. I place a hand over my stomach. Nothing. No more butterflies. Releasing a deep breath, I put down my violin and walk back to Amelia. She throws her arms around me as soon as I get within range of her.

"Oh my God, that was amazing! You were incredible! I'm so proud of you!" she says, wiping away tears again herself.

Laughing through my own, I say, "I told you to save the water-works. At this rate, you're gonna dehydrate yourself and need an IV."

Pulling back, she says, "Oh, shut up. Just bask in the absolute love they have for you. Can you hear it?"

I could. But right on the coattails of that came a bittersweet feeling. I smile brightly at her, but I know she can tell.

Looking into my eyes, she says, "They'll never know that feeling. What it is to be truly adored. They weren't built for it."

I know she's talking about my parents the same way I know she could tell by the dimming of my eyes that I was still bitter about them not being here. I know she's right, but there's still a small part of me that can't help but feel like whatever flaw there was that prevented their love was inside of me instead of them. Out of all the parts of me I hate, I hate that one the most. The part that makes me question my own worth.

Shaking my head to clear the bad thoughts away, I say, "It doesn't matter. You came and that's more than enough. Let me get changed and we can go get something to eat. I'm *starving*."

She stares at me for another second, a second in which I can see the dreaded emotion of pity in her eyes before she pastes on a bright smile and nods. "Pizza?" she asks.

"Fuck, yes. Extra cheese," I reply.

Laughing, she says, "Ok, I'll wait for you outside."

Parting ways, I make my way back to my dressing table, accepting the small pats and smiles from people backstage. As I sit down in front of the lit mirror again, I clean my face up myself this time, wiping away the tear tracks that are clearly visible through my foundation. I really should wear waterproof eyeliner. As I pull my long black hair into a high ponytail, a figure steps into the mirror's reflection behind me. He's tall and dressed in an expensive suit, and as I get a waft of his cologne, I can feel my hormones go on red alert. As I lift my gaze to meet his in the mirror, I'm hit with a zap of ... something. Something I've never felt before. Dark eyes stare into mine in the mirror's reflection, and something in his gaze pins me to the spot. It's a look of ... possession? Infatuation? I scoff inwardly. If only. As I bring myself back to reality, I do a half-turn in my chair to face him.

Adopting the confident persona that's come to shield me like armor, I say, "Hello. Can I help you?"

As he continues to simply stare at me, I feel goosebumps break out along my skin. Just as I'm about to repeat my question, he opens his mouth, and the sound of his voice has the breath catching in my throat, nearly causing me to hiccup. It's deep, with an Italian accent that does things to my insides that aren't spoken about in polite conversation.

"Cio, Bella. My apologies. I watched you play and knew that I had to meet you. Allow me to introduce myself. My name is Dante Gaspari." He holds out his hand as if to shake mine. Tentatively, I extend my own, but instead of shaking my hand, he catches it, bending to bring it to his lips, where he presses a kiss to the top. The kiss is soft, but his grip on my hand is tight. The contrast is both intimidating and intoxicating.

I release a short breath and say, "Thank you, Mr. Gaspari. Myself, along with The Charleston Music Hall, appreciate your patronage."

He waves his hand in a gesture of dismissal. "It's nothing. And please, call me Dante. I must say, I've traveled all over the world and seen many things, but I've never seen anyone play quite like you. Allow me to take you to dinner. I would love for us to get to know each other. You're hungry, si?"

The way he phrases the request doesn't make it sound like much of a request at all, but I'm flabbergasted by the idea that this man would want to have dinner with me. Even just to discuss music, surely there's someone more worthy of his time and attention. The insecurities that I try to keep buried deep threaten to surface. Perhaps it's the heavy focus I'm applying to those insecurities that keep me from wondering why a man like this is looking at a 16-year-old girl the way he's currently looking at me. Still, I find myself nodding before my brain has even had a chance to process everything he said.

Making a mental note to text Amelia and let her know that I'll have to take a rain check on that pizza, I say, "I'm flattered. Yes, I'd love to have dinner with you ... Dante."

It would only be in retrospect that I'd recognize this as the moment that would irrevocably change my life. Recognize that the look in his eyes wasn't just one of possession and infatuation, but that of a predator. And I, the prey, would soon learn what it was to love. Love equaled pain, and I would hate him and myself for allowing those two words to become synonymous with each other.

CHAPTER 17

Deacon

As I walk into the kitchen, I can hear the heavy footfalls of Theo's boots behind me. Stepping far enough into the room to be out of earshot of Siren, I turn to face the not-so-good doctor.

I cut him off before he can even open his mouth by saying, "So what's the real story?"

Theo has been an intense dude for as long as I've known him, but the man standing before me now is night and day different from the one just talking to Siren in the living room. That man actually appeared gentle despite his rough exterior. This man looks ready to commit a murder. Well, he'll have to get in line.

Huffing out a hard breath through his nose, not unlike that of a bull, before it charges into the china shop, he says, "Someone beat the shit outta that girl; that's the real story. She's been carved up like a piece of meat on top of that. Not to mention ..." He trails off, a slight tick appearing in his flexing jaw.

"Not to mention what?" I demand. My nerves are on edge, and my patience is at zero. I've never had any issues with the doctor, but I'll gladly beat the information out of him if he thinks to try and keep it to himself.

Eyes bouncing back and forth between mine, I can tell that he's gauging my mood. Probably trying to decide if he thinks that whatever he's going to say next is gonna push me over the edge or not. He has no idea that I've already swan-dived off that cliff and landed on the rocks below.

Finally sighing in resignation, he says, "Based on her body language and her refusal for any further examination, I'd lay money down that she's been sexually assaulted. Probably more than once."

While somewhere deep down, I think I already knew that knowledge, it doesn't stop the rush of pure rage and adrenaline that shoots through my bloodstream at his words. Turning around to pace, I'm just about to upend my small kitchen table when I feel a firm hand on my shoulder. I whip around to face Theo, nostrils flaring and spoiling for a fight, but he doesn't back down. He doesn't even remove his hand. Instead, he brings the other up to grip the opposite shoulder, holding me still.

"You have to calm down, mon gars. She needs you to stay level. If you don't, she won't. Right?" His eyes hold mine, and he nods slowly in silent encouragement. As I force the heat of anger down to a low simmer, I return the nod with one of my own. "Good. Now, you know who did this to her?"

Another nod. Glancing towards the doorway, I say, "Someone from her past. Someone she thought was dead, but, unfortunately, he wasn't. He came and took her right from her own bed a few weeks ago. We've been searching for her ever since. I found her by happenstance at Kingsley's auction." I don't need to elaborate further. He runs in the same circles I do, so he already knows all about the auction.

A string of French curse words burst from his lips, and he finally removes his hands from my shoulders, stepping away to do a little pacing of his own. As he runs a hand through his already disheveled hair, he says, "Tell me he's actually dead now. Because if you didn't kill him, I just might. I got a thing about men who put their hands on a woman."

I clench my fists at my side, trying to keep myself from flying off the handle again. His anger is only fueling my own. I take a deep breath to calm myself and say, "I honestly don't know. When I got her out of there, she had already done most of the work for me. Slit the fucks throat with a razor." As I glance towards the doorway again, my anger drains away, something softer taking its place. I can't pinpoint what the feeling is, but I don't think I've ever felt anything like it before. If I have, I don't remember it. "She's stronger than she looks," I add.

His pacing slows considerably before he finally stops to face me again. "Good girl. I hope it took. But if it didn't, you need to know. I'm sure you'll find out somehow. You look particularly motivated," he says, a small smirk forming at the corner of his lips.

"Oh, shut up. You don't know me," I say, quietly moving over to the doorway to peek at Siren asleep on the couch again. What I said is true. He thought he knew me, and maybe to a certain extent, I'd let him closer than most, but he still didn't know even a fraction of my story. Of the hate that fueled me. Of the rage that was nearly always there, just below the surface. Of the desperate need for retribution, to avenge my mother so that I could finally let go of the past. Theo had only peeled back a few layers of the onion, and those layers were thick. Come to think of it, they also stunk and would make most people wanna cry, so I guess the analogy is apt.

Coming to stand just behind me, he makes a noncommittal noise deep in his throat. "Mmhmm, right. Don't be *honte, mon gars.* Plenty of people are motivated by much less. She's got a little *lagniappe.* Like a gator, she don't need you to feed her when she got teeth of her own," he says, accent becoming more pronounced as more words from his native dialect slip in. I don't speak French, much less Creole French, but I've spent enough time in Louisiana to recognize many of the common words used by the culture. I don't respond; I just continue to watch Siren closely, but his words play in my head like a broken record. *Lagniappe.* Something extra. Hand gripping my shoulder again, he gives it a firm squeeze before adding, "Give me a call if she needs anything else. I'll send you the bill." With a wink, he heads for the door, stopping to put a pill bottle on the coffee table. Just as he places his hand on the knob, he turns and says, "And Deacon? You tell me how you get on with that research. It would be my pleasure to help you take care of that problem if it's lingerin.'" With that, he opens the door and leaves, quietly closing it behind him.

I stand in the doorway separating the living room and formal dining area for another minute, just thinking. I know what he was alluding to, and the offer to kill Gaspari, should he still be alive, is sweet. But if he did manage to survive the blood loss, I'll make him pray for the death that he's so fortunately evaded twice. He'll curse the day he ever met her and every day since. The last thing he'll see will be my eyes, staring down at him as the light in his own goes out. I was selfish by nature; you had to be when you grew up the way I did. And, like so many other things, I don't want to share this.

For what feels like the thousandth time since Theo left, I find myself sneaking glances at Siren from my vantage point in the chair next to the sofa. Despite all the work I have to do, my brain has decided that I need to take vigil beside her until she wakes up, in case of what, I don't know. But for some inexplicable reason, I can't stomach the thought of her waking up alone. I know she needs rest, but I also don't necessarily like how much she's slept since I got her out of that house. It's almost as if her body is making up for lost time, which wouldn't surprise me at all. I don't think I'd wanna risk closing my eyes if I had been trapped in a house with that sick fuck. Hands clenching on the chair's armrests, I force myself to look outside at the sun that's beginning to dip beneath the tree line. It'll be dark soon, and the crickets will begin their nightly symphony. The sounds of insects and other creatures are about the only soundtrack that plays this far away from civilization. Usually, the gentle chirps of the crickets or the hooting of owls in the surrounding woods are a comfort to me, a soothing lullaby that I've always considered the perfect music to fall asleep to. I mean, who needs white noise machines when you've got mother nature? Now, however, I can't help but wonder if the sounds will scare Siren or if the isolation of my home and otherwise silence will be too deafening. I don't know how long she'll be here, but I want her to feel comfortable while she is. Speaking of comfort, I glance over toward Siren's sleeping form again and, more specifically, her blood-stained and torn clothing. When my gaze tracks up to her face, it's to find her eyes open and watching me.

"Holy fuck, woman, how long have you been staring at me?" I ask, barely repressing the urge to jump out of my skin.

Gingerly sitting up, she says, "Probably not as long as you've been staring at me, you creeper."

My eyes narrow, but internally, I'm bolstered by the bite in her tone. That sass of hers is still in there despite the many thick layers of trauma it's been buried under. She's definitely not 100% but I'll take what I can get for now. Opening my mouth to reply, I quickly close it again, opting to stand instead.

"I'll be right back," I say. Striding through the kitchen, I enter the laundry room just on the other side, rummaging through the overflowing basket of clean clothes on top of the dryer. I finally manage to locate a t-shirt and a pair of sweatpants with a drawstring. Realizing that my own clothes are still covered in dried blood that must've been transferred from her to me, I tear off my shirt and slacks before throwing on an undershirt and a pair of loose fitting basketball shorts. Quickly coming back into the living room, I find Siren exactly where I left her, only now she's looking down at a framed photo in her hands. I know what picture it is based on the frame, and considering no one ever comes here but Merrick, it never occurred to me that anyone else would see it or any of the pictures around the house, for that matter.

"Is this your mother?" she asks in a low tone, and I watch as she runs an index finger over the face in the picture.

The stab of grief is unexpected, not in it's presence but its intensity. I think about my mother all the time, but enough time has passed now that more volatile emotions, like hatred, have dulled the overwhelming sense of pain. I came to the realization a long time ago that those were the emotions that kept you going. Sure, they ate at you, and my soul probably looked like Swiss cheese at this point, but they still gave me a reason to wake up every day. Emotions like grief were probably more healthy to experience, but they also took their toll. A price that I very rarely allowed myself to pay anymore. To experience it now and over such a simple question is disconcerting. I don't like surprises. They usually come with unwanted side effects. Like more *feelings*.

Instead of answering, I hold out the clothes for her. "Here. I don't have any women's clothes, so these'll have to do. There's a bathroom through there," I say, gesturing towards the hallway off the living room. "You can shower and change if you want. Supper will be ready in a bit."

She stares at the clothes in my outstretched hand, then at my face, then back at the clothes. Carefully sitting the picture back on the table next to the couch, she takes the clothes but makes no move to get up. Instead, she sits them in her lap, absently rubbing the fabric of my t-shirt between her thumb and forefinger. Does she realize she's doing that? Based on her gaze on my face again, I think it might be subconscious.

"What?" I ask defensively. Her stare is unnerving, and I barely resist the urge to squirm. I'm a grown fucking man, for God's sake. And I've definitely dealt with much scarier people than Siren Sinclair. I shouldn't be uneasy under her scrutiny, but her eyes are so intimidating. They see too much. Why have I never noticed that before?

Arching a brow, she asks, "You cook?" The note of incredulity in her tone is clear, and maybe it's that, or maybe it's because she keeps having the ability to throw me off kilter, but either way, her words are grating.

"No, I opened a can of Spaghetti-O's for you. You know, since my poor male brain can't figure out how to turn the stove on." I snap. Immediately regretting my actions, I wince slightly. She's been through a lot. I shouldn't have done that. She's still in a fragile state, and the last thing she needs is me biting her head off. I should apol-

"Well, good for you, mastering the can opener. You're a leg up on the rest of your species," she snaps back, effectively cutting off all thoughts of gentleness.

"You...I...wha...," I stutter out, flabbergasted at the audacity of this woman.

"Still haven't quite gotten a grasp on the English language though, I see. Don't worry, champ, I'm sure you'll get there."

Heat floods my face, and I can practically feel my blood pressure spike. Taking a step forward, I open my mouth to give her a piece of my mind. She jumps up from the sofa, bowing up to meet me instead of cowering like any woman in her right mind would after everything she's been through. I guess the questionable words there are *in her right mind.*

"What??" she demands.

We stand there, glaring daggers at each other until, with a growl low in my throat, I turn on my heel and leave the room. Back in the kitchen, I practically wear a hole in the linoleum as I pace back and forth, running a hand through my hair in frustration. It's not her fault. She doesn't know what she's saying. She's just feeling vulnerable and lashing out.

Shaking my head at my asinine thoughts, I stop pacing. No, she's not. I saw her at her most vulnerable. That woman was nothing like this one. This one is more akin to the old Siren, and even as the thought has me breathing an internal sigh of relief at the idea that the feisty wench I met all those months ago is still in there somewhere, the fire her words stoked still rages. Fuck this. If she wants to have it out, we can have it out. Turning around again, I stomp back into the living room.

"You know what..." my angry words trail off when I enter to find the room empty. Quick as a flash, that anger morphs into panic. Turning blindly towards the hallway, I rush around the corner to find the bathroom door at the end slightly ajar. The sound of running water from inside has me slowing my steps and entertaining the thought that maybe I overreacted a little. I highly doubt that any would-be kidnapper or murderer would wanna use my bathroom to freshen up before committing his crime. As I stand in the darkened hallway, I listen to the water bounce off the tiles and, Lord only knows what areas of skin, before it finally turns off. A second later, a towel-clad Siren steps into view of the floor-length mirror within. She's facing away from me but she's not looking at her own reflection either. She appears to be deliberately avoiding eye contact with the mirror. I'm not, though. Shrinking further into the shadows, I press my back to the wall and watch as she removes the towel to dry her arms systematically, then her chest, stomach, and ... am I panting? Why am I panting? I know this is an incredible invasion of privacy, but even my hand scrubbing down my face breaks my attention for too long for my liking. I know I should stop watching; I can't seem to make my feet move. She's just as stunning as I remember. Thoughts of that body have kept me up at night, more times than I'd like to admit. Nearly groaning when she bends at the waist to towel her hair dry, I slap my hand over my mouth before the sound can escape. What's wrong with me? I must be the sickest kind of bastard to spy on a naked woman after she's barely survived Hell for the last several weeks. I'm just about to turn away and attempt to quietly make it back to the kitchen before I get caught, but when she turns around to reach for the clothes sitting on the countertop, the move puts her back to the mirror and, as the light from the bright fluorescent bulbs illuminate the colorful tattoos that litter her shoulders and upper back, I stop in my tracks to stare at a cacophony of angry red slashes, all in different stages of healing. These must be the marks I saw briefly in Kingsley's office. Some appear to be older and have already scabbed over, while others still look so fresh that I know they must be killing her. Unfortunately, I don't get to look for long before she's slipping my t-shirt over her head, effectively hiding the marks from view. As I shake with rage, my first instinct is to barge inside and demand she show me the full extent of her injuries. Another more rational voice overrides that instinct, replacing it with the urge to protect. To take care of her. To coax the information out of her instead of simply taking it. She's had so much taken from her already. I can't be just another man who takes from her without giving anything in return. And aside from money, I don't have anything in me to give. In time, I'll get her to tell me everything that bastard did to her, and if she doesn't wanna tell me, I'll see for myself. She doesn't know it, but there are cameras hidden all over this house. It may be borderline immoral to spy on her, but I can still sleep at night knowing I've done something sneaky, as long as I've gotten the information I need. Not knowing would surely kill me.

Unbeknownst to me at the time, this would mark the beginning of an unhealthy obsession that I never saw coming.

CHAPTER 18

Siren

As soon as I set foot in the living room, I can smell the food. My brain which has been programmed to refuse meals during my recent captivity for fear of being drugged—rebels at the idea of eating. My stomach, on the other hand, takes this opportunity to growl in a way that isn't befitting a proper Southern lady. Oh well. Propriety could shove it. No one had ever mistaken me for a lady before, so the monster that seems trapped in my stomach, currently demanding sustenance, is fitting. When I don't immediately see Deacon in the living room, I'm grateful and take a minute to compose myself. Closing my eyes, I take a deep breath and remind myself for the thousandth time that I'm no longer trapped in that room. The conditioning is hard to break, though. I know there's bound to be an adjustment period. There definitely was the last time. I also know that I'm going to have some long-term mental damage from what happened. Hell, I was still having nightmares off and on, even up to the point that Dante's men snatched me out of my own bed. Thanks to intense therapy and several helpful little pills, I usually went long periods without dreaming about what had happened to me before, but every time I thought I'd finally outrun my demons, they'd find a way to sneak up on me again. Somewhere, in the back of my mind, I'm worried that having lived through the ninth circle of Hell ... for the second time, where the Devil reigned supreme, I might be royally fucked up beyond repair.

No. I give my head a small but firm shake, face scrunching in irritation. No. I won't let this break me. I survived for a reason. I have to believe that. Fate wouldn't let me escape twice just so I could be miserable for the rest of my life. I, Siren Sinclair, won't let that motherfucker break me. The last time was different. I was young, insecure, and had no one. This time, I'm older, wiser, and have friends that actually give a shit about what happens to me. Even if some of them do so grudgingly. I release a little snort because I know Deacon is just as uncomfortable with me being here as I am. It was clear from the moment I set foot inside, his furnishings and decor showed that this isn't just a house to him. I remember the picture of the smiling woman who had just been casually sitting on an end table. I didn't need his confirmation to know that it was his mother. He looked just like her, except for the eyes. Remembering how strategically that and dozens of other pictures, nick-nacks, and books were placed, I can tell that this is *home*. And he clearly doesn't get many visitors here; that much is obvious, too. The man just ... hovers; It's like he doesn't know what to do with himself, having someone else in his space. I can only hope that I'm able to get out of here sooner rather than later. Before he either pesters me to death or I murder him.

Taking one last big inhale, I open my eyes, only to find Deacon standing in the doorway that leads to the kitchen, watching me. He really needs to cut that shit out. How long has he been standing there? He leans against the door jam, head cocked slightly to the side, kind of like a dog when you blow a whistle, and they can't seem to figure out where the noise is coming from. I can't stop the second snort from escaping, even after putting my hand over my mouth. The fact that I can find humor in any situation after what I've just lived through is astonishing. I guess I could put some stock into that whole "mind over matter" thing. Deacon's eyes narrow slightly at my sudden channeling of the bovine variety. Biting my bottom lip, I have to try really hard not to laugh in his face. I'm sure between that and my random sound effects from a minute ago, I look like a total basket case, which, to be fair, I am. If he hasn't figured that out already, he will soon enough.

"What's so funny?" he asks, suspicion lacing his tone

I think about it for a second. "Do you own a dog?"

Suspicion turns to confusion, and now he really is looking at me like I'm a basket case. "Uhhh ... no. Why?" He says the last word as if he's almost afraid to ask. I can't really blame him.

"No reason. Just wondering. Seems like you'd do well with a dog. Have a lot in common," I say, trying desperately to hide the snicker in my voice. I bite my lower lip between my teeth again as he studies me, expression back to one of suspicion.

"Your Spaghetti-O's are ready. Hope you don't mind eating out of the can. I can't get bowls down from the cabinet with my paws," he says, sarcasm coming through loud and clear. Ok, I probably deserved that. Even though he didn't get the full extent of my joke, he obviously got enough to be annoyed with me. What else is new?

"Can't wait," I reply in a deadpan voice before gesturing towards the kitchen. "Lead the way."

Rolling his eyes, he turns on his heel, disappearing into the kitchen again. I follow behind slowly, my brain and stomach still waging battle over whether I'll eat and, more importantly, if I'll even be able to keep it down or end up throwing it all back up. I mean, I've always taken great pride in the fact that I don't have a gag reflex. In fact, at one time, I considered putting it on my resume. I may have to, actually. Who knows if I'll still have a job after all this? I was one of the symphony's biggest draws, but I have no doubt that they've most likely sacked me by now. You can't just not show up to work for weeks and expect to still hold a spot with such a prestigious company. As I step into the kitchen, the scents from before become exponentially stronger ... and they're definitely not from Spaghetti-O's. Intrigued, I walk over to the stove to see a pot of chili simmering on one of the large burners and a cast iron skillet of cornbread sitting on the counter next to it. Eyes narrowing, I slowly turn back to Deacon, who's standing next to a small kitchen table that's been set with ... two disposable bowls and plastic cutlery. I wanna smile, but considering my default is bitchy chic, I can't help the smartass comment that exits my mouth.

"Were you out of clean dishes, or did your last fling just break them all when you didn't offer to make her breakfast the morning after?"

He opens his mouth, probably to tell me to get fucked, but closes it again without speaking. Shutting his eyes, he takes a slow, deep breath in through his nose before exhaling heavily, as if I'm tight-roping the line of his last nerve. When he finally opens them, I'm struck again by just how blue his eyes are, especially this close up. I think I'd prefer them not to be spitting fire at me but I was born and raised in the South. I know how to handle my heat.

In a low tone, he surprises me by saying, "I've never brought another woman here before."

The more I think about it, the quicker my surprise dissipates. It makes sense. Deacon is a hit-it-and-quit-it kinda guy, and this is obviously his sanctuary. I have a feeling that not many people, even outside of women, have been in this house. Given his very illegal extracurricular activities, it's no wonder he prefers to stay off the grid. Also explains the heightened level of security. Doesn't he get lonely out here in the swamps all alone? I briefly entertain the thought of asking him precisely that but then discard the idea, mostly because I wouldn't wanna answer that question myself, should anyone ask. Not that anyone besides Amelia has ever cared enough to ask. I'm not really the type of girl that stays on anyone's mind for very long. Deacon's the hit-it-and-quit-it type, and I'm just the type of girl he'd quit. Correction, *has* quit. Not that I'm bitter about it. I mean, how can I be when I'm technically the one that snuck out first? Hurt them before they can hurt you, right? I ignore the little voice in my head that's asking me how the weather is in Delululand. *Pipe down bitch; nobody asked for your input.*

When I finally reply, there's no heat behind my words. Maybe it's because of what he said or maybe it's the way he said it. Almost as though the words were part of a confession being pulled from him. Regardless, I'm not going to look a gift horse in the mouth, and now that I've showered and changed, the hunger pangs have returned with a vengeance. Glancing back to the stove, I wonder briefly why Deacon cooked instead of actually making me eat something from a can, Spaghetti-O's or otherwise.

I highly doubt it was to impress me. I mean, he's already gotten into my pants so what would be the point? Even though I feel like I made him work for it, to him, I was probably a sure thing. I guess he was right. And now that he's gotten what he wants from me, is there any point in pretending to be a gentleman? I don't spend too long on that train of thought, though, or I'll end up having to deep dive into why he came to rescue me in the first place. I know he put himself in serious danger getting me out of that house. It's anyone's guess as to his true motives. Maybe some misguided sense of obligation? Maybe Merrick asked him to? Who knows. I'll have to think more about this later. Right now, that chili is calling my name.

I stand there awkwardly. "So ... should I serve myself or ...?"

I watch his right eyebrow quirk a second before he says, "Of course not, madame. Let me get that for you." He jumps to attention in such an exaggerated fashion that he wouldn't be out of place on an episode of the Three Stooges. Yet, even though he's clearly being a smartass, he picks up both bowls from the table, taking them to the stove nonetheless. Scooping heaping spoonfuls into each bowl, he cuts a large wedge of cornbread for each of us, sitting it on top of the chili. As he makes his way back to the table, he walks so slowly that I have to suppress another snort. I've really gotta stop doing that. Clearly afraid he's going to drop the food, he takes his time sitting the bowls down before taking a seat himself. Sitting at a table, just the two of us, is weird. He doesn't seem to think so, though, because before I can even ask him if he says grace, he's picked up his spoon and is shoveling a bite into his mouth. I notice something strange as I sit and glance from his heaping bowl to mine. Both bowls have the exact same amount of food in them. I would've expected to have a portion about half the size of his, which is what I'm usually served whenever I eat a meal with someone other than Amelia. It's been that way since I was a child. When they were there, my parents instructed the staff to give me a fraction of the food that they ate. Even by normal standards, the portions I was given were small for a growing child. I knew, even at that young age, that it was because they thought I was too fat. I knew because they told me so, not in a direct way but in every other way that mattered. Buying my clothes two sizes too big so they'd fit loosely, telling the cook that I didn't need dessert, comments about how I'd never win any beauty pageants if I couldn't make it through the swimsuit round. Hell, they even gave me Weight Watchers snack cakes for Christmas one year. The memories used to make me angry, but now I just feel numb. Even though I've gone my entire life feeling significantly less than perfect, I thank my lucky stars that I never developed some type of eating disorder. I knew firsthand what drove people to that extreme, but I guess I always balanced right on the edge of that line without tipping over. I've always hated looking at myself in the mirror, though. Unless absolutely necessary for hair or makeup purposes before a concert, I'd avoid it if I could. I didn't need the constant reminder of why I was never good enough for anyone to wanna keep me. Well, unless you counted an abusive and oppressive psychopath with a fated mate complex.

It takes Deacon five bites of chili before he notices I haven't even picked up my spoon. Swallowing a mouthful, he looks from me to the food before asking, "Why aren't you eating?"

"You gave me too much food," I say. I expect the words to come out in my usual haughty tone, but instead, they sound small, even to my ears.

He looks at me for several seconds, eyes roaming over my face as though he's trying to catalog every twitch and tick, making mental notes so that he can attribute them to some specific emotion later. "I gave us both the same amount," he replies, his nonchalant tone is a direct contrast to the way he's watching my face.

"I can't eat all this," I say. I watch his jaw flex as he appears to be weighing his words carefully, though I'm unsure why. That annoying little voice in my head pipes up again, spewing all kinds of insecure thoughts. Why is he staring so much? Does he think I need this much food because of my size? Is he gonna watch me eat the entire time? These are all thoughts I've heard before, so I squash the voice before it has me squirming in my seat uncomfortably. I prefer to do my self loathing in private, thank you very much.

When he finally speaks again, his words give me pause. "Can't … or won't?"

Pulling a face like someone's stuck something particularly smelly under my nose, I say, "What's that supposed to mean?"

He slowly shakes his head, finally taking his eyes off my face to focus back on his own bowl. "Nothing. You don't have to finish it. Just eat until you get full." He eats another bite or two, then stands.

"Where are you going?" I ask before I can stop myself. Why do I care where he's going? I should be happy that he's leaving me to eat in peace.

"I've got some work to do in my office. There's a spare room down the hall, but I mostly use it for storage, so you'll have to take my bed. It's the room next door to the bathroom you used earlier. I'll sleep on the couch. I've already called Merrick to let him and Amelia know that you're here but if you wanna call her, use one of the burner phones in there." He indicates the drawer next to the fridge. And with that, he tosses the remnants of his dinner in the trashcan near the back door before disappearing through a doorway I assumed was the laundry room. I listen carefully for the opening and closing of another door, but I don't hear anything. Weird. I stand up from my chair, tiptoeing across the kitchen to stick my head around the corner. It is indeed a laundry room, but on the other side is a wall that looks innocuous enough until I take stock of the security panel off to the left. I don't even wanna know what's in that "office." Taking the reprieve for what it is, I sit back down at the table, pick up my spoon, and take a bite of the still-warm chili. My stomach immediately rebels. Not because it's bad. It's good, actually. It's not Michelin Star good, but it's much more than I expected from someone who probably survives on gas station chips and Little Debbie snacks. After the initial wave of nausea, where I'm sure my stomach is wondering if this is some kind of trick, my hunger returns in full force. Practically shoveling the food into my mouth, I finish about half the bowl before I force myself to stop. Could I eat more? Sure. Do I need it? No. I also didn't wanna make myself throw up after only the few sparse meals I was made to ingest during my captivity. As much as it pains me to waste food, I make myself get up and throw the remaining chili in the same trashcan Deacon used before.

Eager to hear my best friend's voice after all these weeks, I pull out the drawer beside the fridge and grab one of the many cell phones. It takes me about five minutes of staring off into space before I can remember Amelia's number. I don't think I've memorized a phone number since the early 2000's. They're all just stored in my cell phone contacts. One of the curses of technology, I guess. Praying that I've dialed the right person, I tap my foot while I listen to the ringing on the other end.

"Hello?" The voice is soft and a little muffled, and it's only now that I realize how late it is, and I berate myself for not waiting until morning to call. I've forgotten that Amelia is married with a baby on the way. She's probably exhausted and was trying to sleep. Even so, just the sound of her voice has a lump forming in the back of my throat. My mind immediately jumps back to another night, not unlike this one, and a phone call, also not unlike this one. Nearly three years have passed, but I'm still in the same place I was before. Battered and bruised, calling my best friend in the middle of the night after narrowly escaping death. I guess I should just be thankful that she doesn't need to come save me this time.

"Hey, bitch." I say, my voice barely more than a whisper as I try not to burst into tears. I don't know why I'm so emotional. It's not like me to be sappy, but try telling that to my stupid chest. The one that feels like it's going to burst from the pressure of holding back the sobs that want so desperately to climb their way up my throat.

There's a loud rustling sound, and a groggy male voice comes through the speaker. "Wh ... what happened?! What's wrong? Is it the baby?? Oh, fuck! What should I do?! Okay, okay, okay, it's fine. Everything's fine." I can't help but smile. Based on the level of freak-out in Merrick's voice, I don't think everything is fine.

I hear Amelia shush him twice before her voice comes through the line again. "Siren?? Is that you? Oh, my God! Are you okay?" The concern and relief in her voice are palpable, and for probably the millionth time during our long friendship, I'm thankful that I have at least one person who's stood by me, even though I know I drive her absolutely insane.

"Calm down, woman, before you send yourself into preterm labor and give your husband a heart attack. The hospital isn't running a two-for-one special tonight. Yes, it's me. I'm ..." I trail off just before saying the word fine. I'm not fine. I'm not sure I'll ever be fine again, but I don't have it in me to explain why right now. Instead, I say, "... alive. I'm alive. I'm with Deacon, but I guess you knew that already."

"You sound so tired. Do you wanna tell me what happened? Where did you go? Did someone take you? Deacon told us he'd found you but didn't give much more detail than that."

"It's ... a long story. I'll explain when I see you. For now, I guess I traded a gilded cage for one made of rickety wood surrounded by swamp. I'm not sure how long I'll be here, but I just needed to hear your voice and let you know that I'll be home as soon as I can."

When she speaks again, I can hear the tears in her voice. They nearly trigger my own, and I have to suck my bottom lip into my mouth to keep it from quivering. "I've missed you so much. I don't know what happened, but I do know that Deacon will keep you safe. He spent a lot of time looking for you when you were missing. You can trust him."

Did he? Taken aback, I don't answer right away. Again, I'm hit with an endless barrage of questions, each one more confusing than the last. I know Deacon and Merrick are best friends, but can I really trust him? I've trusted men before, and look where it got me. I'm not sure I have it in me to hand that kind of power over to another man. Not when there's the possibility of him taking it only to twist and mutilate it before throwing it in my face. Sighing heavily, I say, "I'll keep that in mind. Get some sleep, babe. I'll call again tomorrow at a more decent hour."

She seems reluctant to go but eventually relents. We say our goodbyes, and I hang up the phone and pocket it. I don't think Deacon would completely cut me off from the outside world, but I'm not gonna chance it. Going over to the stove, I put the lid sitting next to it on the pot of chili before rummaging through the cabinets to find a tupperware container for the cornbread. Most of the cabinets are empty, lending further credence to the idea that Deacon doesn't usually cook, not even for himself. There are a few odd things in both the cabinets and the fridge, but not much. Hopefully, I'll either be able to go home soon, or he has some kind of plan to go shopping. I stick the pot and plastic container in the fridge before giving the wall on the opposite side of the laundry room one last glance. It remains stationary, and no sound emits from behind it. My curiosity is piqued, but with the way he abruptly left the kitchen, I don't think he'd welcome me knocking to see what's on the other side. Turning off the kitchen light on my way out, I make my way down the hall to the door Deacon indicated was his bedroom. I'm almost afraid to see what's behind this door, too, but in this case, my curiosity overrides my hesitation. I open the door slowly to find a bedroom that's significantly larger than I expected, given the house's exterior appearance. Hardwood floors run the length of the room, which houses a large four-poster bed against one wall, while a flat-screen TV and entertainment center sit opposite. The furniture is definitely masculine, but, just like the living room, there are small touches here and there that prove this isn't just a place where Deacon comes to get a few hours of sleep. As I step further into the room, I quickly close and lock the door behind me. Old habits are hard to break, I guess. Moving around, I slowly take stock of the finer details. When I reach the entertainment center, I don't know why, but I expect it to be full of something ridiculous, like porn DVD's. Instead, what I find has a smile tugging at the corners of my mouth. There are several gaming consoles, along with a shit ton of video games, of course. There *are* DVD's, however, the majority of them are rom-coms. Cocking my head to the side, I study the titles. Many of my favorites are here, but I don't think that was done by design. I'm more inclined to believe that he actually likes these films, which is surprising. Maybe he isn't quite as one-dimensional as he leads people to believe. Storing that away with the rest of the information I've gathered today that I don't fully understand, I'm suddenly hit with a wave of exhaustion that has me dragging my feet toward the bed without even going to inspect the doors across the room that I suspect belong to a closet. I'll check it out tomorrow. Making my way to the bed, I pause when I pass a free-standing full-length mirror, similar to the one in the bathroom I used earlier. Normally, I'd avert my gaze and walk on by; however, this time, I stop. I turn to face the mirror head-on, staring at my own reflection. A flash of Deacon's face over the kitchen table and how he looked at me flits through my mind. He'd seemed almost ... angry when I made the comment about having too much food. For a brief moment, I wonder if he thought I was giving him some bullshit excuse because I didn't wanna eat his cooking. Sounds plausible enough, but that explanation falls flat, even in my own mind. Suspicion shone from his eyes as if he could see straight through my feeble excuse. If eyes are the windows to the soul, Deacon's living in a glass house. I'm not sure how he's built a career as a fence, where bluffing is a trick of the trade, with eyes like that.

As I look at myself in the mirror, I study my reflection critically, the same as I've done on countless other occasions. Glancing back at the closed door, I impulsively bend at the waist, dragging the loose fitting sweats down my legs before gripping the hem of the oversized t-shirt, stripping it off. Staring at myself, I slowly smooth my hands down my stomach and sides before doing the same to my hips. My belly isn't flat, nor are the areas at my sides. My hips are wide and my thighs press together, no distinct V in sight. I'm hit with another blow to my self-confidence when I realize that I'm probably about 20 pounds lighter than I was before I was taken. Turning this way and that, I inspect every inch of skin I can see. My ass is pert but definitely too big. Pinching the extra bit of flesh surrounding the area where my nonexistent abs are, I promise myself that if I make it out of this house without either killing Deacon or myself, I'm gonna finally sign up for a gym membership. It's a promise I've made myself before but never kept. Maybe this second near-death experience will be enough to finally force me to make some changes in my life. The first of which will be my appearance. Despite my distrust of the entire male population at the moment, I don't wanna die alone. I want to love and be loved. I want to know what that actually feels like, and nobody is gonna love me the way I am now. I can't even blame them. How can I expect someone to truly love me when I can't even love myself?

With that thought, I drop my hands to my sides and turn away from the mirror, not even bothering to put my clothes back on. I never could sleep comfortably unless I were naked. Chalk it up to years of everything you wore feeling too tight. Practically staggering to the large bed, I pull back the thick comforter and crawl in. As I lay my head on the pillow, I'm enveloped by a distinctly masculine scent, and breathing it in, I feel all the tension that's been building within me for weeks, finally starting to release. It smells like the sun and the sea but is also earthy, like moss. It smells like Deacon. A burst of heat shoots through me, but it isn't just the heat that accompanies arousal, though that's definitely present. How it's possible to feel anything even remotely sexual after the ordeal I've been through, I don't know. Maybe it's the familiarity of Deacon. Of his scent, the protective instincts I didn't know were there, or the way his blue eyes look at me like I'm not severely flawed. That warm feeling courses through me, and I realize that it's not just sexual attraction but comfort, a comfortability that puts my fight-or-flight instincts at ease. Not an easy feat with someone like me. Releasing a heavy sigh, I sink deeper into the blankets, turning on my side to press my nose into the pillow. As my eyelids grow heavy, the scent of Deacon surrounds me, and I finally drift off into a dreamless oblivion.

CHAPTER 19

Deacon

Remember that age-old adage that parents used to tell their kids about how sitting too close to the TV screen would mess up your eyesight? It's a miracle I'm not blind, considering how close I am to my monitor right now. The great huffs of hot air from my nostrils are practically fogging up the screen like a damn dragon. As I watch Siren stare at herself in my bedroom mirror, my eyes narrow suspiciously. I fucking knew it. The sinking sensation that began in my gut after her refusal to eat all of her dinner solidifies into a solid block of cement. I had a feeling it stemmed from some misguided notion that she was heavy, though I don't think I ever wanted to be proven wrong about something so much in my life. Jesus Christ. If those feelings are a direct product of her time with that bastard Gaspari, it's just another reason for me to wanna kill him if he isn't dead already. If she had those thoughts about herself before he came along, I wanna hunt down whoever it is that made her feel shitty about herself and strangle them with their own entrails. How can she not see that she's literally perfect in every way? Even her smartass mouth, which frequently makes me wanna stick something in it just to shut her up. Whether that's my dick or food would depend on the situation.

I'd like to say that I never intended to watch her, but that would make me a liar. Every area of my house is equipped with at least one camera, each feeding directly into this room. One monitor is devoted to nothing but small boxes containing the live feeds from all over the house. If I need to get an up-close and personal look at a particular room, I simply pull that camera's feed and enlarge it to full screen on another monitor. On the largest monitor, which sits directly in the center, I watch as Siren looks towards the closed bedroom door, and a wave of unease prickles beneath my skin. Not unlike goosebumps, though I'm not sure if whatever's about to happen is gonna be good or bad. The girl is such a wild card that I never really know what to expect. That notion isn't dispelled when she suddenly grips the waistband of her borrowed sweatpants and drops them to the floor. I'm caught so off guard, that I nearly fall out of my chair. Just as I'm righting myself, she grips the hem of the long t-shirt before hesitating briefly; a moment suspended in time that I have a sneaking suspicion will play on a loop in my head later. Seeming to make her mind up, she slowly drags the shirt up, revealing inch by tantalizing inch of generous thigh. Did I say my nose was pressed to the computer screen before? Right now, I'm so close that I'm pretty sure I'd test positive for radiation. As the hem of the shirt rides higher to reveal the bottom of her ass, I have the briefest moment where I entertain the idea of looking away, turning the cameras off, and allowing her the privacy she deserves. But I don't. Call me a degenerate, but if she stays here for any length of time, she'll come to learn that there's exactly zero expectation of privacy in this house. I have no doubt that if she ever finds out that I've got every room bugged, she'll have my balls for a change purse, and seeing as I happen to like my balls exactly where they are, I'm just not going to tell her.

My breaths are coming faster now as all hesitancy seems to leave her, and she quickly jerks the shirt over her head, kind of the same way you'd rip off a Band-Aid until she's left blissfully naked in front of my bedroom's full-length mirror. I do actually fall out of my chair at this point. As my forehead bangs into the monitor, the chair slides out from beneath my ass, where I've been literally sitting at the edge of my seat, and I fall flat on my back. The momentum has the chair wheeling across the room and into the opposite wall, where it makes contact with a resounding thud. Fuck. This room is soundproof, but I still have the irrational fear that it's possible that Siren may have heard the noise and will come to investigate. Quickly getting up, I drag the offending chair back over, and while muttering a good number of expletives that would've had my mama taking me to church, I reposition myself before looking back to Siren's on-screen image. As sick as it may seem, my recent one-on-one wrestling match and subsequent loss to the office chair has done nothing to lessen the shot of arousal that took hold the second she slid those pants down her legs. In fact, no amount of inner chastisement or the reminder that she's fresh off the heels of weeks worth of trauma can dissuade the erection that's now tenting my pants of the notion that now is not the time or place. Taking my hand, I press the heel of my palm against the nuisance, hoping it'll take the hint and pipe down. I snort at my own pun. Pipe down. I've gotta remember that for later.

Unfortunately, the only thing accomplished by my oppressive hand is a shot of electricity that goes straight to my balls, further decreasing the amount of breathing room in my pants. It doesn't help that my eyes have returned to the monitor just in time to see Siren do a complete 360 turn in slow motion, or maybe it just seems that way because my brain has gone offline. As she faces the mirror again, she appears to be pinching different body parts between her fingers. What the fuck? Eyes narrowing dangerously, I watch as she seems to inspect her body from different angles for several minutes before finally dropping her arms to her sides and turning away from the mirror. I wait for her to pick up the clothes she discarded on the floor, but, to my surprise, she doesn't. She leaves the borrowed shirt and pants where they fell before climbing, naked, into my bed.

My bed.

Fuck, I might as well just tie a bag around my dick at this point because it's already suffocating. My fingers itch to zoom in on that perfectly round ass but I don't. I may be something of a voyeur, but I'm not a skeeve. I do have *some* willpower. At least until I see her chest take a deep inhale, and she turns onto her side, seemingly burying her face in my pillow. Cocking my head to the side, I throw that willpower out the window, and with the tap of a few keys, the camera zooms in on her face. She does indeed have her nose pressed into my pillow, and if I'm not mistaken, there's a small smile playing at the corners of her mouth. As quickly as it took for her to turn from the mirror and lay her head on my pillow, her expression has morphed from one of irritation to one of ... bliss? Contentment? What changed? I sit there, staring for so long that my eyes turn blurry, and I realize I haven't blinked in about a solid minute, my gaze too busy darting

186

from one feature to another as if trying to memorize every detail. In that vein, I zoom out a little, taking in her chest's now slow rise and fall that indicates she's already fallen asleep. As I watch the rhythmic movements of her chest, I think back to the way she was in front of the mirror, and I realize, though she may have exuded the same type of sass earlier as the old Siren, the girl that stood before that mirror wasn't someone I recognize. I almost feel like a shit for watching her when she had her guard down. Almost.

Sudden movement out of my peripheral vision has my senses going on red alert. As my eyes come back from where they've been staring off into space, I relax a little when I see that it was just Siren turning over in her sleep. That relaxation lasts for all of three seconds, which is about how long it takes my woman-addled brain to realize she's turned over onto her back, so deeply asleep that the pain of her wounds must not register. The move has effectively kicked the comforter off the majority of her body. Her entire torso is exposed, as is one entire leg that's bent at the knee and flung wide. Subconsciously rubbing my hand over a mouth that's gone dryer than the Sahara, I feel my already stiff cock swell to a painful degree. Unfortunately, the pressure of my palm does nothing to assuage the intense burst of hunger within me. Even as I berate myself for what I'm doing, I can't tear my eyes away from the screen. As I zoom the camera in, my gaze roams over every exposed bit of flesh I can find. Starting with that outstretched leg that has no business being stretched that wide unless it's to fit my hips there. It's my rotten luck that the blanket is still covering the other leg and the apex of her thighs. Feeling very much like a little kid that's in danger of getting caught looking at porn mags by his parents, I eat up every new vantage point that the zoom feature allows. By the time I reach her navel, I'm breaking out in a sweat, and my dick is throbbing. Moment of truth. Am I gonna do what's best for me and turn the cameras off? Possibly do some much-needed research on Gaspari or my father? Or am I gonna be a complete weirdo and get myself off to the digital image of this woman sleeping in my bed? Fuck it. No one would ever consider me normal anyway.

I lean back in my chair, spreading my knees as wide as the armrests will allow. It takes minimal effort to pull the waistband of my loose shorts down, allowing my erection the freedom it so desperately needs. Gripping my shaft at the base, I squeeze hard, closing my eyes and counting backward from 10 in the hopes that I won't immediately spill in my own hand. As soon as I open my eyes, I realize just how futile that action was. Just seeing the dips and curves of Siren's bare hip and stomach have my hand involuntarily stroking upward, then back down in a hard pump. The move has me gritting my teeth and my hips kicking upward slightly as if I'm not fucking my own fist but instead pushing my way into something warm and infinitely softer. By the time my gaze roves over her naked breasts, my hand is moving at a steady pace that's one or two pumps shy of tipping over the edge into a frenzy. I imagine being in that bed with her, running my tongue around her cute little belly button before dragging it upward to capture first one tight nipple, then the other, in my mouth. I wanna torment her with my tongue until she's begging me to stop, until we're both a mass of sweaty limbs and racing hearts, so that I can taste the salt on her skin. Running my thumb over the head of my cock, I spread the moisture leaking from the tip, using it as lubricant as my hand moves furiously up and down; all the while, my gaze never leaves the computer. As soon as my eyes find her face, I know it's over. I expect my attention to remain there while I finish, but inexplicably, my gaze travels back down to her side, between her ribs and her hip. The spot I saw her pinch in the mirror earlier. There. That's now my favorite spot. The place I'll grip onto while I ride her body hard. Letting out a groan that's a mixture of ecstasy and agony, I keep sight of that spot as I give my shaft one final stroke, angling it upward, coming all over my stomach.

After a moment or two, the rigidity leaves my body, and I practically melt into the chair. What the fuck is wrong with me? Throwing an arm over my eyes in an attempt to shut out my own self-loathing, I release another groan, this one full of frustration and ... *shame?* Maybe. Can I promise I won't do that again? Absolutely not.

CHAPTER 20

Siren

Two weeks. Two weeks trapped in a tiny house in the middle of nowhere with a man-child who knows how to hack into the FBI database but who I suspect can't even tie his own shoes. He's driving me fucking crazy in more ways than one. I thought I had a handle on myself. But, I'm beginning to think all the trauma is catching up with me because one minute, we'll be fighting like cats and dogs, and the next, I'll be imagining squeezing his throat between my hands ... which, given the circumstances, wouldn't be unusual, except in that vision, we're both also naked. It's at moments like this that I start to question my own sanity and just how fucked up my traumatized brain has become. The timing of these thoughts is wildly inappropriate and usually end up taking the wind right out of the sails on my ship, that I've affectionately dubbed "Perpetual Rage", which I *hate*. When these little visions of depravity flash through my brain, causing it to stutter step, he thinks he's won the argument. He has no idea that I've simply lost the plot of the conversation because I'm drowning in a sea of imaginary moans and sweat. I shouldn't be having thoughts like that. It's been two weeks since I escaped Dante's house, and while I know I'm a strong-willed person, I feel like my reaction to everything that happened to me isn't normal. Either I'm repressing *a lot* of feelings, or my mind has turned some kind of corner, leaving the majority of the ordeal behind. Is that even possible? I mean, shouldn't I be a mess? Shouldn't I be unable to function? A normal person would be. Then again, I've never really been normal. While everything was happening, I tried my best not to slip back into the pattern of dissociation that I adopted the first time, worried that I might not come back out. I didn't want to just give up, losing all hope that I'd ever have a life that existed outside of pain. So I fought and tried to remain present as much as possible because if I was feeling the pain, it meant I was still alive. I still had a chance to make it out. And I did, with Deacon's help. Now, I'm wondering just how frowned upon it is to murder the person who's just saved your life.

I was getting stir-crazy. Every day for two weeks, Deacon has gotten up from his makeshift bed on the living room couch, annoyed me for about an hour, then disappeared into that mysterious man cave behind the laundry room. Staying in there for hours, I've been left to my own devices. Alone but somehow still not feeling ... alone. I only see him when he comes out to use the bathroom or get food ... which there isn't much of. The man must live on take-out because the meager offerings in the cabinets and fridge when I got here haven't somehow magically multiplied. I've eaten humble before, but this is just plain laziness. I know the man has money, but it's almost as though he genuinely forgets to eat. He's so caught up in his "research" that by the time he exits the cave, he's hangry. Well, that makes two of us.

I'm sitting cross-legged on the sofa, flipping through the endless streaming services on the flat-screen TV above the fireplace, when I hear him muttering to himself and banging cabinet doors around. I let out a little snort, knowing what he's looking for and also knowing that he won't find it. There's nothing to eat in this damn house. I know I'm slowly finding myself again when I realize that I want snacks: chips, cookies, and ice cream. Like a cow, I need to graze, and I can't do that here. I hate not being in control. Control of where I go, who I see, what I eat. Whenever I've brought up the idea of leaving, Deacon immediately shuts me down, citing the dangers of the unknown. We still don't know if Dante made it out of that house alive, or at least I don't know. Because he doesn't tell me anything. Being kept in the dark about what's going on is annoying enough, but I don't think I can take much more ramen noodles and baked potatoes. He's gonna have to get groceries. I jump up from the couch, tossing the remote down before making my way into the kitchen to tell him just that. As I walk in, I'm greeted by the sight of Deacon bent at the waist, head buried deep in the fridge. God, he's got a stellar ass. Shit! No, focus.

"There's nothing in there. I've already checked. We need food. We're gonna have to go out," I say from behind him, arms crossed as I lean against the door jam that separates the kitchen from the dining room.

His body tenses for a few seconds at my words before he resumes rooting around. From the recesses of the fridge, he says, "We aren't going anywhere. I told you, it's not safe to go out. I'll have groceries delivered and left at the gate." Finally straightening, he turns to face me before adding, "And then I'll go out and get them."

Not one to be subdued, I plaster on my most obstinate face before saying, "No, *we'll* go get them. I can't stay in this fucking house anymore, Deacon. I need to breathe fresh air! I need sunshine!"

Jaw clenching, he replies, "It's ... not ... safe." With that, he walks past me into the living room before starting down the hallway, as if the discussion is over and his word is law.

I'm on his heels in a heartbeat. Following him into the bedroom, I watch him kick off his basketball shorts, leaving himself in a t-shirt and a pair of boxer briefs. His movements are jerky like he's a bowstring that's been pulled too tight and will snap at any moment. He's reaching for a pair of light jogging pants when I say, "It's just groceries. A walk to the end of the driveway. Not the end of the world."

"You're not going."

"You can't stop me."

Eyes narrowing dangerously, he turns and stalks towards me. Instinctively, I back up one step, then two. He continues forwards until my ass bumps into the dresser at my back. He's trying to intimidate me, but it's not going to work. Placing both palms flat on the dresser on either side of my hips, he leans down until he's about half an inch from my face. For a normal person who's been through what I've been through, this positioning would be terrifying. For some reason. though, I'm not afraid of him. In fact, he's actually kinda pissing me off. Face so close that I can feel the warmth of his breath brush across my lips, like the caress of a tongue, he says, "You're pushing it, woman." As we stand there in tense silence, it takes me a moment to realize that there's a distinct bulge in his boxers. I don't dare look down because I refuse to let him win this, but I can see it from my periphery. The longer we stand there, toe-to-toe, the bigger the bulge gets. The knowledge that he's getting off on being this close to me causes a flush of heat to course through my body. My breasts tighten and my core clenches. Without conscious thought, my thighs squeeze together. He's breathing heavily, and I watch his gaze flick to my mouth for a split second before coming back up.

Wait. Did he just *woman* me?? "No," I say, pausing briefly before using both hands to shove hard into his chest. The move is unexpected and causes him to stumble back a step. "*Now*, I'm pushing you. And don't fucking crowd me."

He stares at me like I've lost my mind. I watch his jaw flex, but again, I'm not scared. Have I forgone all sense of self-preservation, deemed him as non-threatening, or just gotten tired of men's bullshit in general? Probably a mixture of all three. Whatever the case, I stand my ground, not backing down. We continue our stand-off for a minute or two before he finally releases a growl that sounds like it's worked its way up from the depths of his soul before turning around, grabbing the pants, and slipping them on. Shoving his feet into a pair of work boots, he pushes past me, heading back through the living room toward the kitchen. Oh, no. He better not be going back into that damn room.

"You know what, fuck this," I say. He's almost made it to the kitchen when I spin in the opposite direction instead of following him, heading straight for the front door. Before he can turn around and stop me, I've gotten the many interior locks undone and flung the door wide open. Ha! Guess for all his security, it works better at keeping people out than in. Walking out onto the front porch, I leap down the stairs and into the bright sunlight. Oh, God, I've missed this. Turning my face up to the sun, I soak in the vitamin D for about 15 seconds before a hand grabs my wrist, spinning me around. Speaking of vitamin D. Mood uplifted slightly by the change in scenery; I let out a little chuckle at my own joke. That is until I see Deacon's murderous face.

"Why the hell are you laughing?" he demands, and it's clear he's spitting mad.

Despite the warmth from the sun's rays, his irritation is like a match to the powder keg that is mine. "Because you're so angry, and it brings me so much joy."

He shakes his head slowly before releasing my wrist like it's burned him. "You're insane. That's the only excuse for it. Rational people don't behave like this." he says, and it's clear from his tone that bewilderment is now fighting for dominance over his previous irritation.

His reaction only brings on more laughter until I'm nearly doubled over. All the while, he stares at me like he's trying to think of a good tailor to have me fitted for a designer straightjacket. Finally, the hysteria subsides, and I straighten, wiping tears from the corners of my eyes. Two seconds later, his grip is back on my wrist, and he's attempting to drag me towards the porch.

I dig in my heels, pulling against his hold, all thoughts of humor evaporating. "I'm not going back in that house, Deacon. Not until you tell me what you've been doing in that cave of yours for the last two weeks."

Stopping, he turns to stare at me. "What? I've been working. Besides, what does it matter?"

"It matters because it's my life. I have a right to know what you've found. Or at least help in some way. I'm tired of sitting by and letting other people make decisions for me. Now, either you tell me what you know, or I'm gonna plop my ass right here in the grass and refuse to budge." I know I'm acting like a child, but I can't afford for him to go back into that room right now. If he does, I'll lose him for another entire day before I get another shot at this.

He's shaking his head before I've even finished my last sentence. "There's nothing to tell. I haven't found out anything. Now, get in the damn house."

I stare at him intently, searching his face for any sign that would tell me, one way or the other, what the truth is. As I watch, he stands perfectly still, but I don't miss the way his eyes dart from mine to stare at a spot just over my shoulder, giving the illusion that he's looking at me while actually averting his gaze. He's hiding something. Lips thinning to a straight line, I cross my arms over my chest before dropping down to the ground. He stares down at me incredulously. That incredulity soon turns into blustering sounds and pacing.

Finally, when he's worked himself up into a good state of mad, he says, "Fine. You wanna be outside, be outside." With that, he turns around, walks off, and leaves me sitting in the grass. Instead of going back inside, I watch him use a scrunchie to tie his hair back before he disappears around the side of the house. Once he's out of my line of sight, I wait a minute, then three, then five, but he doesn't come back. Where did he go?? Soon, I hear a rhythmic whooshing sound, followed by a series of thumps. Curiosity gets the better of me, so I get up and follow the path Deacon took around to the back of the house. As I turn the corner, I stop dead in my tracks. Holy hell. Amidst a large pile of split logs, a very sweaty Deacon swings a heavy ax, obliterating each huge chunk of firewood he sits on the giant stump in front of him. My mouth is suddenly dry, and I feel like I've eaten a bag full of cotton balls. Deacon's shirt is plastered to his back from perspiration, and his colorful tattoos visible through the thin fabric. With every swing, I watch the muscles in his shoulders and biceps flex and ripple. Soon, I notice that my brain must've told my feet to move closer without my consent. Probably to lay on the ground next to him, in the hopes of catching each drop of sweat in my mouth. Jesus, what is wrong with me??

As if sensing my approach, he pauses mid-swing, lowering the ax to the ground before saying, "Leave me be, Siren." He doesn't turn around to face me, and somehow, that only adds to the tone of defeat that laces his words.

Oh, how I wish I could. I feel like a ship lost at sea; for some reason, he's the beacon lighting the way home. Blinking at the absurdity of that thought, my next words come out harsher than I intend.

"Deacon, I'm done sitting in that house, twiddling my thumbs while you do God knows what in that locked room. I wanna see inside." The demand escapes before I've even thought about it. I said weeks ago that I didn't want to know what he kept hidden in there because if it turned out to be something bizarre, I'd be better off not knowing. But now, I realize that my words are underlined with steel. I've made up my mind. I won't change it.

"Absolutely not," he replies immediately. "It's better for you not to know."

"Better for me or you? What are you hiding in there, Deacon? It's not a meat locker full of women's body parts, is it?" I know this isn't the case, but his refusal to entertain even the idea makes me want to needle him.

Letting out an incredulous laugh, he drops the ax entirely before finally turning to face me. "My answer is no. Now, I'm going inside to take a shower, then I've got work to do before dinner. I'll order Chinese. Make a list of things you want from the grocery store." He starts to walk away, then pauses, turning his head and pointing a finger at me. "You can stay in the backyard. Don't go anywhere else, do you understand?"

Is he crazy? Who does this man think he is? I'm Siren-fucking-Sinclair. Not some dog that he can banish to the backyard or bark orders at. So, of course, when he moves back towards the house, I do the opposite of what he said and trail behind him.

"Siren, if you know what's good for you, you won't follow me right now. You wanted to be outside so fucking badly, I'm giving you what you want."

"Guess I don't know what's good for me," I reply, still dogging his heels.

He lets out a roar of frustration, making it to the front door of the house before I do. The last thing he hears before slamming the front door behind him is the sound of my hysterical laughter.

CHAPTER 21

Deacon

As I barge my way into the house, I kick off my boots, sending each one flying in a different direction. The woman was fucking infuriating. Incapable of compromise, stubborn to a fault, and, God help me, the most stunning creature I've ever had the misfortune of fucking. Running my fingers through the sweaty hair that's come loose from the hair tie that I know was there a minute ago, I grip the ends in frustration, hoping the sharp sting of pain will distract from the raging hard-on that woman seems to command like a lapdog. It doesn't work. Now my head just hurts while my dick is practically begging me to go back out there, corner her against the side of my house, and fuck her until she doesn't have the energy to run her mouth anymore.

At the sound of the door banging behind me, I groan inwardly. Looks like I won't have to go back out after all. Turning around to face Siren, I allow my eyes to do a quick sweep up and down her body. The strip of skin showing between the hem of her shirt and the waistband of the oversized sweats, along with the flesh of her upper chest and neck, are flushed the prettiest shade of pink. I have the errant thought that I wonder what other parts of her are that color. Unfortunately, I'm unable to see since she's otherwise covered from head to toe. I had a duffle bag full of her clothes and toiletries delivered the other night while she was asleep, but she's still chosen to wear the borrowed clothes that are too big for her. I know why she's wearing long sleeves and pants, and I hate it for two reasons. One, the motherfucker that hurt her is possibly still out there breathing, and two, that she feels some kind of shame over having all the marks he put on her. It makes me wanna break something—mostly his face. Despite the outwardly projected confidence that I've come to realize she's adopted like a second skin, I've spent enough time with Siren to know a mask when I see one. Nobody knew about masks more than me. I guess like recognizes like.

Huffing like a bull ready to charge, she says, "Hey! I wasn't finished talking to you."

Giving her a shrug that's full of a nonchalance I definitely don't feel, I say, "Doesn't matter. I'm done talking to you."

Eyes nearly bugging out of her head, she says, "Well, that's just too fucking bad because you don't get to dictate how this conversation goes."

Before I can think about the repercussions of such an action, I take a menacing step towards her and say, "You are such a goddamn brat, you know that?"

I regret the move immediately. Not my words, because she is a goddamn brat, but the way I approached her. After what she's been through, the last thing I want is for her to feel intimidated or scared. Her reaction isn't at all what I expected, but, at the same time, I can't say I'm surprised.

Taking a forward step of her own, she replies, "And you're a pig-headed jerk."

Fuck. I can't help myself. I take another step. "Irrational woman!"

Another step from her. "Brainless man!"

Each insult brings us closer and closer to each other until we're nearly nose to nose. I can smell the faint hint of coffee and chocolate on her breath and suddenly, I'm craving something sweet. I don't know if Siren has a sweet bone in her entire body, though. Her very curvy and delectable body. Jesus. The tether I've used to keep my desire for this woman in check is fraying, and I send a quick prayer up to God, begging him to save me from myself. As she stands on her tiptoes to bring her face level with mine, the fraying of that rope that began the first night I watched her on camera—hell, maybe even before then—snaps before the almighty has a chance to intervene. Lunging for her, my mouth bridges the centimeter's worth of space between her lips and mine. One hand gripping the back of her neck to hold her motionless for the onslaught, the other snakes down to cup her generous ass, hoisting her up off her feet. She makes a half-hearted sound of protest in the back of her throat, and for a split second, I think I've gone too far. But the notion is dispelled when her mouth opens for me, her legs wrapping around my waist. I know she's insecure about her weight, but I'm so caught up in this fire blazing between us that she weighs less than nothing. I may or may not have invaded her privacy by listening in on some of her phone calls with Amelia. I've also seen how she looks at her body in the bathroom mirror when she doesn't know I'm spying on her. However, she might as well be a feather for all the manpower it exerts to get her legs up and around my waist. Hanging onto my shoulders for dear life, I feel her short little nails dig into my flesh through the fabric of my t-shirt as her mouth gives as good as it's getting. The sharp sting has tiny little cartoon hearts floating in my vision. Gripping her under her perfect backside, I carry her to the dining room table that I barely use, sitting her down before I break the kiss to yank my t-shirt over my head. I toss it to the floor, but as I grab the hem of her shirt, intent on giving it the same treatment, her hand stills mine just as I've exposed a few more tantalizing inches of her stomach.

Looking back up and into her eyes, I wait with a patience I didn't know I possessed. I can see the war within those dark depths. She must realize that her eyes convey all the words she's not speaking because she doesn't keep the eye contact for long before she begins to drop her head. She knows I'm not stupid. I see way more than she wants me to see, and that's not even taking into account the things she *doesn't* know I've seen. The days and nights I've spent locked in my office watching her when I should've been tracking down the two people in the world that I hate the most and figuring out how they're connected. Gripping her chin between my thumb and forefinger, I raise her face back up until it's inches from mine again and wait until her eyes find mine once more. It hasn't been very long since I got her out of that house, and I don't wanna push her beyond what she's comfortable with. Not until she's ready.

"Even though you're batshit crazy, that doesn't make me want you any less. It's not just the smooth flesh I want. I want the inches raised with scars, the ones marred by burns, those covered in ink, the inches with stretch marks, and every inch in between. I know I'll have to prove that to you, so for now, I won't push you to give more than you're willing. But when the time comes, if you trust me with them, you'll never look at them the same way again, I promise you." I say. For a moment, I fear I've said too much and given myself away, giving away both my intense attraction to her and the fact that I've inspected every inch of her body with a fine-tooth comb, or in this case, a zoom function. But she doesn't question how I know about the marks on her body. Maybe she just thinks I'm assuming what she looks like under those baggy clothes. So I wait because it has to be her choice. I will never allow her free will to be taken from her ever again, not when it comes to this.

I know this must be hard for her. To give over control to a man, especially after all she's been through. To allow someone to see all of her, not just the parts that society would deem pretty. Her eyes bounce back and forth between my own, and I can feel her swallow hard against the hand holding onto her chin. For a second, I have the terrifying thought that she's gonna cry. I honestly don't think I'll be able to handle that. I've never been good with crying females. However, with Siren, I should know better. Jerking her chin from my grasp, she reaches down and grabs the hem of her shirt, taking charge, and lifts it over her head herself. Now I'm the one swallowing hard. She's not wearing a bra. Sitting on my dining room table in nothing but a pair of loose sweatpants, she stares back at me in defiance before saying, "This means nothing."

My mood has improved exponentially, so I smirk before replying, "Keep telling yourself that, brat."

Then I'm all over her. Gripping her beneath the arms, I lift her off the counter slightly so that I can capture one nipple in my mouth; the mixture of pink and tan becoming my new favorite color. The move catches her off guard, and she lets out the sexiest gasp I've ever heard in my life. Letting her head fall back, she moans out my name as I circle the stiff peak with my tongue over and over. Sitting her back down to the wooden surface, I release her breast to lower myself until I'm on my knees in front of her. The position brings my face directly in line with what will be the center of my world for the foreseeable future.

I grip the waistband of the ratty old sweats, simply saying, "Up."

After a brief hesitation, she does what she's told, probably for the first time in her life. Bracing her hands on the table on either side of her hips, she uses them as leverage to lift her ass off the wood just long enough for me to drag the pants down her legs. Jesus Christ on a cracker, she's not wearing any underwear either. I swear, this woman is gonna be the death of me, in one way or another. I grip her hips and jerk her forward until she's teetering on the edge of the table. Spreading her legs apart with my hands on her knees, I let my gaze roam from her flushed face down over her beautifully tattooed upper body—which is still braced back on her hands—to her splayed thighs before me. Aside from the initial bolt of anger, I don't dwell on the number of healing burn marks or the raised lines of flesh that have recently scarred over because they've become a part of the fabric of who she is; she wouldn't be the same person without them. But I know that if I tell her that, she'll balk. So, for now, I pretend like they're not there. It doesn't take much effort when I've got this need for her clawing at my insides. Letting my eyes fall to the juncture between her legs, I feel my mouth fill with saliva at the sight. Which is probably good because I'm gonna want all the lubrication I can get for what I plan on doing to her next. I hook my hands under her knees, and I bring her legs up until they're draping over my shoulders. Leaning in, I give her inner thigh a nip, eliciting a little yelp from her. Smiling to myself, I kiss the spot, softly running my tongue over the small red mark my teeth just made. I slowly make my way up her thigh, peppering kisses as I go until I'm mere inches away from the hottest part of her. Funny, she's pink here too. Chuckling under my breath, I slide my hands up her thighs until I reach her waist, gripping hard onto the flesh just above her hips. Now that I've got her where I want her, I can't have her getting away.

Sure that she expects me to dive straight in with my tongue, I can tell by her small intake of breath that I've surprised her when I instead hover just above her, deliberately prolonging the inevitable. Despite the low rumbling sound climbing its way up my throat in warning, she makes a move as though she means to close her legs to keep me out. I'm not having any of it, and I use the grip on her waist to pull her even closer. Not enough to hurt her but enough to show her who's in charge here. Now that I'm this close, there's no chance in Hell that I'll let her take this away from me. As I finally fully take in the smell that's unique to her and her alone, I release a groan, and my cock twitches in my pants with each inhale. Jesus, the woman makes me feral. I wanna play, but I also need to bury myself so deeply inside her that she'll feel me for days. Taking several deep breaths, which don't really help because all I can smell is her, I try to calm my racing heart and libido. I've wanted this since that first night. Even after our single night together, my cravings for her never abated. Now that she's giving me a second chance, I'm not giving it up. Darting my tongue out, I give her clit a quick flick.

"Fuck!" she cries, her entire body jerking in my hold. As she glares daggers at me, I meet her eyes, and slowly flick out my tongue to do it again. Even though she's more prepared this time, she can't seem to stop herself from releasing a shuddering breath. A breath that's quickly followed by, "I'm gonna murder you in your sleep."

Grinning hugely, I push my way through her wet heat and drag the pad of my tongue slowly over the little bundle of nerves. Then I do it again … and again. Letting out a moan that sounds almost pained, she drops her upper body flat onto the tabletop. Got her. Using the leverage of my hands on her waist, I pull her into my waiting mouth as I eat her alive, alternating between circling her clit and spearing her opening with my tongue. She's soaking wet, practically dripping. Thank God, because when I'm done eating her pussy, I'm going to fuck her until she can't remember her own name. She better remember mine, though, because I wanna hear the reverberating echo of it in her voice as I come inside her.

Lapping at her wetness, I feel her knees tighten around my ears as the rest of her body goes stiff as a board. Hands flying up to cup both breasts, she squeezes her nipples, and the sight nearly has me shooting off in my pants like a rocket. Has there ever been anything so beautiful? As I realize she's close to coming, I tighten my hands to her hips, keeping her body flush with my mouth. I latch onto her clit, and watch her play with her breasts and moan incoherently to the ceiling. At the last minute, I take one hand from her middle and bring it down to push two fingers inside her without warning. Just that quick, her body bows off the wood, hands moving from her breasts to her hair, tangling in the long dark locks as she lets out a scream that I'm glad no one else gets to hear but me. I quickly stand, shedding my pants and boxer briefs, not giving her a moment's reprieve. Squeezing my hard cock, I rub one thumb over the head, spreading the precum that's already leaking from me. As I keep one hand wrapped around my length, I lean over her body, using the other to grip the back of her neck, jerking her up until she's back to a sitting position at the edge of the table. Hair falling like a wild tangle of vines down her back and over her breasts, I hold her face close to mine. I open my mouth to say ... I'm not sure what, because I think I may have devolved back to having the brainpower of a caveman. Before I even have a chance to get anything out, however, her hand clamps over my mouth.

"Don't. Talk," she says on a shuddering breath.

Lips curling into a smile that I know she can feel beneath her palm, I slam my cock into her still-quivering pussy. Mouth gaping open, she trembles out a breath as she removes her hand, leans in, and bites my lower lip ... hard. That's it. I'm only a man, after all—a weak one at that, at least where she's concerned. Losing all semblance of control, I hold her steady as I withdraw to the tip before slamming back in, grinding myself against her. Her cries are like music to my ears, a song that I swear she'll play only for me from now on. Holding her hips tightly, the muscles of my biceps flexing, I fuck her fast and hard until we're both sweating and panting for breath. She's biting and sucking on my neck, and though she's the one feasting, I have this hunger for her that I can't seem to satiate. I have the errant thought that I don't think I'll ever truly be full again.

Feeling her body begin to tighten around me, I release her hips to wrap both arms around her middle, holding us chest to chest. Pulling back my lower body one last time, I push myself into her hard. At the exact same second, I bring my mouth close to her ear and say, "Sing for me, brat."

In a last act of defiance, as if it'll somehow muffle the sound, she buries her face against my neck, unable to stop the scream that's only made better by the sound of my name, seemingly being dragged from her at the end. Tightening my arms around her middle, I feel my cock jerk as I release wave after wave of come deep inside her. I clutch her to me so she can't move even an inch, careful to keep my arms well below the healing wounds on her back. We stay like that for several long moments. Her panting against my neck and me feeling more at home inside her than I ever have in this house. A house that's been my only sanctuary for years.

I'm not entirely sure how to process what just happened or how I feel about it; the best I can manage to do at the moment is ease my grip around her middle to check and make sure I haven't crushed her to death. "Are you okay?" I ask in a soft voice. All traces of the animosity from earlier is gone, wrung from me along with my orgasm. Somewhere in the back of my mind, I'm worried that I've hurt her. She hasn't said much, so I've been left with only the meager amount of info she's told me and what I've seen on the cameras around the house. More importantly, it's the wounds that I can't see that bother me. The internal trauma that she's trying so hard to bury. But I should've known better than to think Siren wouldn't speak her mind if I did something she didn't like. That theory is proven correct when her response finally comes.

"Of course I'm okay," she says, stretching her arms above her head. The move causes her back to arch and her hips to angle in such a way that sends my still semi-hard cock deeper inside her. I hear a tiny moan escape her at the same time that I grit my teeth to hold back the instinct roaring inside my head, telling me to grip her hips and grind her against me even harder. From the look of the red marks on said hips, I have a terrible feeling she's gonna sport bruises matching my fingertips within the next few days.

The thought makes me slightly nauseous. With her chin tipped up, she stares at the ceiling as her upper body relaxes against the table, continuing the conversation as though she isn't subjecting me to physical and emotional torture. "I feel ... high." Lowering her gaze back to mine, she says, "Like I could touch the stars." She wriggles her fingers towards the ceiling. Her voice is languid and dreamy, and in this moment, she's free of all inhibitions and completely at ease with herself. This is what she would look like if the confidence she projected to the world were actually real. She's breathtaking. I'm so wrapped up in the sight of her that it takes me a second for her words to register. My heart quickly picks up pace until it's galloping at breakneck speed. A memory tugs at my mind. *Stars.* Shaking my head to clear it, I mentally wave the similarity away. It's just a coincidence. I tell myself this, even as another part of my brain reminds me that coincidence is just another word for fate, and I don't believe in fate, only the choices that lead you to where you are. And if I'm completely honest with myself, I'm pretty content right where I am, still buried deep inside her. Her walls continue to clutch my length sporadically, and with the way my chest presses against hers, I can feel the fast but steady thump, thump, thump of her heart.

Against instinct, I ease out of her. Grabbing a handful of napkins from the table, I give myself a cursory wipe down, reluctant to remove the remnants of her arousal, before pulling my boxers and pants back up. As I glance back down to where she's now laying flat across my table like a whole ass meal, her thighs still spread enough for me to watch my come leak out of her, and the urge to swipe it up and make her lick it from my fingers is so strong. Next time, I promise myself. And, yes, there will be a next time. Since the day we met, there's been something here. Being trapped in this house with her, I sense that something has evolved and grown. I still can't label it, but I'm certain I don't want it to stop. The longer I stare at her, the more I can see the doubts start to creep back into her eyes. Her legs close, and the loss of that view is almost painful. I watch her sit up and cross her arms protectively over her middle. She still doesn't trust me or my intentions. Probably because I haven't given her much reason to, she doesn't know me, and even though I may have helped save her life, I haven't given her anything else besides the illusion of safety. I realize that if I want whatever this is between us to actually be something, I'm going to have to open up to her. Maybe not everything, because I don't know if she'll condone the plans I have for my father, but I can compromise on the rest. I make a split-second decision that will probably come back to bite me in the ass—time to put up or shut up.

As she fidgets under my gaze, I avert my eyes and blindly hand her a fist full of napkins. Taking them, she quickly uses them before lowering herself onto her feet. She redresses at lightning speed, and within minutes, she's completely covered again. What a pity. But it's probably for the best. If she stayed naked, I'd just end up fucking her again, and we'd never make any progress.

As soon as she's finished dressing and smoothing down the hair that was mused by her own clutching hands, I say, "Come with me. I want to show you something."

She eyes me warily but, thankfully, doesn't ask any questions when she sees me heading toward the laundry room. She follows behind, and when we reach the door on the other side, I can feel her peeking over my shoulder, curious to see how the door opens. I don't bother trying to hide the screen or my movements on the security box. Without my personal biometrics, she'd never get in anyway. As the door opens, I lead the way inside. She follows behind at a distance, slowly taking in the details of the room. The servers along the far wall and the many screens that are currently running line after line of code. When I turn my head to look at the monitors on my desk, my heart flips over when I see that I left one filled with images from the camera feeds throughout the house. Fuck! I never planned on her seeing any of this, so I didn't even think to turn the monitor off. I quickly glance back to see her facing in the opposite direction as she wanders the room, looking everything over, much like she did the first day she came here. Reaching down, I hit a button on my keyboard, and the screen in question goes black. I let out a barely audible sigh just as she turns around at the sound of the noise. I'm fully prepared to fake ignorance if she asks me but I still air on the side of caution and say nothing. A lie of omission is still better than a lie. At least, that's what I tell myself. Thankfully, she doesn't ask, so I don't have to cross that line ... yet.

Facing me once more, she says, "So this is where you go all day. What is it?" She waves her hand around to indicate the room at large.

"My office. This is where I do all my ... research." I try to read her face for any sign of disgust or disapproval as I say, "You know what Merrick and I do for a living. They aren't exactly the safest professions, even under the best circumstances. To ensure neither of us gets killed, I do as much research on prospective buyers, sellers, marks, etc., as possible." She continues to stare at me, those hazel eyes unblinking, and I scratch the back of my neck nervously under her scrutiny. Why am I nervous? My poker face is usually much better. As if compelled by those eyes to continue, I add, "I'm pretty good with computers."

She nods slowly. "I think I knew that, but I didn't know about ... all this." She waves her hand again, indicating the abundance of technology. "So, who are you researching now?" she asks. A momentary look of confusion crosses my features because it's hard to believe she's actually interested in wanting to know more about what I do here. Maybe it's just curiosity. Maybe it's boredom from being stuck in this house with nothing to do. I have a moment where I seriously debate the merits of telling her everything. The words climb up my throat of their own volition, even as I swallow hard, trying to push them back down. I don't know why I want to open up to her. To tell her about my plans for my father, for that piece of shit Gaspari, or for the many other wealthy scumbags that I've stolen from over the years and will continue to steal from until I'm either put in prison or the ground. Or maybe ... until something or someone comes along that alters the course of my future. I've never wanted that before. I've always operated under a single-minded purpose: revenge and restitution. But, just as often as I feel like strangling the woman standing in front of me, I also feel a short supply of air every time she walks into a room, and that's never happened before either. She knows, to some extent, that I'm not a straight and narrow kinda guy, but would she run for the hills when presented with the reality of my nature, or would she stand at my back? I can't be sure and because of that hesitation, I decide that I can't tell her everything. Not yet.

What I can tell her is what directly pertains to her. That, at least, I can be honest about. Sitting down at my desk, I motion her forward. Without hesitation, she walks over to stand next to me. "Sit down, and I'll show you," I say.

She glances around the room again saying, "There aren't any other chairs in here."

I scoot back from the desk until there's enough room for her to slip through. "I'm aware of that," I reply before taking hold of her forearm and pulling her onto my lap. Her posture is stiff at first but after a moment or two, she relaxes into me, her back to my front. I place my hands on the tops of her knees as I lean in to say directly next to her ear, "I need to get closer to reach the keyboard." With that, I use my hands to apply enough pressure on her knees, forcing her thighs wide so they drape over my own. Afterward, I scoot the chair closer to the table, reaching my arms around her warm body so that I can put one hand on the keyboard and one on the mouse. This close to her, that lack of air that I thought about before becomes even more apparent, to the point that I can only smell her. My nose is inches from her neck, and every movement of her head as she looks from one monitor to the other causes her hair to shift, and a fresh wave of her scent invades my senses. I have to restrain the creeper in me who wants to lean in and sniff her like a dog. I've noticed her scent before and even thought to myself that whatever soap she uses makes her smell absolutely edible like coffee and warm chocolate. Now, however, there's an overlay that I know comes from *my* body wash. The knowledge of that, along with the image now being conjured in my brain of her rubbing my soap all over her naked body, has saliva pooling in my mouth. I'm seconds away from biting into the back of the shoulder in front of me, when I realize she's talking to me and I haven't heard a word she said.

"Sorry, what?" I ask sheepishly, willing away the hard-on that I know is forming directly under her lush ass. If she notices that or the husky tone of my voice, she doesn't comment on it.

"I said, why's that one dark?" She gestures to the monitor I turned off when we entered.

Thinking as quickly as my overstimulated brain will allow, I say, "It's broken."

"Oh," she says, tilting her head to the side to glance at me over her shoulder. With a rueful smile, she adds, "I would have thought someone this technologically savvy would be able to fix a broken computer monitor."

With an exaggerated sigh, I say, "Yes, well, there just aren't enough hours in the day to look this good, manage all this technology, and put up with all your mouth."

With a laugh, she elbows me in the ribs and makes as if to stand up. Locking my left arm around her middle, I keep her firmly in place, lifting my hips a little and rubbing myself against her for good measure. The laughter dies in her throat, ending in a small gasp.

Grinning to myself, I reach my right hand for the mouse again. "Let me show you what I've been working on," I say, pulling up several documents onto the screen directly in front of us. "These are the financial records for Gaspari, and several of the men that work for him. The ones I've been able to identify, at least. Aside from my wire transfer for the diamond on the night of the auction, there isn't much money to speak of, coming in or out."

Her eyes are intent on the screen, her head making small movements as she tries to make heads or tales of what she's seeing. At my last sentence, however, her face turns sharply, and her gaze meets mine, with her brows pinched together in confusion. "Wait, what do you mean? No money to speak of? Dante's always had money. A lot of money."

I shake my head. "Not anymore. When he disappeared three years ago, a lot of the deals he was involved in fell apart. Buyers went elsewhere; sellers did the same. Whatever happened to him, it cost him nearly everything. I'm still not sure where he got the diamond from, but without my money from that sale, he wouldn't even be able to pay his own men right now." I watch her face as I speak, gauging her reactions. My suspicions are confirmed when she averts her gaze from mine at the mention of whatever happened three years ago. She knows. I could try to force the information out of her, but if there's one thing I've learned about Siren, it's that when pushed, she doesn't break. She pushes back twice as hard. So, I leave it alone for now. Maybe, at some point, she'll trust me enough to give me the information on her own. At least, I hope so.

Changing the subject, she asks, "Have you found out if he's still alive?" I expect there to be fear in her voice. Terror at the prospect that Gaspari is still out there searching for her. But there isn't. Her words are made of steel, and her face has gone to granite. She wants him dead if he isn't already. She wants this finished. I recognize the sentiment because it mirrors one I've carried around with me since I was 14. I want to end this for her as quickly as possible. I, better than anyone, would know that carrying that amount of weight around for any period of time will destroy you.

Answering her question, I say, "Not definitively. But my connections have alluded to rumors that a doctor, specifically a surgeon, visited the house shortly after we left. The outcome of that visit is still unclear. I'm gonna ask Theo to look into it." If another back alley doctor saved Gaspari's life, Theo would know about it. I haven't yet decided how much information I'll trust the rough-and-tumble doctor with, but right now, the end justifies the means. Just to be sure, I ask her, "Is it okay if I share some of this with him?"

She thinks about it for a second then nods solemnly. "Yeah. Do what you have to do." I know this isn't easy for her, and I'm again floored by the seemingly endless flow of strength inside this woman. A sense of pride fills my chest, and I can't help but stare at her side profile in awe. Despite having gone through Hell *twice*, I've never met another person with so much will and determination to live. As I sit there, I realize that what was once general irritation at everything this woman said or did has morphed into something akin to admiration. Admiration and a gripping need that claws at your insides until you either let it out or it consumes you. Every piece of her I get only makes me want another and another. As I glance at the darkened monitor to my right, I only hope I'm not biting off more than I can chew.

CHAPTER 22

Siren

Deacon's holed up in his office again, and I'm back to sitting on the couch and flipping through Netflix on my own. It's been two days since we tore into each other on the kitchen table, and he showed me the inner workings of his operation afterward. At first, I thought I'd be able to come and go from the vault-like cave now that I knew what he was doing in there. Like, there's no need to close the door if I already know what's inside, right? Wrong. Even though he's continued to keep me updated on any progress he makes in locating Dante's either living body or corpse, he also hasn't let me back into the room, claiming that he won't be able to concentrate with me there. I'm not sure I believe him. I know he's working on something else, something unrelated to Dante. He thinks I didn't see him quickly turn off one of the monitors as soon as we entered the room the other day, but I did. He didn't want me to see whatever he was researching, and considering how open he's being with information about the hunt for Dante, I have to believe it's something completely different. Maybe he's also working on a new job? Some stolen trinket or other that needs to be sold? Or maybe it's something personal he doesn't want anyone to know about? Either way, I can't say that being barred from the room didn't sting a little. I'm not sure why I expected more, especially when I know better than anyone that men can't be trusted not to keep secrets. Unfortunately, the useless organ in my chest still feels tight when I think about it, which makes no sense because I don't feel that way towards him. No, definitely not. Although, against my better judgment, when he doesn't have me bordering on homicidal rage, I can admit to myself that I might actually like him. As for whether he likes me back ... I'm still not sure. I know he claims to want me, and his behavior would indicate the same. But the ever-present voice in my head whispers that I'm just another warm body to him. That he's biding his time with me while we're stuck together. That he could never actually fall for someone like me. Someone with too much excess baggage in both the physical and emotional departments.

Wait, rewind. And no, not on the remote I've been holding that's just dropped into my lap. For a minute, I stare unseeingly at the TV, contemplating my own sanity. Did my brain just use the term *fall for*? Why did I think that? *Siren, you dumb bitch, have you not learned your lesson?* I don't want that, not with *him*. Maybe in 10 years, when I've spent a small fortune on therapy and have gone a sufficient time frame without being abducted and tormented, I'd find a nice man and settle down. Well, as much as someone like me *could* settle down. Based on everything I've come to learn about Deacon, he's not the settling-down type. He's the "I could go to prison any minute so let me fuck your brains out" type. No, I don't want that with him, and I'm certain he would never want that with me. Sure, the sex was phenomenal, and both times, he'd literally made me see stars, but that's all it was. Sex. Don't get me wrong, sex was great, but right now, I'd settle for simple companionship. Nearly three weeks of practically living in solitude was lonely, which also made no sense because I didn't mind being by myself. I was used to my own company, living alone in my Charleston apartment, but I was always free to leave when the voices in my head got too much. To walk around the city and find some trouble. Here, I was stranded in the swamp with nothing to do and no one to talk to but that annoying voice inside my head that only made me think the worst of myself. During these moments, I would usually find solace in my music, but the memories of Dante's house have kept me away from my violin. As I sit on the couch in the living room, I glance over to where the instrument sits abandoned, propped against a wall I remember, in vivid detail, everything that happened that night, but I don't remember Deacon grabbing my violin before we left. How, amid all the chaos, he knew it was important to take it, I don't know. I want to play, but I don't think I can. The violin used to speak to me on a level that most people could never understand. We had our own language. We each understood and appreciated the beauty the other had to offer the world. It took me so long, after my first escape, to be able to hear the music again. This time, I worry that the notes will never come back, and even if they do, they'll fall on deaf ears. I fear it's possible that that process actually started weeks ago. The music came out flat and lifeless when forced to play for a madman. I knew it and he knew it. Despite knowing I'd be punished, I couldn't put my heart and soul into something that was being taken from me by force, stripped away, like layers of armor I'd built up around myself until what remained was a raw and festering wound. One more to add to the many others he gave me, though the significance of this one wouldn't be easily healed by a tattoo cover-up. I used to be able to to make people weep with only strings and a bow. Now, the only person that wept was me, because there was only silence. I glance toward the kitchen, and what I know lies beyond it. I have to admit, if only to myself, that even though all the melodies in my head have gone quiet, over the course of the last few weeks, the urge to go searching for them has grown stronger. I have to concede the possibility that if I want that music back, I can't just sit around and wait for it to find me. I'll have to take it. I'm just not sure how. What if I put the bow to the strings and nothing happens? If I'm not that girl anymore, that musical prodigy, who am I? What else do I have to offer the world?

Running my hands over my face, I stand from the couch and walk to the kitchen to get a drink. Deep introspection made a bitch dehydrated. While standing next to the fridge, with a glass of sweet tea in hand, I take the few steps that allow me to see into the laundry room. As expected, the wall that doubles as the door to Deacon's office is closed, and no sound comes from inside. I know my expression is a sour one. I'm annoyed. I'm going crazy in this house, and if I don't get out of here soon, forget the therapy. I'm gonna have to be committed. I glare at the closed door and the little red flashing light on the security panel, an idea begins to take root. If he's going to hole up in there and leave me to my own devices, then he can't be angry if I get to know my surroundings a little better. I've been like a phantom for over two weeks, floating from point A to point B. From the bed to the couch then back to the bed. Lather, rinse, repeat. I'm sick of the routine. With renewed purpose, I take my glass of tea and begin nosing my way through his house. First, I re-inspect the living room. I've spent enough time in it to know roughly where everything is, but this time, I move around the room slowly, taking in finer details I haven't noticed before. A small figurine of a shooting star amid the many photographs above the fireplace. A handful of loose change. A framed cross-stitch of a sunflower hanging on the wall. A little glass container of seashells on a side table. The items aren't necessarily out of place amongst the rest of the décor, but they don't exactly fit either. Each item varies so much from the rest that I imagine they must have some kind of personal meaning behind them. I store that theory away to investigate at a later date. Making my way down the hallway, I enter the bathroom, opening every drawer and inspecting hair products and toiletries. Again, there are things here that fit the overall mishmash motif, but some seem almost feminine in nature, like they were picked out by a woman. The idea puts a bad taste in my mouth. An old-fashioned crocheted toilet paper cover is sat on the back of the tank next to a potpourri bowl. I didn't think they even made that anymore. Did it still have a smell? I pick up the bowl and bring it to my nose. It does. It smells floral, but I can't pinpoint from which flower. Hydrangeas, maybe? I sit the bowl back down and exit the bathroom, entering Deacon's bedroom. Here, I pause in the doorway, sticking my head back out into the hall to make sure he hasn't come out of his hidy-hole looking for me. When I don't see a 6ft+ surfer lookalike charging down the hallway, I pull my head back inside the room. As I stand in the doorway, I glance around the room to see if anything interesting jumps out at me. I've slept in his king-sized bed every night since I got here, but aside from sleeping, I haven't moved around the room much. Zeroing in on his dresser, I set my glass of tea on top, then proceed to rummage through each drawer shamelessly. Starting from the bottom, I pick over the countless t-shirts and folded pairs of worn jeans. I'm greeted by a sea of socks and underwear when I open the top drawer. Picking through the pieces, I estimate the man owns 400 pairs of boxer briefs. I can't help but let out a little snicker, and my mood is improving by the second. In fact, the thought of Deacon's face if he knew I was elbow deep in his manties has that snicker turning to a full-blown grin. One that remains as I abandon the dresser in favor of searching the closet. My disappointment is palpable when I open it to find only a handful of very expensive suits and several pairs of shoes, ranging from designer dress shoes to dingy work boots.

I'm just about to close the doors when the glint of something metal catches my eye. Turning on the light, I see that it's a small box, similar to the kind used to hold money at a yard sale. It's tucked away on the highest shelf, apart from everything else. My curiosity piqued, I reach for it but pause just as my fingers brush the cold steel. Unlike the dresser and bathroom drawers, something about this box and its location makes me second-guess the idea of opening it. A sudden sense of foreboding penetrates my need for distraction. It's obviously been put there for a reason. Deacon either doesn't want others to see what's in there, or he's placed it there to hide it from himself. Out of sight, out of mind, as the saying goes. Would he be angry if I looked inside? He never specifically told me that I couldn't wander the house or that any particular area was off-limits, but if this were a fairytale, my gut tells me that this box would be the west wing. I gnaw my bottom lip in indecision. Glancing towards the open doorway again, I finally decide, fuck it. I've already gone through everything else. If I'm gonna end up paying the time, I should at least do the crime.

Reaching up, I carefully bring the box down from its resting place. The top is covered in a thick layer of dust, as though it hasn't been moved, much less opened, in years. Sitting cross-legged on the closet floor, I place the box in front of me, staring at it as if it's a snake waiting to bite me. Mind made up, I flip the latch and ease the lid open. What I find inside surprises me. There are more pictures, like those in the living room, but these aren't framed. They look old and worn, the corners frayed, and some show signs of creasing or water damage. Flipping through them, I'm treated to glimpses into Deacon's life growing up. Many of the pictures appear to be of happy times with a smiling Deacon and a woman I now know is his mother. Others seem to be candid photos that, if I had to guess, were taken by one without the other's knowledge. In the ones of Deacon's mother, her face and appearance range from bright and sunny to melancholy. In the latter, her eyes give the impression that she's somewhere else. Somewhere far away. In the individual pictures of Deacon, he's either shielding his face from his mother's onslaught or doing some menial household chore—dishes, laundry, cleaning up trash. In none of the pictures do I see a man that could possibly be Deacon's father. As I reach the end of the stack, the only other thing in the box is a plain envelope that was probably once white but has since faded to a dingy cream color. I pick it up carefully. Deacon's name is written in a distinctly feminine scrawl on the front. I experience a moment of hesitation, as though some part of my brain is screaming at me that I'm about to cross a line I can't come back from. Despite that, or maybe because of it, I can't stop myself from turning the envelope over and pulling out the contents. As I stare at the single worn piece of paper inside, my heart feels like it's beating a mile a minute. The fear of getting caught is like spiders crawling up my back, and I wonder if I'd even hear someone approach over the drumbeat of my heart in my ears. I push past the fear, because I've already come this far and unfold the paper to find a letter. Even knowing that this is a massive invasion of privacy, I begin reading it anyway. I read and re-read the words written by Deacon's late mother, my eyes skimming the page back and forth, trying to comprehend the meaning behind them. It isn't until fresh splotches of wetness land on top of older, dried marks of a similar shape that I realize I'm crying. My vision blurs, and the words become illegible as the tears flow freely down my cheeks, landing on the paper below. Deacon's mother committed suicide. Like puzzle pieces clicking into place, the vacant looks in many of the photos makes sense now. And according to the letter, he never knew who his father was until after his mother died. Did he go looking for him? Did he find him, or is he still searching? So many questions run through my mind and I want so badly to ask him. I want to show him that his secrets are safe with me and that he can trust me with the darkest parts of himself. But I have a feeling, my words wouldn't be welcome. Especially not after I only learned about all this by snooping without his permission. I need to take some time to process everything I've just learned about a man that I once thought of as one-dimensional but can now recognize as just as multifaceted as the diamond he was after the night he found me. I carefully refold the letter and put it back into its envelope. Gently laying the contents back into the box exactly the way I found them, I place it back onto the top shelf before turning off the light and closing the closet. I pray he doesn't notice anything out of place. The good thing is, I'm no longer bored. I've got too many thoughts floating through my head to be bored. The bad thing is that I may be trapped in a house with a man I don't really know.

CHAPTER 23

Deacon

15 YEARS OLD

The white house looms large, even from my vantage point on the sidewalk across the street. Lush green ferns hang in baskets along a front porch that disappears around both sides of the house. A pretty little stone walkway runs from the three-car garage to the base of the brick stairs leading up. Has a set of stairs ever seemed so tall? As I stand across the street, I count them out in my head. One, two, three ... There are only seven but there might as well be a thousand. Around me, the streets of down-town Charleston bustle. Pedestrians pass by, some stopping to give me odd looks while others move around me as if I'm just another Palmetto tree lining the sidewalk. I don't pay them much mind. I know I look like shit, but I can't find the energy to care. After bouncing around through five different foster homes in six months, I've learned to travel light. In addition to the clothes on my back, my small bookbag holds one extra pair of pants, a threadbare t-shirt, and underwear. A handful of pictures and small nick-nacks, a toothbrush, a pack of wet wipes, and a bar of soap in a ziplock baggie take up the space in the front pocket.

Wrapped tightly within the folds of my spare pants is my laptop. That was the extent of my worldly possessions. Well ... that and the letter. Reaching into my pocket, I pull out the plain white envelope. The paper inside is wrinkled and thinning from how many times I've taken it out to read it, but I don't need to take it out now. I know it, word for word, by heart at this point.

Hi, baby.

I truly hope you never have to read this, but if you are, then it means I'm no longer here with you. I know you must be angry with me, but I think somewhere, in the back of our minds, we both knew it was only a matter of time. I hope that one day, you'll understand and be able to forgive me. Please know that I didn't ever want to leave you behind. Life has been so hard. Harder than it should've been. Much harder than it needed to be. And you've grown up so much faster than you were meant to. You had to shoulder the burden of a mother so broken by life that it made her too weak to love herself and find contentment in the life she'd been given, as opposed to the life she wished for. I know none of this has been easy for you, but you're stronger than I ever was. I remember the day you came into this world. I was in such a dark place, scared and alone. But when I finally held you in my arms, and you looked at me for the first time, stars lit up the perpetual night I'd been living in, and I wasn't so alone anymore. From then on, any time life became too much, I'd look into your eyes, and I wasn't so afraid of the dark. But I know, if you're reading this, that it still wasn't bright enough for me to find my way home. The fault in that lies with me, not you. The stars were always shining; I just couldn't keep sight of them. I love you so much, baby. You've always been the best part of me ... and your father. I know I never told you much about the man who helped create you, mostly because it hurt too much to think about the lifetime of memories we should've made together but didn't. Instead, you and I made memories, and I'm hoping, now that I'm gone, he'll pick up where I left off, and the two of you will create memories of your own. I've enclosed the information below with that hope. Just remember, people come and go in life, but stars are constant. They're always there, and as long as you keep sight of them, the darkness can't touch you. Someday, long from now, I'll meet you in the sky, and we'll be together again.

All my love,

Mama

I've also memorized the name and address printed below my mother's signature. My father's name is Martin Hawkins, and I've been standing outside his house for the last hour. After Mama died, social services came and took custody of me. The lady was nice but she looked tired and run down. I guess that made two of us. I'd only been given enough time to grab a handful of things before I had to leave. Turned out we were behind on the rent—the landlord confiscated everything in the house that wasn't nailed down. Sure, I could've scraped together enough from my siphoning software to pay him, but then I'd have to explain to him and the social worker where I'd gotten the money, knowing I couldn't do that. So, in the end, he'd taken the majority of our possessions to sell in the hope of recouping his money. I didn't protest. The only thing I'd really wanted were the photographs anyway. I'd found the letter when I was gathering up the pictures. The envelope was addressed to me, and I recognized Mama's handwriting. I couldn't bring myself to open it then. Instead, I'd stuffed a change of clothes, the pictures, and a few other small things that reminded me of her into my bookbag and left. Later, when I was at the center, waiting to be placed into my first foster home, I'd finally opened the letter. My mother's beautiful script was stained with what looked like water droplets in several places, making it hard to read, but I'd managed. I wondered if the wet spots on the paper were from where she was crying. The thought made me cry, and even though I didn't think I had any tears left in me, I still couldn't stop the lump from forming in my throat at the idea. The letter itself would've been confusing to anyone else, but after living with Mama for 14 years, I knew she likened my eyes to starlight. Just like the fake diamond she'd been buried with. Just like the real one that should've been in its place. She'd never gotten that diamond or the life that she was promised. She'd never gotten a lot of things. I didn't hate my mother for what she'd done. Maybe I should, but I didn't. I hated *him*. Standing across the street from the pretty white house I know belongs to my father, I imagine the entire structure going up in flames. It would be so easy. A little gasoline and the strike of a match. Everything he loved would be gone in the blink of an eye, and he'd know exactly how I've felt for the last year. Or better yet, it would be a bonus if he were inside the house while it burned. It would only be fair. I want him to hurt the way she hurt. The way I hurt. Despite the pretty words of her letter, the only memories I want to make with this man are the kind that'll haunt him for the rest of his life. I want to ruin him. But first, I want him to tell me why. Why he abandoned her, abandoned us. I want to look into the mirror image of my eyes and see regret there. Then I'll find a way to destroy whatever life he decided was better than the one he could've had with us. Only then will I be able to let go of the past.

As I force my feet into motion, I walk slowly, thinking about how I got here. After finding the letter and learning who my father was, I'd told the social worker I had somewhere to go. Granted, I had no intention of ever living with the man, but she didn't need to know that. Unfortunately, I might as well have been talking to the wind. My father wasn't listed on my birth certificate, and she didn't think the letter was sufficient enough evidence to upend someone's life by dropping a kid on their doorstep. Instead, I'd been placed in a foster home with a woman that smoked too much and a man that touched too much. When he started trying to come into my room at night, I'd been moved to a new home. The second wasn't much better. Neither was the third or fourth. I'd split after only four days in my 5th and final foster home. Officially classed as a runaway, the system all but threw my file in the trash. The government didn't care where I was, only that they had one less case to manage. It hadn't taken me long to track down my father. He was famous after all. Well, famous by Southern standards, I guess. Turned out, Martin Hawkins was the mayor of Charleston, SC. An upstanding citizen with a wife and two kids about the same age as me. Rumor had it that he planned on running for governor in the next election. Not if I could help it.

Finally reaching the first of the seven brick steps leading up to the porch, I take them two at a time. Stepping forward, I quickly ring the bell before I have a chance to chicken out. Raised voices come from just beyond the front door, and I can see a figure moving towards me through the stained glass window. My body stiffens, and I brace myself for whatever's on the other side of that door. When it finally opens, I'm greeted by an elegantly dressed woman holding a glass of red wine in one hand and a phone in the other.

She stares blankly in the general direction of my face before saying, "Whatever you're selling, hunny, we've already got two." I don't miss her dilated eyes before she closes the door in my face. If I'm not mistaken, she's drunk, and despite the sugary sweet endearment, her words leave a taste in my mouth not unlike that of artificially flavored banana candy. I recognize her, of course, from pictures I found online. Hello stepmother. Ringing the bell again, I watch from outside as she stops on the other side of the glass before turning around and opening the door again. This time, I don't allow her to cut me off before I can speak.

"I'm not selling anything. I'm here to see Martin Hawkins," I say quickly.

Her face is now pinched, and even the illusion of southern hospitality can't hide her irritation this time. Using the hand still holding the phone to lean on the doorframe, probably to keep herself upright, she says, "Darlin', don't you know it's supper time? We don't do business during supper. That's family time. Come back tomorrow."

"This isn't business, it's personal," I state in a voice that's gone hard as nails. "And I could eat," I tack on. The sarcasm in my voice can't disguise the insinuation. I *am* family.

Blinking hard, she finally focuses on my face. When her eyes meet mine, I watch them narrow slightly before coasting across the rest of my features. Those hazy eyes turn to slits before she lets out a low laugh. One that's completely devoid of humor. Leaving the door open, she turns, effectively dismissing me. As she walks across a large foyer, she yells rather calmly, "Martin, one of your bastards is on our doorstep." Without a backward glance, she puts the phone back to her ear and resumes conversation, disappearing down a hallway.

I stand there on the front porch, wondering if I've slipped into an alternate universe. Is this normal for her? What did she mean by *one of* his bastards? Has this happened before? *Jesus Christ.* A picture of who my father really is is coming into sharper focus by the second. Shaking my head, I take a step back and wait. Within a minute or two, a tall man with broad shoulders and dark hair already peppered with grays steps into the doorway. Looking me up and down from head to toe, he pushes the screen door open, closing the large interior door behind him as he steps out. For the first time, I get a good look at my father. Objectively speaking, I can see why my mother fell for him. He's good-looking in a way that isn't pretentious, which is probably what's gotten him so far in his political career. With his sleeves rolled up and the top collar button of his white dress shirt undone, he looks like a man of the people. That is until he opens his mouth.

"What do you want, boy?" he asks in a low tone. The hostility in his voice is in direct contrast to his laid back appearance. I stand there for a second, just staring at his face, waiting for him to actually look at me. Waiting for some sign of recognition. None comes. In fact, he seems to be deliberately looking anywhere *but* at my face.

Finally opening my mouth, I ask, "Do you know who I am?"

"No, and I don't care. Whatever story you're here peddling, I'm not buying it. Get the hell off my porch before I call the police."

Red hot anger fills me and I have to lock my muscles into place to keep from lunging at him. This piece of shit. How did someone as sweet and caring as my mother fall in love with someone like him? Jaw clenching, I take a deep breath through my nose, reminding myself that if I get arrested, I'll end up back in the system. As I keep my feet rooted to the spot, I glare at him, and he stares in the general direction of my left ear. The longer we stand there, the angrier I get. And finally I lose my temper, my next words burst from me with the force of a shotgun blast.

"Look at me!" Bright blue eyes snap to mine, holding. "Do. You. Know. Who. I. Am?" I demand again.

He stares into my eyes for another long moment before I watch his gaze flick to my hair, then my nose, chin, and jaw, all before coming back to meet my eyes again. I can see the recognition there now. When he speaks, however, it's in a tone that leaves no room for argument. "No," he says.

Liar. He knows exactly who I am. Who my mother was. I can see it in his eyes. My eyes. Realization cements itself into place and every question, every accusation, every need for explanation dries up on my tongue. Any benefit of the doubt that I wanted to give this man for my mother's sake is gone. He wasn't ever stuck in an impossible situation that kept him away from us, and he never intended to keep any of his promises to my mother. She waited her entire life for him and he was here in this pretty house with his drunk wife having supper with the family he really wanted. Disgust crawls up my throat like bile, and a heavy weight settles in my stomach. Without another word, I turn and walk down the stairs, across the cobblestone walkway, and out onto the sidewalk. I don't turn around or look back.

I'm sorry, mama.

I knew what she hoped would happen, but somehow, even before I came here, I knew that it was a pipe dream. He doesn't regret his choices nor is he sorry for anything that happened after. As I looked into those eyes, there was no remorse. There was ... nothing. He recognized me, and he felt nothing. Walking into an internet cafe, I remove my bookbag and sit at a corner table. I pull out my laptop, boot it up, and connect to the cafe's WIFI. As my fingers fly over the keys, all the anger and pent-up frustration drain away, leaving only purpose. Detachment becomes my coping mechanism. You wouldn't make mistakes if you didn't allow yourself to feel emotion. Over the course of the next hour, I dig up as much information on Martin Hawkins as I can, soaking it all up like a sponge. The more I learn, the more I come to realize ... my father's a criminal. A white collar criminal but a criminal nonetheless. As I take all this information in, I'm reminded of that famous saying. What is it? To get into the mind of a criminal, you have to become one? My finger hovers over the button that will begin transferring small amounts of cash and assets from several of his offshore accounts into one of mine. My finger comes down, simultaneously clicking the key and sealing my fate. Consider it done.

CHAPTER 24

Siren

Three days later, and I'm still thinking about that letter. The words float around my head like water circling a half-clogged drain. Or like one of those coin machines you'd see at the mall as a kid, where you fed it a penny, and it would go round and round a type of giant funnel until it disappeared into the dark depths beneath. Well, my pennies just keep circling, never actually going anywhere. The few times I've seen Deacon since then, I'll catch myself averting eye contact, or worse, staring when he's not looking. Hyper-analyzing his mannerisms and facial expressions. It's almost as though the letter has shed light on parts of him that he's deliberately kept in the shadows, but now I can't unsee. If he notices the changes in my behavior, he doesn't let on. He comes out of his cave for meals and the occasional bathroom break but otherwise, I haven't seen much of him. Where that was an annoyance before, I'm now thankful for the distance because the less I interact with him, the less likely I am to spill my guts and admit what I did. The truth is, I feel guilty, and I hate that. I hate feeling guilty. It was a useless emotion. One born out of fear. Fear of knowing you've done something wrong, of telling the truth, and of facing the consequences of your actions. Fear of not knowing what will happen after. I know all about that. After first meeting Dante, keeping everything that happened to me was like a festering wound just beneath the skin. Not seen from the outside but felt from the inside. Which is why I've since tried to live my life as freely and openly as possible. You could never feel guilt if you led an open and honest life. The fact that I now had this new secret eating at my insides was like a blemish on an A+ student's academic record. But as much as I want to come clean and talk about the letter and his mother, I somehow know I'm in no position to demand conversations like that from him when I've been unwilling to give more myself.

So, until I figure out how to handle this situation, I'm stuck here, stewing in a mess of my own making. I'm feeling guilty because of what I did and because I'm still thinking about it. Try as I might to ignore it, certain bits from the letter play on a loop inside my head. The cadence of the words causes a riot of emotions inside me that ebb and flow until they're almost ... melodic. If it were a song, it would surely break your heart. Eyes widening, I turn my head from where I've been staring out the living room window to where my violin case still sits untouched. For the first time in weeks, my fingers itch to feel the bow in my hand, and even though I rarely need to reference sheet music to play a piece, I can see the notes of this particular melody laid out on the paper, plain as day. I nearly cry at the possibility that there may still be some music left in me after all. Perhaps the chaos around me was just so loud that its beautiful notes were drowned out. Somehow, the words of that letter have cut through all the white noise, determined to crank up the volume of those notes.

Sweat beads my upper lip, and I dart my tongue out, swiping at it nervously as I stand and walk across the room. I reach out with shaky hands, and lift the case onto a nearby end table. I stare at it for several long moments before I steel my resolve and decide to open the latch. As the lid comes up, I run my fingers over the instrument, and when I take it out and position it against my chin, it feels like coming home. As I close my eyes, I see the first few notes floating behind my closed lids. On an exhale, I bring the bow up, focus on those notes, and just let myself *feel*.

My insides war with the pull of the new song and the habitual instinct to play Bach, but I have to remind myself that I'm no longer in that house. I'm no longer a puppet being controlled by invisible strings. Still, the conditioning is so deeply ingrained that I start and stop multiple times, useless tears of frustration springing to my eyes. It's as though some invisible barrier stands between me and the visceral need to bring to life the words of love from a damaged mother to her, even now, damaged son. It's only after that first tear spills over and I have to swallow several times past the lump in my throat that my anger sets in, and it's that anger that pushes me to break the habit for good. Finally. I take several deep breaths and try to remember the melody I found in the letter. The first few tries sound rusty, even to my ears, but after a minute or two and a few adjustments, the series of notes in my head begin to vocalize themselves through the strings and then pour out of me like a tidal wave. Eyes still closed, with my cheeks wet from tears, I let out a watery laugh that causes several hitches in the song, but even as I lament the lack of perfection, I have to recognize that it's one of the most beautiful pieces I've ever played, because of the significance of its timing and the emotion behind its source. I'm not sure how long I stand there in the middle of the small house's living room and play, but whether it's 10 minutes or two hours, it'll never feel like enough. When I reach the stage that my neck begins to ache and the muscles in my arm weaken to the point that the bow shakes in my hand, I end the song on a low melancholy note. One full of regret, despair, and longing. For what was and for what could've been. But there's also love there. An outpouring of love. Lowering the instrument, I keep my eyes closed for a moment longer, listening to the resonating sound of the last note. Many people wouldn't hear it, and if they did, it would simply be relegated to ambient noise. But I savor it because the song isn't finished until that note disappears completely.

When I finally open my eyes, I find Deacon sitting in the armchair only feet away, staring at me. He doesn't say anything, only sits on the edge of his seat, his forearms braced on his knees. His mouth parted slightly, and there's a look in his eyes that I can't readily identify. I feel a tinge of uneasiness at the knowledge that the song was inspired by something so personal to him, and he has no idea.

"How long have you been there?" I ask softly. There's no heat in my voice. I'm not angry. I've never been the type to gatekeep my music, so I don't feel any violation over the fact that he watched me play. Especially knowing they're his mother's words put to melody.

He continues to stare at me, and I can see the gears in his head turning. This would be the point where a normal person would either gush about how much they loved the piece or tell me what areas they found fault in and how it could be improved. He does neither of these things. He just watches me, eyes dancing back and forth between my own.

In a somber tone, he finally replies, "Long enough."

To quell my nervous energy, I move to put my violin and bow back into its case. My feet freeze to the spot when he says, "Don't." I glance back at him. He's still staring at me with that laser focus. He motions to the instrument with a tip of his head. "Will you play it again for me?" he asks softly. Not commands, but asks. He's giving me the choice. I don't doubt that if I refused, he'd let me. The stark contrast between this moment and all the times that Dante would demand that I play for him is startling. They're like night and day, the two of them.

With a slow nod, I raise the violin again, position the bow, and begin the song once more. I don't close my eyes this time but keep them open and on his, watching as an array of memories play out behind his eyes, even as his face remains stoic and unmoving. I infuse the song with every ounce of emotion left inside me, willing him to feel what I feel. Wishing I could let him into my head, but I also knew that the amount of sympathy I felt for him and his mother would drown him. It's not a new feeling. It's one I'm used to because this is my process. I compose, I play, and I feel. More than anything else, I feel. But where there's usually a degree of separation that allows for critique, that line has been more than blurred. It's been all but erased. As he slowly leans back, settling into the plush armchair, I can tell that the song is causing its own feelings within him. If only he knew just how similar our thoughts really are. I play the song once and as it comes to a close, I don't need any words from him to urge me to start again. It's all in his eyes. The blue is bright and slightly glassy. *Pleading.* So I play, and I play, and I play. Not because I'm being forced to but because I want to. I want to heal him the way he's been trying to heal me by tracking down the person that hurt me most. If the only way I can do that is through music, I'll play until I can't anymore. Then I'll do it again. And again.

CHAPTER 25

Deacon

I may have to eat crow and admit that Siren was right. There's literally no food in this damn house. I normally only keep enough here for me, which isn't much, considering I'm on the road a lot. To get the right price and keep people out of my business, I always go to the buyer instead of having them come to me. I wasn't lying to Siren when I told her I didn't bring people here. As I look into the barren fridge, the only things staring back at me that are actually edible are a few eggs and less than an inch of milk. The rest, I'm positive, are no good. In fact, I'm pretty sure whatever's in that green tupperware in the back just moved by itself. Giving it a wide berth, I grab the eggs and milk, slamming the door shut with my booted foot. I sit my meager ingredients on the counter as I fruitlessly open and shut every cabinet door, each one more empty than the last. I could scramble the eggs but that sounded like a sad breakfast, even for me. There's no way two eggs will feed both Siren and I. A low whooping sound escapes me as I open the last cabinet to find a half-empty box of pancake mix and a bottle of syrup that's just over a quarter full. I don't know if Siren likes pancakes, but if she does, tough titty because I'm making waffles. I fucking hate pancakes. Even though any sane person would say they're made from the same batter, my brain still tells me that waffles are the superior of the two. All those little crevices to hold lots of syrup and melty butter. Wait ... do I have butter? As I glance back to the fridge, debating the merits of opening it again, on the off chance that something will eat me instead of the other way around, I decide to live life on the edge and risk it. I nearly jerk the door off its hinges with how forcefully I pull it open, as though already spoiling for a fight. Luckily, I don't have a Ghostbusters moment, and whatever's in that tupperware stays put. I don't have to look long before finding a small tub of margarine on the door rack. Hmm ... that'll do. Shutting the door again, I break out my ancient waffle maker and get to work. While I wait for the batter to cook itself into something fit for human consumption, my mind wanders back to yesterday. The day had started like any other in recent memory; I woke up, checked the cameras, took a shower, stroked myself off to the image of Siren sleeping naked in my bed, made some coffee, rechecked the cameras, watched Siren watching TV, ate a few slices of pitiful toast, rechecked the cameras ... again ... and so it goes. By noon, I knew that I wouldn't get any work done if I didn't turn off the monitor with the cameras on it. Not only was I still trying to locate Gaspari, but I was also simultaneously keeping tabs on my father. In the ensuing chaos after Siren's rescue, my vendetta against my father had to fall to the wayside. Now, I'm making up for lost time, so I've spent the better part of every day intercepting emails, tapping cell phones, and tracking his itinerary. After my unfortunate miss at Eugene Kingsley's auction, I've since learned that he did indeed meet with the mystery assassin earlier that night. For all my father's boasting and despite years of practice, the man was a terrible criminal. I could follow his tracks in the middle of a snowstorm. This knowledge should put me at ease but it has the opposite effect. Poor criminals were loose cannons, unpredictable by nature, and bound to do stupid shit. So, knowing that the connection was made that night has just put me further on edge than I already was, being cooped up in this house with the one woman on the planet who makes me question my sanity as much as her own. The pressure to find Gaspari and prevent my father from orchestrating a murder has never been so high. I need him to pay for my mother's death, and I need Siren to be free, once and for all. Two goals, one quickly becoming just as important as the other. As I flip the waffle maker over, I absently rub at a spot in the center of my chest. Thinking about Siren hurts. After only a few hours of absent-minded research yesterday, I'd broken and pulled the cameras back up to find her standing in the middle of the living room, playing her violin. To say I was shocked would've been an understatement. I couldn't hear the music through my office's vault-like door, but the simple fact that she'd taken the instrument out for the first time since she got here was enough to lure me out. What I walked into was something unlike anything I've ever felt. I had to describe it that way because that's what the music did. It made you *feel*, whether you liked it or not. There haven't been many instances where I've cried since the night I found my mother's body, but if I were a man that cried, I would've. As it was, I knew as the song finished, that the image of Siren smiling through a river of tears would stay with me for the rest of my life. The emotions I felt in that moment were too overwhelming to process, and even now,

251

the next morning, I'm still at a loss for words. As I stand there, thinking about how long she stood and played the same piece over and over, as though she somehow knew that it was quite literally altering my DNA, I lose track of time. Before I realize it, there's a faint burnt smell in the air, and the kitchen has gone hazy. *Shit!* I grab a fork and pull the half-burnt waffle from the machine, plopping it onto a paper plate. Huffing out a breath, I close my mind off to yesterday's events, at least for the time being, and focus on the task at hand. Not starving.

Fifteen minutes later, I'm walking out of the kitchen, shoving a forkful of slightly burnt but dripping waffle into my mouth. Just as I enter the dining room, I nearly choke to death.

Swallowing hard several times, I finally manage to get out, "Goddammit, Fed, don't you fucking knock?!"

Sitting at my dining room table as though he owns the place is none other than Mr. FBI himself. As I take a healthy gulp of lukewarm coffee to help finish the job of pushing the waffle the rest of the way down my throat, I look from him to the closed front door and back. My eyes narrow. He didn't trip any of my alarms. And my door was locked. I take a quick glance at the surrounding windows. All intact. How the fuck did this dude get into my house?

The picture of innocence, Alexi holds up his hands, palms out, as if to say *what did I do?* As he puts them back down on the table, his tattooed knuckles stand out sharply in the midmorning sun streaming in through the front window. If I'm not mistaken, I see several other tattoos peeking out from beneath the cuff of his sleeves.

"I'm not sure if you're aware but it's proper etiquette to make extra plates when you have guests. I like waffles too, you know,"

Alexi says, a slight lilt to his words that only hints at the Russian accent I know to be there.

What is it with this guy? Has there ever been a bigger pain in the ass? On some level, his dry and sarcastic sense of humor calls to my own, though. If I'm honest with myself, if it wasn't for his chosen profession being a direct arrow at the massive target that is me, I might actually like him. Though, as it stands, I swear, if he doesn't get out of my house in the next 10 minutes, I may break out into hives. I don't like cops, and this man might as well be a super cop.

"You're absolutely right. Where are my manners? I don't know why I didn't think to make some for you. Oh wait ... maybe it's because I *didn't fucking invite you.*"

If I expected him to fire back at me, I should've known better. Instead, he lets out a deep chuckle before saying, "That's okay. They smell a little overdone anyway."

Glowering at him because I know he's right, though I'll die before admitting it, I move to the table and pull out the chair at the opposite end. As I sit my plate and cup down, I park my ass in the seat and have an internal battle over whether I should wait until he's gone before finishing my food. Fuck that. I dislike cold waffles about as much as I do pancakes, so I pick up my fork and shovel in another bite.

Swallowing again, with much less dramatics this time, I say, "You gonna tell me how you got past my security?"

His Russian accent comes strongly to the forefront this time, and he simply replies, "Nyet."

I don't even bother hiding my eye roll, voicing my earlier thought. "You're a pain in the ass, you know that? Why don't you just tell me what you want? The sooner you do, the sooner you can leave."

Completely ignoring my demand, he looks around the empty space before asking, "Where's Siren?"

In the blink of an eye, I can feel my entire demeanor shift. My eyes return to slits, and the handle of my fork is suddenly biting into my palm. I know he and Merrick have been on friendly terms for a few months now, but I know my best friend. He wouldn't have told the Fed where I lived or that Siren was with me. He knows how much I value my privacy. My mind whirls, trying to uncover how he could've gotten the information. He's obviously hacked into my network, but I have no idea how he did that without me being alerted. Probably the same way he got into my damn house without setting off any of my alarms.

I don't bother to lie. It's clear that super cop knows a lot more than he should, and you can bet your ass that as soon as he's gone, I'm gonna find out how. I'm invasive by nature, and I've also spent a lifetime honing my computer skills. I'm not vain enough to think I'm the best out there, but the idea that this person in particular is possibly better at it than me grates my nerves. Deciding to pick and choose my battles, I say tensely, "She's asleep down the hall."

"No waffles for her either, then." He makes a tsking sound, shaking his head. "Selfish."

Gritting my teeth, because I know he's deliberately trying to piss me off, I say offhandedly, "I would imagine the murder of a government official carries a heavier sentence than the killing of just anyone, right?" I quickly push back from the table, not giving him a chance to reply, saying, "I think I'll chance it."

Alexi lets out a bark of laughter. "Calm down, loverboy; I'm just here for some information."

Despite the fact that he just called me loverboy, I feel some of the tension in my shoulders ease, and I make a conscious effort to loosen the grip on my fork. Letting out a snort, I say, "Based on what I've learned about you, it's hard to believe that I'd have access to any information you aren't able to find."

In a cryptic tone, he replies, "Most information stays put. You can pin point it down to a single source with enough research. What I'm looking for has a pulse and doesn't wanna be found."

Ahhh. Here we go. I knew this was coming. My only hope was that it would be later rather than sooner. I've already got enough on my plate. But I guess, given how much time this particular gnat has been buzzing around our faces, it's surprising this hasn't come up earlier. Alexi and Merrick have been chummy since shortly after he first popped up in our lives, offering to help with the pesky problem of Merrick and Amelia's toxic parents. Usually, you'd welcome the help of a cop when dealing with two dangerous criminals. Unless you also happened to be a world-class thief yourself and are already wanted by an untold number of government agencies. Luckily ... or possibly unluckily, the Fed seemed to know all about Merrick's extracurricular activities already and had no intention of taking him in ... on one condition. At the time, that condition wasn't entirely clear, but since then, we've discovered that Alexi is looking for something himself. Something of value to him. Obviously, well hidden, and yet, somehow, he thinks Merrick will be able to steal it for him. Two things become crystal clear at this moment. My role in all this will be to aid in the search for this hidden thing. And now I know that he thinks whatever it is will lead him to someone. I'd bet my life that it's a woman. Up until now, he hasn't called in the favor from Merrick, but he's still made his presence felt amongst our little group. In the most bothersome ways possible, if you ask me. Like right now. In my dining room.

I sigh heavily. Resigned, I ask, "What, exactly, am I looking for?"

I watch his lips turn up in the ghost of a smile. "You're smart, Deacon. And blunt. I appreciate both." For a moment, he only stares down at his hands, but his mismatched eyes are suddenly a million miles away. After another minute, he lifts his gaze back to mine and says, "I'm looking for a box. A music box, to be exact. A very old music box."

Nose scrunching slightly, I say, "I'm guessing this old music box is either worth a shit ton of money or has some kinda sentimental value? Because otherwise, why the hell would you want some dusty old toy?"

"The toy is hardly dusty and is really only a means to an end. Another clue, leading me on what's been a lifelong goose chase."

What a fucking weirdo. Who on Earth would spend their life running after something, knowing there's a good chance they'd never find it? Pausing, I think back to Merrick's obsession with Amelia. He waited nine years. I guess the answer to that question would be ... a man in love. As if pulled by some invisible force, my eyes flick towards the hallway. When I bring them back, I find Alexi watching me closely.

"Can I trust you, Deacon?" he asks pointedly. What kind of questions is that? Of course not.

"I could ask you the same question, Fed," I say, arching a brow in response.

"Touché," he says. Taking a deep breath, he continues. "I want to help you, Deacon. Not just with this Gaspari problem, but also with the issue of your father."

Taken aback, I slowly sit my fork down before saying, "What do you know about my father?"

"Enough. Enough to know that he's not a good man. I can't say that I know what your endgame is for him, but if I can help you accomplish it while also keeping you out of prison, I'd like to."

My kneejerk reaction is *fuck no*. Cops of any kind can't be trusted. But just the mere mention of my father has my blood set to boiling. So, instead of dismissing the offer completely, I stare back at him pensively, hoping that my silence will make him uncomfortable. I feel a small measure of satisfaction with the idea. But instead of fidgeting, he just continues to look back at me, gaze unwavering. My emotions are conflicting with my brain. My brain is screaming that this is a setup, and if I get into business with this Fed, I'm gonna end up either dead or behind bars. But my gut is telling me that maybe he's just the ally I need. I want something; he wants something. It's nothing more than a business transaction. At least, that's what I tell myself. And, of course, I'd be careful. It's not like we'll ever be besties, but I have to admit I could use the help.

Going with my gut, I make up my mind before I have a chance to second-guess myself. I grab my fork again, loading another generous bite of my now cold waffle. Dammit. Around the food in my mouth, I point my fork at him and say, "Ok. Tell me more about this box."

I watch as that ghost of a smile from earlier reappears before turning into a full-blown grin. The sight causes a reaction that feels like the devil's running his tongue up my spine. I immediately regret asking the question. "Well … it's not so much a box as … an egg," he says, and there's a deliberate pause that I just somehow know is being done for dramatic effect. Unfortunately for me, I'm midway through another bite of waffle when the bomb drops. "A Faberge egg."

Choking for the second time in less than half an hour, I cough, desperately trying to get air into my lungs. All the while, the fucking Fed just laughs.

CHAPTER 26

Siren

"So, tell me, have you murdered Deacon yet?"

I smile out the window at my best friend's voice on the other end of the line and at her words. She knows me so well. Things with Deacon have become ... complicated, and while my gut instinct would be to tell her every little detail, some things feel too personal to share, even with Amelia. Secrets that aren't mine to tell. Things were more manageable when it was just sex. Maybe even better because it was no-strings-attached hate-sex. The kind that starts as an argument and ends in an orgasm. But being in such close proximity, I can't help but learn things about him that make me see him as an actual human being instead of simply a vibrator with legs. The more I learn, the more I empathize. The more I empathize, the less hate I feel, which has turned the hate-sex to real sex, and I'm bordering dangerously on like him. Like, *liking him*, liking him. Ugh, how inconvenient.

When I remember I'm on the phone and my friend has asked me a question, I say, "Not yet, but that could change at any time.

The man opens his mouth and my blood pressure goes up." So do my hormones, but I don't tell her that part.

Amelia's bubbly laughter filters through the burner phone I'm using, and I'm struck again by just how happy she sounds. Most women would be a crabby mess at nearly eight months pregnant, but in true Amelia fashion, she's taken everything in stride and is determined to make the most of every minute of pregnancy. Of course, it helps when you have a husband who's made devotion to you his entire personality.

"You say that but I notice a distinct lack of bite in your tone," she says.

Sighing heavily, I say, "The man is confusing. Wait, what am I saying? Of course, he's confusing. He's a *man!*"

"Usually it's the other way around though, isn't it? You're used to being the one doing the confusing on the poor intellectually challenged male species. Oh, how the tables have turned!"

"Don't gloat. It's very unattractive," I say, but I know she can hear the smile in my voice. Dropping my face into my free hand, I add, "Amelia, I don't think I can do this."

"Do what?" she asks.

"You know ... *feelings,*" I spit out the last word like it's an Atomic Fireball someone offered me disguised as bubble gum.

That laughter comes again before she says, "Wait, there are *feelings?* Like actual feelings? I thought it was just great sex?"

My words come out slightly muffled around the palm still partially covering my mouth. "It was ... I mean ... it is ... fuck, I don't know. Being stuck here with him, I've been forced to get to know him, and you'd think that would've made me wanna light him on fire, but instead, it ... hasn't." I pause while silence reigns on the other end of the line. "Sure, there are times that my hand itches to reach for the matches, but just when I think I've figured him out, he does something that puts me off balance. To be honest, I'm kinda terrified," I add.

Voice growing serious, she asks, "Why?" After a pause of her own, she adds in a low tone, "You know they're nothing alike."

I know she's referring to Dante, and I know the two men couldn't be further apart in every department. For once, that's not actually what scares me. "I know, and it's not that I'm afraid of him. I'm afraid of *me*. He doesn't know the details of my past; hell, no one does, really. Not even my best friend and I'm sorry for that. I have a lot of shame surrounding those years with Dante and I just wanted to forget everything that happened and try to move on with my life."

"First of all, don't apologize. You never asked for anything that happened to you with your words or actions. I believe that wholeheartedly because I know you. Secondly, I know you don't need me to tell you this because you already know, but if you really wanna pursue something with Deacon, you're gonna have to tell him everything. He needs to understand why you are the way you are. Because you have been and will probably continue to carry parts of that with you, maybe forever."

"What if he doesn't want anything to do with me afterward?" I whisper.

"If he runs, he's not worthy of you. If he stays, he'll be getting the better end of the deal. You still have so much beauty to offer the world. He should feel lucky to capture some of it in a bottle for himself."

I bite the end of my thumbnail before saying, "I wouldn't even know where to start. What would I even say to him?"

"I can't answer that for you, babe. I can't tell you what to say and what not to say when I, myself, don't know the ins and outs of everything that happened," she says with what I'm sure is a sad smile.

The rational part of my brain tells me I know what I have to do, it's just the execution of it that's making me feel like I'm going to jump out of my skin. Taking a deep breath, I open my mouth, allowing the nerves to exit along with my next sentence. "Can you talk to Merrick? See if you guys can come here?" I say before tacking on, "Alexi too. If I'm gonna tell this story, I'd like to only have to do it once, and you all deserve to know, considering we're all waist-high in my shit right now."

"Are you sure?" she asks, the concern evident in her tone.

"Not at all. But I'm gonna do it anyway. I'll work it out with Deacon if you can talk to the others?"

"I will, and I'll be with you every step of the way," she says.

"Okay. I'll give you a call later. And, Amelia? Thank you. I love you," I say past the lump that's formed in my throat.

"I love you too. Everything's gonna be fine, you'll see."

I nod even though she can't see me. Saying our goodbyes, we hang up. I drop the phone in my lap in favor of using both hands to cover my face now. Shit, am I really gonna do this?

A loud noise from the kitchen has my head jerking up. A clatter that sounds like pots and pans falling from an open cabinet echoes around the small house, and suddenly, I hear, "Woman, are we making spaghetti or what?"

I can't help smiling despite my anxiety. Yeah, I guess I am gonna do this.

"Go fish," I say over the top of the fan of playing cards in my hand. Deacon narrows his eyes at me from across the coffee table. From our current positions sitting on the floor on opposite sides of the living room's rustic centerpiece, the difference in height between us isn't quite as prominent. So the look of intimidation he's pointing in my direction right now isn't working nearly as well as he'd like. I arch an eyebrow at him, putting on the most serious face I can muster, considering I do have the seven he just asked for. Usually, my poker face can't be matched, but for some reason, the intensity with which he's playing a card game normally enjoyed by small children has my lips twitching with the urge to laugh.

"Are you sure you don't have any seven's?" He asks again, suspicion lacing his tone. After finishing a hearty dinner of spaghetti and slightly burnt garlic bread, made mostly by me because the man was a walking fire hazard in the kitchen, I expected him to retreat back into his man cave, leaving me to fend for myself again. So, I was surprised when he started loading the dishwasher without me saying anything. He further surprised me when he asked if I wanted to play cards afterward. We'd squabbled over what game to play but after a best two out of three rounds of rock, paper, scissors, I'd won and chosen a game based on the typical level of maturity for a man. Go Fish.

I pretend to check my hand again, eyes skating right over the seven staring me in the face. Meeting his gaze again, I say, "Positive."

His eyes narrow further, and at this point, he might as well close them because I'm convinced he can't even see me. He proves me wrong when he says, "You're lying. It's written all over your face."

My lips twitch again, betraying me. Even so, I say, "You don't know shit. Go. Fish," I draw out the last two words dangerously.

He watches me carefully, and I do my best not to break out into a sweat. The urge to laugh is clawing its way up my throat, and if he doesn't break soon and pull a card, I'm gonna lose this battle spectacularly. Seconds tick by until his posture finally relaxes and he reaches for a card from the deck between us. What a sucker. A wide grin breaks out onto my face in my purported victory at having won the battle of wills. His head jerks up, his face morphing from resignation at his impending loss to vindication. He points a finger in my direction. "You're cheating!" He yells a millisecond before lunging over the table at me. A shriek of laughter bursts from me, cards flying everywhere as I attempt to dodge him. I manage to wriggle away as he rummages through the cards I dropped until he finds the traitorous seven of clubs. Holding it up like a war prize, he points in my direction again. "You filthy little cheater."

"That's not mine. You planted that there. You're the criminal here, remember?" I reply as I scoot my butt across the floor, trying to get out of arm's reach.

He advances towards me on his knees, which if I'm honest, isn't a bad look for him. I'm momentarily distracted by inappropriate thoughts of other things he could do while on his knees when he makes his move. Throwing himself in my direction, I barely have time to scramble to my feet before he's wrapped an arm around my waist, hauling us both up, until I'm dangling a foot off the ground, legs kicking wildly back at him. The entire time, I'm laughing maniacally. As he flops back onto the sofa, taking me with him, I bounce on his lap, eliciting a groan from him. My laughter cuts off abruptly, assuming I've hurt him with my weight. I silently pray for his man bits as I grimace, turning my face back to issue an apology. The words dry up on my tongue when he takes hold of my hips, rocking himself into me. Well, clearly, his man bits are just fine. I feel the caress of warm breath as he gently blows my hair, which I pulled up in a high ponytail to the side. I lean back into him as he runs the tip of his nose up the back of my neck, inhaling deeply. Is he ... smelling me? The idea should make me wonder if he has serial killer tendencies, but instead, all I can do is shiver against him, wiggling my ass against the hard ridge now pressing into me.

Mouth close to my ear now, he says, "Stand up and turn around."

I do as he asks, turning to face him. The way he lounges back against the couch, legs spread wide, and hair disheveled from our earlier tussle, reminds me of a rake on the cover of those old bodice ripper novels. I stand awkwardly between his knees, unsure what he wants me to do.

He looks at me through hooded eyes that have darkened to an almost navy blue before using his hands to pat the cushions next to each of his hips. "I want your feet here."

Confused, I ask, "You ... want me to stand on the couch?"

He nods, gripping my hips again to steady and guide me as I step gingerly onto the sofa, placing my feet on either side of his hips. The position is awkward, and I feel off balance until he says, "Put your hands flat against the wall."

It's on the tip of my tongue to call him "officer" and make a joke about whether he's about to give me a strip search but when I glance down to see him slowly lick his lips like a half-starved animal, I think better of it and instead place my palms flat against the wall behind the couch without a word. The move causes me to lean slightly closer to him, and as he grips the waistband of my loose-fitting shorts, his intentions finally become clear. My breath hitches and I close my eyes, unsure if I even wanna watch what he's about to do. This position leaves zero to the imagination and virtually no room for modesty, meaning there's no way to hide anything from him. With my eyes pinched tightly shut, I can only feel my shorts as they're dragged down my legs. I hear a low growl come from him as he realizes that there is no underwear beneath. My eyes spring open at the sound. As the shorts stretch around my calves with the tension of my spread feet, he circles his hand around one ankle, urging me to lift a foot off the couch. I lift one leg, expecting him to simply remove the shorts. He does, but before I can put my foot back down beside his hip, he releases my ankle to reach into that pants pocket, pulling out his phone. Only then does he allow me to place my foot back on the couch. Maybe he thought I was gonna accidentally step on his phone?

I feel open and vulnerable, unsure of what he plans to do next. He leaves me in that state, mind running a marathon of thoughts, as he runs his hands up my bare calves, then the backs of my thighs, making a detour to palm the globes of my ass before coming to rest on my hips again. All the while, diamond blue eyes that have gone sharp enough to slice track the movements of his hands. The position he has me in isn't uncomfortable, but the unease I feel at my bare pussy being inches from his face, combined with the way he's looking at it, is enough to have my thighs trembling. He looks his fill, absently rubbing one thumb in small circles only centimeters above the very center of me.

Releasing one hip, he reaches down and picks up his phone again, unlocking it and opening the camera app. Wariness and insecurities battle the newly discovered instinct to trust him. To trust that he knows what he's doing, and that he won't hurt me. With his phone in his hand, I wait, expecting the clicking sound that would indicate he's taken some lewd photo of me. I don't know what it says about me that, at no point do I open my mouth to tell him to stop. Instead of taking a picture, he swipes the app over to video mode, turns it around and extends the phone to me.

"Take one hand off the wall and hold the phone," he commands. My hand shakes slightly as I take the phone from him. "When you're ready, press the record button. I want you to be able to relive this again later."

His words are like a zap of electricity running up my spine. I feel my body flush with heat, finally centering on the spot he's currently staring at like it's the last meal he's ever gonna get to eat. I aim the camera until it captures his face, then hit the little red button to begin recording. As I do, he returns his other hand to my hip, his fingertips digging into my skin, and he uses them to pull me forward. I try to keep the camera trained on his face, but anticipation and terror make for a poor director. He doesn't seem to mind. The phone seemingly all but forgotten, he leans in, running the tip of his nose up my slit, much like he did when sniffing the back of my neck. The move nearly has my knees threatening to buckle. Thankfully, his grip on my hips is firm, holding me in place for what's to come. I suck in a breath at the first touch of his tongue as he pushes through my wet heat and drags the pad of his tongue from my opening to my clit. Afterward, he licks his lips before curling that wicked tongue back into his mouth, making a show of swallowing my taste. Before I know it, he's jerking my hips forward and burying his face between my thighs. I have a split second where I can't help but think, is this really my life? Here I stand, naked from the waist down, spread-eagled over the lap of a god of a man, filming him as he eats me out. Then, I can't think at all as a loud moan escapes me, my head falling back before I remember that I'm supposed to be keeping aim with the camera. I look back at the phone screen just in time to catch his eyes as they flash up to meet mine through the lens. He runs his tongue up the length of me again, spreading the wetness that's practically leaking down my thighs before circling my clit. Over and over, he drags his tongue across the sensitive flesh until I'm trembling all over. One hand still braced against the wall above his head, I tilt my hips, aching for more. More friction, more pressure, just ... more. I struggle to maintain the camera's focus on the image of his face lapping at my pussy as my moans become higher in pitch and my breathing becomes more and more erratic. The need to come is like the need for air. At this moment, if I don't get it, I have no doubt that I'll die. Running the risk of losing my footing, I remove my hand from the wall, burying it in the hair at the back of Deacon's head. Gripping the sandy blonde locks in a tight fist, I apply pressure and urge him to give me what I need. With an animalistic growl, he latches onto my clit, sucking hard. A scream rips from my throat, and I drop the phone from my hand, adding it to the other that's holding onto Deacon's head for dear life as fire races through my blood and ignites. My legs finally give out from beneath me, and before the spasms have even subsided, Deacon is dragging me down onto his lap. I lean back as he rips the front of his pants down, freeing himself.

He fists his swollen cock, and runs the head along my slit, dragging it through the moisture that the combined orgasm and his mouth have created. In a guttural voice, lips still coated in my wetness, he says, "Ride me, brat. I wanna feel your pussy flutter around my cock with the aftershocks of your orgasm before I give you another."

I rise on my knees as he positions himself at my entrance. Hands braced on his shoulders, the head of his cock slowly pushes inside me. Riding the rush of euphoria, I grip his hips with my knees and slam myself down, taking all of him in one quick thrust.

"Fuck, woman!" he shouts, throwing his head back. He grips my hips hard, fingers biting into my flesh to hold me in place. Unlike any bruise given to me in the past, I relish the idea of waking up with Deacon's marks on me. Because, this time, I'm in control, and I want them. I watch the cords of his throat flex as he stares at the ceiling, breathing hard through clenched teeth. Playful Deacon is gone. This version is feral and slightly scary, but it's the type of fear you feel when playing with an animal you know is capable of biting you at any moment. Right now, I relish the idea of being eaten alive. When he finally tips his chin and his eyes come back to meet mine, that healthy dose of fear mixes with the excitement of knowing I'm about to get fucked, hard. Between one blink and the next, he's whipped my shirt over my head, tossing it to land God knows where. The next thing to go is my bra and I have a moment of unease at the idea. I've never been very comfortable in this position. Gravity and I haven't been on speaking terms for quite a long time. Why? Because she's a bitch. I don't have time to dwell on the insecurities of it, though, because Deacon has my bra off before I can even utter a single protest and already has his mouth on one breast while kneading the other. Sucking my nipple into the heat of his mouth, I let out a little yelp as his teeth bite down on the stiff peak. The pull of his mouth on my breast sends an echoing tug between my legs and the need to move on him is overwhelming. With a devious grin, because payback is a motherfucker, I tighten my inner muscles around him, eliciting the sexiest gasp I've ever heard a man make. High off the power he's giving me, I rise on my knees, gliding myself up the length of him until I'm poised with only the head of his cock inside me.

He releases my nipple with an audible *pop*, gaze meeting mine as he says, "You're playing a dangerous game, brat." His breathing is uneven and there's something in his eyes that borders on madness. I should be afraid, but I've never felt so alive.

I release his right shoulder to grip the front of his throat, leaning down to nip his bottom lip between my teeth before saying, "One I intend to win." With that, I drop back down onto him. He releases a curse that only intensifies the high that comes from being the one setting the pace here.

An incredulous laugh escapes him and he says, "Why is it that whenever you open your mouth, I either hear the Devil calling my name or angels singing? There is no in between." He presses forward, against the hand still clutching onto his throat, and rests his forehead against my collar bone. I can feel the sweat on his skin as it touches mine. In a strained voice, he says, "Siren, baby, I need you to *move*. Or I'm gonna do it for you."

He sounds close to cracking, and the pleading in his tone lights me up from the inside out. Taking pity on him, I begin to glide up and down, slowly at first, but it doesn't take long before I'm whipping my hips at a frantic pace. I'm chasing my own orgasm but I also feel the undeniable urge to reward him for all his hard work, no pun intended. Within the span of moments, the scene before me morphs. We're no longer combatants fighting for dominance. I wrap my arms around his neck, clutching him to me as he grips my hips, helping me rock back and forth. He leans in, capturing my lips with his, thrusting his tongue into my mouth, mimicking the movements of his cock inside me.

Against my lips, he murmurs, "Do you wanna come, brat?"

His words provoke an answering whimper quickly swallowed up by his mouth. As tension builds to a fever pitch, he reaches between us, running his thumb through my slick heat until he finds my clit. He circles the little bundle of nerves while simultaneously lifting his hips, thrusting upward. I tear my mouth from his as my body goes rigid, back bowing until it's only his grip on my hips that's keeping me from tumbling to the floor. There are no thoughts of how my body is on full display for him as my orgasm tears through me. He wraps his arms around my waist, further anchoring me to him and watches as I come apart. As his hips piston beneath me, he fucks me through my orgasm while chasing his own. His eyes remain on me for as long as possible, as if he can't stand the thought of looking away.

With shuddering breaths, he praises me and tells me how perfect I feel against him, how my body was made to take him, and how he wants to be the only man to ever see me like this. How he could watch me all day, and it would never be enough. Every breathless attestation prolongs my orgasm until I finally collapse against him, my lower body still jerking with every movement of his hips. Eventually, he tears his gaze from mine, scraping his

273

teeth down the side of my neck as he clutches me to him, letting out a groan that ends with a broken breath. I feel the pulse of his cock as it releases deep inside me. As the last bit of air leaves his lungs, he whispers, "Mine," against my skin.

CHAPTER 27

Deacon

Time passes. It could be minutes, or it could be hours. I'm starting to believe it doesn't even matter. When I'm with her, they seem to be one and the same. Most moments feel like a lifetime, and yet they're never long enough. If I'm not careful, I'm gonna turn into a total sap for this woman. As we sit on the couch, trying to catch our breath, the cold of the air-conditioning begins to chill my overheated skin. I feel Siren shiver against me from where she sits on my lap, knees still hugging my hips, and I know she feels the same. I hug her tighter against my chest. The way she's molded to me makes it feel like God designed her with me in mind. The more time I spend, whether it's watching her on the cameras or when I'm with her in person, the more my stomach churns at the idea of letting her go when this is all over. Up to this point, this has been the safest place for her. Despite our squabbling, I've never once regretted bringing her here. She's somehow woven herself seamlessly into the fabric of this house, my mind, and my life. But when Gaspari is finally dead, she'll be free. Free to go back home to her apartment and a life that doesn't include me. My chest tightens at the thought, and I war with the knowledge that my chosen life doesn't make a good foundation for a real relationship. I can't give her the 2.5 kids and white picket fence she deserves. Even if I wanted to, I don't think I'm cut out for that kind of life. She may be a hellion now, but I know she'll want those things someday. To settle down with someone and make a family and a home. A home that doesn't include a man with a tragic backstory, questionable sources of income, and even more questionable morals. I don't know how long we have left together in this house, but I intend to make the most of it. So I push all thoughts of my home devoid of her presence from my mind because the more I think about it, the more my chest hurts.

I quickly look around for my discarded phone, finding it lying at an angle against a throw pillow nearby. As I pick it up, I realize that it's actually still recording. My mind races at the thought that it may have captured some video of Siren tormenting me. At the very least, it still would've picked up the surrounding noises after she dropped it. As my finger hovers over the red button, I pause before stopping the video. On a whim, I turn it around to the front-facing camera and pull it back to capture the image of Siren resting against my chest. As I angle the camera towards her face, I realize she's fallen asleep. Something in the vicinity of where her cheek lies squeezes painfully. I sit there momentarily, staring at the reflection of her sleeping form. Her lips are slightly parted, and I can feel her warm breath dance over the tattoos on my chest. Her hair is wet with sweat and stuck to her forehead. The dark circles that were present under her eyes when she first got here are gone. Long dark lashes now lie in their place. Has any other woman ever looked so breathtaking? Drenched in sweat and snoring lightly, she ticks every box I didn't know I had. It's possible these boxes didn't even exist before she came around. I wouldn't put it past her to have created them without either of us knowing. Why do I get the feeling that those boxes will end up being the blueprint against which every other woman will be measured? A small voice inside whispers that they'll all be found lacking in comparison.

Pushing the thoughts away before I dwell myself into an early grave, I turn off the phone and gingerly stand, kicking off the loose-fitting pants that still hover around my ankles. I leave them behind as I carry Siren down the hall and into the bathroom. With my softening cock still inside her, I keep her lower half pressed tightly to my own, prolonging the connection for as long as I can. As we enter the bathroom, I reluctantly pull out of her and sit her down on the counter. The marble must be cold because she startles awake with an audible hissing sound. As she lifts her head to look at me with sleepy eyes, she almost appears ... innocent. When we first met, I never thought she could have an innocent side. Now, I know better. She may not put her vulnerabilities on full display for the world, but I've seen them because sometimes she lets down her guard enough to show me, and other times, without her consent, via a video monitor. In moments like this, when she's half asleep, her default settings of combative and apprehensive are turned off. As she looks at me with lowered lids, there's only trust staring back at me. I'm not sure I deserve it or if she's even aware it's there, but I don't question it. I take it while I can get it.

"Stay there. I'm gonna turn on the shower," I tell her. After making sure she's alert enough not to fall over, I turn and start the water, waiting until it's nice and warm before helping her down off the counter and to her feet. I move to pull us into the shower, but I turn back when I feel a resistant tug on my hand. She gnaws her bottom lip as she glances anywhere but at me. Eyes narrowing, I jerk her hand, catching her off guard, and she stumbles into me. Cupping her ass, I lift her up again, forcing her to wrap her legs around my waist. Whether she likes it or not, we need to get clean. We're both sweaty, and in this position, I can feel the slick residue of my come as it leaks out of her. The knowledge that there's something of me still lingering inside her causes my cock to stir, which only reinforces my determination to bathe us both and stave off the clawing need I already feel to fuck her again. Careful not to slip and end up having to make another call to Theo, I maneuver us into the shower, lowering her back down to her feet. Her stiff posture tells me how uncomfortable she is. No matter the fact that we've been together several times, and despite everything I've done to convince her to the contrary, my gut instinct tells me she'll always feel some level of unease when it comes to being fully naked in front of me. Which is why I had her take that video in the first place. We may have used my phone, but that was only because it was more readily available. With as many cameras as I have in this house, I have plenty of footage for my spank bank. No, that video was for her to keep. I'll send it to her phone later so she can rewatch it when she's alone. Or, at least, when she *thinks* she's alone. I want her to be able to see what she does to me, what her body does to me. So she knows she's not just some time filler but instead something of an obsession at this point. In the beginning, it was a bit of a game. She was beautiful and bitchy, and the combination appears to be my kryptonite because, even after I got her into bed, I couldn't stop thinking about her. That hyper-fixation only intensified when I got the call from Merrick that she was missing. From that moment, it was no longer a game. It became sleepless nights and too much coffee: anxiety and anger. Where was she? What was being done to her? Who the fuck thought they had the right to take something that was mine? There's that word again. *Mine.* Growling it against her skin while pumping my come deep inside her was one thing. The heat of the moment and all that. But thinking it while in control of all my mental faculties is something else. As I roll the word around in my head, I must admit that it doesn't sound ... wrong. I still don't know what this is but I do know one thing. I don't want it to end. If I'm honest with myself, I don't want her to leave. As a terminal bachelor who never allowed people into his space, I can't imagine my house devoid of her energy now. I don't think I want to. It's selfish of me because I know this winding road can only lead to a dead end. Determination makes me want to stay in the car forever, but I know that's impossible.

I keep my thoughts to myself as I step up behind her, leaning down to rest my chin on her shoulder. She tilts her head, and looks at me quizzically. My palms itch with the desire to run my hands all over her. To soap her up and stay here for as long as it takes to watch each bubble pop. But I also don't want to push her further than she's comfortable with. I guess I'll have to find creative ways to navigate around her resistance so she won't realize I'm systematically breaking down those barriers until after all her walls have crumbled to the ground. With a small sigh, I say, "Let's make a deal. I'll wash your hair and you can do the rest."

She thinks about it for a second, but I feel her acquiesce before she even opens her mouth to respond. I don't think she fully realizes how expressive her face and body language are. With my chin on her shoulder, I can feel them relax. Her arms drop to her sides from where I know she was using the fidgeting of her hands as an excuse to hold her arms up in front of herself. It's gonna take time and effort to get her to the point that she can trust that I mean what I say when I tell her that her body is perfect. The effort, I don't mind giving. But time isn't exactly on our side. The best I can hope for is to do everything possible to convince her with the amount of time we have. The faster we find Gaspari and put him in the fucking ground, the sooner she'll be gone. Emotions war with each other as I debate the merits of letting the bastard live longer so that I'll have an excuse to keep her here. But I want her to make the conscious decision to stay. I don't want to trap her here with me, creating another prison for her, albeit one with a nicer guard. Besides, every second that Gaspari is allowed to breathe fresh air is a second too long. Although … there was some merit to the idea of keeping him alive to hurt him the way he hurt her. To torture him, slicing open his skin and watching the blood drain from his body, so that he could feel what she felt. Death by a thousand cuts, right? But no, as cathartic as that might be, he doesn't deserve to inhabit the same planet as her.

As thoughts run riot in my head, I silently reach up for the bottle of shampoo that sits on the little built-in shelf. It's not mine but one I had brought from her apartment. As much as I like the idea of her walking around smelling like me, I recognize the scent as soon as I pop the cap. The familiar hints of coffee and chocolate invade my nose, and it's a smell that has become synonymous with this woman. She has the same brand and scent in soap form and I remember the first night we were together, the way it made her skin taste under my tongue had me practically drooling. Or maybe that was just her. Either way, I can't smell a cappuccino or eat anything with chocolate in it without my cock twitching in my pants. The way this woman affects me is both inconvenient and entirely necessary to my well-being.

I squirt what's probably too much shampoo into my palm while she reaches up and takes down a bottle of her shower gel. As I lather her hair, massaging my fingers gently into her scalp, she adds a generous dollop of the soap to a loofa, running it across her skin unhurriedly. My eyes track the movement of the sponge, and it's not until she turns her head to face me that I realize my hands have stopped moving in her hair.

Clearing my throat so that my voice doesn't come out as a pitiful squeak, I say, "Sorry. Got distracted." Seemingly against my will, I lean down until my nose is about an inch away from the skin of her neck. "Fuck, you smell good enough to eat."

Laughing, she says, "You did that already, remember?"

"And if we don't hurry up and get out of this shower, I'm gonna do it all over again," I warn.

She shakes her head, but I notice her movements are considerably slower as she turns back around and resumes her task. Gripping the sides of her waist, I press my hardening cock against her lush ass. The contact elicits a growl from me and a little gasp from her before she laughs again, though even that comes out slightly breathy. "Okay, okay," she says, speeding up the motions of her hands. After she finishes rinsing the shampoo from her hair, I add the conditioner. As she rinses that too, I watch eagerly as the soap slides down her body along with it. Shaking my head to clear it, I quickly grab my body wash, lathering it up and giving myself a cursory scrub down. She still has her back to me, but as I wash the soap away beneath the shower head's spray at the opposite end, I catch her looking back at me over her shoulder. If looks were physical touches, hers would cause enough friction to make me spontaneously combust. I either need to get the hell out of this shower or I'm gonna have her pinned against the tiles within the next 30 seconds. I'm just about to reach over and turn off the stream of water when Siren turns fully around to face me. The move catches me off guard, but not nearly as much as what she does next.

Gnawing on her bottom lip, she steps towards me, coming just shy of our bodies brushing. For a moment, I think she's going to lean up to kiss me, but instead, she keeps her eyes on mine as she slowly lowers herself to her knees on the heated tiles. My lungs immediately seize up, and I wonder if my brain is leaking out of my ears because all rational thought has fled. The image of Siren staring up at me from her knees with a look of supplication is better than any gem, painting, or artifact that's ever passed through my hands and, somehow, infinitely more valuable.

She places her hands tentatively on the base of my thighs, before slowly running them up until her short nails are tracing the V shape at the cut of my hips. Without any other provocation, my cock jumps as though she's already got her hands on it. At the movement, her eyes drop down and she stares at it, subconsciously licking her lips. Did the temperature of the water just get hotter because I have the sudden overwhelming urge to pass out?

Bracing a steadying hand on the tiles, I try to get a grip on myself. Which, of course, just makes me think of her getting a grip on *me*, and then there goes the temperature again. As she continues to stare, it pulses, a bead of pre-cum appearing on the tip as it begs for attention.

Opening her pretty pink lips, she asks, "Can I taste you?"

My immediate response is, "Does a bear shit in the woods?" It's probably not the most eloquent thing I've ever said, but coherent conversation is difficult when your only working brain cells have traveled down the drain along with your woman's favorite soap.

"God, you're such a man," she says. I don't know what that means exactly, but she doesn't give me time to dwell on it as she leans forward, using her tongue to dab at the pearlescent bead of liquid. I watch as she takes the drop into her mouth, rolling it around on her tongue thoughtfully before swallowing me down. "Could use a little seasoning," she says, a smile playing at the corners of her mouth.

I bark out a laugh, throwing my forearm up to cover my eyes. "Jesus, woman. You do wonders for my ego, you know tha–...". The rest of my sentence trails off on a moan when I feel her lips wrap around the head of my cock. Dropping my arm, I look down just in time to see one hand trail from my hip, wrapping around the base of my dick to hold it steady as she slides her lips further down, taking more of me into her mouth. With every movement of her lips, I lose a year off of my life. I'm pretty sure I may die before this blow job is over. Slapping my other palm against the glass of the shower door, I brace myself for what's to come. As she finds a rhythm, I watch her lips slide up and down my length, and I can feel the glide of her tongue on the underside of my cock, running over the semen inside, already trying to climb its way up. If she's not careful, I'm going to end up coming down her throat.

Bringing one hand down, I run my fingers through the wet strands of her midnight hair and say in a bemused tone, "Sometimes I wonder if I made you up in my head." Her eyes flash up to mine, and with her full lips still wrapped around me, I'm more convinced than ever that she's some figment of my imagination. Something that could only be created in my mind because this type of perfection shouldn't exist. But as her hand tightens around me and begins to pump up and down in time with the movements of her mouth, I'm reminded that she is real. She's real and she's here in front of me, looking up at me like I hung the stars while she's the one making me see them. As her mouth and hand picks up speed, the little fingernails of her other hand dig into my hip as if to hold me in place. My hand tightens in her hair and unconsciously, my hips buck, thrusting my cock deeper into her mouth. As if on cue, she pulls her head back, avoiding the contact that would've had her gagging around the base of my erection before setting back in to continue my torment. I'm so close to coming, and I entertain the sick thought of not telling her so I can catch her off guard, forcing her to take every drop.

Before I can follow through on that thought, I grip her hair in a tight fist, effectively stilling her motions. "You have to stop, Siren. If you don't, I'm either gonna come in your mouth or make a mess of you."

Eyes narrowing as if in challenge, she fights the hold of my hand, regardless of the pain it must be causing her. Tightening her lips around me, she sucks hard, stroking me furiously with her hand. With an involuntary yell, my hips jerk, and I shoot wave after wave of hot come into her waiting mouth. As if hellbent on wringing every last drop from me, she sucks me as deep as she can until I feel myself hitting the back of her throat. Still, she doesn't gag, breathing through her nose as she swallows down everything I have to give her. With a final shudder, I pull her head back, and she reluctantly releases me from her mouth. My legs are shaky and if it wasn't for my other palm still propping me up against the tiles, I have no doubt that I'd simply fall over. Releasing her hair, I reach back, turning off the water that's already started to run cool. After taking a minute to get my bearings, I hold out my hand, urging her to stand. Pulling her to her feet, I look down at her red knees and then back up to her face. She stares back at me with a look of smug satisfaction.

I pull us both from the shower, wrapping a towel around her and then myself. I take her hand again, and lead her down the hall to the bedroom. Next to the bed, I remove my towel and use it to dry most of the excess water from her hair before tossing it to the floor. Her towel is the next to go and before she can utter a protest, I pull back the comforter, pick her up by the waist, and toss her in the bed. She lets out an indignant squeak but still scooches over to the other side to make space for me. Climbing in after her, I pull the blanket over us as I pull her back into my chest.

"I'm not sleeping on that damn couch anymore," I say close to her ear.

"Okay," she says quietly.

"Well, that was easy. I thought you'd put up more of a fight," I say.

She's silent for a moment before she says, in a voice that indicates she's already bordering on sleep, "Seems only logical to have you here if I'm already thinking about you when I'm in it alone."

Stunned, I lie there, taking in the scent of her wet hair on my pillow until long after her breathing evens out and the only light in the room comes from the night sky streaming in through the open curtain. Something changed tonight, and whether she wants to acknowledge it or not, there's no going back to the way it was before. I don't think I'd want to even if I could.

After about two hours of laying next to Siren and still unable to fall asleep, I give up the fight and ease myself out of bed. I feel restless. Too many thoughts and emotions swirling around my head. Siren, Gaspari, Alexi's not-so-old-and-dusty trinket, and of course ... my father. I pull the blanket up over Siren and tiptoe from the room, grabbing a pair of boxer briefs and workout shorts on my way out. Easing the door closed behind me, I head for the kitchen and the coffee maker. I feel drained and exhausted, like I could sleep, but my mind just won't shut off. I need the caffeine if I'm gonna be able to read even one sentence of the numerous emails and text messages I've intercepted to and from my father. So far, he's been careful, making no mention of his little murder plot in his regular correspondence, but I honestly didn't expect any different. He's nowhere near my level of criminal, but he's not a total idiot either. Despite my extensive digging, I've yet to come up with anything I can actually use. Sure, he does a lot of shady shit but what politician doesn't? I need something big, and I know this murder-for-hire scheme is it. Could I save myself all this hassle and just have him killed? Sure. Could I just do it myself? Absolutely. I'd relish the task. But death is too good for him—too quick and not enough suffering. Call me petty but I want him brought down from his current lofty stature to less than nothing. Even that's more than he deserves. Not only for what he did to my mother and me but because the world would be a better place without him holding even a tiny amount of power or influence.

As I stand in the kitchen waiting for the coffee to brew, I swear to God, I'm having an existential crisis, simply staring off into space at nothing. At the machine's telltale hissing that indicates it's finished, I have to blink hard several times to refocus my vision. I pull down a random mug from the cabinet, filling it with coffee and make my way to what I've affectionately dubbed "The Vault". To myself of course, considering no one knows about it besides Merrick and I. Well, and now, Siren. Merrick thought it was cliché, but then I reminded him that most people in our world knew him as The Black Knight. That shut him up real quick. Replaying the conversation in my head makes me smile a little. Our friendship wasn't without its complications, but I'd trust him with my life, and I know he'd say the same about me. We met at a crucial point in both our timelines, when we had nothing and no one else to rely on. I became that person for him, and he became that person for me. As I bypass the security measures to enter the vault, I hesitate when closing the door behind me. My gut is telling me to leave it open, that I can trust Siren with my secrets at this point, but there's still the pesky problem of me spying on her at all hours of the day and night. If I have that monitor up when she decides to walk in, I will lose all control of my bodily functions. Not keen on the idea of shitting myself, I push the door closed, ignoring the little stab of guilt that the action invokes.

For the next several hours, I work in silence, the only sound in the room coming from the quiet hum of the servers behind me and the constant clicking of either my keyboard or mouse. I've combed through so much information that I'm going cross-eyed. I rub my hands over my tired face, cognizant of the fact that I haven't shaved in several days and I've grown quite a bit of scruff. Thank God I wasn't one of those blondes whose beard hairs grow in nearly white. I was lucky enough for my beard to be several shades darker than my actual hair color, so I didn't mind letting it grow out every now and then. Dismissing the notion of proper grooming for now, I sip my coffee even though it's long since gone cold and stare at the screen in front of me. I nearly drop the cup into my lap when my phone suddenly buzzes on the desk beside me. I roll my eyes as I look at the caller ID and the contact I've not-so-affectionately programmed in as "Stranger Danger" but I answer nonetheless, putting the call on speaker before sitting my phone back on the desk.

"Rude of you to call me at such an ungodly hour, you know," I say by way of greeting.

I can practically hear the little uptick of his lips when he says, "It's not like you were asleep."

Eyes narrowing, I reply, "And how would you know that? Aren't most people asleep at 4 a.m.?"

"You're not most people. I also *might* be monitoring your internet activity."

"Is that even legal? If you wanted to get to know me, we could've just gone on a date or something. You'd pay, obviously," I say.

He lets out a chuckle. "Do you really want to lecture me on legalities when you're digging through your father's life with a fine-tooth comb?"

I roll my eyes again. The fact that he's somehow gained access to my system doesn't surprise me anymore. It grates, but doesn't surprise me. I make a mental note to shore up my firewalls and other areas that need to be checked for leaks but he's right. People in glass houses shouldn't throw stones or in this case a boulder, which I'd much prefer.

"Fine, you win this round. I'm assuming you bothered me for a reason?" A thought suddenly occurs to me. "Also, isn't 4 a.m. a little past your bedtime??"

Silence reigns for a few seconds before he says, "I don't sleep much. And yes, I did call for a reason. I think I found the smoking gun you've been looking for."

My spine straightens and even though bringing my face closer to the phone won't change anything, I lean in anyway. "What smoking gun??"

"What's the magic word?" He taunts, and the urge to throat punch another human being has never been so strong.

"Fuckface?" I reply sarcastically.

The chuckle comes again. "Let's save the face fucking for at least our third date, da?" At the growl that emanates from my throat, he continues, "Alright, I'll put you out of your misery, even though it's much more entertaining for me when I piss you off. So ... it would seem that the heir to the Hawkins name has a penchant for random ... what do you call it? Hook-up apps? Fake profiles, of course, with the sole intention of one night-stands and the occasional date rape." His voice hardens considerably on the last few words. From the information I've gathered on him and the knowledge that he used to work in the sex crimes unit, it's no wonder that he finds that type of behavior appalling. Continuing, he says, "To access these apps, he purchases *a lot* of burner phones. He pays cash, but the idiot signed his real name when rejecting the optional device warranties. I had a contact of mine create a fully functioning fake dating app from scratch, essentially a honeytrap that allows me full access to the phone as soon as the app is downloaded. Let's just say the trap was very sticky."

The fact that my half-brother is a piece of shit is no surprise. I've never made any effort to reach out to either of my half-siblings, and I don't ever plan to. If what Alexi is saying is true, it just reinforces the notion that I don't wanna be within 100 yards of my slightly younger bro. While the information is good to know, I don't see how it connects to my father. It would be a scandal but not something a good team of PR people couldn't bury. "Okay, but how does that help me with my problem? You know that's not gonna be enough."

"Patience is a virtue, Deacon," he says, followed quickly by, "And if you keep rolling your eyes at me, you know they'll get stuck that way."

My head jerks around the room, looking this way and that, because I did indeed just roll my eyes again. Is he surveilling me even now? Or have I just become that predictable? Or, worse yet, is he just that adept at learning and memorizing mannerisms and which buttons to push to get which reaction? I don't think I like either of those possibilities, actually. I'm on the verge of cursing him out when he starts talking again, and his tone swaps from taunting and sardonic to all business so quickly it nearly gives me whiplash.

"Well, it appears that the Senator thought it more prudent to use one of his son's already existing burners than to get a new one of his own. It must've gotten mixed up with the others because Jr. reused it after," he says, and I can actually feel my heartbeat pick up speed. I wait ... not patiently ... but still. After another second or two, he says, "I have nearly everything. Emails and texts from your father to the hitman, as well as wire transfer information for what I can only assume is a down payment for the job because the amount sent wouldn't get you a five day vacation at Disney World, much less the guarantee of a dead body."

I jump to my feet, causing the chair to roll backward, bouncing off a nearby table. Running my hands through my hair, I barely suppress the instinct to yell my excitement to the rafters. My elation is short-lived, however, when my mind replays the first sentence of that last bit. I put my palms flat on the desk, leaning down to get closer to the phone again as I ask, "What do you mean, *nearly* everything?"

A heavy sigh comes through the speaker. "I have everything you need to burn his world to the ground, but every bit of information I've gathered is a one-way street. I still don't know who the man behind the mask is or when it's going to happen. That wasn't your father's choice, but his. Apparently, that's how this man operates. If I don't know who he is, I can't prevent Cole Sykes' death. Granted, Sykes is nearly as crooked as your father, but he belongs in prison for his crimes, not in the ground."

Fuck. Frustration bubbles in my gut, climbing up my chest like heartburn. I don't necessarily want the man to die either, but his survival has never been my primary goal. Can I live with him being collateral damage? Can I also live with the knowledge that there's a hired killer still out there, waiting to take his next job? I honestly don't know.

With a sigh of my own, I say, "Bring the phone with you when you guys come. And listen ... thanks, man. I'm sure you've spent more time on this than you would've liked. I appreciate the help." Even though I mean it, the praise still burns my throat, and I'm starting to wonder if I'm actually developing acid reflux.

"Deacon, are you flirting with me?" he asks, effectively ending any sense of obligation I felt to be nice to him.

"Get fucked, Fed."

In a dry tone, he says, "Maybe on our fourth date, but only if *you* pay."

A groan of exasperation escapes me, and just before I hit the red button to disconnect the call, his deep chuckle echoes in my ear, mocking me.

CHAPTER 28

Siren

The ridiculous contrast between Deacon's car and his dirt road driveway only adds to the lightening of my mood. One that began to perk up significantly as soon as the car doors shut, closing us both inside. The sun is shining and the air coming in through the open windows is warm without being sweltering, which is rare in this part of the south. It took a lot of browbeating and even more sexual favors to convince Deacon to take me out, but as loose gravel gives way to the smooth pavement of the main road heading to Savannah, I know it was worth it. He did return the favors which technically makes us even, but I didn't point that out. After weeks of being cooped up in the house, I think we both need this. It did take a lot of convincing, including reminding him that Savannah is a heavily populated little area and that the likelihood of Dante or any of his men spotting us is unlikely, but he eventually relented. Since the day I played for him, something between us has shifted. He still cloisters himself away for long periods of time, doing his "research," but he's begun spending equal amounts of time outside of his cave with me.

Doing mundane things like watching TV, playing board games, and even gardening. Well, he chops wood or works around the yard while I garden. I never thought I'd be the type to wanna stick my hands in the dirt, but you'd be surprised what hobbies you can come to enjoy when you have limited choices. Deacon's taken me out few times in a little boat that he keeps by the river near the house. We've definitely come a long way from the days of him being so overprotective that stepping out onto the porch would start a full-blown argument. The small home and its surrounding swampy landscape have somehow shifted in my mind from feeling claustrophobic to almost ... quaint. In our isolation, Deacon and I have found a routine of sorts. He finally broke down and ordered proper groceries instead of relying on daily deliveries of take-out or the occasional drop off of a meal's worth of food at a time. I loved Chinese food as much as the next person, but if I had to eat one more carton of lo-mein, I'd barf. The now-cleaned and fully-stocked fridge has prompted me to teach him how to cook. Despite that first meal he cooked for me when I got here, I've been convinced that the man could burn water. In actuality, he's proven to be a surprisingly fast learner. Maybe it's because of our newfound relaxation with each other that he finally broke down and agreed to take a day trip to Savannah.

As we make our way down a two-lane highway bordered by dense trees on both sides, Deacon punches the gas pedal, propelling us forward at a speed that would probably scare the shit out of most people. I wasn't like most people. Letting loose a laugh, I tilt my head toward the open window, letting the wind whip through my hair as the sun warms my face. Eyes closed, I smile and release a sigh that seems to take weeks' worth of stress along with it. What's left afterward is a feeling of relaxation and blind trust that Deacon isn't gonna get us killed. That, too, is new. Somehow, over the course of these last few weeks, I've come to believe that when Deacon speaks, the majority of what he says is true. Sure, he bullshits a lot and his sarcasm is off the charts, but I can't pinpoint one instance when I've caught him in a lie. Is he careful with his words? Yes. Is he an expert at evasion? Definitely. But openly lying to my face? No, not from what I can tell. Like I said, we've come a long way. I know there are still things he's keeping to himself, but considering I'm doing the same, I can't really judge him. After talking to Amelia on the phone a week or so ago, I've now boxed myself into telling the group about my history with Dante. She, Merrick, and even Alexi are coming over in two days to discuss the situation. After talking it over with Deacon to ensure he wouldn't flip his wig over the security issues, we decided it was best just to have them come over and get it out of the way. I only wanted to have to tell this story once. If I'm honest with myself, the prospect is terrifying. I don't know how my friends will look at me once they know the full extent of our relationship and that it was my own poor choices that landed me there. After the decision was made, I think Deacon could tell that I was more high-strung than ever, and that could also be a contributing factor that prompted our little outing today.

Once I can see spots from the bright sunlight staining the inside of my closed eyelids, I pull my head away from the window and sink back into the plush seat. Tilting my face to the left, I catch Deacon watching me between glances at the road. He's slowed back down and we've reached a speed that won't rack up a thousand dollars in tickets with even the nicest state trooper on the planet. At this speed, I don't really mind how often he takes his eyes off the road to look at me. Every time I see him glance over from my peripheral vision, my stomach does a little summersault, which is absolutely ridiculous. I'm not a teenager, for God's sake. Still, I can't help the small smile that tugs at the corner of my lips, and it isn't until I see his hand reach up, brushing his thumb over the little quirk, that I realize he's noticed. I can feel my face flush, which apparently is also evident to him.

"Don't go shy on me now, brat," he says.

"Oh, shut up," I retort, though the smile has only tripled in size.

My sass causes a grin of his own to break out, and then we drive in companionable silence. At one point, his hand lifts again, and I expect him to be going for the radio, but, instead, he reaches over, slipping his hand beneath my own, where it's been resting on my left thigh. Palm up, he threads his fingers through mine, squeezing once before relaxing into the hold. It's firm but not tight, and if that isn't the perfect metaphor for our relationship, I don't know what it is. Since I've been with him, I've discovered many things about Deacon. While some are endearing, others have the ability to bring me to a near-homicidal rage. But when it comes to how he treats me, he's like the handhold. Possessive but not oppressive, protective but not domineering, and somehow constant without being pestering. It's an intoxicating combination and one that I've never experienced before. If I'm not careful, I could become attached to him in a way that isn't healthy for a woman with a history of believing the flapping of red flags and butterflies feel the same. If madness is making the same mistake repeatedly and expecting a different outcome, I can't afford to be committed. I've never looked good in white. And yet ... I leave my hand where it is, even curling my fingers around his. I'm clearly a glutton for punishment.

Before I know it, we're entering the city limits, and traffic slows to a pace unique to the south. It's not because there are too many cars on the road or because of people rubbernecking the scene of some fender-bender, but because time and life, for that matter, are just unhurried here. The copious amount of pedestrians doesn't help, though I've seen my fair share of sightseers living in downtown Charleston. While many people would make comparisons between the two cities, each has its own unique charm. Looking through the eyes of a tourist, I'd see a city full of rich history, elegant restaurants, quaint shops, and beautiful parks. Late-night ghost tours, trolley rides, and riverboat dining. With my hand still resting comfortably in Deacon's, I take in my surroundings as we make our way further into the heart of the city. Wondering where Deacon is taking us or whether he even thought to make a plan, I open my mouth to ask just that when the car pulls to a stop alongside a curb directly across from Forsyth Park. The famous white fountain shines like a beacon beneath the midday sun. Deacon finally releases my hand, and almost reflexively, my fingers curl into my palm as if they miss the feel of him.

Turning the car off, he looks over and says, "You wanna walk a little?"

"You're gonna park your car on the street?" I ask, my brows practically rising to the ceiling.

With a deadpan face, he says, "If someone spits within a half block of my car, I'll know about it."

Laughing, I shake my head and follow his lead as he exits the car. Just as he rounds the hood to meet me on the sidewalk, a group of adolescent boys walk by, practically drooling as they point and take pictures of the car with their cellphones.

Without breaking stride, Deacon points at the boys and says, "Don't even fucking think about it. If I come back to your ass print on the hood of my car..."

They take the threat good-naturedly and laugh, making jokes about how much ass he must pull with a car like that before they realize we're together. One of the boys let out a low whistle in my direction, and I blow him a kiss with my middle finger, which just makes them laugh harder. As Deacon reaches my side, he retakes my hand; for whatever reason, it doesn't feel awkward, weird, forced. It feels comfortable and natural. We walk towards the fountain, passing by couples huddled together on wooden benches, families having picnics in the grass, and the countless tourists taking pictures with everything ranging from a cellphone to thousands of dollars worth of camera equipment. While I'm observing them, Deacon's splitting his focus between watching me and eyeballing every person within a half-mile radius, as though he's just waiting for someone to step out from behind a tree and take a shot at us, I can't blame him. Nerves jitter inside me at the mere prospect of running into one of Dante's goons. But soon, the soothing sounds of the water and the chittering of squirrels begging for peanuts, distract me from the threat of imminent danger. That feeling that I've carried around since I was 16, the one that feels like a ball of lead-lined fear, lightens slightly, and I allow myself a little while to just live in the moment and enjoy it. As we pass people, some tip their chins in an age-old greeting that's just another thing unique to the South. We nod back, and with our fingers intertwined, it's so easy to believe that we're just another couple out to enjoy the sunny day and fresh air. I soak in the idea, and my gut reaction is to scoff, but then … I don't. Instead, I entertain the idea of what we'd be like if we were that couple. Then I realize, it would probably feel something like this. Well, minus the impending sense of doom.

The park is crowded today, which is no surprise. Forsyth Park is probably one of the biggest tourist attractions in Savannah. A large two-tiered fountain, modeled after the famous *Fontaine des Mers* in Paris, sits as the park's focal point. Adding to the feeling of refined southern charm are paths lined with large oak trees, their branches heavy with Spanish moss. We pass vendors selling everything from hot dogs to beignets. The smell of fried sweet dough piled high with powdered sugar is generally thought to be more at home in places like New Orleans, but any true Savannahian will tell you that many things about the city mirror that of the Big Easy that have been not only adopted but changed to reflect the individual personality only found in Georgia. They might be famous for their peaches, but Savannah took old-world southern charm to a new level. We reach the park's large white centerpiece, and Deacon allows me to pull him over to one of the unoccupied benches facing the waterfall. As we sit, our hands disconnect and I curl mine into my lap to distract from the way it tingles at the loss of his touch. At the thought, I involuntarily make a sour face because isn't that the dumbest thing that's ever crossed my mind. I don't realize that Deacon is watching me until he lets out a low chuckle.

"I'm not even sure I wanna know what you're thinking," he says, but I can tell by his voice that he's suppressing another laugh.

"No, you don't," I say, adding, "Silly girl thoughts."

He feigns a look around the park, overly exaggerating the movements of his head as it turns this way and that before saying, "I don't see any silly girls. In fact, I only see one girl."

I gaze out over the surrounding area myself, noting a good number of women, several of which are very attractive. "You must be blind because there are girls everywh–" My words trail off when I look back to find him staring down at me, a crooked grin tipping up the corner of his mouth. For a second, I'm caught by the way the sunlight hits his face, making the blue of his eyes sparkle. The suspended moment is broken when a laugh suddenly bursts from me. I start several times to say, "Is this how you pick up women?" but I can't get the whole sentence out without laughing so hard that I double over, clutching my stomach. When the giggles fully subside, I look up to find him watching me with a curious expression. "What?" I ask after I've finally caught my breath.

"It's gonna be my sole mission in life now, to make you laugh like that all the time," He says. His voice is playful, but his eyes are serious. We sit like that for a while, just people-watching and enjoying the warm sun. After a few minutes, he says quietly, "I used to come here as a kid when I should've been in school or while my mother was working. She was a maid brought in to clean up after parties thrown by many of Charleston's more prominent families. After I was born, that all changed. She couldn't get work anywhere, and we ended up moving to Savannah, where she cleaned rooms at a hotel not far from here. When she was working, I'd come here and sit, watching people drop coins in the fountain and make wishes, and all I could think was, why did they waste their money? Didn't they know how many people out there could use that change?" I sit quietly, practically holding my breath, afraid that if I remind him I'm here, it'll break whatever trance he's slipped into, and he'll stop talking. "The more I sat here, the more I realized that they made wishes instead of helping others because people are selfish. Why give away a quarter when a little magic could grant you a million more? But fountains and wishing wells are just like birthday candles or shooting stars. Wishes don't come true, and most of us are left without any quarters or magic."

His words are cynical, and knowing what little I did about his early life, it's no wonder he feels that way. But his comment about shooting stars pulls at a memory buried in my consciousness. The shooting star figurine in his living room. In his mother's letter, she talked about stars. Was the figurine hers? The handful of change on his mantle makes sense now, too. Before I have a chance to respond to his words, he stands, leaving me to look on after him as he walks over to a man sitting on a bench opposite us. There's a shopping cart beside the bench, piled high with bags and odd items. The man is dirty and looks tired. As Deacon approaches, the man's face turns wary, as if expecting some kind of attack. Reaching into his pocket, Deacon removes what looks like a hundred-dollar bill, handing it to the man. I can't hear exactly what the man says to him, but I don't need to. I can see his face. Deacon walks back toward me, taking my hand again and pulling me to my feet. He steers me closer to the fountain as he digs into his pants pocket again with the other hand. As we reach the railing, he pulls out a shiny quarter. Surprised, I look up at him. With sad eyes, he lifts the hand still clutching mine, turns it over, and places the quarter into my open palm. "You deserve to be a little selfish," he says. He curls my fist closed, gesturing towards the fountain. "Make a wish. Just in case."

I look from him to the fountain, then down at my closed fist. I open my hand slowly and stare down at the quarter. He waits patiently for me to toss it in, but I stare at it for a long moment before shaking my head. Without a word, I turn and walk over to the man on the bench, handing him the quarter. He doesn't say anything but, again, I don't need to hear it. The look on his face is the same. I walk back over to Deacon, who's staring at me with an intensity that would alarm most people. Again, I'm not most people.

This time, it's me that latches onto his hand before asking, "Where to next?"

His hand tightens around mine almost imperceptibly before he leads us around the fountain and down another path exiting onto Bull Street. As we leave the park behind, the number of tourists drops drastically, leaving more room for other sounds to come through now. A few blocks away, jazz music can be heard pouring out into the street from one of the many restaurants or lounges in the area, but, by contrast, it's quiet enough now to also hear the calling of birds or the sound of a housekeeper beating the dust off of an area rug that's slung over the porch railing of one of the many large townhouses nearby. It's such a beautiful day, and I find I'm lucky that Deacon has a good grip on my hand because more than once, I nearly trip over a crack in the sidewalk or face plant into a parking meter, too busy looking up at the large oak branches and the way the sun filters through the dripping moss. I can only blame the distraction when, in my lack of awareness, I take two full steps past Deacon when he abruptly stops on the sidewalk. My momentum, combined with the grip on his hand, lightly jerks me back. Of course, he takes full advantage of my loss of equilibrium, using the force to spin me towards him and into his chest. I brace for impact with my hands on his chest, and he steadies me with strong hands gripping my hips. He bends slightly and for a moment, I think he's about to kiss me. Our mouths are only an inch apart now and I can feel the warmth of his breath across my lips. My eyes slide closed, and I wait, lips parted, my heart kicking against my ribs, not from fear, but from adrenaline. A rush that I'm coming to recognize is unique only to moments with him. After a second or two, when I realize nothing is happening, my eyes snap open to find him just where he was before, only now there's a sparkle in his eyes that says he knows exactly what he's doing.

I clear my throat before I speak, but my voice still comes out as a husky rasp. "Why'd you stop? I wouldn't complain if you wanted to feel me up, but maybe we should wait until we get back home," I say, and almost as soon as the last word leaves my mouth, I wanna take it back. It's his home, not *ours*. Why did I say that?

If he catches my blunder, he doesn't say anything. Instead, he lifts a hand, using his index finger on the side of my chin to turn my face to the right. It takes me a second to realize what I'm looking at. When I do, I let out a squeal unbecoming of a proper Southern lady, jumping up and down excitedly. I turn back to face Deacon, finding him smiling down at me, pearly whites on full display. With his hair down and the ends catching in the breeze, he looks more relaxed than I've ever seen him.

Returning the smile, I say, "You brought us here on purpose? How did you know?" The "here" in question is Mercer Williams House, featured in one of my favorite movies, Midnight in the Garden of Good and Evil. Even knowing that the movie was filmed in Savannah, the now infamous house owned by Kevin

Spacey's character is a place I've always wanted to visit but never got around to. Did he know that? For all his computer skills, I don't think something like that would've come up in a background check.

He shrugs nonchalantly. "Know what?" he asks, but that smile still lingers. I glare at him, but there's no heat behind it. "Do you wanna go inside?" he asks.

Glancing between him and the house, I hesitate. "Ummm ... I don't think we can. Unless you're planning on breaking in? Though, isn't that Merrick's forte?" I arch an eyebrow at him.

"You'd be surprised what crimes you don't have to commit when you can just pay the right people," he replies, adding, "Besides, it's a museum now, so it's open to the public."

I'm pulling him towards the entrance before he's even finished speaking. He laughs but allows me to drag him inside. Throughout the tour, he appears to be interested in everything I excitedly point out. By the time we leave, dusk is setting in, and the gaslit lamps lining the streets are already on.

Ever vigilant, he says, "We should be getting back. There's less visibility at night." Meaning it's not so easy to see the people around us and any potential danger lurking behind every corner. I nod and we make our way back to where his car is, thankfully, still parked and in one piece. I sink into the passenger's seat and close my door just in time to see him lean down and inspect the hood as he rounds the car to get in behind the wheel. He doesn't appear murderous, so I'm guessing there wasn't an ass print in sight.

Just before he starts the car, I turn to him and say, "Thank you for today." Then, because I don't want to make the moment awkward for either of us, I turn my head to look out the window as he starts the engine, and we speed off for home.

There's that word again. *Home.*

CHAPTER 29

Siren

"We're gonna have to go out again," Deacon says as he exits his man cave and enters the living room.

I look up from the book I've been reading, some old bodice ripper novel I found, and I can't help but wonder if it's something that, like I suspect so many other things in this house, belonged to his mother. It's endearing how little touches of her are all over his house. As someone who's experienced very few examples of true love, I can only go based on my limited knowledge and what I've observed from others around me. It's led me to the belief that there are many different types of love and, based on that assumption, there are infinite ways of expressing that love. Some are pure and innocent, like a child's love for a parent. Some are toxic and unhealthy, like the emotions I felt for Dante. But, there are also some that are complex and can't be defined by any terms in the English language, instead refusing to be shrunk down to fit a specific mold. From what I've observed, love is both messy *and* euphoric because you can't have one without the other, or how would you be able to recognize either? Finding the balance between the two was where you found real love. Deacon keeping items belonging to his late mother and making them a part of his everyday life proves that he loved her very much, despite her problems and the circumstances that I think surrounded the end of her life. I think the love he has for his mother falls into that third category.

Sitting the book upside down in my lap so I don't lose my place, I say, "We? And where are *we* going?"

He sits in the chair beside the couch, elbows resting on his knees. "Yes, *we*. Do you really think I'm gonna leave you here alone?" he asks with a raised brow. I narrow my eyes in mock suspicion.

"Why? You afraid I'll burn the house down?"

He snorts. "No, I'm more afraid you'll *clean*." He scrunches up his nose, his facial expression and tone as he says the word "clean" making it seem like he finds the prospect abhorrent.

I give him a deadpan stare, but I can't really argue, considering that I vacuumed yesterday and cleaned out a microwave that had basically built its own ecosystem out of leftover food particles. "At some point, you'll either have to call in a cleaning crew or just bulldoze the house and start fresh. You know that, right?" I'm being extra dramatic with that last part, but even I know that the first suggestion is nearly as outlandish. He confirms that theory as soon as he opens his mouth.

"First of all, no. No cleaning crew is coming in here. I can count on one hand the number of people that've been in this house, and I'd like to keep it that way." I try really hard to squash the little flutter in my belly at that. Meanwhile, he continues, "Secondly, it's not that bad. I know how to mop and stuff. I can do it myself."

I arch an eyebrow at him because bullshit. I mean, I guess the fact that I didn't die of fright when I looked at the underside of the toilet seat implies that he does indeed do at least the bare minimum of cleaning. That didn't make the house clean. Besides, what else was I supposed to do with my free time when *all* my time was now free? I can't get on social media, and my only link to the outside world is phone calls with my very pregnant best friend, she has her hands full preparing not only herself but her husband for a new baby because, apparently, having a child is a scarier prospect than breaking into the Louvre. Amelia didn't need me calling and chewing her ear off because I was dying of boredom in this house. Okay, there I go again, being dramatic. I wasn't actually dying. If anything, I'd become somewhat compla-cent in my new environment, to such an extent that it doesn't feel new anymore. I won't say no to another excursion, but I definitely didn't expect it to be so soon.

Intrigued by the prospect of going out again, I let the cleaning thing go and instead ask, "So, you gonna tell me where we're going or not?"

"I have a job. Merrick isn't the only thief I fence things for, you know. Given the current circumstances, I would put it off, but the client is a long-standing one, and what I have is payment for a favor that was done a while back. If I don't deliver, it'll cause problems in the future," he says.

I check the book I was reading to memorize the page number before setting it beside me, then scooch to the edge of the couch and say, "Okay, when do we leave?" My sudden eagerness elicits a laugh from him.

With a shake of his head, he stands up. "Be ready in an hour," he says before retreating back into his cave. Just before I hear the whoosh of the door, he yells, "And I *mean* an hour! You don't need to primp!" I sit there for a second, marveling at the man's ability to compliment me somehow while also chastising me. I'm gonna ignore the second connotation and instead believe that he means that I don't need makeup or my hair done to look good.

Still, I jump up from my sitting position on the edge of the couch and rush down the hall to change my clothes. Pulling on a pair of well-worn skinny jeans and an oversized t-shirt sporting a picture of a violin and the words, "I don't make mistakes when playing, only spontaneous creative decisions." I slip on a pair of sneakers, just in case we have to make a run for it. The man is a criminal after all. I do my hair up in a quick French braid because I don't care what the newest generation of influencers say; the French braid is still the tits. Running into the bathroom, I throw on some foundation and mascara, which I definitely do *not* consider "primping." I do have a moment when I wonder why I'm even putting in this much effort when I'll probably end up sitting in the damn car the whole time. I imagine being closed up in Deacon's car because, of course, he'd lock me in while he makes some shady deal in the alley behind a seedy bar or something. I wave that thought away like a gnat in front of my face. No fucking way am I staying in the car. If he doesn't want me going out into the alley with him, then he can park me at the bar, and I'll do tequila shots with the bartender until he's done. Hell, maybe I'd even test that possessive streak I've seen hints of by pretending that my primping *is* for the bartender. As I double-check my hair in the mirror, I can't help but make a note of the space on the bathroom counter that Deacon cleared off to allow room for my makeup bag and skincare products. My toothbrush sits alongside his in the holder and my hairbrush has distinctive blonde strands in it. I don't need these little reminders that we're basically cohabitating at this point, though. Funny enough, for all my blustering about being bored and wanting to get away from this house, my thoughts of actually leaving have become fewer and fewer over these last weeks. Not because the prospect seems so unrealistic right now but because every time I try to envision returning to my quiet apartment, my stomach knots up, and I feel a little sick. I try to push those thoughts away whenever they creep up, but it's difficult when that one gnat turns into a swarm of gnats. I combat the swarm by telling myself that whatever's going to happen will happen when it happens while a little voice inside my head quietly whispers a prayer that it doesn't.

Pointing at my reflection in the mirror, I say quietly, "You are not falling in love with this man." My face is stern but my tone sounds unsure, even to my own ears. With a shake of my head, because I know I'd look insane if anyone could hear this, I exit the bathroom. I rush back out to the living room, through the dining room, kitchen, and laundry room. Pressing the button on the security panel that I now know works like an intercom system, I yell into the small speaker, "I'm ready!"

Less than a second later, a series of beeps sound, and the wall slides open. Deacon stands there, a funny look on his face. Bemusement? What does bemusement even look like? As if snapping out of some kind of trance, he says, "It's literally been 15 minutes. There's no way you're ready to go before me."

I hold my arms out wide and do a little spin as I say, "And here, I bet you thought I was high maintenance. You don't know m—." My last word is cut off as I complete the spin, only to suddenly have Deacon backing me up against the washing machine. Reaching around, he palms my ass with both hands and buries his face in my neck, giving me little kisses and teasing licks against my skin that have my entire body shivering.

"I swear to God, I'm gonna give up coffee and opt for just sniffing your neck every morning," he says, his voice muffled against my skin. And with that, I might as well just melt into a puddle because the crazy version of me just telling herself off in the mirror seems to have left the building entirely. Instead, I tilt my head, allowing him better access. As his lips make their way up my neck, one hand grips my ass while the other coasts up the opposite side of my body. As he passes my jaw, the tips of his fingers brush the back of my neck near the hairline just as his mouth hovers over mine. My head tips back, my eyes slide closed, and my lips part, our breaths mingling. I wait for a beat, quite possibly the one that poets often talk about getting skipped. Wait for the feeling of his mouth on mine but my eyes pop open when the hand that was just at the base of my neck suddenly gives my braid a firm tug. As soon as my eyes clash with his, he slams his mouth down, swallowing my gasp of surprise. *Thump.* There it is, making itself known with the power of not only the missed one but the one after. From there, horses gallop in my chest. He doesn't touch me anywhere else except the hand on my ass and the one now using my braid as a leash to guide my head this way and that, the different angles allowing him to deepen the kiss and I swear to God, the man is trying to suck my soul from my body. It might very well be working.

He eventually pulls away with a tug on my bottom lip, the suction from his mouth evoking the need for me to follow him. My mouth tries to do just that, but the grip on the end of my hair stops me, and he releases my lip with a slow *pop*. We're both breathing heavily as we break apart, and he looks down at me with eyes that have darkened to cobalt. If I didn't know any better, I'd swear entire galaxies swirled in those eyes.

"If we don't stop, we're never gonna make it out of this house. Hell, we might not even make it out of this laundry room. Have you ever been fucked against a Kenmore before?" As my lust-clouded brain tries to process what he's just said, he wiggles his eyebrows at me, adding, "Spoiler alert, there is no gentle cycle." He knows he's being ridiculous, and yet, somehow, he still finds a way to make it hot. Out of the two, however, ridiculous wins out because I immediately burst out laughing. He grins at me, then just before turning to lead the way out of the laundry room, he *winks*. This fucker knows precisely what he's doing. And I'm falling for it, hook, line, and sinker. I shake my head in astonishment but follow him nonetheless.

It doesn't take long before we're in the car and on our way. When we start to head east on the interstate, I think that the meeting must be in Charleston. Despite it being my hometown, my hands suddenly grow clammy, and the galloping horse is back in my chest, only now for an entirely different reason. There hasn't been any significant progress on locating Dante that I know of but even so, the irrational part of my brain whispers that he's taking me home and dropping me back off in my dark, cold apartment. Clammy turns to sweaty as drops of perspiration bead my upper lip and forehead despite the air conditioner going full blast. I might be on the verge of having an anxiety attack, but why? I don't know. Am I afraid of being alone? I never used to be, but even if I was, I don't think that's the reason I don't wanna go back. Trying to get myself under control, I reach up to tuck a small piece of hair that's escaped my braid behind my ear. When I realize my hand is shaking, I quickly lower it into my lap. Without warning, a hand reaches across the middle console, sliding under mine, linking our fingers together like before. Without thought, I grip his hand like a lifeline, even though I know he can feel the tremors. I don't look at him out of the twisted notion that avoiding eye contact will somehow minimize my embarrassment.

"Hey," he says, his tone gentle but firm. I still won't meet his gaze but nod slightly to indicate that I'm listening. Without warning, our speed decreases, and the car swerves into the emergency lane. The *thump thump thump* of the tires as they roll over the hazard lines mimics the sound of my heartbeat in my ears. As the car comes to a stop, he reaches over the steering wheel with the opposite hand, putting it in park. Gentle pressure from the hand interlocked with my own steadily increases until I finally lift my gaze. Immediately, he releases the extra pressure, but not my hand. Looking at me with concerned eyes clouded with confusion, he tilts his head, studying my face, before glancing out the front windshield at the large green sign in the distance, indicating the distance to Charleston. A look of revelation takes hold and he looks back at me, simply saying, "You stay with me. Where I go, you go. Understand?"

No, I don't. I don't understand any of this. Whatever this is, I didn't plan on it. I didn't want it. Now, I'm afraid that I won't know how to function without it, and that feeling is terrifying. It literally feels like we were fighting five minutes ago, and now I'm having an anxiety attack at the thought of not being stuck at his stupid house. My mind is telling me that this isn't normal, but that stupid horse in my chest is just running wild, refusing to be tamed. His words have the desired effect, though. My breathing slows, and so does my heart rate; the ringing in my ears no longer drowns out the sound of everything else around me. As I look down, I realize I've got a death grip on his hand, the knuckles on both turning white. I make a conscious effort to loosen my hold, but he doesn't take the reprieve for what it is and let go. Instead, he rubs gentle circles with the thumb of the hand still tangled with my own.

"Good?" he asks, angling his head to catch my eye.

I nod. "Good." He looks at me for another second or two, then gives a satisfied nod, again reaching over with the opposite hand to put the car back into gear. He navigates us back onto the highway with one hand on the wheel and the other still clutching mine. I still have no idea where we're going, but the trip seems like a good metaphor for my life—seemingly stuck somewhere between my past and present, unsure of the final destination. But he's here and holding my hand, so I let go of the reins.

CHAPTER 30

Deacon

As we near our destination, a thought occurs to me. I don't think I've ever held a woman's hand before, not like this. To lead her to bed or on a dancefloor, maybe. Never just sitting in a car while driving down the highway. I try to picture doing it in other scenarios with other women; in each one, the image of the woman begins hazy before slowly morphing into midnight hair and chocolate eyes. The body type of the mystery woman is wrong, too, at first. Too tall, too thin, too ... not *her*. I can't shake the feeling that she's ruined me for all other women. Not just with her body, but also with her mind, her wit, and her mouth. I watched her in the bathroom while she was getting ready earlier. I heard what she said. At first, I was sure I'd heard wrong. But after rewinding the feed and playing it back about 47 times, I'm convinced that what I heard was correct. She's falling for me. It's clear that she's trying to fight it, and I'm not entirely sure what I've done to nurture those feelings, but they're there regardless. I thought that hearing that word from a woman's mouth when directed at me would make me run for the hills. But each of those

47 times I replayed that line coming out of her mouth, the words stoked something in me that I know I've never felt before. I think it's possible that there's been a bed of lit coals inside me since the night we met. It flared to a small flame the first time we slept together, lying dormant while she was missing but never truly extinguished. The only thing it took for that fire to light again was the two of us being forced into a living situation that neither of us expected. Since the minute she stepped foot in my house, she's become a fixture there, and that fire has only grown until now. The sound of that word coming out of her mouth in the bathroom mirror was the equivalent of pouring gasoline on that flame. I don't need to ask myself if I want her to fall in love with me because I already know the answer. Yes, I do. Will the fire rage so hot that we eventually burn out? I don't know, but I do know that I wanna find out. I can't stop my hand from giving hers a little squeeze at the thought. It's an involuntary reaction but one that I'm coming to recognize as my mind and body latching onto her. To ensure she's here, that she stays here, and that she's real. The gentle pressure I get in return only adds more fuel to that growing fire.

"We're almost there," I say, tipping my head at the sign indicating the exit I intend to get off at.

She looks at the sign and sits up straighter in her seat. "We're going to Beaufort?" she asks, and the excitement is back in her voice. I much prefer that to the fear I heard earlier.

Grinning, I say, "Yep. We're meeting my contact at the Beaufort History Museum."

Her head whips around to face me, surprise making her eyebrows nearly reach her hairline. The face makes me laugh, and it's clear that she assumed we'd be meeting the person at some backwater hellhole. I think living in my house in the middle of wooded swamp land has given her the wrong impression of what kind of criminal I actually am.

"What exactly are we dropping off? And why the museum? Shouldn't it be closed at this time of night? Oh my God, you're not actually gonna try and rob the place, right? I mean, isn't that Merrick's job?" she says.

Laughing again, I say, "Calm down, brat. I'm not robbing the place. I know my area of expertise, and that definitely isn't one of them. As for the rest, you'll have to wait and see."

"You mean you aren't gonna try to lock me in the car?"

"This car has very little trunk space and I wouldn't trust you with the rest of it alone," I say jokingly.

With a grin, she says, "Good. That's smart. Maybe you're not as dense as you look."

"I have my moments," I reply.

As we coast down the streets of downtown Beaufort, I marvel again at how little recognition cities like this get. Beaufort is very similar to Charleston or Savannah because it is another picturesque waterfront city, rich in history and culture. The large Gullah population lends to the already extensive repertoire of local artists calling Beaufort home. Nestled in the heart of the low country, the city aids in the escape from the stress and worries that come with the more densely populated areas of the South. As we round a corner and the museum comes into view, I have to shake my head ruefully at another perfect example of how Southerners have the ability to turn what was arguably our history's most bloody battle into a tourist attraction. The Beaufort Museum wasn't always here to educate the next generation about the perils of secession and how nearby Parris Island was the

Spanish's first major settlement, even before Plymouth. In fact, the museum initially used to house volunteer artillery following the Revolutionary War. Built in 1798, the building now housed several exhibits dedicated to the abundant history of the area and how it played a much larger role in the course of US history. I'd taken tours several times over the years but the majority of the information my brain now housed on this building wasn't because I was a bit of a history buff, though you'd be surprised what someone who was would pay for historical relics. Once a criminal, always a criminal, I guess.

We drive two blocks past the museum, pulling into a parking garage just as my phone chirps in my pocket. I take it out and read the text on the screen before turning to Siren. "We're gonna walk from here, just as a precaution. I've set all the security feeds within and around the museum to loop until we're back home. No one should see us coming or going, but my contact isn't too worried about it anyway. She said to go to the back entrance."

"Wait ... she? Your contact is a woman?" she asks, and if I'm not mistaken, there's a hint of green in her tone. Suspicion thinly veiled by nonchalance.

I lean over the middle console and give her a quick peck on the lips because her scowl is just so fucking cute. "Yes, it's a woman. I will answer all of your questions soon. We're on a clock. We've gotta go." With that, I get out of the car, leaving her looking slightly bewildered in the passenger's seat. The delay only lasts the span of a few seconds before she swings open the door and slams her way out. I wince and issue a silent apology to my poor, abused car. I know what kind of woman I'm dealing with, so I should've expected that type of reaction. Maybe that's exactly why I did it. Knowing she's jealous gives me a sick kind of satisfaction, considering that the mere idea of her with anyone else makes me wanna commit homicide. As she nears, I reach out and grab her hand again. I'm encouraged when she settles into step beside me instead of pulling away. Maybe she isn't plotting my downfall the way her RBF would allude to. We walk hand-in-hand the two short blocks to The Arsenal.

As we approach the back door, it swings open to reveal a woman dressed in a tan button-down blouse and a dark brown pencil skirt. I cock my head in curiosity. I happen to know that this particular woman is more suited to black, and her favorite accessory used to be a lock picking set. The attire choice is interesting, matching the blonde hair that's been pulled up into an elegant updo. The nearly platinum, threaded with streaks of gold, isn't her natural color, which can just be seen coming through at the roots, but it compliments her honey-toned skin and almond-shaped eyes.

We stop a few feet away from the woman, and I can feel Siren fidgeting beside me. I use the grip on her hand to tug her closer and say, "Siren, this is Isadora Harper. Former thief and tomb raider extraordinaire. Isadora, this is Siren, my ... person." Okay, so nobody ever accused me of being the quickest, but it was on the tip of my tongue to say "girlfriend," and we haven't had that conversation yet, so I don't wanna get maimed. Though, considering the narrowing of Siren's eyes at the classification of "person," I think maybe I should've just taken the chance on embarrassing myself. It would've bruised my ego if she'd contradicted me, but it would probably hurt less than the retribution her eyes promise now.

Siren releases my hand and steps forward first, extending her hand to the other woman. They shake and I nearly breathe a sigh of relief, thinking things might be okay until Siren opens her mouth and says, "So, you're literally Dora the Explorer?" I have to bite my top lip to keep from cracking up.

Isadora arches a sculpted brow and looks down her nose at Siren through the wire rimmed glasses perched on her nose. "Gosh, I've never heard that one before." Both women continue to stare at each other, the handshake no longer shaking but just holding, and I pray they aren't doing that thing that guys do when they're trying to intimidate each other by strangling the other person's fingers.

A sudden burst of laughter splits the night air as both women dissolve into giggles. Their postures relax and they finally break the handshake, Siren stepping back to my side. Isadora looks at me and says, "She's a bitchy one. I like her." Siren gives me a shit-eating grin, and I just shake my head because I will never understand how the female brain works. Isadora steps back to let us in, and we follow her inside. Walking down a long hallway, I realize we're near the restoration room. I recognize the layout from the blueprints and hacking the security feeds. As she leads the way, she says to Siren, "I think what Deacon meant to say was that I'm an archeologist that just so happens to be a reformed thief. I specialize in Egyptian antiquities. Speaking of...?" she says as she uses a keycard to enter an airlocked room. One that's filled with historical artifacts, though not my bread and butter. The door closes behind us, and she turns to me. "Do you have it?" Her eyes, which are hard to see behind her glasses but I know to be the most unusual mixture of honey and moss, are alight with excitement, and she's practically bouncing in her three inch stilettos.

I take pity on her before she breaks an ankle and reach into my pocket, pulling out a brown drawstring pouch. I hand it over, trying not to laugh at how gently she takes the bag, even though I can tell every muscle in her body wants to snatch it away from me. She walks quickly over to a table nearby, places the bag down, and opens the top. Siren and I follow her over and her excitement must be rubbing off because Siren is now hip to hip with her, leaning over to see what's in the bag. Isadora reaches inside and pulls out something small wrapped in a tan piece of cloth. I don't have to tell her to be careful. She knows what she's doing. She handles the unfolding of the cloth just as carefully as the contents because she knows the cloth is just as old. With each new layer unfolded, the women's heads get progressively closer to the item. The moment of truth finally arriving, Isadora unfolds the final piece, revealing ... a bug. A solid gold bug, but still a bug. The heart scarab dates back to the Middle Kingdom and is worth exponentially more than its weight in gold. All business now, Isadora slides on a pair of gloves before picking the scarab up to examine it. Turning it over in her palm, she looks at the etchings on the bottom, tilting it to allow Siren to see while she explains its history in rapid fire. Isadora was a funny thief. I likened her to the Egyptian version of Robin Hood. Except she stole from the rich to give back to the land of her ancestors what was rightfully theirs.

As I glance around the room at some other pieces positioned on the surrounding tables and stands, I ask, "So, what are you doing in a museum in Beaufort, South Carolina?"

She looks up from her position, hunched over the beetle, and her glasses have slid down to the end of her nose. She uses one finger to push them back up before saying, "I'm the new curator here. I also might be hiding out."

"You're curating for The Beaufort History Museum??" I ask incredulously. That bit is way more surprising than the fact that she's hiding out from someone. That's just one of the perils of our lines of work.

"Listen, it's a stepping stone, okay? I'm trying to go legit, and it's difficult to do when the field you studied happens to enable your tendency to steal." Siren snorts out a laugh at that, shrugging and making a face that conveys a very "makes perfect sense to me" attitude. Isadora gives her a grin, and if it weren't for their vast differences in appearance and heritage, you'd swear they were sisters conspiring against the world.

"So, should I even ask who you're hiding out from?" I say.

She shakes her head, a piece of wavy blonde hair escaping her bun. She lets it dangle, which isn't surprising. I'm sure she's used to it by now. The mass of dyed blonde waves usually escape whatever messy ponytail she's attempted to pull them up in. "Nope. You don't wanna know. Let's just say, I can't go home at the moment." Home being Cairo.

"But you'll let me know if you get into trouble and need help?" I ask, glancing at Siren in the event her mood switches and she suddenly decides to claw my face off. She doesn't. She gives Isadora a worried look before glancing at me.

The Egyptian princess shakes her head again, more blonde strands flying. "I definitely will *not*. I can handle myself."

I roll my eyes, and am just about to open my mouth to argue when Siren cuts me off. "She'll call me instead. You know, chick support is better than guy support, anyway. Men don't know how to give advice for shit." That elicits a laugh from Isadora, and she gladly takes out her phone to program in Siren's number, giving her own in trade. I stay silent but shake my head. *Women.*

The newly minted curator finishes up with the scarab, wrapping it back up and tucking it away inside a brown leather bag that she slings over her shoulder. We follow her out, and once she locks the back door to the museum behind us, she turns to me. Holding out her hand, she says, "We're square. Thanks, Deacon. It means a lot." I shake her hand with a nod. Turning to Siren, she holds out a fist for her to bump. She does.

Grinning, I take Siren's hand and pull her away as she puts her fingers to her ears in the universal signal for "call me". Just before we round the corner, she calls out, "It was nice meeting you, Dora!"

We make our way back to the car at a much slower pace than the one we took on the way in. Soaking in the night air, I breathe deep. Or as deep as you can do in some of the most ridiculously humid weather in the United States. Looking down at Siren, I say, "Wanna walk a little?"

She nods. "Sure."

Tucking her into my side, we bypass the parking garage and walk a ways in the opposite direction. We'll make our way back eventually, but I'm not in a hurry. Tomorrow's gonna be a tough day for her. Merrick, Amelia, and Alexi will be at the house tomorrow night, and I have a feeling that whatever Siren is gonna say will turn my world upside down in one way or another. For now, I just wanna be a couple, out on a late-night stroll around the city. We don't need to think about tomorrow. We can pretend it's just the two of us beneath a blanket of stars tonight.

CHAPTER 31

Siren

I clutch tightly to Amelia's hand as we exit the bedroom. Maybe it's just my imagination, but the hallway leading from the bedroom to the living room has never seemed so long before. From here, trekking the distance seems daunting. I know it's only because I dread what waits at the other end. My truth. Like an episode of Scooby Doo, the gang's all gathered tonight to discuss … me. Or, more accurately, the issue of Dante's whereabouts, and why he took me in the first place. Well, to them, this was the first place. To me, the second. But they don't know that, and the time's finally come for me to tell someone my deepest, darkest secret. That at one time, I was not only capable of murder but was convinced I'd actually committed one. Surprisingly, living with that knowledge was easier than you'd think. Easier than remembering all the things that came before it, anyway. And definitely easier than the idea that someone would eventually find out what I did. Now, the time's come when I need to actually put a voice to the actions of my past.

Releasing a shaky breath, my footsteps halt. Beside me, Amelia stops, too, turning to look at me with pitiful eyes. The emerald green of my best friend's gaze glitters with unshed tears, the water only lending to the multifaceted color. I hate seeing pity in her face, but I brace myself for the eventuality that it's only going to get worse.

"I don't know if I can do this," I whisper.

Amelia takes my other hand in hers, and turns me so that we're face-to-face. "You can. You're the strongest person I've ever met. You survived, and the retelling of it will never be as scary as living it over and over in your head every day." The conviction in her voice and the unwavering confidence she has in me cements my resolve. I straighten my spine and give her one firm nod of my head, but I still hold tight to one of her hands as we take the remaining steps down the hall and enter the living room. As we walk in, all heads turn towards us, and it's as if I'm back on stage, standing in front of a large crowd, about to play a song that I don't really want to play, but I know I have to because they want it and I know it like the back of my hand. The three men take up so much space in the small living room, bringing the walls in and making the air thick. I don't realize how long I've been standing in the same spot, focusing on breathing until Amelia gently squeezes my hand. Looking at her, she nods and finally releases my hand to sit next to her husband who's perched on one end of the sofa. Alexi sits in the armchair beside the couple stoically. His lack of emotion is actually helpful in this instance. As much as I appreciate my best friend's sympathy and support, enough emotions are playing bumper cars inside me already. The less that I have to deal with externally, the better. As I survey the room at large, I realize that Deacon is the only one not sitting, instead choosing to stand between me and the others. My romantic side whispers that it's because he needs to be closer to me. His hands are in the pockets of his worn jeans, and at first glance, his stance would appear casual, but I know better. He radiates aggression, and if I'm not mistaken, there's a trace of apprehension when my gaze meets his. He knows whatever I'm about to divulge is gonna be bad, and he's already spoiling for a fight. Despite my anxiety over the situation, I feel the sudden urge to go over and calm him. To soothe his worry and assure him that everything will be okay. But I can't because it won't. Right now, the only person having to live with the knowledge of what happened to me is me. Once I give voice to the nightmares I endured, everyone else in this room will have to live with them, too. I don't want that for them; these friends have somehow become more than friends. But I'm a firm believer in the philosophy that you can't know where you're going if you don't know where you've been. So, in order to move forward and finally put an end to this, everyone has to be on the same page, with the same knowledge. As I look into Deacon's eyes, I hope mine aren't projecting everything I'm feeling right now. I don't want him to see that I'm terrified that, after he hears everything Dante did to me, he won't look at me the same way. He won't want me anymore. Because I can't be sure that my eyes aren't giving me away, I tear my gaze from his as I walk over to sit in the only other empty chair in the room. The story, if told in its entirety, will be long, so I guess I should make myself comfortable. I keep my gaze trained on the floor, focusing on a small piece of frayed fabric on the area rug as I start at the beginning of what will be a turbulent tale.

"I was 16 when I met Dante. He came backstage after one of my concerts. He was charming, and flattering and I was ... starved for affection. So when he asked to take me to dinner, I said yes. It didn't matter that he was much older or that I was underage. I thought I was in love, and as many of the great love stories can confirm, that trumps everything, including the age of consent. In the beginning, things were wonderful. He took me to parties, dinners, and dancing. We traveled, and he made me feel beautiful." My voice drops to a whisper before I add, "I'd never felt beautiful before." I pause to draw in a deep breath before continuing. "The decline started small. Little comments here and there about how much I ate, how absent my parents were, and how often I was on my own. He took advantage of the fact that I didn't have anyone keeping tabs on me while at the same time, using it to further isolate me. He weaponized my loneliness. Over time, he made me think the only person in the world that loved me, could ever love me, was him. The process was so gradual that I didn't realize what he was doing until I was already living with him. By that time, it was too late. I was already a prisoner, held by an invisible leash. One made of insecurities and fear, and each link in the chain was stronger than the last. I couldn't wear what I wanted, I couldn't go out, I couldn't talk to my family or my friends." My eyes flit to Amelia's and my bottom lip trembles. "I wanted so badly to call you, but so much time had passed that I was afraid you wouldn't recognize my voice. I didn't. I didn't know who I was anymore." A tear slips down her cheek, one to mirror my own. "Then I no longer had the option to call anyone. That's when the real pain began. There had always been punishments for bad behavior. If he thought I'd looked at another man at a party, whether I had or not, I didn't get to eat for a day." Releasing a small, humorless laugh, I add, "He said I could afford to miss a meal or two." I shake my head ruefully. "After a while, the punishments morphed from stolen liberties to actual pain. A belt, a piece of cord ... a razor." I close my eyes as the memories flood me. "Every time he'd cut me, he'd tell me how much he loved me. He'd remind me that he was the only one in the world who cared about me; if I loved him, I'd wear his marks proudly. His brand on me, each one, meant to teach me a lesson. To behave, to not try to get away, to be what he needed me to be. Property. Subservient. Eventually, I did become what he wanted. But he still kept hurting me. Sometimes, it was just physical punishment but, sometimes, it was more. My first time was with a belt looped around my neck and fresh blood on my back. It only got worse from there." I see Deacon's body stiffen in my peripheral vision. I keep going, knowing that if I let his anger distract me, I won't be able to get through the rest. "At some point, I started going somewhere else, drifting away until I couldn't feel what was happening anymore. But every time I drifted, it got harder and harder to come back. I was afraid that one night, I'd simply float away. That was the night I finally made the decision to get out. I think he believed that he'd finally broken me down enough that he didn't have to worry about me trying to escape. He became lax, no longer locking the door when he came in or out, as though I would never have the audacity to go against his rules—the arrogance. One night, after he fell asleep, I slipped out of bed and tried to run. One of his men caught me just before I reached the front door. I put up a fight, which he didn't expect. The noise woke Dante up, and I heard him coming down the stairs after me. I managed to knock the guard out. I don't know how, but when I looked down, his gun was in my hand. I'd never held a gun before. It was heavier than I thought it would be," I say, bemusement tinging my tone. "When I looked up, Dante was in front of me, reaching for me. So I lifted my arm and pulled the trigger. My hand shook so badly that the first shot missed, but the second and third shots didn't. I just kept pulling the trigger long after he'd dropped to the floor and the gun ran out of bullets. There was so much blood, and he wasn't moving. I dropped the gun, and I ran. I took someone's car, I don't remember whose. Probably the guards. The keys were inside, and there was a wad of cash on the middle console. In bare feet and a blood-stained t-shirt, I checked into a cheap roadside motel and dialed the only number I could remember." I glance back to Amelia. She's sitting with one hand held protectively over her belly while the other grips Merrick's tightly. Her face is wet with tears. His hand rests on her back, and he's sat forward in his seat on the sofa. His overprotectiveness and need to comfort his wife is evident in his every move. It actually makes me smile a little.

"I was afraid for a long time after. I didn't sleep or eat much. When I did sleep, I'd wake to the sounds of my own screams. The nightmares were almost as bad as the experiences. I was constantly looking over my shoulder. But when one month turned into two, then three, and no one ever came after me, I assumed he was dead. Then I had to stomach the knowledge that I'd taken someone's life." My eyes meet Alexi's now. "It was surprisingly easy to stomach." His face remains passive, save for a slight quirk of his lips. I continue, "I buried what happened to me and tried to move on with my life. To actually *live* my life. Then I climbed into my bed one night and woke up in someone else's. I'm not gonna lie; when I realized who I was trapped in that room with, I went a bit hysterical. Then I got pissed. Really pissed. It was clear that history was doomed to repeat itself but this time, I fought back." Picking at my nails to keep my hands from shaking, I whisper, "It didn't change the outcome, though." I focus on that spot on the rug again. "So when the urge to float away came, I took it, and this time, I prayed not to come back. Because I knew that if I did, I'd be lucid enough to do something far more drastic than killing someone else. I was prepared for that." At the sound of Amelia's small sob, I finally look up again. But instead of looking at her, my gaze finally meets Deacon's. He's still standing but far enough away, so that his presence over me doesn't feel intimidating. His eyes, though, they're intimidating. The clear blue practically crackles with electricity. His jaw is tight, and he's gone from his hands in his pockets to his arms crossed over his broad chest. His breathing is hard and heavy, and his nostrils flare slightly with every inhalation. The urge to look away is strong, but I don't. I keep my gaze trained on him as I say, "So, now you know. I'm fucked up beyond repair."

He doesn't say anything, only continues to stare down at me. I wish I knew what he was thinking. Scratch that; I don't think I wanna know. Because, despite all my bravado, deep down, I'm a coward. I've spent years running from my past, and even before that, most of my life was spent accepting scraps because I never thought I deserved any better. As Ms. Jane Austen famously said, "My good opinion, once lost, is lost forever." Any good opinions I may have had about myself were lost a long time ago. Now that I've finished my story, the room falls silent and I realize I'm exhausted. Whoever said emotional stress didn't take as much of a toll as physical stress could fuck right off. Amelia is the first to stand, coming over to lean down and try to hug me. I've never been big on hugs, but with the addition of her belly in the way and the fact that I'm still sitting, it isn't that hard to bear.

Before she releases me, she whispers, "I'm so proud of you." I squeeze my eyes shut to keep them from producing more stupid tears.

Merrick rises and stands next to her as she straightens, one hand at the small of her back. He rests the other briefly on my shoulder. Glancing down at me, he says, "You did what you had to do. He earned it. If he's still alive, we still have a debt to settle." I don't miss the way he said "we," as though my problems are their problems. I guess that's what real families did for each other. His brown eyes are unwavering in their intensity, and I have no doubt that the same man rubbing the base of his pregnant wife's back is capable of murder under the right circumstances. I give a small nod of agreement. They step away to share a few words with Deacon, but I don't hear them. I feel like a zombie as I stare off into space. That is until I realize that Alexi has moved from his spot across the room to the end of the sofa closest to me.

"*Istseleniye nevozmozhno poschitat', vzvesit' ili izmerit'. Ono menyayetsya kazhdyy den', prosto otkryvaya glaza.*" At my blank look, he smiles softly and translates. Healing cannot be counted or weighed or measured. It's re-defined every day, simply by opening your eyes.

On that note, he stands and makes his way over to the others. The time that follows is a blur. They could be talking for minutes or hours while I sit, staring off into the distance. The three of them leave quietly soon after, and I'm thankful for the lack of goodbyes. I think they could tell after all I've divulged, I don't think I have much left in me to say. As Deacon closes the door behind them and I listen to the sounds of their cars pulling away, I stand. I know I'll have to talk to him eventually, but every minute I stall is another minute that I don't have to see the rejection on his face.

Without turning around, I say, "I'm tired. I'm gonna take a shower and go to bed." Not giving him a chance to reply, I make a beeline for the hallway and run like the coward I am.

CHAPTER 32

Deacon

I listen to the sound of the shower running, the pitter-patter of the water on the tiles mimicking the thoughts bouncing around inside my head. There is no rhyme or reason to their direction, and like the water going down the drain, refusing to be captured. I know tonight was hard for her, but I don't think she has any idea how difficult it was to stand there and listen to her explain all the ways that that bastard violated her. My growing feelings for the woman now hiding out from me beneath a spray of hot water have only reinforced my silent pledge to be the sword with which she ends that fucker's miserable existence. What worries me more than the murder of another human being, if you could even call him that, is the way she wouldn't meet my eyes after our friends left. The way she ran from the room, as though she couldn't bear to see pity on my face, and there was pity. But there was also pride and fear, and what I'm beginning to suspect is devotion of the lifelong kind. Of course, I'm sorry for everything she went through, and if I could've spared her that, I'd do it in a heartbeat. But she underestimates just how powerful she is. How strong and resilient. The fear came when she talked so flippantly about ending her own life, and knowing that there could've been a scenario where we didn't end up together terrified me. Then I remembered the scene I walked in on when I found her in that house. She was still fighting, and the pride I feel in knowing she never truly gave up overrides everything else—all the negative emotions like pity and anger and sorrow. There will be a time for revenge, but for now, I need her to look into my eyes and see the pride there. I want her to see the devotion growing exponentially every day I'm with her. She's running from me, but even more so, she's running from herself. I need to prove to her that my opinion doesn't mean shit. She needs to accept herself wholeheartedly, flaws, and all, or she'll always doubt my intentions towards her. As the water turns off, I straighten and take a deep breath, heading down the hallway—no time like the present.

Coming up behind Siren as she stands in front of the bathroom mirror, I place my hands on her hips, pulling her back into me until her ass is flush against me. Releasing her hips to coast my hands down the front of her generous thighs, I dip my left hand between her legs, cupping her while my right-hand runs up and over her exposed belly. Leaning down, I press a soft kiss on the top of her shoulder.

As my right hand roams, she quickly grabs it, stopping me in my tracks. "Don't." Eyes briefly meeting mine in the mirror, she quickly glances away again as she tries to angle her body away from her own reflection. No, no, no. This won't do. We've come too far and made too much progress for her to regress back to the girl who doesn't want me to see her naked.

Sliding my hand out from under hers, I reach up, pinching her chin and angling her face back to the mirror so she can look at herself. At us. At how well we fit together. Her petite stature is a direct contrast to my height—all her soft curves mold perfectly to my hard edges. Ever defiant, she jerks her face from my grasp, glaring at my reflection in the mirror.

"What do you want from me, Deacon?" She asks.

There's a flippant response, poised and ready, on the tip of my tongue, but I pull it back at the last second. Going with my gut instead, I keep my gaze locked on hers as I reply, "Everything." Pressing the heel of my left hand more firmly against her heat, I elicit a small moan from her, her head dropping back to rest against my chest as I say, "This." *Your secrets.* My other hand settles on her stomach again. "This." *Your insecurities.* Dragging that hand up, I cup one breast in a firm and possessive hold, conscious of the way my thumb rubs small circles just over where her heart lies. I wonder if she notices. "This." *Your trust.* Releasing her breast, I run my hand up her neck before slipping two fingers past her slightly parted lips. "This." *Your smart mouth.* She bites down on my fingers, not enough to hurt but enough to get my attention. *Oh, baby, you've had my attention for a long time.* Sliding my now wet fingers from her mouth, I track the tips up the side of her face until they're resting against her temple. "And this." *Your mind.* Back down, my hand travels until it's trailing down the side of her neck, over the back of her shoulder, and across the healing marks there. "This too." *Your pain.* She releases a heavy sigh, and I can practically feel the fight drain out of her. I wrap my arms around her waist, enveloping her in a tight but unrestrictive hold. Burying my face in the side of her neck, I kiss a path up to her ear before lifting my eyes to meet hers in the mirror again. No singular moment has ever felt so important as this one. "I still see you. Not despite everything but *because* of everything, I see you, and I want all of it."

At first, she appears unaffected by my words. As if attempting to maintain the status quo, she says in a lighthearted tone on the surface, but I can detect a slight wobble in her voice, "This conversation's getting a little heavy, don't you think?"

I consider my answer carefully. On the one hand, I don't think I recognize the person standing behind her in the mirror. He's broody and deeper than my usual shallow puddle. But, on the other hand, I think I'm beginning to recognize the feelings I see behind my eyes as they roam over her face. Probably because of those new and unfamiliar feelings, my reply is anything but light. "You're strong enough to hold it."

Her brows crease in consternation, and her following words come out in a barely discernible tone. If I didn't actually feel them climb up her throat, I'm not sure I would even hear her. "I'm scared. I've always been so easy to throw away. Like trash. I don't know how to do this." Like a lance to the heart, her words cause a rush of emotions I don't know how to handle. In the past, I've never allowed myself to get too close to a woman because all my energy has always been focused on revenge. I didn't want the inconvenience that came part and parcel with a relationship. I didn't want to have to answer to anyone else, depend on anyone else, or care about anyone else. If I'm honest with myself, that was the crux of it. I wouldn't allow myself to care about someone on a deeper level because if anything ever happened to that person, I'm not sure I'd survive it. Hell, look at me. It's been fourteen years since I lost the last person I cared about in that way, and I still carry that around with me every day, like a cement block tied around my ankle. But Siren is different. Without conscious consent, she's become attached enough that I fear something happening to her would be heavy enough to sink me straight to the bottom. In doing so, she's brought new life to emotions I thought were long dead. Emotions that have no place in my hollow chest. It scares me, too. But not enough to make me wanna give her up, and that, too, makes her different from every other woman who came before her.

Nuzzling her neck gently, I whisper, "Don't think, just feel." I'm not sure if the advice is for her or myself. Maybe both. I know she'll take a lot of convincing, but I have to prove to her with my actions that I'm nothing like Gaspari and that she's safe with me. That I'll never intentionally hurt her. Placing my forefinger on the side of her chin, I turn her face to meet mine. Those chocolate brown eyes peer back at me, and I know what I'm asking of her is something monumental, but I'm gonna ask for it anyway. "Trust me?"

She stares for a long time, breaths shallow, and I wonder if she's about to panic and bolt for the door. Instead, I watch her lip tremble slightly before she tucks it between her teeth and slowly nods. I try my best to hide the pent-up sigh waiting for her answer has caused as I turn her in my arms until we're face to face. Hands grasping the backs of her thighs, I hoist her up, carrying her the few short feet to the bathroom counter before sitting her down. Going back to the mirror, I turn it, angling the glass until we can see ourselves again. When I look back, I find her gnawing her bottom lip, wariness written all over her face. She's embarrassed. I open my mouth to speak when, like a switch being flipped, I watch her expression morph from one of anxiety to that of a seductress. Leaning back on her hands, she gives me a smoldering look from beneath lashes that have lowered to half-mast. Irritation flicks through me. I know what she's doing, and I don't like it. I don't want the version of her that she gives to everyone else. I want a version tailor-made for me, and I know the only way I'm going to get that is by trimming away all the bows and frills. I want the raw material—the layers underneath that she doesn't let anyone see.

"You don't have to do that with me," I say solemnly.

A look of confusion passes over her features before she straightens, subconsciously bringing her arm up to block her midsection from view. "Do what?" She asks. But I can tell by the look in her eyes that she already knows what. I tell her anyway.

"Fake confidence you don't feel. You don't ever have to do that with me," I repeat. Putting my hands on her knees, I gently pry them apart, wedging my hips between them as I step in closer. I swear I must have the willpower of a saint because I manage to keep my eyes from straying down to where she's now open and exposed for me. It's a testament to how far we've come that she doesn't move to close them again. Making a split-second decision that may come back to bite me in the ass, I lean down until my mouth is close to her ear before revealing the secret I've been keeping while locked away in my office. Well, one of them, at least. "I've watched you, you know. In here ... and in the bedroom. All around this house. I've got cameras everywhere, and I've seen every inch of your body." Her breath hitches, and I'm sure at any second, she's gonna haul off and slap me. So I quickly continue before she has the opportunity because if I'm going to end up unconscious, I should at least try to plead some of my case first. "I've got a little ... problem where you're concerned. You're under my skin; no matter how often I scratch this itch, it remains just out of reach. And believe me, I've scratched plenty, even when you didn't know it. I've sat in that computer room and watched you shower, watched you when you're changing clothes, watched you sleep, and ..." Pause. "Watched you when you stare at yourself in the mirror, pinching different parts of your body that you think are a problem. And do you know what I was doing each and every time?" Another pause. Her breathing is coming faster, and she's beginning to squirm on the countertop. Smiling devilishly, I lean in and nip her earlobe with my teeth. "I was fucking my own fist and calling out your name." A tiny whimper leaves her. Gripping her hips in my hands, I pull her forward until the hard ridge in my pants is grinding into what's become an altar I'd gladly worship at for the rest of my life. I'm so caught up in her, that my brain only momentarily pauses at that thought. I'll have to come back later and analyze that "rest of my life" part in further detail. Right now, I can't think beyond the feel of her. One stroke, two, three. Every pull elicited a new sound from her lips, and the combination of friction and her moans is driving me up the fucking wall. But I have a point to make, so I force myself to focus, at least for now. "I've seen every inch of you," I say again. "And what I haven't seen, I've felt. You're perfect, and there's nothing about you that I would change. Not a single dip or curve. Not a single bounce or jiggle. You're so accustomed to using and being used that you've lost sight of your true worth. You're not trash; you're treasure. I deal in valuables, remember? I know a gem when I see one. Let me prove it to you."

As she leans back, I brace myself for the hit I'm sure is coming. Instead, she looks at me quizzically, her head leaning to the side as if she's trying to work out a math problem, and the answer is eluding her. Unfortunately for us both, I don't have the answer yet either. So I stand there, waiting patiently for her to decide what she wants to do. Eyes bouncing back and forth between my own, I watch as she slowly lowers the arm that was draped protectively over her middle. Fuck, yes. That's all the encouragement I need. Swooping in, I capture her mouth with mine, swallowing her little gasp of surprise. An idea takes hold as she reaches up and wraps her arms around my neck. I grasp her hips again, lifting her and lowering her down from the counter until she's standing between me and the bathroom sink. Breaking the kiss, I slowly turn her around, returning us to our original positions, her back to my front. Reaching up, I smooth her long, dark strands of hair over one shoulder, exposing her back to both my view and the mirror's. I feel her stiffen slightly, but she doesn't protest as I run my hands over the mixed pattern of tattoos and scars littering her back. I'm careful not to hurt her. The wounds are closed now, but the pink skin is still new in many places. This close, I can finally see every mark that that bastard put on her. As I take a moment to inspect each raised inch of flesh, she stands straight as a board, allowing me to see everything she's tried so hard to hide. Anger like I've never known courses through me when I see the crude outline of letters and even a fucking heart. I don't let the anger show though; instead, I temper it by leaning down and running my lips softly over each mark. What sounds suspiciously like a hiccup escapes her, and as my lips venture lower, she begins shifting on her feet. I slowly lower myself to my knees behind her. A move that puts my face right in line with her mind-blowing backside.

"Lean forward," I say huskily. "But keep your eyes on the mirror. I want you to watch."

For once, she does as she's told, and I send a silent prayer to God, thanking him for making her bite that forked tongue of hers. Bending at the waist, she leans her upper body forward until her front rests on the countertop, her face turned towards the mirror that sits just to the right of us. She sucks in a breath when her breasts press against what must be cold marble. I can't help but wonder if the coolness of the stone has her nipples hard. I'll find out soon enough. As I run my hands up the backs of her thighs, I palm the generous curves of her ass, massaging the flesh until it turns from pale cream to a pretty pink. Speaking of pink.

I grip her thighs from behind before saying, "Feet apart."

Again, without argument, she widens her stance. The move opens her up, and I can't stop myself from reaching up and running my thumb over her entrance, collecting the wetness that's gathered there before using it to rub several deliberately slow circles around her clit. She releases a moan, and I watch as her eyes begin to slide closed.

"Uh uh, eyes open, brat. You watch what I do to you. Not just where I'm touching but my eyes. I want you to see that there's no place in the world I'd rather be than buried between your legs." As our gazes clash in the mirror's reflection, I grip the fronts of her thighs to hold her in place before leaning in to nip the globes of her ass with my teeth. She lets out a sharp cry, and for a second, I wonder if I've hurt her. That is until she widens her stance, arching her back and offering herself to me as if it's my fucking birthday. You know, I've always been a sucker for cake. Releasing a deep chuckle, I run one finger up and down her slick heat before pushing that finger deep inside her. Instead of pulling away, she pushes back against me, silently begging for more. Always one to oblige, I add a second finger, pumping them in and out of her until she's running her short nails across the marble counter, searching for purchase. She won't find any. I fuck her with my fingers for only a moment or two before sliding them out of her. Watching her face in the mirror, I bring them to my mouth, painting my lips with her taste. As my tongue darts out to swipe across my bottom lip, I release a guttural growl that only eludes to the monster I've been keeping under lock and key. As much as I'd like to let the demon out to feast, tonight is about her, and for once, I'm going to allow someone to see me as something other than one-dimensional. Someone less concerned with their own pleasure and more focused on drawing out parts of her that she doesn't even know exist.

Gripping her thighs again, I lean down and drag the pad of my tongue over her clit, swirling it through her wetness before spearing it inside her opening. I alternate between the two until I feel her thighs begin to tremble beneath my hands. As I tighten my grip, I bury my face in her pussy, sucking her clit into my mouth. A high-pitched cry bursts from her, and I glance up at the mirror to see if she's done as I asked or succumbed to the pleasure I'm giving her. As my gaze finds hers, a rush of pleasure, stronger than anything I've ever felt, courses through me at the sight of her eyes, wide open and locked on mine.

Between this breath and the next, she falls apart and comes against my waiting mouth. All thoughts of being patient and gentle disappear, and as the beast within me breaks free from its cage, I can only pray we both survive it.

CHAPTER 33

Siren

My legs give out from beneath me until I'm held up only by Deacon's grip on my thighs. The next thing I know, he's shooting to his feet and looming large at my back. A strong hand grips the hair at the base of my neck, lifting my head from where my flushed cheek has been pressed to the cool marble of the counter.

Angling it towards the mirror again, he says roughly, "Look. Look at you. How could anyone, including yourself, see you as anything less than a goddess?"

Before I even have a chance to reply, he's using his free hand to pop the button on his jeans, freeing himself to the bathroom air that's gone thick and steamy in a matter of minutes. I watch in the mirror as he fists his length, stroking once, twice, before lining the head against my entrance. Gripping my hip, he pushes inside me in one powerful thrust. As I cry out, I try to lower my head, but the hand in my hair tightens, pulling my upper body higher until I'm standing straight with my back pressed to his chest. I can feel the muscles in his torso flex, just as I'm sure he can feel the muscles of my pussy clench around him as he grinds against my ass.

"Fuck, woman. If you don't stop that, I won't even make it to become a two-pump chump."

I don't know how he can make me laugh at a time like this, but somehow, he manages to do it. That laugh is cut off midway when he pulls back his hips, withdrawing until only the tip of his cock remains inside before pushing slowly back in. His mouth hovers close to my ear now, and he holds my head still with the hand still fisted in my hair.

"Watch me fuck you, brat. Watch me worship your pussy the way it deserves."

Helpless to do otherwise, I watch in the mirror as his cock slides in and out of me. His manic energy from only minutes before seems to have disappeared, leaving in its place something else. Something ... new. His strokes are slow and unhurried. The sight of him transfixes me, not just his body but his face. There's a look of, I don't know, wonder in his eyes. As if what he's feeling is just as new to him as it is to me. The longer I stare at his face, the slower his thrusts become until he pauses entirely. We stand like that for a long moment, unmoving. My entire body vibrates in his hold. The hand in my hair releases, and slowly, he eases out of me before turning me around to face him. Tipping my head up to meet his gaze, his eyes offer more questions than answers, but as he lowers his head and gently rubs his lips over mine, I forget what it was I was even looking for. As my mouth opens for him, he doesn't thrust his tongue inside as I expect but instead traces my bottom lip before dipping in, as though savoring the taste. Before I know what's happening, I'm literally being swept off my feet. Scooping me up, he walks out of the bathroom, leaving the mirror and the scent of sex behind. He carries me down the hall and into the bedroom as if I weigh nothing. Kneeling on the bed, he lowers me down until I'm lying in the center of the mattress, his strong body hovering over me. Of their own accord, my knees fall open to make space for him. As he braces his weight on his hands on either side of my head, he lowers his towards me, and for a moment, I'm sure he's about to kiss me again. At the last second, however, he rests his forehead against mine, our noses brushing lightly, breaths mingling. Maybe it's the romantic side of me that I didn't know existed before I met this man, but the moment seems thick with ... something. Something that can't adequately be expressed with words. It can only be felt. Absorbed, reshaped, and grown in size before being given back. Only for the process to begin again, over and over, until that feeling has grown so much that your insides can't contain it anymore, and it has no choice but to burst free. I wonder what will be left of me when that happens.

As if sensing the mounting tension within me, he echoes his words from earlier. "Don't think, just feel." I am feeling. That's the problem. I'm feeling too much. Desperate to break this spell that's woven its way around us, I reach up, hooking my hand behind his neck, bringing his mouth to mine. With a helpless groan of defeat, he thrusts his tongue inside, stroking over my own. Hips shifting, he lines himself up at my entrance and pushes inside again with one deep stroke. The strength of that thrust pushes me several inches up the bed. I hardly notice, but he does.

Seated deeply within me, he pauses and says, "Wait." Reaching over, he grabs a stray pillow beside us and tucks it between my head and the headboard.

A feeling of bemusement settles over me. No one's ever done anything like that for me before. No one ever cared enough. It's at this moment that every insecurity instilled in me by my parents, classmates, and even Dante ... evaporate. At least for the span of time that I'm in this bed, all doubts as to my worth vanish, and, for the first time in my life, I feel beautiful. Blinking away the sudden film that's clouded my vision, I avert my gaze, turning my head to the side hoping he won't notice. I should've known better. The man sees too fucking much. A finger on my chin tilts my head back to face him.

"Eyes on me, brat," he says, and the nickname that he's used to needle me all these weeks suddenly sounds less like an insult and more like an endearment. Maybe I'm imagining that, or maybe the gentle way he says it has me questioning every life choice that led me to this moment. To this bed and this man. Regardless, I give him my eyes just as one useless tear escapes. His gaze tracks the movement of the drop until it disappears into the hair at my temple. He says nothing but reaches up to brush the wetness away with his thumb. Then he begins to move. Hips rolling, he strokes in and out of me at an agonizing pace. Every time he pushes inside, little sparks of electricity light up my entire body. He watches me the whole time, blue eyes practically sparkling. Soon, our breathing is becoming choppy, and I can feel the tightening in my lower stomach that signals my impending orgasm. Weight still braced on his arms, each thrust comes a little faster, a little harder until I'm arching my hips up to meet him. The sound of flesh hitting flesh echoes in the quiet room, the only other sounds coming from the wild night outside the bedroom window. Crickets sing in time with my moans. Frogs croak in time with his. A rhythm of sounds, all merging into a song unlike any I've ever heard before, the melody unique and ours alone. As the music swells, I keep my eyes on his, just like he wanted. So bright, so blue. I'm suddenly hit with a memory of two bright blue spots on a blood-stained wall. Those spots kept me grounded when all I wanted to do was float away. A similar desire strikes me now but in a completely different way. Just like before, I focus on those bright spots, but, unlike the last time, it's not because I fear the elevation. Quite the opposite. This man makes me want to *fly*. But I don't want to soar alone. I want nothing more in this moment than to take him with me.

Reaching up, I place my hands on either side of his face, this time ensuring *his* eyes stay open and on mine. Soon, the movements of his hips become increasingly uncoordinated, our breaths coming out in a series of grunts and gasps. With every passing second, that blue becomes brighter and brighter until it's nearly blinding in intensity.

"Just like stars ... "

The whisper escapes me before I even realize I've spoken. Something flashes behind his eyes. Surprise? Confusion? Fear? I'm not sure, but I'm too far gone to care. My body goes rigid; I open my mouth and cry out, the release tearing through me in a way that has little pinpricks of light swimming in my vision. But those spots are bright and blue and constant. I don't wanna close my eyes or risk losing them altogether. I want to feel like this for the rest of my life. Worshiped, adored, protected. All too soon, however, Deacon's head is lowering into the crook of my neck, and with one last hard thrust, he presses firmly against me, emptying himself inside me with a groan.

CHAPTER 34

Deacon

What the fuck just happened? With my face still buried in Siren's neck, my labored breathing has very little to do with having just experienced the most mind-bending orgasm of my life and everything to do with three little words. Funnily enough, not "I love you."

Just like stars.

Those words, combined with the way she gripped my face and stared into my eyes, has me on the verge of a panic attack. There's no way she could've known what those words mean to me, and yet, as they tumbled from her lips, they carried such a heavy sense of connection with them. Very much like dots on a road map, only I'm not ashamed to admit that, in this moment, I feel lost. That wasn't just some phrase thrown out in the heat of passion. Each word resonated with the force of a bomb blast hitting me dead center in the chest. If I were a man who believed in silly things like wishes and fate, it would be so easy to believe that my mama had somehow sent her to me. How else could I explain the tide of feelings that have been slowly dragging me under for weeks? The way my throat tightens to near suffocation at the idea of letting her leave this house. The way I find myself reaching for her in my sleep or the way I've come to crave the smell of fresh brewed coffee and chocolate. Something isn't right. Whatever this is, it's gone way beyond sex or fixation or even the need to protect. I can't explain it, and I'm not sure I'd want to, even if I could. Some things transcend human understanding, and whatever this feeling is that Siren's planted within me has taken root, and I have a bad feeling that trying to remove it will do permanent damage to my insides. I never thought that anything could be as painful as losing my mother, but something tells me that uprooting this particular tree would make it so that nothing would ever be able to grow in its place. Internally, I'd be a barren wasteland. *Fuck.* Is that what the Fed feels like all the time? No wonder they called him The Ghost. I give my head a slight shake against Siren's shoulder because I don't wanna be thinking about that fucker while I'm buried inside my woman. And she had become mine. I'm still unsure in what capacity, but I know that she belongs to herself first and me second—no one else.

Siren releases a small yawn, and the noise breaks me out of my internal emotional struggle, causing my lips to curl into a smile against her shoulder. I lift my head, brushing her sweat-soaked hair back from her face. She looks up at me with heavy-lidded eyes. I need to pull out of her before I do something stupid, like start this process all over. Gently easing my way out, I lay down onto the mattress beside her. She stays as she was, legs spread wide, arms thrown up over her head, and the knowledge that I'll be able to go back on camera later and capture a screenshot of her just like this has my dick hardening again. *Down, boy.* The way she looks right now, you'd never know this was the same woman who didn't want me looking at her naked body earlier. She's now completely at ease with herself and me. I turn onto my side, propping myself up on one elbow so I can look down the entire length of her body. She glistens with sweat from her forehead to the apex of her thighs. As beams of moonlight kiss her skin, it's almost as if she sparkles everywhere ... like a diamond. I think back to the auction and how much I paid that bastard Gaspari for the Oppenheimer Blue. I'd give that times 100 to have this exact view before bed every night. As much as it feels like a betrayal to my mother, this diamond shines so brightly in this moment that all other gems might as well be colored glass. Pretty to look at but lacking in substance. This gem, on the other hand, has it all. Cut: she's the perfect shape and size, especially for me. Color: the blush of her swollen lips after we kiss, the mauve-toned flesh of her nipples, and the creamy white of my come as it leaks out of her. Clarity: she knows what she wants, and she's not gonna settle for anything less. Carat: no unit of measurement on Earth that can quantify her.

Moments later, she still hasn't even attempted to cover herself, and I look up to find her asleep. I'm starting to wonder if this woman has some form of narcolepsy or if being around me makes her so bored that she passes out. As I lean in closer, I hear a faint sound coming past her barely parted lips. I pull back, face breaking out into a grin. She does indeed snore. They aren't loud but they're there nonetheless. And isn't that just the cutest fucking thing I've ever seen. Now that she's fallen asleep, I don't feel so guilty about staring at her, mostly because she isn't awake to tell me to fuck off. My gaze travels over every inch of exposed skin, stopping where her hips meet her thighs. As if fed by some compulsion, I reach my hand out, running a finger through the slit between her legs. When I lift it again, the proof of our mixed arousal is wet and sticky on my fingertip. I take a quick glance back at her face but she hasn't moved a muscle. So, I take that finger, and I use my come to draw a small heart around her belly button. A sudden flash of the same symbol crudely carved into her back hits me, and I reach down to quickly swipe the substance away, but then I stop. The sentiment may be the same but our vast differences show themselves in the method of delivery. Leaving it there, I slowly drag that finger up her body until I reach her face. There, I use the remnants to paint her full bottom lip. When she wakes up, she'll lick her lips and be reminded of everything that happened tonight. As she takes in my taste, she'll crave me the way I do her. I can't be the only one falling in this situation because I fear that I'll never actually hit the ground if she's not there with me. Nearly as exhausted as she is now, I scooch down until I can rest my head in the crook of her arm, between her breast and shoulder. Wrapping my arm around her middle, I pull her in tight, molding my body alongside hers. Her skin is warm, and soon, the little purring sounds of her quiet snores prove to be the perfect soundtrack for sleep.

It's the jittery feeling that wakes me first. The room is dark, and a faint whining sound comes from somewhere. It takes me a minute to orient myself and figure out what's going on.

When I realize that the shaking sensation I felt against my face is coming from Siren, I lift my head to look down at her. Her body is drenched in sweat, and I realize the sound I heard is coming from her, too. Right before my eyes, those twitches turn to jerking movements that soon turn into full-blown thrashing. Her wet hair is plastered to her forehead and shoulders as her head moves side to side on the pillow. In the time it takes me to realize she's having a nightmare, the whining sound from before becomes whimpers and indiscernible pleas muttered under her breath. Though her eyes are closed, tears leak from the corners, and I have no idea how long she's been trapped in the throws of whatever dream she's stuck in. I don't have to guess what the dream is about, though. I just don't know how to handle situations like this. My first instinct is to wake her up, but I don't wanna do anything that's gonna startle her during those few precious seconds between asleep and awake. The decision, however, is taken from me as she suddenly tips her head back, opening her mouth and letting loose a scream so loud it could shatter glass. Fear takes hold of my throat, making it hard to breathe. Fuck this. Putting my palm against the side of her face, I turn it towards me so that when she opens her eyes, my face will be the first thing she sees. At my movement, she startles awake with a gasp, like she's been trapped underwater for minutes and is desperate for oxygen. As her eyes adjust to the dark, she takes in greedy gulps of air.

"Shhh, it's ok. It's just me. Look at my face," I say in as soothing a tone as I can manage. She focuses on me, eyes zeroing in on mine. Her bottom lip trembles and another tear escapes as she blinks up at me. As she looks into my eyes, her breathing begins to even out, her body going from rigid as steel to boneless, like all the fight in her has gone, leaving only exhaustion in its wake. In a quiet voice, I ask, "How long have you had these nightmares?"

She tries to look away, but I apply pressure with the hand still cupping the side of her face, forcing her to look at me. After a moment, she says, "Nine years, give or take."

Jesus. A thought occurs to me, and with a look of consternation, I ask, "Have you had them since you've been here? And don't fucking lie to me, Siren."

It's a testament to how drained she must feel because usually, me talking to her like that would get her back up, and she'd shut down. But this time, she doesn't. She only nods hesitantly. Annoyance flares inside me. At her, at myself. How did I not know? Why didn't I hear her? My house isn't *that* big. I still should've known something was going on, even from the living room couch. Furthermore, why didn't I see or hear it happening during any of the wakeful hours I spent watching her on camera? Because I'm busy berating myself and her, I don't notice her moving until she's turned onto her side and wrapped her arms around my waist. The tip of her nose brushes my chest, and I can feel the remnants of the tears staining her face. There's only a split-second in which I freeze, blown away by the fact that she's seeking comfort from me, a man, because of trauma given to her by another. By the next second, my arms instinctively go around her, one hand stroking her hair while she shakes slightly against me. We stay like that for a long time. I know she needs rest, but I also don't want her to fall asleep and go back into the dregs of the dream. So, instead, I talk to her. Senseless chatter and nonsensical things. About me, about my life. Things I've never told anyone, not even Merrick. Maybe if I can draw her into the details of my life, it'll be enough of a distraction from the horrors of hers.

"When I was a little boy, I used to have nightmares. They centered around my mother, and for years, I would wake up in a panic, rushing to her room to check and make sure she was okay. When I'd find her sleeping peacefully, I could finally breathe again. Then, one night, when I was 14, I had the nightmare again, only this time, I never woke up." I speak in a whisper, and even though I tell myself it's for her benefit, it's not really. The pain of talking about my mother seems slightly less if I only give it half a voice.

Her response is slightly muffled against my chest when she says, "She died, didn't she?"

I stare off at the wall on the far side of the room, swallowing past the lump in my throat. "Yeah. Drug overdose. I found her in the living room, pills scattered across the ratty carpet."

She's quiet for a long time, but I'm too overcome with my own emotions to worry about what she thinks of me now. Her voice, when it comes, startles me a little, "And your dad?"

My brows knit together, and I debate not telling her because I don't want to be defined by who my father is. I don't want to be associated with the man at all. But we're beyond the point in whatever this is where I can lie to her, so eventually, I tell her the truth. "He's a United States senator. I never knew him. I never even met him until after Mama died. Eventually, I went looking and found him living in a pretty white house with a wife and two kids. I knew what the outcome would be, but I didn't really go there to be welcomed into the family. I went to see what was so much better about the life he'd chosen over the one he could've had with us. The truth is, everything about it was better. He had money, his kids had expensive clothes, and I'm sure they never worried about where they were getting their next meal from. Thinking about it objectively, the decision seemed like a no-brainer. All I wanted to know was why he fed her the lie."

"Because he's a selfish prick?" she says, finally pulling her face back so that I can see her features, even in the dark. She lays her head on the pillow beside mine so we're face to face on our sides.

A look of sardonic amusement flits across my features. "He was definitely that. Mama was only 17 when they were together. Like a true politician, he sold her the dream. He gave her a ring and everything. It was nothing more than costume jewelry, but he promised her he'd get her the real thing when he turned 25 and gained access to his trust fund. So she waited ... and waited ... and waited. By the time she found out she was pregnant, he was married to someone else and wouldn't have anything to do with her. Still, she waited." My voice breaks and I have to grit my teeth to keep the tears at bay. I look off to the right so that I don't have to see the pity in her eyes. I guess I wasn't too manly to cry after all. "She wished on stars, threw coins into fountains, and stared at that stupid ring every day. She nursed her pain with opioids, preferring the dream version of him to the real version of me." The resentment I had convinced myself wasn't there rears its ugly head. "He promised her the world and she died alone on a threadbare couch, her last moments still spent living inside her head."

She doesn't say anything but reaches up, running her thumb under my left eye where a tear has managed to break through my toxic masculinity. When she finally speaks, instead of asking questions about all the trauma I just dumped on her, she says,

"Tell me something good about her. A memory you're fond of, maybe. Do you have any of those?"

Without hesitation, I nod and say, "Yes, I do."

"So, tell me something. A moment, frozen in time like a photograph."

I think about it for a minute before a sad smile touches the corner of my mouth. "I think I was probably about eight years old. I got into a fight at school with some kid. I don't even remember what the fight was about, but I was prone to fighting at that age. The school called my mother at work to come pick me up. I was sure she was gonna be angry with me because she barreled into the principal's office like a bull-in-a-china-shop. Instead, she cursed him out. She told him that she didn't need to know the details of the fight because she knew her son." Nostalgia morphs my sad smile into a real grin. "We left and instead of going back to work, she took me to get ice cream." When I focus again on Siren's face, she's smiling too.

"You feel that?" she asks. Before I can respond, she adds, "That's love and it overrides everything else. That's your photograph, and you can take out that picture any time you want, look at it, and relive that moment. You don't have to lock all the photos away. You get to pick and choose which pictures to keep and which to discard. Eventually, your mental album will be full of photos of the two of you when you were happy."

I stare at her, eyes dancing over her features, trying to figure out where the fuck she came from. She shouldn't be real, but she is. I wasn't looking for her, but I was. I didn't want this, but now I do. Leaning in, I place a soft kiss on her lips. Not the kind meant to entice, but a thank you for doing the same thing for me that I've done for her. She saw me and wanted me anyway. Suddenly, something she said pings off the walls of my mind, and adoration turns to suspicion. *You don't have to lock all the photos away.* Pulling back from the kiss, I ask in a low tone, "Have you been snooping in my closet?" She gnaws her bottom lip, glancing away. That's a yes. "Did you open the metal box at the top? Did you read the letter?" I ask. I know my mother mentioned stars several times in the letter, but I don't remember her ever writing the exact words Siren repeated back to me just before she climaxed. There's no way she could've known, but a lot of things make more sense now, and I wonder if she found the box the same day she played that song for me. Her eyes meet mine again, pleading with me for absolution of what she thinks will amount to a cardinal sin. But I'm not angry. In a way, I'm relieved. The majority of my most painful memories were locked in that box. Now she knows nearly all my secrets. She's stitching together the tattered scraps of my being, and slowly, I'm becoming more and more whole, a picture beginning to form. Not of a broken boy with a lifetime's worth of trauma but that of a man reaching out to someone for help, desperate to be saved. Some pieces are still missing, but if the picture doesn't come together to reveal Siren as that someone, the entire puzzle will go in the garbage.

"Is the diamond for her? Your mother? It would seem very much like you to promise her not only a real stone but the biggest one in the world."

Laughing because I've become a forgone conclusion, I flop to my back, slinging one arm over my eyes. "You're such a nosy brat and far too intuitive for your own good."

She creeps up until her face is hovering over mine. Prying my arm away, she looks at me. "It's time to stop hiding. Behind a computer screen or a pseudonym, if you have one. Step out from the shadows and into the light with me. Let's both do what we need to do to lay these things to rest. You'll never be happy otherwise, and I'll never feel truly safe until that fucker is dead."

Nodding, I reach up to cup her face in my hands and kiss her, her hair falling around us like dark curtains blocking out the moonlight. If she's content to enter the shadows with me when necessary, how can I do any less than the opposite for her?

CHAPTER 35

Deacon

"The doctor has put her on bed rest. They're saying the baby could come any day now, but it would be best for her to take it easy and try to get to 40 weeks." Merrick's voice comes through my phone's speaker from where it sits on the desk next to me. Even without having to see his face, I can tell he's close to freaking out, and it takes a lot to freak Merrick out. I can't say I wouldn't feel the same way in his position, though. You wait nine years to finally get the love of your life, only to have her almost die in your arms. Thankfully, she lives, and now you're having a baby together, and there's the possibility of complications. Something potentially happening to her or the baby. I'd probably be freaking out too.

"Everything's gonna be fine," I reassure him, trying to put as much conviction into my voice as possible. I mean, I'm not a doctor. I have no way of knowing if everything will be fine, but that's what you do when your normally stoic best friend sounds close to spiraling. "How's Amelia taking this news?" I ask.

Merrick releases a heavy sigh, the crackling on the other end of the line making me thankful that I don't have the phone directly to my ear. "She seems fine. Not worried in the least, but I don't know if that's a front she's putting on for my benefit or if she's actually okay. You would think that basically stalking someone for nine years, then being married to them for nearly a year, would make me a little more intuitive to her tells. But she's either really good at faking it, or she actually isn't worried, and I'm not sure I wanna know the answer, honestly."

"Well, women know what's going on with their bodies more than we do, so if she's not concerned, I think it's best for your own mental health to take that at face value. Otherwise, you're just gonna make yourself a nervous wreck," I say seriously, shelving my usual dialogue of banter and sarcasm.

There's a lot of rustling going on in the background as he says, "Yeah, I'm sure you're right. The thought of losing her terrifies me, though. I barely survived the first time, and, granted, it worked out in the end, but what if this time it doesn't?" More rustling. "*Fuck!* Where did I put that blood pressure cuff?!"

"Dude ... calm down. Find a seat and take a few deep breaths. If she sees you like this, it's just gonna stress her out. Talk to her and tell her how you feel, but don't look for a problem before there is one." Damn, I give sound advice. Too bad I'm shit at practicing what I preach.

"I just need a distraction. Tell me, what's going on over there? Any news on Gaspari or your father? I know Alexi found something but we haven't gotten to discuss what that something is." he says, the rustling finally stopping. I can physically hear him sit down as he expels a big puff of air. I hate to be that friend that's always talking about their own drama, especially when he's going through the wringer right now, but if immersing himself in my bullshit will help take his mind off his problems, I'll oblige.

I scrub my hand over my face, then click several buttons on my keyboard to pull up the data I extracted from the burner cell Alexi dropped off the other night. "I've got my father dead-to-rights on the assassination plot. Unfortunately, I still haven't figured out when or where the hit will occur. I've sent an anonymous tip to Cole Sykes to let him know that his life may be in danger, but I don't think he or his staff are taking it seriously. I could out my father right now, but I'm not sure that would prevent Sykes' death. If anything, I'm worried that releasing the information I have will only push the hit to happen sooner rather than later. As for Gaspari, I've got nothing. I'm almost positive he's still alive but other than the little bits of video feed I found of a doctor coming and going from the house right after I got Siren out, there's been no movement. He's either covering his tracks like no one I've ever seen or he's simply gone to ground. I have a hard time believing it's the latter because, after everything he put Siren through, I highly doubt that he'd just let her go without a fight." I wouldn't. But then again, I would never have hurt her like he did. Flashes of what she described the other night still play through my mind, each one only increasing the desperate need I feel to avenge her. I want him dead nearly as much as she does now. Releasing a sigh of my own, I add, "I think we're gonna have to do something to draw him out. I'm tired of waiting. I wanna end this. For her, for me, for all of us."

"Use me as bait."

The feminine voice comes from behind me, nearly giving me a heart attack. I whip around to find Siren standing just inside the vault doorway. Since the other night and my confession about the cameras, I've taken to leaving the door to this room open. I don't have anything left to hide from her. My secrets have been laid bare for her to see, and she's still here. As much as I want to keep her as far removed as possible for her own safety, I've stopped thinking of myself as her protector and started thinking of the two of us as a unit. A partnership with open communication and rational discussions, all of which are about to fly out the window.

I give Siren a death glare. She simply returns the sentiment. "Have you lost your fucking mind?" I ask, my tone making it very clear that there's no way in hell that's happening. There's gotta be another way.

"Deacon, I'm just as tired of waiting as you are. I need this to be over," she says, and her eyes pleading. "I *need* it to be over."

I stare at her for a long time. Time in which Merrick simply sits there, silently waiting for the climax of what I'm sure he believes will be an epic battle. But as I look at Siren, I don't feel the need to fight. For her, definitely. With her, no. Still, there are too many "what ifs" for this type of plan to work. Addressing her, I say, "How would we even do that? In what scenario would we be able to get him the information that you're out in public and set a scene for him to feel comfortable enough to make a move?"

Merrick's voice chimes in from the speaker. "He's right, Siren. Even if we could drop the information in a way that wouldn't make him suspicious, where would be a location that's safe enough to protect you but open enough for him to feel like he could take you without anyone being able to identify him?"

She blinks, looking at the floor for a minute before lifting her head again and saying, "My parent's annual masquerade party. It's one of the few things my parents return home for. It'll be in the same house I grew up in, so we'll know the layout better than anyone. It'll be crowded, and everyone will be wearing masks, so he'll feel like he can slip in without being seen." Looking at me, she says almost desperately, "You know it's a good plan. It's probably the best we're gonna get. Please, Deacon."

Fuck. I hate it, but she's right. It might be our only opportunity. As much as I'd like to keep her to myself, I can't hide her here forever. Eventually, she'll want to return to some semblance of a normal life. The thought that that life might not include me almost has me ready to take up the fight again. But for the first time in my adult life, I have to set aside my own wants and needs in favor of someone else's. I can't rule her life for her or I'll be no better than him.

"It's a decent plan, Deacon. And the only one we have right now," Merrick says cautiously, as though he can sense that I'm balancing precariously on a knife's edge.

Resigned, I say, "When's the party? We need to know how much time we have. We have to do recon, prep, and work out the timeline."

The smile that blooms over Siren's face is nearly enough to quell the waves of nausea rolling through my stomach at the idea of that fuck getting within 100 yards of her. "It's in a week. My parents won't give me the time of day after I walk in but they'll expect me to be there. If we plant the seed that I've confirmed my appearance, I think he'll take the bait."

A week. It's not nearly enough time for my liking but again, it's not my decision. The only thing I can do for her is shore up every possible loophole that would allow him to execute whatever plan he'll concoct to get to her and make sure that by the end of the night, he'll finally be put in the ground where he belongs.

Merrick's voice chimes in from the speaker. "What do you need from me? How can I help?"

"You've got enough on your plate. We can handle this. Take care of Amelia and yourself. We'll keep you updated," I say firmly. I know him, and if I said I really needed him here, he'd want to come. But I don't want him to have to make the choice between Amelia and me because I know if she said she needed him there more, I'd lose. As I look at the woman across the room from me, I don't fault him for that. When you find that person, the Earth shrinks down until everything that matters is standing right in front of you and that person *becomes* your world. Everything else blurs, your focus centered on the part of your soul that now lives and breathes and looks at you with chocolate brown eyes like you're her savior when, in reality, it's the other way around.

CHAPTER 36

Siren

Contrary to what men believed, a woman can only spend so much time in the bathroom. I know I have to come out at some point but I can't stop myself from leaning heavily on the white marble surrounding the sink and taking several deep breaths before glancing up at myself in the mirror. Cocking my head to the side, I try to see myself the way Deacon seems to see me. For the first time in my life, it's actually not that difficult. Over these many weeks, the volume of that little voice that's always plagued me seems to have been turned down, to the point that I barely even hear her anymore. At first, it was hard to combat the years of ingrained degradation, ridicule, and self-loathing. With Deacon's help, I've been learning to love myself: my weight, scars, and many flaws. Even though I know I shouldn't need a man to validate me, if I'm honest, it hasn't hurt. Sure, I probably could've done it by myself but there's just something about walking into a room where a man who sees you as the epitome of feminine beauty is waiting, who makes you light up from the inside out. That's how he makes me feel. What truly makes me believe that it's real is the fact that I get the same look whether I'm dressed as I am now, in a stunning silk gown or in sweats and a baggy t-shirt. I've come a long way from that insecure high school girl who was defined by the fact that she was always a little more than slightly overweight. I've also come a long way from the scarred young woman who was left behind in the wake of Dante, not once but twice. I no longer see haunted eyes and pale cheeks staring back at me from the mirror. I'm scared, but I know what I have to do and am resolved to see it through. If Dante is still alive, he'll be here tonight because he knows this is where I'll be. Not only because it's my family's home but because we've deliberately made the information known. I've resigned myself to being bait because I may not get another chance to end this once and for all. I'm sick of running, being afraid and always looking over my shoulder. I want a life, a real life, and not just the feeling of living on borrowed time. I wanna be able to trust men again. One man, in particular. A man I know is waiting for me outside the bathroom door. I know he's not too happy about using me to lure Dante out. He made that very clear, but considering it's our best shot, he didn't really have a choice. In the end, as much as I could tell he wanted to fight, he recognized that it had to be my decision.

Smoothing my hands down the hips of my floor length blue silk dress, I do a quick turn to see the back. I still don't necessarily like having my scars on display, but I also know that with everyone here wearing masks, my tattoos will stand out like a beacon. That was the main reason I chose this dress. Its halter style top came all the way up to my neck in the front but exposed my entire back. Between that and the slit that reaches nearly to my hip bone, I might be exposing more skin than I'm covering. It's not my usual red, and as much as I could use the boost in confidence that the color affords me, something tells me that Deacon's reaction to how the dress fits me will be all the boost I need. I do one final check of my hair and makeup in the mirror before pulling the small navy blue mask from my clutch and putting it on. It fit very much like a pair of glasses, the ties made of metal instead of ribbon, and they weave their way seamlessly through my updo, hiding any visible lines. I move to the door, opening it wide, and, just as expected, Deacon stands sentinel right outside. I hate to admit with his hair pulled back in a low ponytail, he cleans up pretty good. His suit is the same dark blue as my mask; his tie and half domino nearly match my dress perfectly. Did he do that on purpose? No, he had no idea what dress I'd be wearing tonight. I didn't choose one until we got here. As I step out into the corridor, his attention pivots in my direction, away from where he seems to be surveying the ballroom below. At the sound of my heels on the marble tiles, those bright blue eyes meet mine before slowly perusing my body. That look might as well be his fingertips ghosting over me. Everywhere his eyes touch, corresponding goosebumps spring up. Barely suppressing a shiver, I feel the warmth accompanying the light I mentioned before. I embrace the heat and place one hand on my hip, sauntering closer to him. As I watch, his jaw flexes, and his eyes darken dangerously. He's too easy.

He takes a step closer to me, and I hold up a hand as I say, "Don't even think about it. No touching. I spent nearly two hours on my hair and makeup, and I'm not about to let you fuck it up by making me all sweaty."

Eyes molten glass, he says, "Your hair and makeup aren't the only things I wanna fuck up, and I promise you, it wouldn't take much from me to make you sweat. Besides, you knew what you were doing when you picked out that dress." Stepping forward until his chest meets my outstretched hand, he forces my back to the wall behind me. In a low voice, he says, "You're wearing my favorite color, did you know that? It makes me wonder if what's underneath matches."

Even though my breathing has become slightly erratic, I still arch a brow, somehow managing to look down my nose at him despite the fact that he's a head taller than me. "Who says I'm wearing anything underneath?"

Letting out a low growl, he says, "Careful, brat. You keep teasing me like that, and I'll have you back in that bathroom and bent over the sink before that forked-tongue of yours can voice a single protest. If I recall correctly, you have an affinity for bathroom countertops now. Besides, I guarantee that if you're not wearing my favorite color under that dress, you're wearing my second favorite." He gives me a lascivious grin before adding, "Pink."

I can feel my cheeks flush at his words ... which is absolutely ridiculous because I don't get embarrassed. Especially not by dirty talk about how pink my pussy is. For some reason, though, the way this man speaks to me makes me wanna climb him like a tree ... or find a chainsaw and cut the tree down to a stump. My feelings change from minute to minute. As much as I wanna push the envelope and see where it takes us, I know we don't have time for this. We need to stay focused. So, I do my best to erase all thoughts of finding some random closet and letting Deacon fuck my brains out. Instead, I use the hand that's now trapped between us to give his chest a hard shove. Thankfully, he allows the distance, stepping back, but not before giving me a cheeky little wink. As he turns back to the railing that overlooks the ballroom once more, he holds out his arm. For a moment, I'm struck at how seamlessly he transitions from the grumbly bear I've spent weeks holed up with to this gentleman straight out of a Regency romance novel. With a look of bemusement, I place my hand gracefully in the crook of his elbow, and we make our way down the corridor. Just as we near the top of the grand staircase, a ridiculously muscular man in a sharp black suit and matching domino reaches the top step, turning in our direction. Panic flares inside me before my brain registers that the man is far too young to be Dante. Yet, he seems familiar.

Like puzzle pieces clicking into place, my suspicions are confirmed when Deacon groans next to me and says, "Fucking Hell. Did Merrick call you or did you tap my damn phone too?"

The other man brings a hand up to his face, subtly scratching his jaw with his middle finger. It's then that I notice the tattoos on his knuckles. Ah, so it is the hot FBI agent. Lips curling in a deliberately enticing smile, I project an amount of sex appeal that would normally be based on false bravado but has somehow shifted into actual confidence and say, "Wow, Deacon. I knew this dress was dangerous but I didn't think the way I'm wearing it was a crime." Meeting Alexi's eyes, I hold out my hands and wrists together and turn them upwards before saying, "I'm ready to be cuffed, Agent Kapranov." The innuendo in my tone is clear not only by the quirk of Alexi's lips but also by the possessive hand that suddenly appears on my hip, pulling me against a hard body. A small spike of fear at the possibility that I've pushed too far has my spine straightening, but as I look up to see Deacon's murderous gaze not on me but on the man opposite, a sudden realization hits me like a ton of bricks in the face. He's not trying to rein me in at all. He's looking for the Russian's reaction. I don't doubt that he'd be ready to throw down if Alexi so much as looked at me inappropriately, despite the fact that I started it. I stand there dumbfounded while they just stare at each other. Dante would never have allowed me to get away with that type of behavior. He would've jerked me up, taken me home, called me a whore, and punished me. It dawns on me that Deacon's never once made me feel like I'm doing something wrong by being ... me. Sure, we've swatted at each other, but he's never made me feel cheap or filthy or damaged.

While I grapple with this newest revelation, Agent Kapranov keeps his eyes on Deacon but replies to me. His Russian accent is front and center, proving just how comfortable he is with us now, "Siren, I don't think there's a prison on Earth that could hold you once you decide you don't want to be held."

I think about his words for a long moment. Was that for Deacon's benefit or is there some deeper meaning in it? The other night at the meeting with what I've now come to consider my own little found family, I finally unburdened myself of the secret I've held for three long years. While there was a range of emotions from most of the room, from horror to sympathy, very little was shown from the stoic FBI agent. Almost as though what I was divulging wasn't exactly new information to him. Or maybe he's just emotionally constipated; who knows?

My thoughts are interrupted when Alexi steps forward, face going back to all business. Lowering his tone to barely more than a whisper, he says, "To answer your question, yes, Merrick called me. That call should've come from you, but we'll talk about that later. We have a bigger issue to deal with. I think he's here. Gaspari, I mean. A car registered to one of his men was picked up by a street camera not far from here. The windows were dark, but there was definitely more than one person inside. I'm not sure if he's actually in the house yet or if he is, even how he got in since we're watching all of the entrances, but I believe he is indeed planning to make his next move tonight."

As Deacon glances down at me, concern is clearly written on every line of his face. I read it in his eyes, too. "I don't like this. I don't like being on the defensive, and I don't like leaving you vulnerable."

"We talked about this. It's the only way to lure him out. If he's out there, I'll never be free until he's dead," I say, shooting a furtive glance at Alexi as I finish the sentence. If the Fed cares about me making another murder attempt, he doesn't let on. He looks entirely unbothered. Maybe because he knows Dante deserves to be six feet under a prison instead of in one. Or perhaps because he's got more than a few skeletons in his own closet, so the notion of taking a life doesn't even phase him.

"You don't leave my line of sight for a second, understand?" Deacon stares at me, waiting for a response. For a moment, I want to argue, but looking into his eyes, I see concern and apprehension and fear. So, I let the words die on my tongue. As I nod my agreement, he turns to Alexi and says, "Let's finish this then."

Holding out his arm again, he begins to lead me down the stairs. Turning back, I see that Alexi has disappeared. I have to assume this is part of some telepathically-made plan because Deacon doesn't even turn back to look. As we descend the stairs, my eyes dart back and forth around the foyer below. On the one hand, I feel confident that I could recognize Dante in the dark, so spotting him, even with a mask, should be easy. On the other hand, I'm terrified that literally anyone down there could be working for him. As we near the bottom, Deacon's other hand rests over the one I have placed on his arm, giving it a gentle squeeze of reassurance. As I glance up, I find that he's not even looking at me. He just somehow knew that I was on the verge of panicking. I swear to God, every time I think I've hardened myself to the idea of this man, he does some stupidly sappy shit like this, and I practically melt for him. Taking the comfort where I can find it, I take a deep breath and try to slow down my racing heart. As we mingle around the foyer, we pass face after face, each one masked, but even so, I can discount the majority of them. Too tall, not tall enough. Too old, too young. Many men are with other women, which isn't entirely out of the question for Dante, but I have a feeling that he'll be on his own. Less baggage to deal with when he decides to make his move.

"He's not in here. Should we go into the ballroom?" I ask Deacon in a hushed tone.

After another quick perusal of the area, he nods and leads me towards an open set of large French doors. The music, which was low in the foyer, becomes much louder as we enter the main ballroom of my family's home. I always liked this room. With its high ceilings, the acoustics were fantastic. When I was younger, I would set up a chair in the middle of the vast empty room and play for hours. The only people able to hear me were the hired help and they pretended like I wasn't even there. Something I was quite used to by that point. But that was fine. I always played for myself anyway. It wasn't until much later that I lost the ability to play for *myself*, instead being forced to play for someone else. Just another thing to hate Dante for.

I look around the crowded ballroom, but nothing jumps out at me as being overly suspicious. Looking up at Deacon, I say, "Can you dance? It'll give us a chance to survey the room without being too conspicuous."

He gives me a wounded look as if my doubting for even a second that he doesn't know how to dance has broken his heart. Without saying a word, he leads me to the middle of the dance floor. Pulling me in close, he clasps one of my hands in his own, and I feel the other hand come up to rest just above the curve of my ass. The touch is deliberately low and definitely not appropriate for the setting and I wonder if he's doing it subconsciously or if it's just another tactic. Maybe he thinks that by making Dante angry, he'll make a mistake? Either way, I absorb the touch like a sponge. I no longer automatically flinch when he touches me in places like that. Places I used to believe had a little too much padding. Now, in fact, I wait with bated breath for those touches to turn into the feel of his fingertips digging into my flesh.

Suddenly, I feel the thumb of his hand start to make small circles against the bare skin of my back. Those blue eyes bore holes in mine as I look up at him. "You're the most beautiful woman here, did you know that?" he says, his tone so serious that I actually start to believe him.

Still, I scoff as I retort, "You haven't seen every woman here."

Without hesitation, he says, "I don't need to." Then he's pulling me closer, and we're swaying in slow circles, in time to the music. The man actually can dance and for a moment, I let myself pretend this isn't a life-or-death situation and we aren't in the middle of a plot to try and trap a criminal mastermind with more lives than a cat. For a moment, we're just two people dancing with each other in a crowded ballroom. Two people who fight as much as we fuck. Who's love language is trading barbs until tension is mounted so high that it's combustible.

Wait. Love language? *Love?* No. No, no, no. Mouth dropping open in shock, I berate myself, acknowledging that this is not the time or place for this kind of revelation. Not that I can think of any good time or place for this kind of revelation, but still. When you're the worm dangling on a hook, waiting for a giant fish to come try and gobble you up, it wasn't the best time to realize that you might be in love with the most stubborn man on the planet. A man who drank cold coffee and had hair almost as long as yours. A man who ate off of paper plates and left cupboard doors open. A man who ... would sit and listen to you play for hours and never take his eyes off you. A man who covered you with a blanket when you fell asleep on the couch. Who left you the last fried wonton despite having grown up starving. Who tucked your hair behind your ear so he could see your face better.

Fuck. I'm in love with Deacon Taylor. I let out a little puff of air before picking my jaw up off the floor. So this is what this feels like. How could I have ever mistaken what I felt with Dante for this? This is ... annoying. And perfect. *Double fuck.* I will away the glassy film that's developed over my vision as I force my mind to get back to the task at hand. I'll have to worry about this love situation later when the timing is better. Like never. As I take in one masked face after another, it's clear that Dante isn't here.

"This isn't gonna work. He's not here. Maybe Alexi's intel was wrong?" I say, "Or maybe he just knows there's no way for him to get to me if I'm standing with you in the middle of a crowded room."

"Well, you're not going anywhere on your own, so don't even think about it," he replies.

Huffing, I say, "You don't have to. But maybe you could ... pretend to. Give him a chance to make his move. I'll go to the bathroom. You can watch me, in case he makes an appearance. If he follows me, he'll be cornered in there."

Before I've even finished, he's shaking his head. "No, I don't like that idea."

"Fine. Then you come up with something," I say. He opens his mouth, then closes it. He knows he doesn't have a better plan, and he hates it.

Giving his head a small hard shake, he says, "Goddammit. Fine. But if he hasn't shown up by the time you come out, we're leaving. We'll go home and reassess the situation. Try to come up with another plan."

Home. I don't think he realizes that the way he said it makes it sound like *our* home. But I can't point that out or even dwell on that at the moment. He's right. If he hasn't shown himself by the time I come back, he may not be coming at all.

"Okay," I say simply. I see his eyes narrow behind his mask like he doesn't really believe that I'd give in that easily. Probably because I normally would put up more of a fight, but being in settings like this makes me remember the times that Dante used to parade me around, and it makes my skin crawl. Disengaging from Deacon's hold, I walk towards the hallway leading to the bathroom. At the last second, Deacon grabs my hand, and I feel his warm, calloused palm against my own.

"Five minutes," he says, voice like steel. Nodding, I reluctantly release his hand and make my way through the crowded room. I take the turn that will lead me down the hallway and nearly run right into another woman's back. Stopping short, I see a line of about 12 women standing in the hallway, all seemingly waiting for their turn in the bathroom. *Shit.* Making a split-second decision, I bypass the line and go through an open archway at the end of the hall that leads back to the foyer. Knowing there's another guest bathroom on the other side, I quickly cross the foyer, praying there isn't a line for this one. I'm sure Deacon will be following not too far behind, and I know he's going to explode on me for switching things up, but it can't be helped. Thankfully, as I round the corner, I don't see anyone waiting outside the large white door. As I turn the knob, I enter the bathroom and let out a sigh of relief. The music from the ballroom is now much lower, and I rub my suddenly aching temples with my fingers, trying to soothe away the pain that's starting to form there. Stepping up to the mirror, I open my small clutch and take out some blotting powder and apply it. I've gotten my lipstick nearly to my mouth when I hear it. The hand in front of me begins to shake involuntarily. The music is barely discernible here, but I would recognize that song from a mile away. *Bach.* Could it just be a coincidence? I don't think so. Immediately dropping the tube of lipstick in the sink, I bolt for the bathroom door. I've just gotten it open when a noise behind me has my head whipping around. A masked figure, dressed all in black, is suddenly right behind me. Somewhere in the back of my mind, I know I should try to scream, but I can't. Jerking me forward, he quickly covers my nose and mouth with a rag. My arms and legs flail uselessly as the man picks me up off the floor, dragging me back into the bathroom. Once inside, I know it's only a matter of seconds before I black out. I can smell the chloroform and already see the dimming at the edges of my vision. With my last few functioning brain cells, I go limp, causing the man to have to hold up my dead weight. You wouldn't think that would be surprising, but this is the one time

I'm thankful for my size because, as all rigidity leaves my body, the man is left grappling for purchase. Because he's not prepared for the move, the hand holding the rag over my face falls away as the assailant tries to use both arms to lift me. Taking advantage of the distraction, I lift my right foot, slamming the pointed heel of my stiletto down onto the man's toes. At the same time, I spin my upper body to the right, throwing my elbow out blindly. I must hit my target because my elbow connects with flesh and a muffled bellow of pain follows a cringeworthy crunching sound. The man releases me altogether to grab at the area of the mask where his nose must be located. I throw my body weight forward and grab for the door handle, flinging the door wide and running as fast as my heels will carry me. As I bolt down the hall, my shoes skid, clicking loudly against the marble flooring. Soon, I burst into the entryway, party guests look up from their champagne with a mixture of confusion and nosiness. I try my best to skirt around anyone in my way but push several people aside in my haste to reach the ballroom. It's only there that I risk a glance behind me. Breath heavy, I scan the sea of faces for a masked kidnapper, even knowing how foolish it would be for him to chase me out into a room full of people. So instead, I quickly look around the room, eyes flicking from one face to another, looking for anyone that shows signs of a broken nose, black eye, or any other similar injury. When the only faces looking back at me are those I've seen all my life at one party or another, I turn back to the ballroom to search for Deacon. I weave through the crowd surrounding the dance floor but don't see him. Maybe he got lost somewhere between the first and second bathrooms. Even as wary as I am of venturing down another hallway on my own, I'm fully prepared to do that if it leads me into Deacon's arms.

However, when I enter the first hallway again, the only thing I see is the line of ladies waiting for the restroom. They stand casually chatting or looking impatient, dancing from foot to foot as they await their turn, utterly oblivious to the danger lurking in this house. While the hall is clogged with people, nowhere do I glimpse a tall figure with sandy blonde hair pulled back in a tie. Where is he?? My heart is pounding, and I'm bordering on hysteria now. I turn back to the ballroom blindly, skirting the edge of the crowd again. I don't want to leave the safety of being around the throngs of people but I need to find Deacon and tell him what just happened. Dante may still be somewhere in the house, and if so, we need to find him. Just as I round a particularly large group of women gossiping with each other, a hand reaches out from a shadowy alcove just off the main ballroom. My fight or flight instincts immediately kick in, and I lean my head down, biting the top of the hand now gripping my wrist. There's a grunt from whoever it is, but the hand doesn't release me. Just as I'm about to start screaming, the details of the hand register, and it's then that I realize that I recognize those tattoos. I instantly stop fighting and allow myself to be pulled into the shadows of the alcove, where I come face-to-face with Alexi. His features are set in granite, and for a moment, I experience a flash of fear, but as soon as he takes in my disheveled appearance, his face softens to one of concern.

"Siren, what happened? Are you okay?" he asks, his voice barely above a whisper, conscious of the many ears surrounding us.

I'm shaking my head furiously before he's even finished his question. "No, not really. Someone just tried to grab me from the bathroom. I need to find Deacon." My voice is laced with panic, and I make a move to pull away in favor of continuing my search. Unfortunately, Alexi's death grip on my wrist prevents me from barreling back into the crowd.

"Wait," he says, and the next thing I know, he's pulling me behind him, back the way I just came. His broad shoulders carve a path through the gawking women still loitering in the hallway to the bathroom. Some openly drooling or giggling behind their gloved hands while most simply stare in shock. I have to admit that the FBI agent doesn't fit in here. He emanates an air of danger, mystery, and raw power. We quickly bypass the line and subsequent bathroom door before Alexi opens another set of French doors further down the hall, that I know lead to a private sitting room. Shutting us both inside the dimly lit room, he faces me.

"Tell me everything," he commands, and it's on the tip of my tongue to argue, but the look in his eyes tells me that now isn't the time. Speaking of time, we're running out of it.

"Deacon and I decided we'd have a better chance of Dante showing himself if he thought I was alone. So I left the dance floor to pretend to go to the bathroom. As you can see," I gesture towards the closed doors and the gaggle of women that can still be heard from the hallway, "it was too crowded. I knew there was another bathroom on the other side of the foyer, so I followed this hallway around to that ballroom. Deacon was only feet behind me, so I assumed he'd just follow me to the second bathroom. When I got inside, it was empty, or so I thought."

He doesn't crowd me, but the aggression suddenly pulsing off of him in waves is nearly visible to the naked eye. He nods before saying, "I heard the orchestra start the song and knew something was wrong."

My nervous hands start to tunnel into my hair when I remember that it's pinned up. Dropping my hands to my sides, I say, "I heard it through the bathroom door and tried to get out. That's when someone grabbed me. He put a rag over my face. It must've been covered with chloroform because I could feel myself getting ready to pass out. The only thing I could think of was to drop to the floor. He tried to catch me, dropped the rag, and I stabbed him in the foot with my heel before elbowing him in the face. I heard a crack, so I'm pretty sure I broke the bastard's nose. It gave me enough time to make it out of the bathroom, and from there I just ran. I knew if I could get back into the ballroom, I'd be marginally safe with all the other people around. I expected Deacon to be there, but he's not."

"I saw you go down the hall. Deacon followed behind you. I never saw him return to the ballroom; he's clearly not down here. *Pizdec!*" he swears. I'm not sure what the word means, but I don't have to speak Russian to hazard a guess.

Looking confused, I ask, "Deacon wasn't outside the other bathroom when I got out. Where could he have gone?" Fear grips me and I feel like a toy dangling from the vice of a claw machine, unsure if I'll be dropped at any second. Unfortunately, I don't think there will be a soft cushion of stuffed animals for me to land on; rather, the hard reality that Deacon is either alone somewhere in this house with a psychotic kidnapper or, worse, missing.

Alexi watches me closely. Reaching up, he grips my upper arms, halting my downward spiral and forcing my gaze back to his face. His grip is firm but gentle. "We'll find him, don't worry. I had cameras set up around the house. If he went somewhere, we'll know. But first, we need to call Merrick and Amelia. Let them know what's going on."

What is it with these men and their cameras? I don't waste time berating him, though. Instead, I say, "Are you gonna call, or should I? I'll have to borrow your phone if you want me to call. I think I dropped my clutch somewhere, and my phone was inside."

"I'll call. Hold on," he says. Taking his phone from his pocket, he dials a number. Suddenly, I hear Merrick's voice faintly on the other end. I stand, feeling completely useless, while he quickly explains what's transpired. He then tells Merrick that his car is in the alley next to my parent's home and we'll be leaving soon. I open my mouth to tell him that I don't want to leave without Deacon but he holds a finger up to me as he brings the phone down, ends the call and immediately places another. He speaks in rapid fire Russian, none of which I can understand, as he paces back and forth in front of me. While he speaks, I focus on breathing, trying desperately not to hyperventilate. What if Deacon isn't here? What if something bad has happened to him? What if I never get to see the reaction on his stupidly good-looking face when I tell him I'm in love with him? All these questions and more swim through my brain until I'm one giant ball of nervous energy.

Finally hanging up with whoever he was talking to, he turns back to me. The look on his face has my pulse stutter stepping. Fuck. It's bad. Oh my God. I bend at the waist, trying to get air into my lungs. Hand pressed to my stomach, I have to fight the urge not to be sick while simultaneously trying not to pass out. A strong hand soon rests on my back, and on instinct, I flinch away.

Turning to face Alexi, I ask in a barely-there whisper, "He's not here, is he?"

He shakes his head slowly before speaking. His tone is emotionless but there's an underlying thread of worry that even I can make out. "The cameras caught him following you down the hallway, but he went back towards the kitchen instead of across the foyer to the other bathroom. He must've gotten turned around. About the same time you came running out, he entered a room just off the kitchen. Possibly a pantry or linen closet, I'm not sure. A few minutes later, someone came out pushing a serving cart. It wasn't Deacon, and they didn't go to the kitchen or the dining room. They pushed the cart past the kitchen and out the back door, where a car was waiting. They moved something from beneath the linen cloth of the cart into the trunk. Something big."

He says the last few sentences as though he's telling me there's rain in the forecast for tomorrow. How is he so calm? Oh, right, it's not his world that's falling apart right now. It's mine. As I sink down slowly into a nearby chair, my sightless gaze roves over the room, from the shiny material of Alexi's shoes to the window that overlooks the gardens outside. As I stare out the window at the night sky, stars wink in the distance, and a feeling of calm settles over me. That calm is quickly eaten away by rage which is a much healthier emotion than fear, in my opinion.

Popping up from my chair, I say, "Fuck this shit!" Alexi stares at me with an arched brow before a small grin tips up one corner of his mouth.

"So, what do you wanna do, *pevchaya ptitsa?*" he asks.

Fed up, I take a deep breath. There's no fucking way, after everything I've gone through, that I'm not going to get my happily ever after. If Deacon is the stars, I'll move Heaven and Earth to reach them if I have to. I refuse to live in the dark any longer.

Alexi's typically deadpan stare meets mine, and I can see the resignation. He already knows what I wanna do, and not only is he gonna let me do it, clearly, he's gonna help me. My spine straightens as I rip my mask off completely. "Let's finish this," I say.

CHAPTER 37

Deacon

The first thing my brain registers as it comes back online is an overabundance of saliva pooling in my mouth. You would think having a rag full of chloroform shoved in your face would give you some kind of dry mouth, but, in fact, the first thing I feel is the urge to puke my guts up. Nausea churns in my stomach, and even though I haven't yet opened my eyes and have absolutely no idea where I am, I'm tempted to give in to the insistent demand to empty my body's contents on the floor of whatever fresh hell I've found myself in. Instead, I take several deep breaths, swallowing down mouthful after mouthful of spit, willing the feeling to pass. I have no doubt that when I open my eyes, whatever predicament I've found myself in will have the impulse to vomit coming back, and I really don't have time for that right now.

After the initial urge to throw up has passed, the very next thing to enter my mind is … where is my woman? My eyes spring open, and I immediately regret it. The room around me spins and my head feels like it's gonna roll off my shoulders. I've had hangovers before but this is like a hangover on steroids. I don't drink nearly as much as I used to and there's a reason for that. I'm too old to experience this feeling. My party-going days are long behind me, and the fact that I have all the symptoms without the benefit of getting completely shitfaced, quite frankly, pisses me off. After several long blinks and even more deep breaths, I slowly reopen my eyes, taking in the room around me. At first glance, it would appear to be an apartment, except it's nearly empty. The space is large and open, with only one set of windows directly to my left. The moonlight pouring in through those glass panes is the only source of light in the entire room, falling directly over my strategically placed chair. One that my wrists and ankles have been zip-tied to. From what I can tell, the chair is old in the way that antique furniture made for showing off instead of sitting is old. In other words, it's uncomfortable as fuck. It could be the lack of padding in the seat, or it could be, I don't know, the fucking zip ties. I attempt to shake off the remnants of the drug in my system, slowly turning my head left and right, trying to figure out if Siren is in the room with me. Was she taken, too? I have to admit, if my hands were free, I'd be punching myself in the balls for not seeing this coming. We were so focused on Siren being the target at the party that it never even occurred to me that that motherfucker Gaspari might come after me instead. I guess he was still sore about the whole leaving him for dead thing. Tragic.

After a quick perusal of the space, I've determined two things. One, it's not exactly an apartment as I first thought. It's an empty loft of some kind. Maybe at one time, it had been a warehouse or a mill and was in the process of being renovated to become luxury lofts. Well, whoever owned it was gonna have a hell of a time selling it with my blood all over the place because I'm pretty positive that I wasn't tied to this chair so that Gaspari could give me a lap dance. The second thing I realize after looking over the area is that Siren isn't here. At least not in this room. If she's being kept somewhere else within the building, I need to get out of this pin cushion of a chair and find her. The realization that Gaspari isn't in the room with me is also troubling. If Siren was taken along with me and she is here, I'd much rather have the bastard in here tormenting me than doing God knows what to her. The very idea has red clouding the edges of my vision. Tugging at the zip ties around my wrists, the sharp sting of plastic cutting into flesh barely registers. I don't have time to care about pain. Uninvited images of Siren being tortured or assaulted bombard my brain, and within seconds, drops of my blood hit the hardwood floor from where I've thrashed against my bonds to no avail. Again, it doesn't hurt. The self-inflicted pain is nothing compared to the absolute hysteria I feel at not knowing where she is. My heart feels like it's gonna burst free from my chest, and I'm breaking out into a cold sweat, my skin clammy as the panic takes hold. I don't know what I'll do if anything happens to her. I'm seconds away from spiraling completely when a voice speaks up from behind me. Blood turns to concrete in my veins, slowing to a crawl and it's suddenly hard to breathe oxygen. The owner of that voice has only spoken to me once, but I hear in my head every day.

"I'm sorry it had to be like this, boy," the voice says, the smooth cadence of his southern drawl nearly enough to hide the fact that his words hold no emotion, no remorse. Closing my eyes, I finally let the pain come. The pain of the past washes over me like scalding water, leaving behind new scars to add to the old. How did I not predict this? For all my digging and spying, I'm obviously thick as shit. I thought I had everything I needed, so

I stopped monitoring him. Clearly, the worst mistake I've ever made.

As the man finally moves from the shadows behind me, stepping into the beam of light streaming through the window, eyes the same shade of blue as mine stare back at me from a face that would look weathered and wrinkled if it weren't for the plastic surgeon I know he keeps on retainer. To the South Carolina State Senator, appearances were everything, after all.

My voice is low and deceptively calm when I finally speak. "Are you? Somehow, I find that very hard to believe."

My father cocks his head to the side, taking in my sweat-soaked features and the hair that's come loose from its hair tie and now sits plastered to the sides of my face. The longer he looks, the angrier I get. Everywhere his eyes touch, my skin burns as though allergic to his scrutiny. Letting out a humorless little laugh, he says, "You really do look like me. Except, if I remember correctly, you inherited that blonde from your mother. She was a cute little thing, though a little too trusting and far too naive."

At the mention of my mother, white-hot rage engulfs me, overtaking any remnants of pain caused by this man's actions. In this moment, if my hands were free, I have no doubt that they'd be wrapped around his neck. As it is, my nostrils flare as I try to breathe past the anger, reminding myself that expelling energy trying to fight my way to him now will only tire me out and make it impossible to find an escape angle. I glance down at the floor and take several calming breaths before slowly lifting my eyes to his. "You're gonna wanna be careful with your words, old man, and you better pray that I don't get free because every bad word you speak about her will equal one pound of flesh I'll remove from your bones while you're still alive."

I can tell he's taken aback at my words. Something akin to fear flickers in his eyes and I take small comfort in knowing he's afraid of me. He should be. He doesn't know me or what I'm capable of. I've waited my entire life for this moment, though, I didn't picture it going exactly like this. I watch as he takes a small step backward, running a hand that's shaking slightly through his sleek hair. Despite the obvious tells his body language is giving, he says, "You must've inherited that psychotic streak from your mama too. No son of mine would dare talk to me like that. I'm thankful now more than ever that I turned you away all those years ago. If I'd made the mistake of taking you in, I would've had to sleep with one-eye-open. Not that it matters now. You won't be going anywhere."

"You didn't turn me away. If you recall, I'm the one who gave you my back. It didn't take more than a few sentences out of your mouth for me to realize what a piece of trash you are. You didn't deserve to breathe the same air as my mother, much less raise the son she single-handedly kept alive for 14 years."

He stews on that for a minute before saying, "Hmm, 14 years? So what happened? She die?" The nonchalant way he spits out the last word makes me wanna throw up. In fact, everything about this man makes me wanna throw up. With his selfishness and disregard for human life, it's no wonder he excelled in politics.

"Yeah, she died. After you promised her the world to get in her pants, only to knock her up and then disappear," I say.

He lets out a laugh. The sound is like nails on a chalkboard, making every hair on my body stand on end. "Like I said, naive.

But your mama was no angel, boy. She knew I was engaged to be married when she let me fuck her. Sure, it took some convincing. Pretty words, hearts, and flowers. It was a lot of effort, but in the end, I got what I wanted—her cherry. You're just an unfortunate byproduct. You can hate me, but if you think about it, I did her a favor. She needed to grow up."

Disgust tears through me. Not only at his words but at his complete lack of any kind of empathy. He made mention before about my psychopathy and I'm more convinced now than ever that every drop of my psycho was inherited from this man. He's a sociopath. He doesn't care who he has to destroy to get what he wants; that much has been clear for years. What hits home now is that he's incapable of feeling remorse for his actions. Thoughts of all the lives he's obliterated and the people he's stepped on over the years don't keep him awake at night. Forget about sleeping with one-eye-open. I bet this bastard sleeps like a baby. As fiery rage transforms into a kind of resigned loathing, I want nothing more than for this man to shut the fuck up. I'm not interested in anything he has to say. I've gone far past the need for explanations or apologies. I honestly don't care anymore. The only thing I want is retribution. I want to snuff out his life and then never think about him again. The same way he did with my mother. But I'm not an idiot. I know that my current predicament isn't ideal, and as much as I'd like for him to just close his mouth and get on with whatever he has planned, I know I need to keep him talking if I want the opportunity to get loose.

Changing the subject entirely, I glance around the empty room and ask, "Where's Siren?"

He shrugs, unconcerned. "How the hell should I know?"

Confusion fills me even as hope that she may not even be a part of this begins to take root. "What the fuck do you mean? Didn't you take both of us?"

A look of annoyance passes over his features before he shakes his head. Moving away from me, he begins to pace back and forth, disappearing into the shadows for a moment before returning to the light. Over and over, he repeats this process, seemingly ignorant of the fact that it's incredibly stupid of him to take his eyes off me, even for a second. I subtly test the strength of the chair's arms and legs by shifting my weight from left to right slightly. Thankfully, it doesn't creak, but a distinct sway tells that while the chair may be an antique and well made, someone clearly doesn't value their things. Like most old shit, if it isn't cared for, the quality of it degrades over time. The joints of the chair aren't as strong as they used to be, and I wonder if it would splinter apart with the right amount of force. I keep one eye on my father as I continue to gently shift my weight from side to side, working the screws and bolts loose. Eventually, he replies with a shrug, "It was supposed to be both of you but good help is hard to find, I guess."

You guess? What the fuck is actually going on here? Clearly, he's the one that drugged me at the party, but maybe someone else was supposed to do the same to Siren and failed? I can only pray. His phrasing however, gives me pause. If you had hired someone to do a job and they didn't get it done, surely you'd be positive about the fact that said henchman isn't worth a shit? Pressing further, I say, "So she's not here? This is just between you and me, then?"

Shaking his head, he says, "I don't know if they got her, but, either way, this situation doesn't really even have anything to do with me."

A look of incredulity crosses my features. "Then why the fuck am I here??" I demand.

A second voice sounds out from behind me, and my head jerks around to see who the newcomer is. I can only make out his profile in the darkened room due to my limited mobility. Even through the hint of a rasp, the Italian accent and glowing end of the cigar are unmistakable, though.

"Haven't you figured it out yet, *Bastardo?* Your father needed something taken care of. I wasn't going to take the job, but then you stole my Sirena, and I found out who you were. Your father was all too happy to trade your life as payment for a job-well-done." The otherwise soft shuffle of expensive loafers sounds like bombs going off, every step reverberating around the room as Gaspari finally enters my line of vision. He's dressed in slacks and a tucked-in button-down. His hair is perfectly made up, the salt and pepper strands slicked back with enough gel to lubricate a slip n' slide. His wrist is adorned with a very expensive Rolex, and gold cufflinks accent the ends of his sleeves. Probably all paid for with *my* money. One hand holds the still-lit cigar while the other holds a long metal pipe. To what I'm sure is his everlasting irritation, none of this distracts from the long, angry-looking scar running the length of his throat. The flesh is healed over, but the skin is still new. As I take it in, I notice that it only extends to within an inch or so of his carotid artery. I guess that explains how he's standing in front of me right now. It also explains the raspy tone of his voice. I would imagine speaking past such an ego crusher would be difficult. Coming to stand directly in front of me, he looks down his nose as he adds, "Now, I suppose, in addition to killing you for touching something that doesn't belong to you, you'll also serve as bait."

Bait. To catch Siren? For the first time since I woke up in this room, I'm actually glad I'm sitting because I'm sure the relief I feel at this moment would have my legs turning to jelly beneath me. She's not here. She got away. I can only hope that Alexi got to her in time and got her out of that house. If she knows what's good for her, she'll stay away. And if he knows what's good for him, he'll lock her up until all this is over, one way or another. Face turning to a mask of false bravado, I eye the pipe in his hands before saying, "Nice try, Mario, but she won't come after me. She doesn't care enough. We were just fuck buddies." The words burn my tongue like acid, and the immediate urge to take them back claws at my insides. But if he thinks she means more, he'll use it against me. He'll use me against her the same way if he thinks she has deeper feelings for me. Even in a dire situation like this, I can't drown out the voice in my head that whispers, *God, I hope she does* because I'm in love with that smart-mouthed witch. I'm not sure when it happened because it was such a gradual process that I don't think I was ever fully cognizant of just how deeply she was burrowing herself beneath my skin. Every little thing she did, from sniping at me to playing her violin for me long into the night, just pushed me closer and closer to the inevitable realization that I love her. I know what love is and what it feels like. I loved my mother, so I recognize the feeling. However, what I feel for Siren is so much more complex and multifaceted ... like the diamond. Every angle sparks a new sense of wonder and awe. Then you take a step back and look at it as a whole and realize it's the most beautiful thing you've ever seen and probably the most precious thing you'll ever hold in your hands. That's how I know it's love. Chip away at it and have no doubt, it'll cut you. But hold it up to the light, and every facet will burst with energy until it's all you can see. Until it's all you *need* to see. A diamond doesn't ask permission to shine; it just does. Siren didn't ask permission to invade my life. To carve her way into my chest and fill that space that's been empty since I was 14. She just did it. God knows it isn't perfect, this love. She filled that space with as much piss and vinegar as she did with gentle touches and endearments. But I don't want perfection; I want *real*. I just hope I make it out of this alive so I have the chance to tell her. If I die before I can profess my undying love for her, she's gonna be *pissed*.

A sudden burst of pain hits the side of my face, radiating outward, followed quickly by an equal explosion of pain in my gut. With a grunt, I hunch over as Gaspari pulls back on the pipe he's just whacked across my face and into my midsection. When I'm finally able to take in oxygen again, the simple act of breathing hurts like a motherfucker. Pretty sure I've got at least one broken rib and I can feel blood trickling down my face. I can see my father's shoes shifting side to side out the corner of my vision. As I lift my head to look back at the bastard that just hit me, my body shifts, and I realize that the force of the blow has also aided in further compromising the integrity of the chair. The pain will be beyond belief but if I get an opening, I think if I tilt myself sideways, the chair will break apart. I'll still have bits tied to my wrists and ankles but at least I'll be mobile. Two against one aren't great odds, but I don't have much choice right now. I've gotta shoot my shot if I get it, and the only way I'm gonna get it is by making Gaspari mad enough to make a mistake.

Coughing out a painful laugh, I say, "Ouchies. Was that because I called you Mario? I mean, come on, man. You're Italian and you just hit me with a lead pipe." With a glance at my father, I gesture to Gaspari with a tilt of my head, saying, "Do his voice but say "Issa me, Luigi." To my astonishment, the sperm donor that gave me life actually lets out what sounds like an involuntary snort. The single second of humanity costs him dearly.

With an enraged roar that I know must hurt like a bitch echoing off the bare walls of the room, Gaspari tosses the cigar to the ground, reaching behind him to pull a handgun from the waistband of his slacks. Between one blink and the next, a shot rings out, and I watch my father drop to the ground. Alive one second, dead the next. A pool of blood collects on the hardwood floor around him as his eyes stare sightlessly at the ceiling. I wait for a wave of grief that never comes. A burst of anger that's also suspiciously absent. But there's nothing. All my thoughts are preoccupied with the need to get back to my woman. To find her and prevent her from being lured out here and into a trap tailor-made just for her. Don't get me wrong, I always envisioned myself being the one that eventually ended my father's life. An eye for an eye and all that. His death for my mother's. But somehow, over the last few months, my need for revenge against my father has been overshadowed by my need to avenge Siren. To kill Gaspari and free her from the chains that have held her down for years. So, am I mad at the fact that my father was killed by someone else? Surprisingly, no. The end result is the same; now, only one person is standing between me and the object of my desire instead of two. And, if I had a choice, I know without a shadow of a doubt that I'd much rather Gaspari's than my father's death come at my hands. As the madman in question turns back to face me, he aims the pistol dead center at my chest as if he knows there's a piece of her tucked away in there and is determined to get her out. I close my eyes, trying to come to terms with the probability that I may not make it out of this room. If I don't, I refuse to give him the satisfaction of seeing the light leave my eyes. I don't have to wait long before a loud bang sounds, I assume, to herald my eternal dirt nap. But I feel no pain. I open my eyes to the realization that the sound came from behind me as the door was being kicked off its hinges. Men dressed in black suits and pointing guns of their own flood the room, surrounding Gaspari and myself. I nearly breathe a sigh of relief before my brain takes more detailed stock of the men. These are no Feds. The few pairs of eyes that aren't trained on the two of us look back towards the door as someone else slowly enters. With my back to the door, I can't see who it is. Still I know immediately that I'm in much bigger trouble now than I was 10 seconds ago as I watch every bit of color drain from Gaspari's face, leaving it whiter than the ghost of the Senator whose blood will forever stain the floorboards of this room. As the newcomer enters, the sound of dress shoes on hardwood is accompanied by the rhythmic clicking sound of ... a cane. As the man finally comes into view, the only thought reverberating through my brain is *oh, shit*. Though we've never met in person, I don't need an introduction. I know exactly who he is.

It's Ilya Kapranov.

CHAPTER 38

Siren

"Oh. My. God. Can you pull over so I can drive?" I ask Alexi, as my patience flies out the window along with my hair. Why did this man have the windows down? Air conditioning, hellooo? Maybe he feared I'd throw up in his precious car without the fresh air. He needn't worry. There was no way I'd ever get car sick from the speed he was going.

"Why would I do that?" he asks, and the calmness in his tone is infuriating. If I hadn't seen him exhibit at least a little human emotion over the months that we've known each other, I'd swear he was a robot. Maybe it was just a Russian thing? Though I was starting to wonder if his deadpan attitude had anything to do with what I've now dubbed his "long-lost love."

"Oh, I don't know, maybe because you drive like someone's dear old granny, and I'd like to make it there before somebody gets killed?" I retort. My nerves are getting the better of me, and it's making me even more bitchy than my usual bitchy. Does he deserve my aggression? No, but what I said was true. He does drive like a little old lady.

He releases a long, suffering sigh that can be heard even over the whipping of the wind blowing through the car, probably because he knows I'm on the edge of a cliff and is trying to breathe through the urge to push me off himself. "He's not going to die, *pevchaya ptitsa*," he says, but I watch the speedometer climb steadily as he applies pressure to the gas pedal. That's the second time he's called me that, and I have no idea what it means, but it better not be Russian for "pain in the ass".

I reach for the button on the inside of the door, rolling up my window before turning to him. "How can you be so sure?" The new level of quiet in the car allows for the shakiness and uncertainty to be clearly heard in my voice, the fear of the unknowns beginning to bleed through the pent-up rage I've been harboring like a miser since realizing Deacon was taken.

He glances over at me to meet my eyes, and for a second, I'm about to screech at him to keep his eyes on the road, but with almost laser focus, he slides seamlessly through the other cars on the interstate, even through his peripheral vision. "Because he has something to live for now besides revenge. And something to lose," he adds the last part as if the loss of said thing would be worse than dying. Maybe it is. The overwhelming sadness I feel at the thought makes my heart ache for him. If there's one thing I've come to learn about Alexi, it's that he may not say much, but what he does say is cryptic but telling. I have a feeling most people get the former but not the latter.

Rolling up his window, we sit in a silence that's somehow both comfortable and tense as we speed down the highway. A few minutes later, Alexi's cell goes off in his pocket. Pulling it out, he glances at the caller ID before answering, not in English but in Russian. So, not the FBI, then. I let him conduct his business while I alternate between staring out the window and looking at the clock on the dashboard. I still don't know exactly where we're going. All Alexi said was that he had a rough idea and that we'd get more information on the way. I assumed from contacts within the FBI. Based on the low, raspy string of Russian coming through the other end of the phone, maybe not.

A few minutes later, Alexi hangs up with a word that sounds oddly like "speedo." Usually, that would make me laugh. Now, not so much. Without taking his eyes off the road, he says to me, "Gaspari is indeed alive. He's holed up in an old building just outside of Savannah that's being converted into loft space. According to my contact, he's not alone." I'm glad I'm already sitting down because the relief I feel at his last sentence would be enough to make my legs give out. If he's not alone, that means Deacon's still alive. We've still got time. However, if the windows were still down all that relief would have somewhere to fly when he adds, "Deacon's father is there."

His father?? The Senator? "What? Why? What does he have to do with this?"

"Martin Hawkins was trying to hire someone to kill one of the men running against him for his senate seat, though we didn't know that someone was Gaspari until now. I don't know why he's there now, but I'm sure we'll find out when we get there."

"Why haven't you called in the Feds?? SWAT? You know, the cavalry? Are they gonna meet us there?" I ask, and the edge in my tone has returned full force.

He shakes his head. "Nyet. A full-scale invasion will only turn what's already a precarious situation into a shit show. Gaspari will either kill everyone, including himself, or he'll run and go to ground. The best way to end this in the way you desire is for only a choice few to know about it." The way I desire. He's got a funny way of describing murder. Then again, from what I've learned of him, murder seems to be in his genetic pool.

I ask another question to take my mind off the idea of Dante killing everyone in the building. "So, if you didn't call your brothers in black, who did you call? You were speaking Russian."

His brows pull together, and for a moment, I don't think he's going to answer. Just when I'm about to turn and face the dark night outside again, he says, "Let's just say I have my own Deacon. He just happens to live on another continent."

"If you already had a hacker in your back pocket, why do you need Deacon's help finding the music box?" I ask.

He lets out a low chuckle. "I should've known he'd tell you about my little visit. Considering he's helping me locate it and I need Merrick's help to get it, everyone would know eventually." He briefly takes his eyes off the road again, glancing over at me. "Deacon may be a hacker, but he's also considered one of the best fences in the country. Between the two, he has his finger on the pulse of the criminal underworld in a way that most people don't. He has a lot of connections, and those connections have connections. Additionally, up to this point, my man in Russia has been unable to find her."

Her? That's an interesting way to describe an inanimate object like a music box. "Don't you mean it?" I ask though I think I already know the answer. I think I've known for a while.

"Isn't that what I said?" he replies.

"No, you said her. You said your man hasn't been able to find her. Who's her?" I know I'm being invasive, but considering the man probably has files on all of us tucked away in a safe somewhere, I don't really feel bad about it.

He glances down at the speedometer that's currently reading nearly 100mph. In a low voice, barely audible over the engine's roar, he says, "My wife."

My eyes go so wide they nearly fall out of my face. Wife?? Deacon never said anything about Alexi having a wife. I'm positive he would've told me that. Does he even know? When Alexi looks at me again, the sadness behind his eyes causes an involuntary lump to form in my throat. I was right when I dubbed her the love of his life. It's right there in his eyes. I don't know precisely how long he's been searching for her, but it's clearly been too long. Why is she hiding from him? Or was she taken by someone? If she did run, what made her do it? I've got so many questions, but before I can voice the next one, he's exiting the highway and pulling onto a dark road. There are very few houses here and even fewer lights. Dense woods line both sides of the narrow road, and the oaks are heavy with moss, which only adds to the feeling of being closed in. If I were claustrophobic, I'd be freaking the fuck out right now. As it is, I was raised in the south, and even though I was born with a violin in my hand and a silver spoon in my mouth, I still feel just as comfortable on a back road leading to nowhere as I do in a concert hall performing for hundreds. Maybe more so.

The further we travel down the darkened road, the creepier the area becomes. Who the hell would wanna build luxury apartments way out here? It isn't until I start to smell the distinct scent of marshy water that the answer to that question comes. Regardless of how far from civilization the building is, if it's directly on the edge of the Savannah River, people will pay a pretty penny to live there. Waterfront property is worth a fortune. Within a few minutes, the car slows, and Alexi pulls down a roughly carved-out dirt road. If the headlights hadn't shone on it, I would never have seen it, which I guess is the point. Backing his car into the thick foliage, he turns off the engine.

"We have to walk from here. Lower our chances of being detected. Do you know how to shoot a gun?" he asks before quickly answering his own question. "What am I saying? Of course, you do." He reaches into the glove box in front of me and pulls out a small pistol. As he hands it to me, I'm surprised by how light it is. Based on my only other experience with a gun, I expected it to be heavier. While I move it around in my hands, he points to show me where the safety is, how to turn it off, and how to cock the gun. Looking at me with grave eyes, he adds, "This time, aim for the head." I nod. I appreciate how blunt he's being. I think he knows that if he handles me like glass, there's a good chance I'll break. I also appreciate that, for all his brutishness, he hasn't once told me some dumb shit like to wait in the car while he takes care of it. No, he just equips me with what I'll need to get the job done, should the opportunity present itself. I don't know much about Russia or the Bratva, but I always thought the men liked their women subservient. I guess they broke the mold when they made this one.

Alexi opens the car door, motioning for me to do the same. We both get out, with Alexi removing his suit jacket and button-down shirt and tossing them into the backseat. Wearing a black fitted t-shirt and slacks now, we close the doors as quietly as possible. As he moves around the front of the car to my side, I'm able to see two full sleeves of intricately woven tattoos. From what I can make out, they're beautiful. I don't think I've ever seen him dressed in anything less than a full three-piece suit before, and it's no wonder. Those tattoos are a lot to take in, the few on his knuckles and hands only hinting at what lay beneath the sleeves of his shirt. I tighten my grip on the cold metal of the gun in my hand. It makes me feel like some badass female character straight out of a movie. As Alexi begins to walk, I follow, but before I can take more than a few steps, I notice my feet sinking into the ground a little. I glance down and see that it's because of the spikes on my stilettos. As near to the water as we are now, the ground is thick with mud and has the distinct smell of swamp.

I click my fingers once, getting Alexi's attention. As he stops and turns to face me, I brace myself on the hood of his car before lifting one foot, then the other, snapping off the heel of each shoe. Tossing them to the side, I reach down and rip the bottom of my dress off until it hits right at my knees instead of dragging on the ground. Much better. Feeling like Buffy at a vampire-infested prom, I look back up to signal to Alexi that I'm ready, only to find him smiling at me. Well, as much as a man whose heart is currently in hiding can smile. I give him a small one in return, and we start walking. I don't know where the hell we're going, but he seems to, so I follow behind him, periodically glancing around to ensure no one is watching us.

Within minutes, a clearing starts to appear in the distance. In the center sits a huge building that I'd guess was, at one time, maybe a mill or a factory of some kind. It's clearly under renovation. and several smaller buildings surrounding it are midway through the construction process. Before we can reach the edge of the clearing, Alexi puts an arm out to stop me from going any further. Reaching into his pants pocket, he removes something tiny, placing it in his ear. As he begins to whisper something in Russian, I realize it must be a two-way earpiece. Whoever his hacker person is must be on the other end, feeding him information. They go back and forth for a few seconds, Alexi's words clipped and barely loud enough for me to hear, even standing right next to him. That is until I see his entire body stiffen, and he lets out a very angry-sounding word that's clearly a rather vile curse. My heart kicks wildly in my chest and I wait on pins and needles for him to tell me what the hell is happening.

When there's a lull in the conversation, he looks at me and says, "We may have a bigger problem than just Gaspari and Hawkins. We may indeed get that shit show after all because there's a very good chance that my father is inside that building too."

His father? The mob boss? Whispering, I say, "What the fuck is your father doing here?"

He says something into the earpiece, then pauses to listen to the reply. Finally, he says, "I believe Gaspari may be in possession of something that belongs to my father. Clearly, he wants it back."

"FUCK!" I whisper. "Wait. Maybe that's a good thing? Your father would help us, right?" I ask.

"Nyet. I haven't seen him in several years. In fact, I've done everything in my power to stay off his radar. I have no doubt he'll be happy to see me, but not in the way you think. He won't help us. Not unless there's something in it for him." He speaks a few more sentences into the mic. After another moment, he says, "There were only three guards on site. Two patrolling the grounds and one inside the building, probably guarding the door to wherever Deacon is being held. If my father is in there, he won't be alone. Which means there's a good chance those guards are already dead and have been replaced with ones of his own. Either way, we're running out of time. We have to move."

Just then, a shot rings out, echoing into the still night air. My stomach jumps to the general vicinity of my throat. Panic grips me, and I grab onto Alexi's arm. I'm not sure if it's to steady myself or just for confirmation that he heard what I heard.

With hardened eyes and a set jaw, he says, "I think that would be our queue to take the safety off your gun now. I don't want you to hesitate. Shoot first and ask questions later. I don't care if you can't see who it is or you don't know whose side they're on. If it moves, shoot it."

Fear emanates from me, permeating the air around us. Not fear for myself or what we're about to walk into but fear that we might already be too late. Pushing past the terror that's turning my guts to jello, I nod. He sets off, and I follow closely behind. We skirt the edge of the clearing until we're close to one of the smaller structures being built. Alexi holds up one, two, three fingers and points to the building. Nodding, I wait until he counts again before following him quickly to the side of the building. He presses his back to the wall so I do the same. If you'd asked me a few months ago if I'd be playing Mission Impossible while trying to save the life of a man who's upended mine, I would've called you crazy. We do this from one building to another until we're close to the main warehouse or factory or whatever the hell it is. Alexi motions to a door on the side of the building. It's only then that I notice there's a man standing guard outside. Whether that's Dante's guard or one that belongs to Alexi's father, I don't know. He holds up a hand in the universal gesture for "stay here." As I watch, he slips into the shadows surrounding the building, effectively disappearing. Even knowing he's there somewhere, I can no longer make out his outline. That is until he reappears directly beside the man at the door. Between one blink and the next, he reaches up, twisting the man's neck at an impossible angle, the muscles in his arms bulging with the effort.

There's an audible cracking sound, and the guard collapses. Alexi takes the brunt of his body weight before quietly lowering him to the ground. With a curl of his index finger, he motions me over to the door. We finally enter the building that, thankfully, isn't locked. As I follow closely behind him, I can just hear the faint hum of speech coming from his earpiece. His contact must be giving him information on the building and its occupants as we go. I hold onto the gun with both hands now, my finger hovering over the trigger, just in case I have to lift and fire unexpectedly. The interior of the building is dark, and there doesn't seem to be any electricity hooked up yet. I wait for Alexi to produce a flashlight so we can see where we're going but he doesn't. I assume it's because he thinks the light would give us away. I take one hand off the gun, fisting it in the tail of his t-shirt as he moves, apparently able to see much better in the dark than I can. Loud noises come from the ceiling above us—another gunshot and a thud, followed by a yell of pain. My ears strain, trying to identify the source of the noise. Is it Deacon or someone else? It didn't sound like him, but that could just be wishful thinking on my part. I'm so focused on listening for more noises from above that I run directly into Alexi when he suddenly stops abruptly.

He turns his head to look at me over his shoulder before saying in a hushed tone, "Siren, if you accidentally shoot me in the back, I'm going to be very upset with you."

I grimace, whispering back, "Sorry. I can't see where I'm going. Why'd you stop, anyway?" I see the vague outline of his arm lift as he points at something. Blinking hard, I can just make out a flight of stairs directly ahead of us. Ah, so that's why we stopped.

"Lead the way, boss," I say, saluting him with the hand still holding the gun. I don't know why sarcasm is my default setting when I'm nervous. I feel like I'm coming unglued at the seams, so naturally, I need to deflect with humor.

He quickly dips his head out of the way and, in a tone that I'm sure would equate to yelling if we weren't in a life-or-death situation right now, he says, "Jesus Christ, you're a menace. Would you stop brandishing that thing around? And don't call me that."

"What? Boss?" I ask.

"*Da.* I'm no one's boss." The vehemence in his harsh whisper leaves no room for argument. Whoops. I may have struck a nerve.

Resting my hand on his forearm, I say, "Okay, okay. I won't do it again. Scout's honor." I was never in the Girl Scouts, so I'm sure I'm not doing the sign correctly. Even so, I salute him again, the cold steel of the gun barrel resting against my forehead for a brief second.

"*Bozhe, pomogi mne,*" He says under his breath. Again, why do I get the feeling that he's calling me a pain in the ass? Lifting his hand, he grabs the gun, jerking it and my arm downward. "You're gonna blow your damn head off and give away our position."

Click.

The sound of a gun that definitely isn't one of our own being cocked registers in my brain only a second before a heavily accented voice says, "I think it's a little late for that, *prizrak.*" Alexi closes his eyes as if pained. Slowly leaning my head to the side, I see a man with dark hair and even darker eyes pointing a gun at the back of Alexi's head. He must've come down the stairs, and between not being able to see shit in here and the fact that Alexi is built like a tank, I never even saw the man coming up behind him. I wince because if Alexi hadn't been busy preventing me from accidentally shooting one of us, he would've been facing the other way and probably detected the threat himself.

"*Yebat'*," is Alexi's only reply. I don't need a translator for that one because I feel like he and I are on the same page right now. *Fuck.*

CHAPTER 39

Deacon

"Well, well, well. Isn't this an interesting situation?"

Understatement of the century, old man. From all my research into Alexi, I know that Ilya Kapranov is only pushing 65, but the years of terrorizing a good chunk of the Russian population have clearly taken their toll. His once-black hair is now fully gray. His face sports more wrinkles than a gator skin handbag, and his dark eyes are sunken into sockets that are rimmed with dark circles. He looks like the fucking Crypt Keeper. I pity the tailor that had to fit this walking corpse with the very expensive three-piece suit he's currently wearing. The clicking sound from only seconds earlier came from a long black cane topped with the silver head of a wolf. As the man's hand shifts on the cane, I see that the wolf's eyes are actually made of large red rubies. It probably cost a pretty penny, and even though my brain would usually switch to autopilot and start calculating the resale value of such an item, I'm having a hard time focusing because of, you know, my impending death.

At Ilya's words, I both hear and see Gaspari's feet shuffle further away from the man. He's afraid, too. Good. It doesn't take a rocket-scientist to figure out why the old bastard is here. He wants the diamond, though I have no idea if he's aware that Gaspari sold it to me or I just happened to get zip-tied in the wrong place at the wrong time. It seems like a bit of a clusterfuck if he hired Gaspari, who then hired my father, to kidnap me in the hopes of getting it back. As Ilya takes stock of the scene, I stay silent, watching him. With the exception of my hands, which are now furiously trying to extricate themselves from the plastic cuffs, I don't move a muscle. Maybe if I don't breathe, he'll forget I'm here—fat chance. His gaze moves from my father's rapidly cooling body to Gaspari, who continues to shift on his feet and watch the other man warily, the proverbial smoking gun still clutched in one of the hands hanging limply at his sides. When the old man's gaze finally turns to where I'm still sitting, bound and helpless, we lock eyes, and the sudden urge to vomit hits me like a ton of bricks. There's less than nothing behind those eyes. It's like staring into a well, the bottom so dark that you have to wonder if there even is a bottom. A lot of puzzle pieces begin clicking into place regarding Alexi's personality. I don't think I'd have made it out alive if I'd grown up in the same house as this man. It's no wonder Alexi came to the US and entered into law enforcement. If even half the rumors about Ilya Kapranov are true, he's the definition of a nightmare, and I'll bet Alexi wanted to be the polar opposite of the monster that raised him. Trapped under that dead stare, if I were a lesser man, I'd probably shit myself right now. Ilya takes that moment to part his lips and smile at me and I can practically feel my asshole tighten. His teeth are black, but not because they've gone rotten, as you might first assume. He's had them capped that way. I didn't even know you could do that, but it's fucking terrifying, which I guess was the goal. Beads of sweat dot my upper lip and I try my best not to let him see that my guts are threatening to come up my throat. I can tell by the way his smile widens that he knows exactly the effect he has and that even my iron will is no exception.

Gaspari takes another small step away from us, and the lethal-looking men surrounding us take a step forward in unison, guns at the ready. Without taking his eyes off me, Ilya speaks to him. "Where is it, Dante?" he asks. They're only four short words, and yet each one feels like what I would imagine having bamboo shoots shoved underneath your fingernails feels like. My hands involuntarily clench into fists on the armrests of the chair.

"Wh ... where's what? I don't know what you're talking about, Ilya." Gaspari says, and the lie can be heard screaming from beneath the many layers of fear, even to my own ears.

The old man finally looks away from me to face the Italian, who looks to be about two seconds away from pissing himself. If I weren't in the same boat, I'd laugh at how quickly he went from a supervillain to the unnamed extra that dies within the first five minutes of a horror movie. Any intimidation factor he previously possessed has been overshadowed by the radiating evil coming off this small, decrepit old man. Ilya makes a tsking sound and shakes his head, not unlike that of a disappointed father. Except, I highly doubt Gaspari's in for a grounding unless it's the kind that comes with a satin-lined casket. Or, in this case, a black garbage bag.

Ilya sighs heavily, as if he's already weary of this conversation. "Kneel," he commands, but instead of waiting for Gaspari to get on his knees, it becomes very clear very quickly that the single-worded command has a dual purpose. As if they share one mind, the guard closest to Gaspari steps forward, raises his gun, and fires a single shot, taking out his right kneecap. The Italian buckles to the floor with a loud thump, screaming in pain. Despite the fear for my own life, I can't prevent the smile from curling up the corners of my mouth. Maybe if I'm lucky, Kapranov will torture and kill Gaspari before me, at least allowing me to witness his death if I'm not going to have the pleasure of being the one to dole it out. A long string of Italian expletives is interspersed with whimpers and sniffling. When the man now resting on his only remaining good knee, finally lifts his head back up, I get a sick kind of thrill to see tears mingling with drips of snot running down his face. His eyes meet mine, and the hatred I see in them is a direct reflection of mine, only mine are also alight with humor whereas his are alight with humiliation.

Ilya Kapraov takes that moment to follow Gaspari's gaze, his eyes returning to focus on me. Fuck.

"Who are you, boy? And why are you shackled to that chair?" His voice is curious, but I don't have any delusions that it's because he plans to set me free, even if just to piss Gaspari off. His tone would indicate that his curiosity is more geared toward the possibility of using me for something. Leverage maybe? I watch the old man, weighing my options carefully. I could lie, but I'd certainly end up with fewer knee caps than Gaspari. Or I could tell the truth and pray that, by some miracle of God, there's some favor I can do for him in exchange for my life. All things considered, it would seem there's really only one option. Even though talking to the man makes my insides squirm, I opt for the truth—or at least part of it.

"My name is Deacon Taylor, and I'm tied to this chair because Gaspari is a pussy and can't handle me in a one-on-one fight. I would ask you to untie me, but at this point, I'd basically be doing the equivalent of kicking a puppy."

The old man lets out a low chuckle, but there's no humor in it. In fact, the laugh sounds very much like what I'd imagine a robot attempting to mimic human emotions would sound like. Turning to Gaspari, who still kneels on the hard floor, blood dripping from the mangled remnants of his right knee, Kapranov asks, "Is that true, Dante? Who is this man to you?"

Practically spitting venom, he says, "He stole something from me. Something worth a hell of a lot more than your precious diamond." His eyes bore holes into mine, and even past the ringing in my ears set off by the blow of the lead pipe against my face and the two subsequent gunshots, I still muster the gall to blow him a kiss. He attempts to lunge for me, buckling in agony when the realization of his current circumstances catches up with him. During this exchange, Ilya watches us both carefully, those cold, dead eyes giving nothing away. As Gaspari collapses to the ground once more, his brain must finally register the words he just spoke and the fact that he's given himself away. He just practically admitted that he stole the diamond. Or that, at the very least, he knows why Kapranov is here.

The old man taps the end of his cane on the floor slowly several times before saying, "We'll come back to the matter of my diamond. I must admit, my curiosity is piqued. What could possibly be worth more than the largest blue diamond in the world?" Gaze swinging from Gaspari to me, he asks, "Are you a thief, Mr. Taylor?"

Nodding my head slowly, I recall what Alexi said to Siren at the masquerade. "Yes, though you can't steal something that refuses to be held."

Ilya lifts an eyebrow. For the first time since entering this room, Hell, maybe for the first time ever, genuine interest crosses his expression. After a moment of silent contemplation, he lets out another low laugh, this one holding no more emotion than the first, however. "Ah, a woman, then?" he asks, though it sounds like more of a forgone conclusion than a question posed to either of us. "I would be very interested to meet the woman that two such formidable men deem more valuable than the Oppenheimer Blue."

Fat chance, old man. If I'm lucky, said woman will be hidden away in a safe house under FBI protection by now. It's literally the only thought keeping me from jumping off the deep end. Suddenly, there's a commotion in the doorway behind me, and a man's voice says, "*Izvini*, boss. I'd bet good money that this is the woman in question. She's obnoxious, but ..." The man pauses before continuing, "... she did come with a gift."

Slowly closing my eyes, I pray that it's not who I think it is. But, to coin a phrase often used by my mama, if I didn't have bad luck, I'd have no luck at all. I can't see the door behind me, but I don't need to when a voice that's been both a thorn in my side and the rose attached to it says in a loud voice, "What's more obnoxious was your Dad having the audacity not to skeet you into the toilet. You smell like fish tank water, and if you could keep your sweaty ass palms off me, that'd be great. I do know how to walk, you know."

Goddammit, woman. If there were ever a time to keep your mouth shut, it would be now. Chair legs screeching in protest against the hardwood floors, I shift around until I can see what's going on behind me. The foul-smelling man in question pushes a spitting-mad Siren into the room before stepping back into the hallway. The gun he's currently holding points at someone outside of the room, but I don't have to be psychic to guess who it is, and I'll bet he wants to be here even less than I do. The guard gestures with the gun, and sure enough, the broad frame of Alexi Kapranov steps slowly into the room. Those mismatched eyes meet mine, then move to Gaspari, who's still lying in a heap on the floor next to my father's lifeless body, before finally landing on his own father. Well, shit. This situation is getting increasingly out of hand by the second. The way we're going, I wouldn't be surprised to see a full three-ring circus in here next. If the look passing between father and son is any indication, I need to figure out how to get us out of this and fast ... before the elephant in the room stomps on all of us.

CHAPTER 40

Siren

The mouth-breathing Russian that pointed the gun at the back of Alexi's head downstairs now ushers us into a large empty room. I say empty, but that's not exactly true. There are so many people that we might as well be throwing a rave, except I'm not sure even I could dance in a room filled with this much tension. As my gaze zeroes in on Deacon, who's tied to a chair with a swollen and bleeding cheek, every other person in the room simply fades away. Everything around him goes dark and all ambient noise is drowned out by the sound of my own heartbeat in my ears—one that's rapidly increasing with fear … and pure feminine rage. As the smelly Russian releases me, probably to usher Alexi into the room using the gun that I have no doubt is bigger than anything else he's packing, I use the opportunity to rush over to Deacon. Taking his face into my hands, I gently run my thumb underneath the rapidly swelling bruise that surrounds the split skin on his cheek. Somebody hit him with something. My gaze quickly takes stock of the rest of him, but thankfully, I don't see any other injuries, at least not on the surface.

"Why the hell did you come here?" he asks in a whisper that's half anger, half desperation. He stares up at me with those blue eyes, and I know the anger is only a mask for the desperation. I don't know if he was afraid before I entered the room but he is now. Considering how thick he is, I'm sure it's fear for me instead of for his own life.

"Don't be a fucking idiot. Of course, I came." My voice softens, and I add quietly, "Do you think I'd let you die before telling me you love me?" I shake my head slowly. "You're not that lucky. Now, tell me who hit you."

He opens his mouth to respond at the exact same time that something akin to a growl sounds from a few yards away. Slowly turning my head, I see Dante kneeling on the floor, supported by only one leg. The other seems to be hanging on by a thread and I mean that literally. Good, it'll make what I'm about to do a lot easier. I have no doubt in my mind that he's the one that tied Deacon up and beat the shit out of him. Well, karma's a bitch. Without a second thought to the consequences or anything else going on around me, I turn and launch myself at him. Closing the short distance at record speed, I tackle him at full force. The momentum, combined with his injury, prevents him from being able to brace himself, though by the time he realizes my intent, it's already too late anyway. He falls backwards with a cry of pain, likely because the half of leg beneath his obliterated knee is now folded beneath him. Straddling his waist, I apply my full weight and press down hard, remembering all the times he called me fat or told me that no one else would ever want me because of how big I was. Well, enjoy suffocating to death. As he screams in pain, I rear back my arm, punching him in exactly the same spot as the bruise Deacon now sports. There's a sickening crunch, and I'm not sure if it comes from his face or my knuckles, but either way, it evokes a rush of satisfaction and even more adrenaline as his head whips to the side.

"That's for putting your hands on what's mine, you piece of shit!" I spit in his face. He lifts his arms, most likely to go for my throat, but that proves to be a mistake on his part. Leaving himself wide open, I land another blow, this time to his ribcage. With a grunt, his hands quickly change course, aiming to guard himself instead of attempting to overpower me. It doesn't do much good. If he blocks an area, I just go for another. The more pain I cause him, the more my rage builds, compounding on itself until I'm practically frothing at the mouth: every slight, every injury, every sexual assault, every night of torment flashes before my eyes. The screams continue, but it isn't until strong hands grip my biceps and wrench me away that I realize there's one scream that echoes above all the rest, and it's coming from me. It's a purging of every ounce of emotion this man ever evoked—lust, infatuation, and love. Humiliation, degradation, and pain. Fear, doubt, and loathing. I internalized all of those emotions, projecting the nastiest of them on myself. It wasn't until I met the man currently strapped to a chair and bleeding, that I started to see my own worth. Not because *he* saw value in me but because he made me believe in its existence in the first place.

It takes several pairs of hands to drag me off and away from Dante. Once the red haze clears from my vision, I begin to register more of what's going on around me. It's pandemonium. Deacon is yelling and fighting desperately against his bonds. Alexi is cursing in both English and Russian but hasn't moved and seems content to let me murder Dante with my bare hands.

Unfortunately, I don't get that privilege as I'm dumped unceremoniously at the feet of a man whose presence I'm just now noticing. As I look up from the floor, he stares at me like I'm a venus fly trap, kept under glass to be studied. It's a good analogy, actually. Because if he or any of his men come too close, I'll bear my teeth and fucking eat them. As he continues his perusal, I stare right back, refusing to be cowed by another man ever again. Even one that could potentially end my life here and now. Instead, I push my sweat-slicked hair from my face and force my shaky legs to cooperate as I stand, brushing something invisible off the remnants of my ripped gown before facing the old man in front of me. Despite the evil emanating from him, he's not much taller than I am, especially as he leans slightly on a long black cane. He's dressed immaculately, but a designer suit on this man is the equivalent of wrapping a bow around a paper bag full of dog shit right before you light it on fire and leave it on someone's porch. The two just don't go together.

In a tone that bleeds curiosity, the old man opens his mouth to speak and, Jesus Christ, what the Hell is wrong with his teeth?! "I can see why they're so infatuated by you. There's fire in your veins. I bet you can still feel it, can't you? The ecstasy that accompanies the dispensing of pain." He sounds almost ... aroused. I can only thank the Lord that I'm no longer eye level with his crotch. "As much as I enjoyed that little show, *dikaya koshka*, I'm afraid I need Dante alive for the moment." Turning in the general direction of his son, he says something in Russian.

Alexi replies in English. To piss his father off or because he wants us to know what's being said? "Yes, I know you've been looking for me, which is precisely why I've been so difficult to find. There's nothing to discuss. I'm not coming back."

Ilya Kapranov's eyes narrow and his gaze jerks to meet Alexi's, flitting away just as quickly. Instead, Ilya seems to be focus on some spot over Alexi's right shoulder. Tracking his gaze, I don't see anything. Why won't he meet his son's eyes? Is it because of guilt or fear? In English this time, he says, "We'll discuss this after I take care of my business here."

Alexi takes a step forward, and several guns are drawn upward and pointed at him by the guards. However, I also notice that many of them look uneasy on their feet and make no move to protect their master. Interesting. Alexi slowly turns his head towards the men, and one by one, they lower their weapons until only one or two are left. Holy shit. Looking into Alexi's face, I understand completely why they're afraid. It's as if a mask has come down over his already stern expression. This face is terrifying, much more so than the old man who sired him. As he stares at the remaining two guards, he speaks to his father, "I don't care what you do with Gaspari but the other two are off limits."

At his words, the men around us look back and forth between each other, and I'll bet no one has ever dared talk to their boss that way before and lived to tell the tale. Meanwhile, Ilya's nostrils flare, and he slams the end of his cane on the floor beside him with enough force to chip away a small hole in the wood. "Know your place, boy!" He's seething, and his face is turning more and more red by the second. He doesn't like being embarrassed in front of his men; that much is clear. It's also clear that this isn't the first time he's been challenged by his son.

Finally facing his father again, Alexi replies cryptically, "I do know my place, father. I also know that if I wanted it, I could take it at any time." His words are simple enough but there seems to be some hidden meaning in them. The two men are locked in a staring contest now, except again, Ilya isn't quite looking Alexi in the eye. Finally, he grits his teeth, turning and waving toward the two remaining men with their firearms still pointed upward. Immediately, they lower them as if they already desperately wanted to do so, but only sheer force of will kept them from cowering under Alexi's gaze.

Ilya takes several steps closer to Dante, who has now managed to get himself up and into a sitting position. Towering over the other man, Ilya says, "Tell me where it is, Dante. And don't try to lie because we both know that you already outed yourself earlier. I know you have it, and you know that you won't leave this room alive if you don't hand it over."

Spitting out a mouthful of blood onto the floor directly next to one of Ilya's shiny leather shoes, he says, "I don't have it. I sold it." His dark eyes brighten slightly as he glances slyly over at Deacon. That is, until Alexi casually walks over, pulls a switchblade from his pocket, and flips it open, cutting Deacon's zip ties. None of Ilya's men make a move to stop him. With the sight of Deacon, now unrestrained, combined with the imposing figure of Ilya Kapranov hovering over him, Dante has to realize he's fucked. So, naturally, he plays the only card he has left. "What if I could point you in the direction of who has it? Would that information save my life?" he asks.

Cocking his head to the side as if in contemplation, Ilya finally says, "I'll consider it." What a crock. Even I can tell he's lying straight through his gross black caps.

Dante takes a second to make his decision before probably coming to the conclusion that he doesn't have much of a choice. He's out of options, and he knows it. My heart kicks wildly in my chest, and the air around me grows thin. I know what he's about to do because I know who has the diamond. Once he gives voice to the words, no amount of pleading with this old man will be able to undo them. This is all my fault. I dragged Deacon into this mess. Yes, he was after the diamond long before he found me at that auction, but if he hadn't saved me from Dante's home, he'd never have any reason to hold a grudge against him. It would've been a simple business transaction, and sure, maybe Ilya still would've come after the diamond anyway, but the trail would've died with Dante because if there's one thing I've learned about Deacon, he wouldn't have left any breadcrumbs behind for Ilya to follow.

As fate finally catches up to me for what will probably be the last time, Dante lifts his hand, pointing the finger at Deacon before saying, "I sold it to *him*. Then he repaid me by stealing my woman." The last sentence is thrown across the room like acid. Deacon's jaw clenches, but he doesn't say anything. He wants to kill Dante but knows that if he moves, Ilya's men will shoot him.

Ilya looks to Deacon with the expression of a man who's finally found the right spot for the last piece in a jigsaw puzzle. The picture is now complete. "Ah, so that's why you were here, bound and bloody, when I entered. Tell me, Mr. Taylor, do you have the diamond on you right now?" His words are deceptively soft, but there's a deadly undertone, warning him of the consequences of lying to him. I don't think Deacon has the diamond on him, but if he does, I don't want him to have to give it up. I know what it means to him, what it would've meant to his mother.

"No, I don't have it with me. Otherwise Gaspari would've just taken it, killed me, and run like the coward he is." I can practically see that earlier acid that Dante tossed his way being thrown right back.

Reaching into the inside pocket of his suit jacket, Ilya removes a gun, pointing it directly at Deacon between one blink and the next. I release a yell of surprise and terror, reflexively stepping between Deacon and the loaded gun. Before he has a chance to push me aside, I move out of his reach and closer to Ilya until the barrel of the gun is flush with my chest. Somewhere in the back of my mind, I knew this was how it would play out, and I've resigned myself to my fate. I escaped one monster only to trade myself to another. But instead of letting my head run away with the fear and anxiety of what I know is to come, I remember Deacon's words from the night he made love to me for the first time. *Don't think, just feel.* Looking over my shoulder, I make eye contact with him. His blue eyes blaze with emotion. As a single tear slips down my cheek, my voice doesn't make a sound when I mouth, *I love you.* His nostrils flare and he attempts to take a step forward but the sound of the gun pressed to my chest being cocked stops him in his tracks. Steeling myself, I give him a small nod of reassurance and resignation before turning back to face the old man.

In a voice barely above a whisper, I say, "Please don't. Take me instead. Let him go and I'll serve you, in any way you desire. *Any way.*" I have no idea where I got the nerve to consider myself as valuable as a giant blue jewel. But I've gotta shoot my shot, no pun intended. If there's even a minute chance that I can get Deacon out of this building alive, I have to try. We stand like that for several seconds, him studying me, his gun cocked and aimed at my heart. I barely breathe and hope against hope that the stuff Amelia and Merrick have relayed to me about this man and his penchant for breaking women is true. I'm counting on that sadistic streak to tempt him into making a deal with me.

Deacon speaks up from behind me, but I don't turn around to face him. I can't. "Siren, what the fuck do you think you're doing? There's no way in Hell I'm letting you walk out of this room with anyone but me." I ignore him. It's not up to him. This is the only way to save his life.

For a moment, I wonder if Ilya will accept Deacon's words as a challenge, which would ultimately help my case. However, after several moments of contemplation, he says, "As tempting of an offer as that is, *dikaya koshka*, I'm going to have to pass. There's no reason to prolong the inevitable if he doesn't have the diamond. I'll simply kill you all and then track it down myself." My stomach pitches, and I bite the inside of my cheek to keep my chin from quivering.

Without warning, the warmth of a large body hovers behind me. Two hands grip my biceps, pulling me back into a familiar chest. One I've traced the contours of late at night in the dark. The smell of sea and earth envelops me, and I close my eyes, waiting for Ilya to decide he wants to pull the trigger, killing two birds with one stone. Instead, shock has my eyes popping open again when Deacon speaks, his voice coming from directly behind my head.

"Let us go, and I'll bring you the diamond," he says. "On one extra condition."

"Go on," says the Russian, and my heart sinks. Try as I might, I can't prevent the tears from sliding down my cheeks. I don't want this. I don't want him to give up one of the only things that have kept him going since his mother died. The only two things keeping him alive were the search for the diamond and revenge against his father. Now his father is dead, under circumstances that I'm still not clear on. And he's prepared to offer the diamond in exchange for my life. Despite my newly discovered confidence and the value with which I now see myself, I know I'm not worth this. It's a bad trade, but Ilya seems to be entertaining the idea.

Suddenly, a hand reaches around, placing two fingers on my chin, turning my head around. Meeting Deacon's eyes, I shake my head. "Don't. It's not worth it," I say quietly.

"You still don't get it, do you, brat? The diamond is my past. *You* are my future." He looks back to the old man and says, "I'll give you the diamond if you let us walk out of here and ... she gets to be the one to kill *him*." His gaze flicks to Dante's still-sitting form. Hatred blazes in his eyes but he can do little about it considering he can't even stand. At Deacon's words, my head whips back around in shock.

"What?" I demand.

"He owes you a debt. You never needed me to save you. You saved yourself," he says. I glance down, but those same two fingers dip under my chin, tipping my head back up to bring my eyes to meet his again. "Go be your own savior," he says. After a moment, I nod, turning back to face Ilya who looks at me with a kind of sick amusement on his face. He's enjoying all of this like it's his favorite soap opera. As the old man thinks about Deacon's proposal, we wait with bated breath.

Finally, he says, "How can I trust you'll deliver the diamond once I let you leave? What's to prevent you both from simply disappearing? Not that I wouldn't eventually find you, but I'm getting too old for hunting." He pauses, and I just know that at any minute, he's gonna give his men the "okay" to shoot all of us. But after a moment, a sinister smile tips up the corners of his lips, and he says, "I'll agree, but I have a condition of my own." I should feel elation at his words, but instead, all I feel is trepidation. What else does he want? We don't have to wait long for the answer. Uncocking the gun that's been aimed at me this entire time, he lowers it to his side and, using his black cane to do a half-turn, faces his son. "You'll deliver the diamond to me. At home."

I'm already shaking my head when Alexi looks over at us. He can't go back to Russia. There's a reason he left, and it's clear that he hates his father. There's also the matter of the search for his wife. If he returns to Russia, he'll most likely be giving up that search. As he looks back at me, his mismatched gaze shows a sad sense of resignation. With full knowledge of the Hell he'll be walking back into, he still gives a single nod and says, "Done."

The epitome of smugness, Ilya turns back to me, lifting his hand and holding out the gun. I can see Dante begin to squirm backward from my peripheral vision. As I take the gun, testing its weight in my hand, I notice that it's very similar to the one Alexi gave me downstairs. With one last reassuring squeeze, Deacon releases my arms. I grip the gun in my right hand, finger already hovering over the trigger. Am I really about to do this? Both times before, my actions were in the heat of the moment, my fight-or-flight response on high alert. This time, I'll be killing a man in cold blood. Do I have it in me to do that? *Fuck yes, I do.*

As I walk towards Dante, he finally seems to find his voice, "Sirena, you don't know what you're doing. You've tried this twice before, remember? It didn't take because you never really wanted me dead. You and I are destined to be together. You need me. You'll be lost without me!"

Glancing back at Deacon, I say, "Not if I keep sight of the stars." He looks at me with eyes that have gone a little glassy and a small smile on his face. He gives me a nod of encouragement.

Without another word, I turn back to Dante and lift my arm, aiming directly at his face. Without a second thought, I pull the trigger, the bullet hitting him right between the eyes. The force of the shot blows him backward, and what's left of his head makes a large *thump* as it hits the hardwood floor, blood immediately pooling around it. Not even affording him a backward glance, I walk back to Ilya, handing him back the gun.

With Deacon by my side, I look over at Alexi. He nods and says in a stoic tone, "Good girl."

Ilya steps into the line of vision between Alexi and me, effectively interrupting our quiet conversation. Addressing his son, he says, "You have one month to get your affairs in order here, then you'll come home. *With* my diamond."

Alexi stares at his father with a blank expression, and I can practically see the life draining from his eyes. I'm hit with a pang of guilt so strong that it actually hurts. "*Soglasovannyy.*" The switch to Russian when addressing his father seems significant, though I don't know why.

Ilya motions to three of the guards standing alongside the far wall. Once they've stepped forward, he gestures to the bodies of Dante and Deacon's father. "Clean up this mess." And without another word, he turns and walks from the room, taking the remainder of his men with him.

CHAPTER 41

Deacon

The drive back home is quiet. Having been the victim of a kidnapping, I didn't have my car once Alexi, Siren, and I got outside the building where Ilya's men were hard at work disposing of the bodies of my father and Gaspari. After a short trek through the woods, we finally reached Alexi's sports car. We piled inside, and he took us back to Charleston, where my car still sat outside of Siren's family home. Alexi, too, was suspiciously quiet during that time. I mean, he was already a man of very few words but there was something ... off about him now. I have to wonder if it has anything to do with his promise to hand-deliver the diamond to his father. I didn't need to do a lot of digging on him, though I had, to figure out that he and his father hated each other. He'd never said much about his upbringing, but if even half the rumors about his father were true, growing up in his house must've been Alexi's personal Hell. Now, in saving our lives, we'd doomed him right back there. Despite my earlier misgivings about the Fed, there was no way I'd allow him to walk into the lion's den without backup. Merrick and I would see the hunt for this music box through, and we'd do whatever we needed to get him back out of Russia.

Surprisingly, out of all the things I regretted tonight, losing the diamond was at the bottom of the list. I meant what I said to Siren. I love my mother, but Siren is my future, and if I have any hopes of keeping her, she needs to know that she takes precedence over everything else. Pretty jewels and old promises included. I'd like to think Mama would understand and be happy for me. I finally have something more to live for than simple revenge. Within the month, I'll be handing over the diamond to Alexi, and that'll be that. Siren and I had a lot to talk about, not the least of which is me still being slightly pissed off at her for stepping between me and a potential bullet. But that conversation isn't for now. For now, I want to get the both of us home, where I know we'll be safest. That is if she even still wants to stay with me. The possibility that she won't nearly has my throat closing up. Back in that warehouse, she said she loved me, but there's always a chance that it was simply a confession made to make me feel better because she knew she was probably going to her death. So I wouldn't feel like all this had been for nothing. I don't wanna believe that. I want her to want me ... no ... *need* me, the way I need her. I didn't know what kind of life we'd have; my life was mostly played out in the shadows. In contrast, she literally lived in the spotlight. Talk about opposites attracting. I must admit that I knew something special was there from the moment we met, even if it took my head longer to catch up. Something that set her apart from the countless others that came before her. That feeling has only grown over these last few months. I'm not entirely sure that, if she says she wants to return to her old life, I'll be able to let her go, and that scares me nearly as much as the idea of her leaving because I can't definitively say that there are limits to what I'd be willing to do to keep her. When I think about it, I feel sick to my stomach. Siren will be the second woman ever to take up space in my heart. The first one left me, and I barely survived it. My gut tells me I wouldn't be so lucky this time around. If we get home and she starts packing her shit, I'll be on my knees so fast it'll be embarrassing. Fuck pride. I'll beg if I have to.

Before I know it, we're coming up on the entrance to the long dirt driveway. A low vibrating feeling starts beneath my skin as we turn in and follow it to the house. The car slows as we pull up out front. I put it in park, but simply sit there, both hands clutching the steering wheel like a lifeline. I wait for Siren to tell me to turn the car off and unlock the doors, but she doesn't. I find out why when I glance over toward the passenger's seat. She's asleep again. There goes the narcolepsy, though I'm starting to believe her body is simply making up for not having a good night's sleep in nine years. Her head rests against the spot where the window meets the door, long black hair acting as a curtain over half of her face. Gently, I reach out and tuck the offending strands behind her ear. As I stare at her, I remember the last time we did this. I brought her home the night of the auction, and she fell asleep in my car. Very much like that night, her clothes are ripped and bloody. She has smudges of dirt on her face, and something that looks like sawdust sprinkled throughout her hair. She must've picked them up while she was wailing on Gaspari like a woman possessed. I honestly don't think I've ever been more proud of her than I was at that moment. If she was afraid, she sure as hell didn't show it. Instead, she took her power back, raining down a world of hurt on the man who's made her life miserable

451

for nearly 10 years. As I look at her now, my chest aches at how beautiful she is—dirt, blood, and all. I can't let her get away. I just can't.

I release a long-suffering sigh, laying my forehead down on the steering wheel. From my current position of dejection, I don't realize she's awake until she speaks.

"What are you doing?" she asks, her voice still thick with sleep.

I sit up and open my mouth ... but nothing comes out. Fear has me in a chokehold and I don't even know where to begin. So, instead, I just shake my head, turn off the engine, and open the door. I can see her looking at me perplexed as I slam the door shut. I hustle around the front hood to open her door, but she beats me to it. Figures. I should've known better than to think she needed me to help her get out. As she climbs out of the car, I hold out my hand the same way I did when we visited Forsythe Park. My heart resumes beating when she slips her hand into mine. Together, we walk up the front steps and go into the house. She walks ahead of me, and I pause as I close the door behind us. We both desperately need a shower, a change of clothes, and maybe even a few ice packs. But I can't wait that long. The not knowing is killing me; if she intends to go, it'll be better just to rip the band-aid off. It'll be the equivalent of ripping a band-aid off of an amputation, but it's better than the alternative of dying a torturous death via anxiety.

"Can we talk?" I ask.

She turns to look at me from the center of the living room. Assessing my dire expression, she says, "Sure. Do you wanna sit?"

I shake my head. "No, I don't think I'd be able to stay still that long."

Her expression changes from one of confusion to apprehension. Still, she opts to stand as well. "Are you gonna yell at me for getting between you and Ilya Kapranov? Because if you are, you should know that I'm not sorry. I was desperate, and it was the only move I had left."

I wanna be angry at her. I wanna rant and rave about how careless she was with her own life, but I don't. The anger I felt in that moment has faded away, leaving only understanding. I would've done the same thing for her, so how can I be mad? I open my mouth to say something, though I'm not sure exactly what. What comes out, however, surprises even me.

"I don't think I can do this without you," I whisper.

Her brows pull together. "Do what?"

"Life," I simply say. "I don't think I can do life without you. In fact, I know I can't. You've become such an integral part of me that you've practically embedded yourself in my DNA. There is no me without you anymore."

She stares at me with wide eyes, the chocolate brown warm and inviting, but I don't dare step closer. As much as I want to touch her, I can't crowd her. She has to have space to decide what she truly wants. So, instead, I begin to pace back and forth across the living room. All the while, she watches me, waiting for whatever comes next. Stopping in front of the mantle, I look down at a picture of me and my mother. Sitting next to it is the little porcelain figurine of a shooting star.

I pick it up, turning back to face Siren. "This was hers, you know. I never believed in wishes before I met you. But from the moment you entered my life with the force of a wrecking ball, everything you did felt like a tiny little wish I'd unknowingly made came true." Looking down, I rub my thumb over the small star. "I think it's quite possible that I've been wishing for you my whole life. It just took my head some time to catch up to my heart."

Sitting the figurine back down, I pick up one of the coins sitting next to it and walk over to take her hand, dragging her into the kitchen. She doesn't offer any protests, which I'm thankful for because I need to get all this out before she tells me to kick rocks. Before she reminds me that we're from two different social classes and girls like her don't end up with guys like me, a guy with a tragic past, a criminal present, and an unknown future. I pull her with me as I walk to the kitchen sink, plugging the bottom and turning on the tap. It's no fountain, but it'll have to do. When I look at her, she's watching me warily, probably thinking I've lost my mind. Maybe I have. Still, when the sink has filled about halfway, I stare into her eyes as I hold the quarter in my palm for her to see.

"Let me make one more wish?" I ask, my gaze pleading. Her chin begins to wobble, and I know I have to do this now because soon, I'm not going to be able to stop myself from touching her. My breathing is shallow, and there's a slight ringing in my ears as I stand there, waiting. I can't even allow myself the luxury of passing out because if I do, she might be gone when I wake up. She reaches up and brushes away several tears from her cheeks before giving me a jerky nod. I sag with relief. Gently tossing the coin into the water, I watch it sink to the bottom before looking back at her beautiful face. The tear stains have made tracks through the dirt on her face, yet I still want to lean down and kiss those tears away. But I've still got my wish to make. "Stay with me. Build a life with me. I need to wake up every day knowing that the woman I'm in love with is sleeping right beside me. I need you to understand that I breathe for *you* now. If you walk out that door, you'll leave me gasping for air, and there won't be enough oxygen in the world to save me. I don't know how we'll make it work, but we will. I'll do whatever it takes. Just please ... don't leave me."

She looks up at me, teary eyes flitting this way and that as she tries to get a read on my face. I don't try to stop her because I know she needs to see the truth beneath the masks I've so strategically worn all my life. That I'll be lost without her. Like her namesake, she called to me and if she leaves me now, I'll drown.

Suddenly, to my surprise and horror, she bends at the waist and buries her face in her hands. Great sobs wrack her body, and I reach out a hand to do ... something. I want to comfort her, but don't know how to help her if I don't know what's wrong. When my hand is only an inch or two away from her shoulder, her head jerks up, and her eyes pin me to the spot.

"Do you know why I stepped in front of that gun?" she asks with a sniffle before letting out the cutest little hiccup I've ever heard a woman make. Her words, however, throw me for a loop. I shake my head, not because I don't know but because I need to hear her say the words for it to be real. "Because I was prepared to give up my life for yours. To become a slave to a man just as evil as Dante, if not more so. But you know what the funny part is?" she asks but doesn't give me time to answer before she continues. "I didn't even have to think about it. It was an involuntary reaction. No hesitation, no second guessing. I didn't think, I just felt," she says, tossing my words from the other night back at me. Reaching up, she grips both sides of my face like she did that night and says, "Deacon, you've done so much for me. You helped me find myself, even the parts I'd repressed. Pieces of myself that I'd broken down to fit a mold that never came in my size. You gave me the confidence to keep myself whole and believe that anyone who can't swallow that can choke. You did that. I never would've found *me* if it weren't for you." She pulls my face down until my forehead rests on hers, but our eyes are open. As brown meets blue, she adds, "I kept sight of the stars, and I've found my way home. *You* are my home. I'm in love with you, you fucking idiot, and I'm not going anywhere."

Relief and elation fill me in equal measure, and my arms come up around her, squeezing her against me. Burying my face in her hair, I breathe in the scent of coffee and chocolate, and even with a hint of sawdust, I know I want that combination to be the last thing I smell before I leave this earth.

EPILOGUE

Siren

2 MONTHS LATER

As I step out onto the dark stage, I feel like my life has come full circle. There are many similarities to how this started, yet, everything is different. There is no spotlight. There is no audience, save one. Nearly 10 years ago, I stepped out onto this stage to a packed house and played Bach's Chaconne, unknowingly capturing the attention of a monster. Unknowing that my life was about to be irrevocably changed forever. The horrors I endured afterward turned me into a completely different person. Still, despite how hard I tried to rework myself into the model of perfection, that goal was never achievable because there was still a core of *me* buried deep inside. My innate personality refused to bend to anyone's will. Many in the psychological field have researched the question of, "how does trauma affect you?" I can't speak for everyone, but I've come to believe that every piece of trauma I went through molded me into the person standing on this stage. Am I more than just my trauma? Absolutely. That core part of me that allowed itself to be buried out of a sense of self-preservation never actually died. She came out when I needed her most, and that proves to me that every day I survived was another day I was able to safeguard that part of myself. She knew when the time was right to claw her way to the surface. She did it on countless occasions, each one ensuring I'd live to open my eyes again. And she did it when I needed to defend myself and the people I love. She's doing it again right now.

As a low overhead light gradually comes on, it creates just as much shadow as it does illumination. I smile because it's the perfect setting for my crowd of one, and for what I'm about to do. Coming up to the stage, my hands were clammy and nausea wreaked havoc on my insides. The sight of a darkened theater and only my violin sitting onstage would be enough to give anyone anxiety. I've done a lot of work on myself over the last two months: therapy, medication, and open communication with the people closest to me. I've been officially diagnosed with PTSD, anxiety, and bouts of depression. Despite all of those things, I've continued to push myself past invisible barriers erected by my brain that, very often, tell me that I'm weak. That I still need to safeguard that core part of me. That history is bound to repeat itself. I suppose, in a way, it's right. Tonight is a perfect example, though my brain is going to be severely disappointed in the outcome.

Picking up my violin, I place it to my chin and bring the bow-string up, poising it just so. As my heart rate picks up speed, my gaze sweeps through row after row of empty seats. My eyes dart from left to right, then down to up, before finally reaching one of the private boxes on the upper balcony. Just as my attention lands on the box's sole occupant, a dim light matching the one above my own head glows to life over Deacon's sitting form. In true Deacon fashion, he's not dressed as he should be, but neither am I. Instead of red satin, there are blue jeans, and instead of a tux, there's simply a plain black t-shirt and pants. As soon as we make eye contact, the nerves turning my insides into a curdled milkshake dissipate entirely.

"Are you ready?" He asks from above, his voice echoing around the large room in a way that makes the sound reverberate louder than any amount of trauma could ever combat. I used to think that relying on someone to fix me meant I wasn't strong enough to do it alone. I don't think that any longer. The strength I feel now is my own, but the bond that's formed between mine and his, has made me feel invincible. It was never that I couldn't do it alone but that another person, this person, helped me find that part of myself that I'd buried deep, and it wasn't until he reached into me and pulled my soul out to meet his that I became cognizant of the fact that I could do anything.

My chin still perched on my violin, I say, "I'm ready." And I realize, as the first notes of Bach begin to echo off the walls, that I am. I'm ready to let go of the past. To bleed away all of the pain and misery that followed a night very similar to this one. I play the song only once because that's all I need. History won't repeat itself, and neither will the song. Lowering my instrument, I realize that my eyes are completely dry. I didn't cry this time, and that proves to me that the song no longer holds power over me, and neither does the man that turned it into a weapon of punishment. As the reverb of the last note dies off, I look up to the box again. Deacon is standing now. He doesn't clap or holler or otherwise cheer me on. He simply stands there, a look of pride overtaking his features. "I think I'm ready to go home now," I say.

Home.

Our home. After the culmination of the ordeal two months ago, I realized that I don't need a big house, a fancy car, or designer clothes. In fact, the house that had started as a claustrophobic little box was now the only place I wanted to be. Don't get me wrong, I'd still play because ever since the day I read that letter, the music has come back in full force. But I no longer need to go out and stir up trouble. I no longer need to drown out the voice in my head because she's been noticeably quiet. Our house in the woods is home; of course, we'll build onto it as we need to, but for now, the most important thing in my life resides inside it. My very own shooting star, there to help me shine anytime I feel the darkness creeping in.

Amelia gave birth to a beautiful baby boy about a month ago, and Merrick was a complete marshmallow for that child. Granted, he had no fucking idea what he was doing, but the look in his eyes whenever he stared down at his son made my chest ache. Another thing that made my chest ache, though in a completely different way, was thinking about Alexi. One month ago, he came for the diamond. As he stood in the living room of our tiny house, he might as well have been made of mist. He wasn't there anymore. What had taken his place was a specter, and the nickname he'd tried so hard to outrun made so much sense now. The visit had been brief, Deacon handing over the diamond gladly, but as we'd walked Alexi out the front door to his car, it felt like a funeral procession. I had the sneaking suspicion that we'd sent him to his death, and there wasn't much of him alive to begin with. After he was gone, Deacon and I agreed that, with Merrick's help, we'd track down the music box and continue the search for his long-lost love. He gave up his life for us, and the least we could do was to find his and give it back.

I both see and feel movement to my left, turning to find Deacon standing just off stage. I was so lost in my own thoughts that I never saw him leave the box. Putting my violin back into its case, I approach him, handing the case off. He puts his arm around my waist and, much like that night ten years ago, I leave the theater arm in arm with a man. As the circle comes to a close, the biggest difference is that this time, it is the one fate chose for me. It was written in the stars, after all.

Want more?

TURN THE PAGE FOR A
SNEAK PEEK INTO THE
NEXT BOOK IN THE *THICK
AS THIEVES* SERIES.

PROLOGUE

Alexi

9 YEARS OLD

I try my best to stave off the shivers. Not the easiest thing to do when you are trapped in a meat locker surrounded by slaughtered pigs ... and other things hanging from hooks on the ceiling. This isn't my first time in the ice box; I know it won't be the last. It was a punishment disguised as training. Conditioning me to the cold in the event I was ever taken by a rival and held hostage. In reality, I knew it was just another sick way for my father to torment me. I was only nine, and I'd already seen things that would have most grown men shitting their pants. I'd done things that would have most grown men shitting their pants. It came part and parcel with being the only legitimate son of one of the highest-ranking men in the Bratva. I didn't know why my father hated me so much, but I felt it in everything he did. As though each breath from my lungs was an offense to him. I couldn't say the same for my younger brother, Rurik. You would think that being a bastard in the most literal sense, he'd get it much worse than me. That was usually the way of people in our position. Or, at the very least, he'd be locked in this freezer

467

beside me. But no, my father doted on Rurik if a man like that was capable of such a thing. Sure, my brother endured plenty, but it was nothing by comparison. I'd come to the conclusion that it was because my father saw something in Rurik. Something he didn't see in me. Himself.

Ilya Kapranov was a cruel son of a bitch that reigned over his men with an iron fist. It was why he'd kept his position and territory for as long as he had. People feared him, although sometimes when their eyes strayed to me, I thought I saw fear, too. Not that I could blame them. Some of the things I've done during my short life were too heinous for even the confessional. If there was a God, he'd already washed his hands of me. I couldn't really blame him either. The fact that I hated every second of it didn't really matter. Whatever it was, I still did it. Because, even at nine, I knew it was either them or me. Sometimes, I wondered what the point of it all was. If my only purpose on this earth was to suffer and make others suffer, why bother? But then my mind would flash with a vision of my father lying in a pool of his own blood at my feet, and and even though the image is only in my head right now, the idea of it someday becoming a reality kept me going. As my teeth begin to chatter, I bring myself back to the present and try to focus on regulating my breathing. Too fast or too slow, and I know the effects of hypothermia are setting in. From my previous times here, I've also learned to look for things like confusion and sleepiness. Both were symptoms of an impending death sentence. I'm not sure how long my father intends to leave me here this time, but I know I have to try to show as little weakness as possible. Difficult to do when your body begins to betray you and the uncontrollable tremors started. Still, I would know better than anyone that, in this house, there's always someone watching. My gaze flicks upward briefly, and I keep my head perfectly still as my eyes find the little blinking red light that indicates that the camera in the top corner opposite me is on. I know the old man isn't watching himself but, rather, one of his trusted men. He doesn't want me to die. Then the game would be over. With that in mind, I repeat to myself over and over that someone will get me out before I freeze to death. I don't know how long I stay that way, legs crossed in the middle of the box. Time doesn't exist here, only the cold. Only the blank stares that came from the eyes of the dead men hanging on hooks alongside the hogs. Only pain. I welcome it. Pain means I'm still alive.

The loud click of a handle, followed by a rush of warm air, accompanies the man who finally opens the door. Still, I don't move even while every nerve in my body screams to scramble for the door. For the promise of heat. Glancing again at the little red light, I stay in my position on the floor of the freezer for several more long moments. I want him to know. He didn't break me. He'll have to try harder next time. And, of course, there will be a next time. There always is. As the man's shiny black shoes come to stand in front of me, effectively breaking my stare down with the camera, I finally bring myself to my feet. My hands clench into fists at my sides with the effort it takes to keep my balance in front of the lackey sent to pull me out. Not even to him will I divulge the fact that my legs feel like jelly, and the cold mixed with oxygen deprivation has my head swimming like a small fish in a pool full of sharks because that's exactly where I am. A pool full of sharks, the largest of which just loves to watch me swim for my life, knowing that he can devour me whole at any time. But someday, I'd be the biggest shark in the tank, and all the other sharks will either swim away in fear or turn on each other in a feeding frenzy. Either way, there would only be one shark left. Me. Because, as much as I hated the blood that coated my hands, in this life, you either ate or you got eaten. I was a villain origin story in the making when, deep down, all I wanted to do was play the hero. Unfortunately, I wasn't in the position right now to choose. Maybe someday.

Once I'm sure that my first step isn't going to result in me face-planting into the hard floor, I turn on my heel and head for the open door, leaving the other man to trail behind me. Outside the meat freezer, I both welcome the warmth and hate it. The pinpricks on my skin feel like a thousand tiny knives stabbing me all over. I grit my teeth and stand just outside the door, giving my body a minute to acclimate under the guise of waiting for the other man. Finally, looking at the face of the underling with the shiny shoes, I see that it's one of my second cousins. Most of the men who work for my father are in some way related to me. The fully grown man lowers his head immediately, refusing to meet my eyes. That happens a lot. I wasn't sure if it was because they were afraid of me or because they thought something was wrong with me. Maybe it was both. I didn't speak much, and I very rarely exhibited emotion. Sometimes, I thought that that was the reason my father went out of his way to hurt me. Because he wanted to see me *feel*. But little does he know, I feel plenty. I hated him, and even that word didn't seem to do justice to the amount of raw emotion that I kept buried so deeply that only I'd know where to find it when the time came. I hid it well because I refused to give him the satisfaction of knowing that the majority of what I feel is terrifying. He'll know when I want him to know. Until then, we'll play this little game of him trying to force a reaction and me giving him nothing ... until the day comes when I decide it's time to give him *everything*.

BOOK COVER BY CANDICE CLARK

EDITED BY YVETTE MITCHELL

2024

About The Author

CANDICE CLARK IS AN AVID ROMANCE READER-TURNED-WRITER WHO LIVES IN SOUTH CAROLINA WITH HER MAN-CHILD HUSBAND AND SMALL DAUGHTER, WHO HER MOTHER ALWAYS WARNED WOULD BE JUST LIKE HER. SHE WAS RIGHT.

IN ADDITION TO WRITING, SHE WORKS FULL-TIME, OWNS AN ETSY BAKERY, AND HAS A THOUSAND OTHER HOBBIES THAT ALLOW HER TO COMPLAIN ABOUT HOW STRESSED OUT AND STRETCHED THIN SHE IS.

SHE'S A DOWN-TO-EARTH, MIDDLE-AGED WOMAN WHO FEELS 97 MOST DAYS AND SUFFERS FROM CHRONIC PAIN AND MASSIVE ANXIETY. SHE HOPES TO USE THESE CHALLENGES TO WRITE RELATABLE CHARACTERS WITH RELATABLE PERSONALITIES IN AN EFFORT TO HELP IMPROVE THE REAL-LIFE PERCEPTION OF MENTAL HEALTH STRUGGLES.

BEGINNING HER READING JOURNEY AS AN EARLY TEEN WITH TITAN AUTHORS LIKE NORA ROBERTS AND JOHANNA LINDSEY, SHE IS EXCITED ABOUT COMBINING CLASSIC WRITING STYLES AND PLOTTING WITH THE MORE EDGY SUBJECT MATTER COMMONLY FOUND IN TODAY'S INDIE AUTHOR COMMUNITY.

Printed in Great Britain
by Amazon